Praise for Barbara Ann Wright

The Pyradisté Adventures

"[A] healthy dose of a very creative, yet believable, world into which the reader will step to find enjoyment and heart-thumping action. It's a fiendishly delightful tale."—*Lambda Literary*

"Barbara Ann Wright is a master when it comes to crafting a solid and entertaining fantasy novel...The world of lesbian literature has a small handful of high-quality fantasy authors, and Barbara Ann Wright is well on her way to joining the likes of Jane Fletcher, Cate Culpepper, and Andi Marquette...Lovers of the fantasy and futuristic genre will likely adore this novel, and adventurous romance fans should find plenty to sink their teeth into."—*The Rainbow Reader*

"*The Pyramid Waltz* has had me smiling for three days...I also haven't actually read...a world that is entirely unfazed by homosexuality or female power before. I think I love it. I'm just delighted this book exists...If you enjoyed *The Pyramid Waltz, For Want of a Fiend* is the perfect next step...you'd be embarking on a joyous, funny, sweet and madcap ride around very dark things lovingly told, with characters who will stay with you for months after."—*The Lesbrary*

"This book will keep you turning the page to find out the answers... Fans of the fantasy genre will really enjoy this installment of the story. We can't wait for the next book."—*Curve Magazine*

"There is only one other time in my life I have uncontrollably shouted out in cheer while reading a book. [*A Kingdom Lost*] made the second...Over the course of these three books all the characters have blossomed and developed so eloquently...I simply just thought this whole novel was brilliant."—*The Lesbian Review*

Thrall: Beyond Gold and Glory

"[I]ncidents and betrayals run rampant in this world, and Wright's style successfully kept me on my toes, navigating the shifting alliances...[*Thrall*] is a story of finding one's path where you would least expect it. It is full of bloodthirsty battles and witty repartee...which gave it a nice balanced focus...This was the first Barbara Ann Wright novel I've read, and I doubt it will be the last. Her dialogue was concise and natural, and she built a fantastical world that I easily imagined from one scene to the next. Lovers of Vikings, monsters and magic won't be disappointed by this one."
—*Curve Magazine*

"The characters were likable, the issues complex, and the battles were exciting. I really enjoyed this book and I highly recommend it."—*All Our Worlds*

"Once more Barbara has outdone herself in her penmanship. I cannot sing enough praises. A little *Vikings*, a dash of *The Witcher*, peppered with *A Game of Thrones*, and a pinch of *Lord of The Rings*. Mesmerizing...I was ecstatic to read this book. It did not disappoint. Barbara pours life into her characters with sarcasm, wit and surreal imagery, they leap from the page and stand before you in all their glory. I am left satisfied and starving for more, the clashing of swords, whistling of arrows still ringing in my ears."
—*Lunar Rainbow Reviews*

Paladins of the Storm Lord

"This was a truly enjoyable read...I would definitely pick up the next book...the mad dash at the end kept me riveted. I would definitely recommend this book for anyone who has a love of sci-fi. An intricate...novel one that can be appreciated at many levels, adventurous sci-fi or one that is politically motivated with a very astute look at present-day human behavior...There are many levels to this extraordinary and well written-book...overall a fascinating and intriguing book."—*Inked Rainbow Reads*

"I loved this...The world that the Paladins inhabited was fascinating...didn't want to put this down until I knew what happened. I'll be looking for more of Barbara Ann Wright's books."
—*Lesbian Romance Reviews*

"*Paladins of the Storm Lord* by Barbara Ann Wright was like an orchestra with all of its pieces creating a symphony. I really truly loved it. I love the intricacy and wide variety of character types...I just loved practically every character!...Of course my fellow adventure lovers should read *Paladins of the Storm Lord!*"
—*The Lesbian Review*

Coils

"Greek myths, gods and monsters and a trip to the Underworld. Sign me up. This one springs straight into action...a good start, great Greek myth action and a late-blooming romance that flowers in the end..."—*Dear Author*

"A unique take on the Greek gods and the afterlife make this a memorable book. The story is fun with just the right amount of camp. Medusa is a hot, if unexpected, love interest...A truly unexpected ending has us hoping for more stories from this world."
—*RT Book Reviews*

House of Fate

"[F]ast, fun...entertaining... *House of Fate* delivers on adventure."
—Tor.com

By the Author

The Pyradisté Adventures

The Pyramid Waltz

For Want of a Fiend

A Kingdom Lost

The Fiend Queen

Thrall: Beyond Gold and Glory

The Godfall Novels

Paladins of the Storm Lord

Widows of the Sun-Moon

Children of the Healer

Coils

House of Fate

Visit us at www.boldstrokesbooks.com

CHILDREN OF THE HEALER

by

Barbara Ann Wright

2018

Credits
Editor: Cindy Cresap
Production Design: Stacia Seaman
Cover Design by Sheri (graphicartist2020@hotmail.com)

Acknowledgments

A big thank you to my readers, Angela, Deb, Erin, Matt, Natsu, Pattie, Ross, Sarah, and Trakena.

A continuing thank you to Bold Strokes Books: Radclyffe, Cindy, Sandy, Ruth, Stacia, and Sheri. You're forever awesome.

I love you, Mom.

Thank you, Wonder Woman.

A Selected Cast list can be found at the end of this book.

PROLOGUE

Enka crept past the trees and into the fields surrounding the human city of Gale. No one moved atop the wall—the palisade, they called it—but still she walked carefully, gesturing to her fellows to do the same. Among the trees, the brown and silver bodies of the drushka mixed well with their surroundings, but here, among so much nothing, they stood out like bright leaves on still water. The whorls that covered their skin could not hide them among grass and dirt, and any moment she expected a shout from the human wall.

When she had first come to Gale, she had walked boldly, wanting to speak to their leader, their god. She had thought to use the power of the scent to seduce the Storm Lord into giving her weapons or lowering his defenses, but he had threatened her instead. He only wanted hoshpis, the large insects of the swamp that the humans used for food and clothing. The humans had traded such with other drushka, the renegades, but Enka did not want to be tricked into an alliance. She did not really seek trade, only information that would give her an advantage over them.

The humans had conceived their own destruction instead. The Shi had been happy to deliver their death to them.

When Enka reached the gates of the settlement and still went unchallenged, she stood straighter and smiled in satisfaction. The second time she had come here, long after the hoshpis had been delivered, she had done so stealthily and alone. The hoshpis she and her band had gathered had been dosed with spyralotus leaves, and she had smelled the scent change in the humans who had eaten them. A harmless change until she had scattered veira pollen in the human wells. When it mixed inside the body, it became a powerful poison.

Thesta, Enka's second, pushed gently on the gates that led into Gale. They swung open, but they should have been guarded. When Enka had sneaked in before, she had done so at night, scaling the wall, but this was far easier.

Thesta peeked inside and grinned, showing her sharp teeth. She put her spear to her back, and the wood clung there, a gift from the Shi, the same as they all had: a living piece of their queen. Thesta stepped inside the gate, and the rest followed. Enka let her own knife cling to her waist. She still had poisonous claws on the tip of each middle finger, the paralyzing poison that coursed through every drushkan female, enough to incapacitate any human she met.

As Enka studied the streets of Gale, she saw no need for either claws or weapons. It seemed nearly deserted, and the air stank of sweat and sickness. Human detritus lay untended in the streets, wagons and rickshaws and other words she had learned her first time here. She supposed she should not have bothered to learn those terms, either. The humans seemed finished.

One of them lay in the shadows along the street. His light brown skin was splotchy and pale, his lips tattered and flecked with foam. Enka bent over him, hissing at the stink of the poison and something more. This one had fouled himself, but his chest still rose and fell with shallow flutters. One eye blinked rapidly, mouth working as if he knew someone was there but could not respond. The other eye stuck firm, encased in yellow crust.

Enka left him to die.

"Spread through the city," she said to her band. "Find any humans who have not succumbed, any healthy or able to walk." They ran to do her bidding.

Elsewhere in the city, other hunt leaders would be bringing in their bands and searching for survivors. Other agents of the Shi were moving east, keeping watch for the renegades and their human allies. The Shi still sensed the mind of the renegade Anushi queen now and again; she could not have gone that far into the plains. This poisoning of humans would lure her back and let her know that the Shi would never stop chasing her, that any humans who associated with her would meet the same fate.

Enka leaned against a wooden pillar on the front of a building and waited for her band. She watched the dying man breathing his last and knew the Shi would be pleased. Nothing the Anushi queen did would save her human allies, but the Shi would let her believe it was possible. They were the source of her freedom. They would be her downfall. Truly, there was no escape.

❖

Fajir stood in her stirrups and shaded her eyes against the sun. Beneath her, the ossor danced sideways. She'd run the insect hard already, but she would need it to run harder before the day was through. It flapped its vestigial wings against her legs, clacking its mandibles and drooling. Her instincts said to slow the creature, but her sense of vengeance cried out for her to keep going.

In the distance, the large tree moved away from Sun-Moon territory at high speed. It was another wonder she didn't have time to marvel at. At Celeste, city on the coast, there weren't many trees, and those they had would not begin to rival the monster that had visited them, the home of the strange, alien drushka. It was bizarre enough to see the massive tree; it was nearly impossible to believe it could move as well.

"The tracks are easy to follow," Nico said from her side. "Even if we couldn't see it."

She glanced to find him watching her instead of the tree. His cheeks were tattooed with large teardrops, just as hers were. All widows bore the same marks. They'd lost their partners, the person they were raised with, who was to share all aspects of their life. And like her, Nico's dead partner had also been his true love. His was killed after losing her way. Hers was killed by a plains dwelling raider. By the customs of their people, they were supposed to spend the rest of their lives making sure no other partner died as theirs had. But Fajir had been asked to be a palace guard when her Lords had come from the sky, and Nico had pledged his life to Fajir. He'd said she would never lose her way while he lived.

Now, though, Fajir had an opportunity she'd never thought possible. One of the humans riding the walking tree, Cordelia Ross, had said she would help Fajir avenge her dead partner by hunting down the man who'd killed him. She'd offered the pledge in exchange for the life of another plains dwelling vermin, and Fajir had agreed.

But then Cordelia had left Celeste without fulfilling her promise, curse her! Well, Fajir would make that right soon enough.

She settled in the saddle and put her feet to her ossor again, urging it forward. Gentle tugs on the reins wrapped around its antennae kept it on track for the giant tree. Cordelia would either help or watch Fajir hunt her friends and family to the ends of Calamity. If she had to, Fajir would make her see the horror in being alone.

Three people had already departed the tree and headed north. They were likely more plains dwelling vermin. And even though revenge was closer than ever before, Fajir longed to pursue them, kill them, and rid the world of more of their kind. But she told herself to keep her mind on her goal, and her soldiers didn't question her. The opportunity for true vengeance didn't come along very often, and they all wanted to see it done.

But once she caught up to the tree and made certain Cordelia would honor her promise, her soldiers would have to leave her. She couldn't deprive the Lords of this many guards at one time, not after their city had been devastated in the war with Naos, the one-eyed goddess who still resided among the stars. Too many of their people had been killed, and they would need not only protection but help rebuilding. As soon as her vengeance was done, she would return and aid them, too.

Or perhaps, after vengeance was done, she'd take her own life, and she and Halaan would reunite in whatever lay beyond.

CHAPTER ONE

Cordelia floated above Pool's tree, watching the drushka and humans crawl through its branches like ants. To her spirit eyes, the massive tree shone as a column of white light, brighter than the setting sun. A beautiful sight, it eased the fear that wound through her like rot.

The last time she'd ventured out as a spirit, Naos had severed the long silver cord that attached to her body. Doomed to float around forever, unheard by anyone except the drushka and unable to touch anyone or anything, she'd never felt so alone. She hadn't known she could feel so deeply, and that scared her nearly as much as the mess she was in.

Now, after three days of nightmares, she'd told herself to get the fuck back up. She would use every weapon in her arsenal to help her people. After all, she'd helped Simon Lazlo defeat Naos, and he'd tied her body and spirit together again using their shared attachment to the drushka. The white light that infused Pool's trunk, that infused all drushka, wound around and through Cordelia's silver cord, letting her feel Pool and hear the drushkan babble of voices even louder than she could before.

It still freaked her out a little. And she could feel Simon, too. After he'd been healed by Pool, he'd developed his own drushkan attachment. He'd said his first love had been botany, so he easily took to communicating with the arboreal aliens and their moving tree.

Even before she'd almost been eaten by Naos, being so connected with another person, let alone a whole tribe, would have made Cordelia's skin crawl, but now she could see the comfort in it. If any mad gods tried to kill her again, Simon and the drushka were only a thought away.

Cordelia looked for Simon now. A human mind among aliens, he was easy to spot, a darker flame instead of white. He sat near the base of Pool's tree, using his micro-psychokinetic powers to heal some plains dwellers of a deadly disease, a task he'd began before Naos and the Sun-Moon had pulled them all into a war. But that was done now, and after this stop, they were on to Gale.

And a host of other problems.

Cordelia took another look at Calamity's plains, the rolling hills dotted by rocks and ditches, the occasional river snaking in the distance. She floated as high as her spirit cord would allow, seeing farther than any scout. In the distance, a group of people rode hard from the east. Probably more plains dwellers coming to see the walking tree or wondering about missing kin. When Naos had raised her army, many plains dwellers had flocked to her banner, and other clans had gone looking for them, though most would be going home with only grief for company.

Cordelia floated down, following the cord until she spotted her body on one of Pool's massive limbs. Her head rested in Nettle's lap, and through the link to Pool, Cordelia felt Nettle's worry and love. She'd never liked the idea of Cordelia leaving her body, liked it even less after Naos. Cordelia lingered a moment, watching Nettle's lean form, the whorls on her dark skin, her long fingers stroking Cordelia's hair, the poisonous claw on her middle fingers rolled into her palm to prevent an accidental scratch.

Sensing Cordelia's affection, Nettle raised her head. Her short, thick red hair had flattened on one side where she'd been leaning against a branch. Her lichen-colored eyes searched the air, but she wouldn't be able to see Cordelia's spirit, only sense her. She wrinkled her narrow nose, and Cordelia heard one clear thought:

"Sa, my heart's friend, return to me now."

With a chuckle, Cordelia slipped into her body with all the ease of donning a favorite shirt. She opened her eyes and stared into Nettle's worried face. "Sorry if I scared you."

Nettle's thin lips turned down. "If you were truly sorry, you would remain in your body where you belong."

Cordelia sat up. "I couldn't let memories of Naos keep scaring me."

"I know this. I only wish you to be safe." She looked away and smiled. "And I do not wish to argue with you now."

Cordelia sighed. The "now" meant there'd be more arguing later. She started to look forward to Gale's problems if it meant she'd be too busy to explain the need to conquer her fear.

"Liam awaits." Nettle gestured along the branch to where Liam stood, arms crossed, green eyes pinned on them. All he needed was a tapping foot to make the picture complete.

"Ah. You're going to let him argue with me instead. I get it."

Nettle didn't answer, so Cordelia strode to Liam, bracing herself for a lecture. He'd never been happy on the plains. Like her, he'd given up being a paladin lieutenant when they'd first left Gale, given up weapons and powered armor, but that wasn't the reason he'd been so angry. The Storm Lord, god of Gale, had killed her uncle, the mayor, and Liam's mother, captain of the paladins. Liam had wanted to stay in Gale and get his revenge, but they'd had to wait eight months before the fight came to them. After Simon killed the Storm Lord, Cordelia hoped Liam's anger would find an end, but he'd just found other things to be mad about.

"I wasn't gone long," she said before he could start.

"Why go at all? Naos's army is done. The Storm Lord is dead, and we're making peace with the plains dwellers and headed back to Gale. Why tempt fate by leaving your freaking body?"

She walked past him, quickly losing her taste for a lecture. "Shouldn't you be down hobnobbing with the plains dwellers? They like you."

"Simon and Horace have it well in hand."

Two healers united in power; she'd felt just how potent that could be. She couldn't help giving Liam a leer at the "well in hand" comment since Simon and Horace were also lovers.

Liam snorted a laugh, still the same beneath his anger. Reach had told Cordelia that while she'd been off fighting Naos, Liam had been getting the plains dwellers to talk to one another and make peace. A good job had calmed him down. Now, if he could find another such task in Gale, the nagging might stop. And he could take all the talking, as far as she was concerned. She was more than sick of it.

"Have you spoken to the paladins and yafanai we captured near Celeste?" she asked.

He sighed deeply, and she nearly grinned, happy to deflect him. Some of their captives were still desperately loyal to the Storm Lord. Others seemed to be wavering, especially since the Storm Lord had killed Jen Brown, captain of the paladins since Cordelia left.

That particular death hurt more than a little. Brown hadn't exactly been a friend, but she'd been a compatriot, a good soldier. She'd always watch a fellow paladin's back. Her former lieutenant partner, Jon Lea, was now the leader of the "failing faith" party. But with their powers subdued by Simon, the captured yafanai seemed to still be on the Storm Lord's side. Most of them, anyway. And many of them, paladin and yafanai both, were spreading a crazy rumor that the Storm Lord hadn't died, that he'd flown off to fight Naos in space. The fact that no one had found his body, only his armor, convinced them it was true, even though Simon assured them he was dead.

"They still insisting he rode a lightning bolt into space?" Cordelia asked.

"Some are very convinced."

"Don't tell me you're starting to believe it?"

He shook his head. "I know he was just a man, but a few have let Horace read their minds, and…they saw it somehow."

"I bet it was the Sun-Moon fucking with them. Then they stole his body after Simon left, but before we could get there. A little parting annoyance to remember them by."

"Dirty fuckers, if that's the truth." He shrugged. "I'll put that to the captives, see what they think." He looked at her sideways. "Or you could."

"Oh, no. A few rounds of bullshit, and I'd be punching the truth into them."

Nettle grabbed her arm. "Sa…"

Even though she was firmly in her body, Cordelia felt it as Pool's mind touched Nettle's, though she didn't get as clear a message as when she was spirit walking. Pool was anxious, giving a warning: "Fajir approaches."

"Shit." Cordelia put a hand to her wooden blade, a gift from Pool, an ever-sharpening weapon. "With how many?"

"A group of ten, all widows."

Looking for revenge? They hadn't parted with the Sun-Moon on good terms, not exactly, but in the end, Simon had saved Celeste from

Naos and promised to hurt the Sun-Moon bad if they ever came looking for trouble again.

The branches lifted Pool to where Cordelia stood. Taller than the rest of her drushka, well over six feet, Pool loomed over them. Her long green hair flowed over her shoulders, the mark of a queen. She frowned hard, pulling all the whorls downward on her brown face.

"I thought we had seen the last of these people, Sa."

Cordelia nodded. "Me, too. If they've come for trouble, they're going to regret it."

Her stomach shifted as the tree lowered all of them to the ground, but she was happy for the assistance. She didn't know how long it would have taken to climb the trunk of Pool's massive tree; she hoped she never had to find out.

They left Simon and Horace to their healing work, though Pool sent several more drushka to guard them. The plains dwellers they healed would defend them, too, Cordelia had no doubt, if only to save their own skins. A host of drushka and humans waited for Fajir's arrival. She wouldn't stand a chance.

But why come at all? Cordelia searched her memory for all her conversations with Fajir, most of them angry. She sucked in a deep breath as she remembered the dank dungeon under the Sun-Moon's palace. She'd been looking for Mamet, a plains dweller who'd gotten caught in all the fighting. Fajir hated plains dwellers, wanted to kill them all because one had killed her partner. She wanted to torture Mamet for that pain, even though Mamet had nothing to do with her partner's death. Cordelia had to bargain for her freedom, and she'd only had one thing to offer.

"Shit," Cordelia said again. When Nettle looked at her, she leaned in close. "She's here about my promise."

Nettle sucked her teeth, the sign of drushkan confusion, before her eyes widened. "I had forgotten!"

"Me, too. Stand down, everyone. I know why she's coming." They all glanced at her, and she rubbed her forehead. "In order to get Mamet back, I, uh, had to promise Fajir I would help her find the plains dweller who killed her partner. I'd hoped she'd forget in all the fighting, but I guess not."

Liam gawked. "You're going to help her find this person, and then what? Kill them?"

"No, she can do that herself." But even helping left a bad taste in her mouth.

Liam still frowned as if they'd eaten the same thing. During the fight between Naos and the Sun-Moon, Cordelia had tried not to kill any humans, and the only death she'd delighted in had been the Storm Lord's. She'd been ready to kill Naos, but in the end, that hadn't been necessary. After she helped someone hunt a fellow human being, she didn't know if her hands would ever feel clean again.

"Maybe I can convince Fajir to let it go," she said.

"Maybe *we* can," Nettle added.

Cordelia gave her hand a squeeze. "I didn't want to ask."

"You will never have to."

Before Cordelia could kiss her, Liam butted in again. "Just tell Fajir to fuck off, then!"

Cordelia considered it. There were only ten people with Fajir, after all. "I'll talk to her first. Let's match her ten for ten with others standing by in case this turns nasty."

Cordelia and Nettle were two of the ten that went out to meet Fajir, taking Liam as well as Reach, a healing shawness, and several others. The drushka would maintain a telepathic link with Pool, who promised to come herself if Fajir proved rowdy.

As the widows came closer, all of them riding ossors, Cordelia's stomach did a turn. Fajir was human, too, as were all those who rode with her. Cordelia gritted her teeth. Killing them by defending herself was different than hunting someone down. Fajir's life didn't compare to Nettle, Liam, or Reach. It didn't compare to any of Cordelia's friends and new family. She could stand a little blood on her hands if it meant her loved ones would live another day.

Fajir wore a satisfied smirk that made Cordelia want to punch her in the face. She used to think she and Fajir were a lot alike, but Cordelia hoped she'd never looked this cocky. She'd thought of Fajir as the woman Cordelia might have become if she'd surrendered to the urge to sink into a life of violence after her parents' deaths. She used to go on drunken street brawls with Liam, the two of them punishing whomever they could for the shit life threw at them, but neither had ever been as murderous as Fajir.

And Cordelia wasn't as angry anymore, not after seeing how big the galaxy was, not after seeing how many people cared about her, depended on her. The living were more important than the dead, and if she could learn that, maybe Fajir could, too.

Fajir dismounted, her long black hair trailing around her shoulders. Tall and willowy, she didn't look very powerful, but Cordelia had witnessed firsthand how skilled she was with the bone sword on her hip. Her fellow widows stayed mounted, letting her come forward alone. Cordelia knew part of Fajir didn't care whether she lived or died. It was one of the things that made her so dangerous.

Before Fajir could speak, Cordelia said, "Miss me?"

Fajir's smirk widened into a genuine smile that reached her gray eyes for half a heartbeat, then she shrugged. "You remember your pledge?"

The words were casual, but her fingers twitched next to the grip of her sword, and she leaned forward slightly as if she might leap. Cordelia bet her muscles were as taut as ballista strings underneath her Moon embroidered robe. She wouldn't be put off by assurances that the pledge would someday be fulfilled, and she wouldn't be bought by anything else Cordelia could offer.

Everyone was silent, waiting for Cordelia to refuse. Then Fajir would attack and be killed. But her fighters were skilled. They'd made it through the attack on Celeste, after all. Some on Cordelia's side could die. Liam, Nettle, Reach: they were all on the front line. Cordelia herself might die just when her people needed her the most.

And the way Fajir's gaze skated over everyone in Cordelia's group told her that Fajir would go for the pain before she'd seek the kill. She knew that losing loved ones hurt more than the threat of one's own death. She'd probably told her fighters who to target first.

It made Cordelia's blood boil, but she had to find the least bloody way out of this for her conscience to rest. She gestured to Nettle. "The two of us will come with you."

Fajir nodded. "I will send my fighters back to Celeste and keep two ossors for you." She waved behind her. "I'll wait for you over that ridge." It was a good vantage point. She'd be able to see exactly who was coming, the sort of cautious move Cordelia herself might have made.

"We'll get our gear."

As Cordelia turned away, Fajir said, "Wait." She tossed a ceramic jar to Nettle, who caught it easily. "We use this when breaking in young ossors. Spread it on your body, and they should not shy from you." So she'd noticed that the animals didn't like Nettle. Or maybe Cordelia had told her at some point. Or maybe she was just guessing.

Cordelia told herself she had to stop admiring this woman. "Thanks."

Nettle smelled the jar and winced. "What is it?"

"They sweat it out," Fajir said as she mounted.

Nettle was still grimacing when Fajir rode away. Liam had the same look but probably for a different reason. Reach stood at Nettle's shoulder, both of them smelling the jar, but Cordelia bet they were more freaked out by the smell than by the thought of rubbing bug sweat on their bodies. She supposed it was no different than drinking mead made from the hoshpis in Gale.

"She didn't even say hello to the rest of us," Liam said as they all walked back to Pool. "I guess she's not interested in diplomacy."

"Did you expect so?" Nettle asked. "That one dwells in the past. Everything else is nothing to her."

"Do you think she can change?" Cordelia asked.

Nettle spread her hands. "If she were drushka? Perhaps. Humans seem more stubborn." She glanced at Cordelia. "All but you."

Liam snorted, but Cordelia ignored him. "I love you," she said to Nettle, not caring that everyone else could hear, that Pool would know. It probably meant all the drushka would know, but at the moment, she didn't care about that either. It was too soon after the fight with Naos to hold back what was in her heart.

Nettle grinned. "And I you, though you pick the oddest times to say so."

"Better odd than never spoken." Cordelia paused, thinking over the phrase. "That sounded better in my head."

"I shall make that into a drushkan saying," Nettle said. "Better the sudden flood than the long drought?"

"No, no," Reach said. "Better a sharp wind than utter stillness."

Cordelia laughed. "They both need a little work."

As soon as they were back at Pool's tree, Liam pulled Cordelia aside again. He'd worked up the same anxious, angry look she was getting used to seeing, but she supposed she should be thankful he didn't lecture her in front of everyone.

"It'll be all right," she said. "She'll keep following us if I don't go."

"So let her follow us, and if she starts any trouble—"

"You'll kill her? As far as I know, she's never done anything to you." She looked at him closely. "I'd expect Mamet to want to kill her."

"And Horace. She kidnapped him, remember?"

"So you want to kill her on his behalf?"

"No!" He walked in a tight circle, hands resting on top of his head, a frustrated pose she remembered from their childhood. Without his mother to make him crazy, maybe he was desperate for something else. "I'm just so sick of everyone else's shit."

She barked a laugh. "I won't argue with that. But if I started killing everyone who annoyed me, well…"

He nodded and pulled her into a quick hug. "Don't get in too deep with her. From what you've told me, she's an asshole. She isn't you. You aren't responsible for her."

She returned his hug, slapping his back. "Noted. And if she does manage to kill me, avenge my death."

He breathed a laugh. "You got it. I'll bring all the drushka down on her, too. Right?" he asked as Pool stepped up beside him.

"Indeed," she said, looking faintly amused at her daughter's lover. Or former lover? Liam had mentioned that he hadn't seen Shiv in the days since they'd left Celeste. And he was too scared to ask her if they were through. That was probably the source of all his tension, and Cordelia hoped he'd work it out soon enough. She'd hate to have to get between them.

"Well," Cordelia said as Nettle joined them with two backpacks. "We've got gear, mounts, and two pledges of bloody vengeance. Looks as if we're all set."

"More than two pledges," Pool said. "If you count one drushka, Sa, you must count us all. Let her know just how many would seek her death."

Cordelia was touched beyond measure, and warmth spread through her body as she nodded. "I will."

She and Nettle donned packs and strode toward where Fajir waited with their mounts. She'd kept one fighter with her, a small, stocky man Cordelia had seen before at her side. Maybe they'd decided an even number was preferable. Cordelia didn't look back at the humans and drushka who'd become her family, telling herself she'd do what she had to and get the fuck out as quickly as possible.

❖

Simon Lazlo watched the captured Galeans and fought the urge to fidget. A few craned their necks and peered at him with equal parts fear and discontent. Lieutenant Jon Lea stared, no expression lighting his face, the same way Simon remembered from the long night's siege in Gale. Lea had urged the other Galeans to listen to what Simon had to say; he'd lost his faith in the Storm Lord, but others weren't quite there yet. They sat in separate groups: those willing to listen, and those who were convinced that Simon and the other "renegades" would be punished when the Storm Lord came back from heaven.

Simon had already told them what had really happened. It didn't seem to matter that he let some read the truth in his mind; under Horace's watchful eye, of course. In the end, he'd told them he didn't need them to believe him. He'd help Gale however he could. They seemed as if they didn't know what to do with that information. All in all, he'd rather go back to healing the plains dwelling Svenal, but that work was done. The disease was no more, and the Svenal would be able to have children again. How they'd make peace with the other clans they'd attacked, he had no idea. He could only worry about one people at a time.

He leaned toward Liam, who'd urged him to speak with the Galeans again. "What more do you think I can do to convince them?"

"We can't go into Gale with a host of captives who are going to fight us at every step. They need to know we're going to help them." He gestured at the Galeans with a pointed look, as if Simon was a wand he could wave to clear everything up.

Simon's temples burned. "I'm not going to use my power to make them believe you, and I'm not going to let you bully Horace into doing it either."

Liam held his hands up, drushkan fashion, but his eyes were wide with sincerity. "I'd never ask that. And if I knew it was happening, I'd stop it."

Simon's anger evaporated. He usually kept his shields tight, trying not to read people without their permission, but some emotions still came through loud and clear, like Liam's genuine feelings. Simon couldn't hear human thoughts like Horace could—except for Cordelia, anyway—but his micro-psychokinetic powers always told him what they were feeling, their current hormone levels, and the way their body responded to what they were thinking. It helped him pinpoint the skeptical Galeans, but they already knew what he could do. Some of them had powers quite like his, so no one could say he was using anything they didn't know about.

"Sorry," Simon muttered. "I was around people who'd use any means necessary for far too long."

Liam smiled. "I understand. I never thought belief would be harder to combat than a disease, especially to people who can read minds."

"You'd be surprised." Simon ran a hand through his hair, remembering life on the *Atlas*. Even though his regenerative powers had kept everyone on the satellite alive for hundreds of years, they'd still enjoyed tormenting him. And since he'd believed he deserved it on some level, he'd endured it. Yes, belief was hard to combat.

The Galeans continued to argue in soft voices, casting the occasional look in Simon's direction. Jon Lea stared with half-lidded eyes. Simon wished Horace was beside him. Even though their powers always connected them while they were near each other, Simon missed his physical presence. But Horace was babysitting Pakesh, the plains dweller boy who'd eaten some of the drug the Galeans used to give the yafanai their powers. The plains dwellers had stolen it and fed it to one of their own, and now a teenage boy had macro-psychokinetic powers and telepathy he barely knew how to control. Simon and Horace were helping him learn, but it was slow going. One of them had to be near him at all times to keep his powers in check, or he could wind up hurting someone. Among his own people, he'd avoided that by spending most of his time alone. From the conversations Simon had with him, he'd missed being around people.

The Galeans looked to him as a group as Simon stepped close. "Have something to ask?" He tried not to sound impatient, but public speaking had never been his strong suit. Even after all he'd been through—leaving Dillon, burning out his own power, seeing that power return, getting kidnapped, getting shot, connecting with the drushka, and finally being comfortable with his place in the universe—his anxiety disorder still reared its head at the most inopportune times. He supposed he should try to fix it, find out what was different in his own brain and reorient it, but messing with himself at such a level scared him. If he did it often enough, how much of him would be left?

"How did you do what you did at the drushkan tree?" one of the paladins asked. "When you made us…go still?" He frowned, clearly confused. "We were fighting, and then I don't even remember what happened."

Simon nodded. When he'd emerged from a cocoon in Pool's tree, he'd felt more powerful than even before he'd burned his power out, more in tune with the rhythms of the body. "I think of it as…interrupting. I shut down all the systems in your body simultaneously, putting you in a state of suspension." Like the original colonists had been aboard the *Atlas*, but he didn't mention that. They might remember stories, but that was the tale of their ancestors, two hundred and fifty years in the past.

Some of the yafanai stared with open mouths. Even the paladins glanced at one another, and he knew what they were thinking. Dillon had taught them to be on the lookout for new weapons.

"No, I won't teach you how to do it," he said before they could ask. He doubted any of them could manage it, anyway. Only Horace's augmented power could come close to Simon's own, and he wasn't going to be augmenting anyone else.

With a sigh, Simon leaned against Pool's trunk. They'd brought the Galeans to the ground so they might be more comfortable, more willing to listen. Simon bet Cordelia Ross would have beaten the truth into them, but Liam had told him that she was off jaunting with some widows, and even with the violence she'd no doubt encounter, Simon wished he was with her.

"You knew him as the Storm Lord," Simon said, "but to me he was Colonel Dillon Tracey. He was a soldier in Pross Co., the company that employed your ancestors to colonize a world far from here. He was human, like me. And like me, he was given powers during the accident that stranded us here." He pointed upward, but the satellite wasn't yet overhead. "What you call the unwinking star is the *Atlas* satellite platform, the broken ship that brought us here. One of the crew members convinced the others that we should be gods, so that's what some of us did. That same person launched your ancestors to the planet, and two hundred and fifty years later, here you are."

They watched him without moving. He'd never laid out the facts this baldly before.

"And they lived that long because of you?" Lea asked.

Simon nodded. "Your micros can tell you that cell regeneration is possible, even if they can't manage it."

Another hurried, whispered conversation produced some nods.

"And besides you and the Storm Lord," Lea said, "there was the Sun-Moon."

"Two lieutenants who were merged during the accident," Simon said. "Christian and Marlowe. Then there was Dué, also known as Naos, the person who started the plains dweller war. There were ten others, seven now, petty officers you probably won't hear from as they weren't as powerful as the rest of us. Dillon called them breachies."

"But the Storm Lord..." One of the yafanai shook her head and waved her hands impotently. "No yafanai could do what he did!"

"You're right. As far as I know, electrokinesis was unique to Dillon. I don't know why. Even Dué, who had all our other powers, didn't have his. And unlike many of us, it was his *only* power. He didn't create the plant that gives you your powers. He was not a macro or a telepath, and he certainly could not fly, to space or anywhere else."

"You created the yafanai," Lea said.

Simon nodded, happy he didn't have to say it himself. "Botany is my specialty. Biology is a close second. But even with everything I can do, I can't fly either."

That got a chuckle from some of them, but others shook their heads, and he knew they were fighting with a powerful telepathic memory implanted to confuse them. It had to have been a parting gift from the Sun-Moon, and if he'd discovered it while he'd still been close to Celeste, he'd have been tempted to strike at them as he'd threatened to do if they ever went against him or his friends again.

The Galeans fell to murmuring. He'd already told them the story of how he'd defeated Naos along with Cordelia in her astral form. They knew that was why the plains dweller war had ended. And he'd told them what had happened to Dillon, but whether or not they'd ever be able to reconcile that with their own memories, he had no idea.

"However you see things," he said loudly, "the fact is that we're headed back to Gale, and Dillon is gone. The paladin captain is dead, many of the yafanai are dead, and there will be a power vacuum. You're going to need people like Liam Carmichael and Cordelia Ross. You liked and respected them before. They've never given up on you, even though it's been nearly a year since they were last home. You can put your city back together as it was before Dillon and I ever came here, before the boggins or any of it. You can have your lives back."

At that they went quiet, thoughtful.

"I won't fight you," Lea said, head tilted as if Simon had given him something to think about. "And I'll tell others to wait and see, but if you try to push us, we will fight back."

"Understood." Still, Simon leaned forward as his power threatened to rear within him. With Dillon dead, he wasn't prepared to take even implied shit anymore. "You'd lose, but since I'm not looking to push anyone around, I suppose it doesn't matter."

He walked away before they could reply, back to where Liam waited with Reach.

Reach looked past him at the captives. "They smell differently than I remember."

"How so?" Simon asked.

She spread her hands. "Perhaps they are eating something different."

Simon let his powers play over them again. He was still keeping the yafanais' powers under wraps, but he didn't sense any wounds or changes to their system. "I don't sense anything wrong."

Liam shrugged. "As long as they're not sick, why is it important?"

But Simon had been through too much to not be suspicious of sudden change.

"Maybe the old drushka showed them something new to eat," Liam said. "Some of the paladins mentioned the drushka had started trading with the Storm Lord. Though I can't imagine why since they hate us so much."

"Maybe it was an 'enemy of my enemy is my friend' sort of thing. I wouldn't be surprised if they got into bed with Dillon," Simon said. At their curious looks, he added, "Figuratively." He sighed. "Or literally."

"Doubtful the old drushka had good intentions," Reach said. "They would not suddenly become friendly just because one human leader was replaced by another."

Liam shrugged. "So they found something new on their own."

"There is only one way to be certain," Reach said.

"How?"

"Ask." She clapped them both on the shoulder before moving toward the Galeans.

Liam chuckled, and Simon put his hands over his head and stretched. "Well, they're in your hands now," Simon said. "I've told them everything I know."

"They seemed more open to you than they did me."

Simon shrugged. "I used a little carrot and a little whip."

"Pardon?"

"Honey and vinegar?"

Liam shook his head. "Don't know what you're talking about. Sorry."

"Sometimes I forget how old I am. I used persuasion and intimidation, an old trick of Dillon's, though I'm probably not as frightening." It made him shudder to think Dillon had taught him anything. "And now I'm going to find Horace."

Liam waved good-bye, and Simon walked toward the tent he and Horace shared since they'd been camping with the Svenal. Horace suggested they stay in Pool's tree, but as comfortable as he was getting with the drushka, Simon didn't want to sleep so far off the ground. Even though Pool made little resting cubbies in her bark, Simon couldn't shake the idea that one wrong roll in his sleep would send him plummeting to the ground.

Outside of the tent, Horace sat with Pakesh. Their eyes were closed as they communed, and Simon let a trickle of his power join theirs. Horace was not only teaching Pakesh how best to use his power, he was working on Pakesh's brain slowly, trying to alter it so it could better handle the power that had been thrust upon it. It was the same kind of work Simon and Horace had once done on Natalya, but for her, it hadn't been enough. The power had driven her mad. Of course, Pakesh was nowhere near her level. That was good. Maybe their days of battling mad power-wielders was behind them.

Pakesh's youthful brown face had a telling air of serenity. After a few moments, he opened his brown eyes, pushed his thick black hair off his forehead, and smiled. "Hello, Simon."

Horace echoed the greeting in Simon's mind, and Simon could feel how happy they both were to see him. A bit of training had unearthed the real Pakesh: a kind, considerate boy of fifteen who thought about girls with every breath, it seemed.

"Hello yourself," Simon said. "How's it going?"

"Wonderful!" Pakesh beamed. "I'm learning so much."

Simon sat beside them and took Horace's hand. "He's a very good teacher."

Horace gave him a squeeze. "Thank you."

Pakesh glanced at their clasped hands, then looked away with a shy smile and a bit of an eye roll. Simon supposed he would have done the same as a teen if he'd seen anyone older displaying affection. It didn't help that Pakesh viewed anyone over eighteen as old.

As if sensing Simon's irritation, Horace said, "You're excused, Pakesh. Go find your friends. I'll follow you." He tapped his temple.

The idea might have freaked out most people, but Pakesh grinned again, and feelings of relief poured from him. He'd never liked hurting people with his power, feared it, actually, the same way his people feared him. The new friends he'd made were ex-Galeans and drushka, people used to mind powers. He nearly leapt up and strode away, calling to someone as he went.

"You're irritated," Horace said. "The Galeans giving you trouble?"

Simon sighed. "I'm sick of worrying." He brushed Horace's light brown hair off his forehead and looked deep into Horace's kind brown eyes. "I'd rather turn my attention to more pleasant things." He lifted Horace's hand and gave it a kiss and a nibble.

Horace's eyes widened. "Simon Lazlo, are you trying to distract me when there's still work to be done?"

"What work? Pakesh is fine. The Svenal are fine." He scooted closer and gently kissed Horace's neck. "I think you can use a break."

Horace chuckled, and Simon leaned in to the vibration along his throat. Horace clasped the back of Simon's head and gasped lightly. Simon moved from his neck to his lips, but Horace stopped him with a raised hand. "Some of the Galeans weren't feeling well, and I promised to take a look."

Simon sat back. "Why didn't they ask me? I was just there!"

"It was one of the yafanai. Will. I've just…known him longer."

Simon cocked his head. "Known him, eh?"

"Are you jealous?" Horace asked with a mischievous grin.

"Should I be?" It was mostly in jest, but a tendril of worry wormed through his heart. He'd spent too many years being suspicious.

Horace wrapped an arm around his shoulders. "I've never known him, not like that. And I've never loved anyone like you, Simon." He leaned forward for a slow kiss. "I'll never love anyone else."

Simon's mouth worked for a moment. He hadn't expected a proclamation with such...finality. His chest went cold, the surety in Horace's voice frightening him almost as much as the idea of Horace leaving, but before Simon could sink into the scared feelings, he pushed them down and leaned in. "I love you, too."

They kissed again, more passionately, their power wrapping them together.

"Well," Horace's voice said in Simon's mind, "maybe work can wait a *little* longer. The tent is right here, after all."

CHAPTER TWO

The place where Halaan had died was more a collection of hovels than a village. Cordelia couldn't even see Celeste in the distance. It seemed like a place to keep, breed, and tame ossors, judging by the sheer quantity of animals in the pens. Cordelia bet it had been a prime target for raiding back in the day. If Halaan's death was any indication, it was still raided from time to time. The Sun-Moons had put a fence around it, and several guards patrolled nearby, doing the same job Fajir and Halaan had done.

One look at Fajir's face had gotten them through the guards. Every Sun-Moon worshiper they'd met had been unnerved by her tattoos alone. Her expression was as dark as a thunderhead, wobbling briefly to grief before it came rushing back to anger. She rode straight for a spot near one of the pens and stared into it as if she could still see her partner on the ground.

Cordelia wondered why they'd come here at all. Fajir knew that an Engali had killed Halaan; she just didn't know which one. And according to what Mamet had said, the Engali didn't always stay clumped together. They were a large clan, and sometimes bands of them would go off hunting—or raiding, apparently—and be gone for months. Packs of them would go to stay with relatives, and other clans would come to join them. To know where Halaan's killer had gone, they'd have to speak with some Engali first, as any trail from this spot was nearly a year old.

"Which way did he go?" Cordelia asked.

Fajir pointed, and they began to ride again. She seemed determined to take them through every point of Halaan's death and what happened afterward. Cordelia was waiting for a chance to try to talk her out of vengeance, but this particular stroll through Fajir's past left no opportunity. Still, Cordelia didn't want to have a hand in anyone's death, and not just for her own sake. What would she do if the killer was standing beside Mamet or Samira at the time? How would she explain that?

Cordelia glanced at Fajir's solemn face and then Nico's. He seemed more relaxed but still wary, scanning the surrounding landscape much as Nettle did. But Nico's glances often wandered to Fajir. Maybe the best way to get to Fajir was to go through him.

Sunset caught them on the plains before they met anyone else. They might not *ever* meet anyone, might travel all the way to the mountains in the north without meeting a single soul. That would be a relief, except Fajir would insist they keep searching. She might drag Cordelia around the plains for years. The plains dwellers moved constantly, and Cordelia didn't know their patterns, though Wuran, chafa of the Uri, had told her that they often camped close to water. So the Engali would probably follow one of the many rivers and streams that crossed the plains, especially to the north and south. Fajir probably knew that.

Cordelia wished Pool was nearby so she could communicate with Nettle without speaking. As they made camp, she gave Nettle a few pointed looks, then glanced at Fajir. Nettle sucked her teeth slightly. Cordelia repeated the looks, then wandered toward Nico, hoping to have a word alone with him, hoping the Sun-Moon had given him Cordelia's language the same way they'd given it to Fajir.

She plopped down beside him, and he glanced at her, a questioning look in his dark blue eyes. Nettle moved next to Fajir and struck up a conversation. Fajir stared at her for a few moments before answering in fits and starts.

"How did you come to be here?" Cordelia asked softly.

Nico turned from looking at Nettle and Fajir and blinked at her.

"Do you understand me?" she asked.

He nodded. "I haven't…spoken your language much since the Lords gave it to me." He spoke haltingly, his accent thick, and his voice surprisingly light, almost feminine. "I am here because I follow the seren."

Cordelia nodded. She understood following the leader, but that didn't explain the way he looked at Fajir when her back was turned. "Is she your lover?"

He sat back, eyes wide as if she'd slapped him. Being a widow meant having no partner, but Cordelia didn't know if that meant they could never love anyone else. Partners didn't necessarily become lovers, though Fajir and Halaan had been. By the shocked look on Nico's face, she guessed he'd been lovers with his partner, too, and that their vengeance might keep them celibate forever.

"No," he said quietly, gaze darting toward Fajir.

But Cordelia noted the flush in his tanned cheeks and a spark in his eyes. Fajir might not wish it, might not even know about it, but there was something there on Nico's side. Well, that answered her question about why he'd come.

"Do you think this is the right thing to do?" Cordelia asked. "Will killing this man bring her peace?"

"True vengeance will help Halaan rest." He smiled and glanced into the distance.

Cordelia sighed. If Halaan was able to rest, Fajir's vengeance would be satisfied, and Nico would be clear to make a play for her. Well, that meant there was no help here. Nettle and Fajir were still talking, so Cordelia decided to find out everything she could about Nico in the meantime. Maybe there'd be something she could use.

"Were you always a guard?"

He shook his head, staring into the flames of the campfire he'd built. She wondered if that would be his only answer, but then he said, "My partner and I guided lost travelers. We liked the solitude of living in our outpost, hosting the occasional patrol. Sometimes, we even helped plains dwellers who'd gotten separated from their clans. Shira died in a storm, looking for a lost child. Now I make sure others don't share her fate."

Cordelia frowned. "So...you're helping the lost by being a guard?"

When he glanced at her, he had tears in his eyes. "Fajir is lost, and I am helping her find the path again."

Maybe once they found their target and Fajir killed him, Nico would propose, take Fajir to a house in the middle of nowhere, and set up shop again. Cordelia wondered if Fajir would ever go for it. Maybe Nico wondered the same thing.

Cordelia wiped the dust off her boots and tried to look nonchalant.

"And once she finds her path, she'll go back to being a guard, and you'll go back to helping lost people on your own?"

He frowned hard and glanced at her, clearly uneasy with the idea. Cordelia kept her face neutral.

"It's admirable," Cordelia said. "Helping others, making sure no one dies like your partner did, even if it means you have to be alone in the end." She stopped there, only a little ashamed, but that was better than having to kill someone. She could see she'd planted a seed of doubt. Maybe now Nico would try to slow this expedition, giving Cordelia more time to convince Fajir that vengeance wasn't worth risking her own life or Nico's.

Cordelia lay down to sleep, satisfied.

The next day, they spotted a plains dweller camp in the distance. Fajir wanted to ride ahead but listened to Cordelia's words of caution. They dismounted and secured their ossors with screw-like tethers that sank into the ground. Nettle spotted an outrider circling the camp, a sentry, a likely source of information.

Fajir sneered, her hand twitching near her bone sword. Cordelia prodded her in the arm. "We can't kill the sentry. He can tell us if your man is in this camp." And she hoped like hell that he wasn't.

"We must take him unawares," Fajir said. "If he sees us, he will alert the clan."

Cordelia rubbed her chin. She didn't trust Fajir to keep her cool. She kept her own weapon near at hand.

"I will bring him." Nettle was off through the grass before anyone could protest. When the sentry rode past ahead of them, Nettle reared from the grass and pulled him backward out of the saddle, snagging the reins of the animal at the same time.

Cordelia bent double and ran as best she could, hoping the long grass was enough to hide her. The sentry was limp, eyes half-lidded, his breathing shallow. Nettle had scratched him, paralyzing him. Cordelia grabbed him before Fajir could and dragged him back the way she'd come. When Fajir moved to get his legs, Cordelia said, "Grab the ossor!"

Fajir frowned and did so. Nettle grabbed the plains dweller's legs instead and wrinkled her narrow nose in Cordelia's direction.

Unless a person had a bad reaction, drushkan poison wore off in about an hour. They sat and waited, not really speaking. When the sentry came around, Nettle stayed out of sight, not wanting to scare the man any more than they had to. When the sentry's eyes opened enough to focus, Nico knelt at his side.

"Make no noise, friend, and you will live," Nico said.

The sentry blinked at the three of them, and his brow glistened with sweat. "Who are you?"

Cordelia hoped Nico hadn't been lying. She'd defend this man if she had to. "This woman is going to give you a description," she said, nodding at Fajir. "Tell us if the man she describes is in your camp."

"Dusky skin," Fajir said, her voice flat. "Light green eyes with flecks of brown. Light brown hair. A small scar on his chin, and a bigger one near his temple." She must have seen that face every night in her sleep.

"What do you want him for?" the sentry asked. "Who are you?"

"I'm Jenna; this is my sister and her friend," Cordelia said. "And the man she's describing got me pregnant."

Now the sentry gawked at her. Nico and Fajir cast glances at each other but looked at the sentry again, clearly going along with her story.

"We met when he was on a raid," Cordelia said, trying her best to sound wistful. "We…dallied." That sounded pretty classy, better than screwed. Or fucked. "I didn't know I was pregnant until long after he'd gone, and now I've come to find him."

The sentry blinked for a few moments and struggled to sit upright. Cordelia let him, trusting that Nico could pull him down if he tried anything. "He didn't give you his name or tell you where to find him?"

Cordelia shrugged and tried to look as if it didn't matter. "I just know he was Engali."

The sentry seemed skeptical until Nico sighed. "I…dallied with a young raider once. It was a hurried affair, and we simply called each other 'my love.' "

Even classier. The sentry's sigh said young people were all the same. "Why did you grab me?" he asked. "Did you think we'd try to hide the father? A child is always welcome!" He looked around, probably seeing from the terrain that he wasn't far from camp, but he still eyed them with suspicion.

Cordelia shook her head. "Sorry about the tackle. My sister's really upset." Luckily, Fajir looked positively murderous. "She grabbed you before I could stop her."

The sentry shook his head. "Come meet the elders. I don't know anyone who looks like that, but the Engali clan is huge." He puffed up a little. "Maybe one of the elders knows where to find him."

"We're in a hurry," Fajir said, sounding slightly strangled.

The sentry gave them all a frustrated glance. Cordelia put her hand on Fajir's arm, not knowing what she'd do to repay such a look.

"There's no need to be so angry," the sentry said to Fajir. "I don't know how it is in Sun-Moon lands, but here in the plains, having a child outside of a bonding ceremony is perfectly natural. Your sister will be honored among us."

"Just tell us where the next Engali camp is," Cordelia said, "and we'll be on our way."

He gave them directions as best he could, telling them to watch for certain landmarks that only a plains dweller might recognize. Before they parted, the sentry stood and touched Cordelia's arm, then Fajir's. "All will be well. You'll see! Next time, just ask."

Cordelia tightened her grip on Fajir. "Time to go, sis." She nearly dragged Fajir back to their ossors. Nettle came out of the grass to join them when the sentry was out of sight, but Fajir's gaze kept swiveling back toward the camp.

"Keep going," Cordelia said.

"He touched me!"

"Yeah, keep your eyes on what's ahead of you." Cordelia bit her lip. "We might not find him, you know. He could be dead already."

Fajir's expression was unreadable, but she mounted her ossor without another backward look. Cordelia wondered what that meant for Halaan if his killer was already dead.

"We're going to have to speak to more Engali," Cordelia said. "And you're going to have to keep your cool." When Fajir didn't respond, Cordelia sighed, seeing that she'd have to make this more personal to make any headway. "Did you hear that the Storm Lord is dead?"

Now Fajir glanced at her, confusion replacing anger. "So?"

"He's the one that killed my uncle. I didn't kill him myself, but I know the man who did."

Fajir stared, clearly waiting for more.

"It didn't really make me feel better. I mean, I'm relieved that he can't kill anyone else, but my uncle is still dead."

Fajir snorted. "And once the Engali vermin is dead, he won't kill anyone else, either."

"It sounded like an accident when you told me about it in the palace."

"Save your breath."

Cordelia resisted the urge to smack her. "Look, I know you don't care about your own life, or about mine or Nettle's, but what if Nico is killed during this quest for vengeance? How would Halaan feel about that?"

"Nico's life is his own. I would not dare tell him how to live it."

Well, shit, that wasn't going to work. She tried to think of something else.

"Your words are nothing but ashes in your mouth," Fajir said. "Don't try to lead me astray. Just do as you promised, *sister*." She kneed her ossor forward, out of earshot.

❖

As night fell on the plains, Shiv wandered away from her mother's tree and sat cross-legged in the long grass with her little sapling in front of her. It had grown faster than a normal tree, even faster than a normal queen's tree, but nothing about her or her mother was typical. Queens were not supposed to bear their own children. When one queen died, a queen-to-be ascended in her place, and another was born at that moment with green hair, changed at her birth. The newborn became the queen-to-be, and the other queens moved to the next tree in line, so that each one would one day be the ninth, the great Shi, leader of all drushka.

Except for Shi'a'na, Shiv's mother, Pool. When she separated from the drushka, Shi'a'na would only know one tree forever. She had missed the communion of other queens, and out of loneliness, she had borne Shiv. The daughter of a queen would always be a queen, which was why they were forbidden. There simply were not enough trees.

But now, Shi'a'na had learned to make another tree and had given it to Shiv, though it would not be able to carry her for many years. She would care for it before it would care for her. And still, she had no tribe but her mother's. One day, long in the future, she would take the Anushi tree when Shi'a'na died, but then who would care for this little tree? Who would be its queen? She had often wondered, too, how she could be a queen without a tribe.

Now she knew. Now she had to resist pushing her thoughts through her tree, knowing what would happen when she did. Whenever she connected with the tree this deeply, feeling as one with the soil and sun, feeling the wind through branches, she felt *him*, her tribe of one.

"Lyshus," she whispered. She had never been a queen before, but now she had a tribesman all her own, and the connection to him was so definitive, so electric. He was not connected to Pool. He was hers.

When Simon Lazlo had been injured, Reach had placed him in one of the Anushi's birthing pods in order to keep him alive. The pod's original occupant, only a few days from being born, had been ejected early. Reach had said it would not make a difference. The last stages of birth served to bathe the infants in the sap of the Anushi and the blood of its queen, tying the infant to the rest of the tribe. But Shi'a'na had been busy fighting, so Shiv had fed the child her own blood. She never dreamed that would make him skip over her mother and bond with her. After all, she was not a proper queen, and Shi'a'na was so much more powerful.

"Lyshus," Shiv said again, unable to resist calling him. But the natural order of things wanted her to have a tribe, so it had given her one.

She felt him stand in her mother's branches and turn in her direction. His parents were with him, and through him, she heard as they tried to coax him back into their embrace, but he fought them. Only a week old, and he was already so independent, like her. Like the tree, he grew faster than he should, though all drushkan children could toddle from birth, and all were born with teeth.

Shiv had tried to deny contact with him, knowing it hurt the parents when he pulled away, but Lyshus had seemed hurt and confused when Shiv shunned him. He did not understand why she would deny him, and she was tired of trying. She had shared these thoughts with no one, not the parents, not Shi'a'na, not Liam. She had tried to keep to herself, tried to meditate through these feelings, but Lyshus's anguish ate at her like rot in the roots.

"Lyshus," she said again. She was lonely, had been so most of her life. This was why. She had been tied to the Anushi tribe through her mother, had been able to speak to them as her mother did, but it was borrowed power. This was real; it was alive. It was meant to be.

She felt it as Lyshus fled his parents, sliding down through the Anushi's branches. He could not speak yet, could not fully understand what was happening, but he knew she needed him, that they were one tribe. She blocked out the feelings from the parents. They would be Shi'a'na's problem, but after that thought came the touch of Shi'a'na's mind as she sought the source of the parents' alarm.

When her mother tried to touch Lyshus's mind, Shiv's anger flared, and she denied the contact.

"Daughter?" Pool asked through their connection.

"No, Shi'a'na. He is mine! My tribe!"

Shiv felt her mother's shock but also acceptance. She knew the pull of the tribe. She understood it. But she was forced to split her attention between many individuals. Perhaps she could guess how intoxicating it could be to have a tribe of one.

Shiv felt a sense of relief. Now her mother knew. Maybe she would explain it to the rest of the tribe. Maybe she could explain it to Liam, tell him why she had been distant. It was cowardly to avoid him, but she never knew what to say. His touch was invigorating, but now that she had Lyshus, she knew where she belonged, knew what she had to dedicate herself to. It was the same reason her mother could never have more than a casual lover.

Lyshus raced through the long grass, short legs carrying him quickly. Shiv opened her eyes, and Lyshus leapt into her arms. He grinned; his skin was dark brown, almost as dark as hers, and little buds of hair were red over his scalp. He opened his mouth wide. Over his long leather shirt, Shiv found a *nini* tied to his waist by a bit of vine. She held the wooden bauble, and he grabbed it, shoving it in his mouth. He settled in Shiv's lap and crunched on it contentedly. Shiv was glad Reach had taught her this trick. She had never cared for a small child before, but Reach had cautioned her that they liked to chew on everything: wood, clothing, other drushka. A chewing child was a happy one. So all parents tied a *nini* around their child lest they become the chew toy.

Shiv felt the probing thoughts of her mother again and blocked them. She would not be able to do so forever. Her mother was too strong.

For now, she seemed content to probe and retreat, but she would never allow someone in her tribe to keep secrets. All drushka were too open with one another for that. And someday, Shiv would need Shi'a'na's advice.

For now, she cuddled Lyshus and listened to his contented little mind. She stood, and he swung around her, knotting his small fists in her shirt and dangling down her back. She climbed high into her mother's branches while her sapling and her tribemate clung to her. There were predators on the plains at night, and neither Lyshus nor her sapling could defend themselves. Shiv found her small cubby and lay down inside, lighting a candle so she could watch Lyshus at play.

He chewed on his nini, occasionally grinning around it. She passed a hand over his head, and his little hair buds tickled her fingers. When the first bud fell, she thought it a trick of the light, maybe a stray piece of dirt instead of a bud of hair. When the second fell, she leaned close, thinking him infested by some insect, but as she searched him, all the hair began to fall from his scalp.

She sat up sharply. Was he sick? Injured? She stroked him, and all the buds fell, but he seemed happy. She had never heard of such an illness. She wondered if she should call Reach, but there, just under his skin, new hair was already growing, pushing out the old, and she had helped it along.

Perhaps this was normal with infants? The new hair seemed lighter than the first. Maybe infants shed many coats before they grew their true color. She sucked her teeth, wondering what this new color would be, wondering if it would set him even further apart from his fellow drushka. What would they think of her tribe of one?

Shiv searched in the pouch at her waist and found some berries she had been saving. Quickly, she chewed then spat the juices in her hands. She rubbed them softly along his scalp, turning the tips of the new buds red again. She would find a way to ask Reach, but until then, she would help him hide.

❖

When the new day dawned, Pool took to her little cupola of bark halfway up her massive tree. Slivers of wood held her to the trunk as she commanded the tree to walk, and she took comfort in its familiar rhythms. Undulating roots propelled it over the ground while its branches swung to balance it. It took only a fraction of her attention. After two hundred years as a queen, moving her tree was as a flick of the wrist.

Her mind played over her tribe. Most of them looked ahead. They would reach Gale this day, and many wondered what would become of them there. They had ventured from the swamp because it was no longer safe for them in their home. After the last attack by the old drushka, Pool realized that the Shi would never let them go. She wanted all the queens under her sway.

They had ventured on to the plains because Cordelia Sa Ross and her people were banished by their Storm Lord, and Pool had already seen how their fates were intertwined. The Storm Lord had no love for the drushka either. Merging with Sa's tribe had seemed the wisest course, and now Pool thought of them as members of her tribe, too. She could even touch Sa's mind, and she could hear Simon Lazlo through the tree, through her drushka. Two human leaders tied to her; her people thought of them only as family, but Pool had learned how to think deeper, how to see the best course for her people's survival along with her affection.

Most of her people were excited to be venturing closer to the swamp. They hoped to return to it someday, but the Shi had a long life in front of her, and who knew what her successors would think? And Pool herself might not live that much longer. She needed something more stable for her tribe, and she did not know if they could find that in the swamp. It could be that they *could* find peace living so close to the human settlement with the Storm Lord dead. She doubted the queens would bring their massive trees outside of the swamp itself, and without them, the humans might be able to resist an attack, especially with Pool by their side.

She sensed some agitation among her people, worry for their future. And she sensed a pall of anguish and knew at once who it was: the parents of Lyshus, the young tribesman of her daughter.

She had not foreseen that the child would attach solely to Shiv. Blood alone should not have merged them. A queen had to open her mind to new tribemates and draw them in, a queen's power Pool had never shown Shiv. It had seemed to happen between the two automatically, a worrying thought.

At first, Pool had been surprised that her daughter denied her access to Lyshus's mind, but on further reflection, it made sense. Pool would not let another queen communicate mind-to-mind with her drushka. Why should Shiv be any different? But she had never had someone under her branches that was not bonded to her. Even in the old days, when drushka could go from queen to queen, they first underwent a ritual of bonding where they drank their new queen's blood and bonded to her mind. No one took such a move lightly.

Now, though, Shiv's mind circled Lyshus's like a thorn wall. They spent nearly every moment together. The pull of a tribe of one had to be great indeed. But the anguish of the parents was a rotten hole among Pool's drushka. She tried to send them soothing waves, but she knew they missed their child. Maybe they should switch their allegiance to Shiv; then they could all be together.

Pool could not help sneering at the thought. She had kept the same tribe for hundreds of years, generations upon generations. She could remember the ancestors of all of her drushka, and she did not want to give any over. If she had been part of the old drushka, she would not have been so attached. She would have moved trees, gotten new tribes, switched members as mates were bonded and children left the branches to find adventure with another queen.

Pool sighed at her own hypocrisy. She wanted to stay free, had taken the lessons humans had taught her and rebelled against her own people, but she wanted everyone else to follow her rule. She did not want her daughter to have a larger tribe if it meant taking drushka from Pool herself. She sent her mind over the rest of her drushka again, trying to lose herself in their anticipation. She would deal with Shiv and her tribe of one soon enough, when things were settled. She chuckled; this was what humans called denial.

She felt a twinge at the edge of her consciousness, another drushka out on the plains. She thought at first it was Nettle returned, but no, Pool did not know this mind, and it stood between her and Gale. He was not hers, so she could not delve into his thoughts directly, not as the Shi could. She reached with her telepathic call, searching for another queen, but there was none nearby.

Without a word, she sent some of her people to fetch this lone drushka. He had to know she would sense him. She searched again for others but found only one. What did he hope to do? A spy? A messenger? A bloom of hope wanted her to believe he was a renegade, running from the old drushka. If one went, many would follow.

But better to be cautious. She sent a message to Simon Lazlo, asking him to bring Liam. The three of them descended from her tree as her drushka brought the spy through the long grass. Simon and Liam seemed in charge of the humans in Sa's absence, though Pool still thought of the humans as hers, and she knew they would obey her, especially where drushkan matters were concerned.

"Why would one of the old drushka be way out here?" Simon asked.

"And only one," she said.

Liam rubbed his hands over his long brown hair. Several strands had escaped the tail he tied them in, and the dark spots beneath his eyes said he had not been sleeping well, if Pool remembered her human expressions correctly. She knew her daughter was not spending much time with him. It had to be hurting his feelings. Perhaps he could convince Shiv that it was better to open herself and her tribe to Pool.

She shook her head and put that worry away for now.

"There could be more in Gale," Liam said, hands resting on top of his head.

"Great," Simon said, his sigh turning the words to sarcasm. He looked more at peace than Pool ever remembered, even when he had emerged from his pod. Then he had been focused and angry, if calm. With his dark blond hair, he could have passed for drushka at a distance, though he was a bit on the pale side, and no drushka had his blue eyes. Liam's green eyes were almost as deep as her own, as Shiv's.

"There is only one way to know." Pool turned as her drushka brought the spy out of the grass. He walked meekly, head down in her presence. His long yellow braids swung around his head. She stepped close, towering over him, over all her drushka. She grabbed his chin and made him look at her, though his silver eyes tried to shift away. He was young, barely older than her daughter. He let his chin rest still, signaling obedience.

"Your name?" she asked, keeping her voice low and soothing.

He licked his lips. "Sest."

She turned his head back and forth. The whorls in his face carried a hint of yellow across his silvery skin. "Named for the sunrise. I see it."

He swallowed but did not move. If she wished to kill him, he would stand and wait obediently. Was this the only kind of drushka the queens bred now? She liked to think her drushka would spit in the eyes of their captors, queens or no.

"Your queen?"

"Yunshi."

"The sixth," Pool said. She had been among those Pool had fought in the swamp. She shuddered as she remembered how dominated they had all been by the Shi's mind. They were not themselves anymore, just pale copies of the Shi, puppets. "Why are you here?"

"To see if you would come for the humans."

Pool took a deep breath. Liam knew a little drushkan, but Simon would be ignorant of all they said. "And what has happened to the humans?"

"The Shi knew you would return to help them. If you did not come on your own, I was to find you and tell you they were in danger."

So the Shi had done something to the humans of Gale. Did that mean they were now dead? "Shawness," she said to Simon in the human language. "Can you read his emotions?"

Simon frowned at Sest. "I'm not well-versed in reading drushka, but he seems…fine. Passive."

His mind taken over by the Shi? At the moment, it did not matter. "What did the Shi do to the humans?"

"The poison she gave them has run its course."

Pool sucked her teeth. "Dead?"

"Soon."

Pool gestured for her drushka to take Sest into the branches. "We must hurry to Gale. The old Shi has poisoned its people. Reach told me she thought our human captives smelled differently. Perhaps they left their home just in time to escape the worst of the poison."

"I'll tell Horace to give the humans another check," Simon said.

The branches lifted everyone, and Pool commanded the tree to move faster before she had Sest brought to her again.

"Do you wish to come into my branches, young one?" she asked him.

For the first time, his face twitched as if someone was trying to break through. "Your branches? What…what of my queen?"

"I will help your queen." She wondered if Yunshi acted like this:

nearly asleep until given a command by the Shi, like a toy waiting to be given life by a child. The thought had Pool grinding her teeth. It was clear the old drushka would not leave the humans alone, would not leave her alone. They would force a fight no matter how far she roamed.

Sest's face still had not settled, and he seemed in anguish. "I want…"

Pool reached into her belt and drew the little knife Shiv had once made. She cut the pad of her thumb and held it out, letting it be his choice.

Sest stared at the golden blood that curved around Pool's hand, rocking back and forth before he lunged forward and crammed her thumb into his mouth.

It was not the ceremony she remembered, but it would do for now. She pressed their foreheads together and opened her mind to him. As her blood passed into his body, his mind opened, too. She drew him in and made him part of her. He looked at her in wonder.

"Ahya," she said with a smile. "You are mine. Now, tell me all you know."

CHAPTER THREE

Cordelia called another halt so she could rest her aching thighs. The ossors seemed as if they appreciated stopping, too. Each of them was drooling, heads drooping and mandibles slack. Fajir huffed impatiently, but she knew more about ossors than Cordelia; she had to know how tired they looked.

"What's the plan?" Cordelia asked as she stretched. "We keep asking until we find your guy, then what?"

Fajir stared into the distance and said nothing.

Cordelia sighed, going through arguments in her head. She rubbed her forehead as a headache began to build. "What if he's already dead?"

Fajir shrugged. "There are always more."

Cordelia shook her head. "No killing innocents."

"Why do you care?"

"Why don't you? I know you care what happens to your own people. What about other innocent people?" She breathed deep, trying to get her temper under control.

Fajir glared. "The vermin killed—"

"No, one of them did the killing." It would be so much easier to grab Fajir and beat some fucking sense into her, but Cordelia kept her fists down. For now. "And you could have gone on this revenge quest long before now, but you didn't."

"The Lords commanded—"

"Bullshit!" She vaguely realized she was yelling. Her legs were sore, she wanted to go home, and she did *not* want to help kill some random plains dweller she'd never met. She didn't know if she could sway Fajir, and she was quickly losing the will to try. Liam had been right. She should have told Fajir to fuck off.

Nico stepped up. "Seren Fajir couldn't go on this hunt alone, and no one offered to come with her before."

"Fuck that," Cordelia said. "She could have suggested it. I know *you* would have gone with her. Why did she have to wait and bother me?"

Fajir's hand flexed near her sword, and she had thunder in her gaze. Cordelia's temper yielded like dust before the storm. If Fajir *wanted* a beating...

Cordelia sauntered around Nico. "Oh, I think I get it. You didn't go after Halaan's killer because you didn't want your pain to be over; you'd gotten a taste for killing." She pointed a finger at Fajir's chest. "So when I offered to help, you couldn't turn me down without giving away your bloodlust. Well, now your vengeance quest is going to end, Fajir. Either you accept your partner's death now, go home, and find some peace, or you kill your Engali, but then you won't have an excuse to kill anyone else." She cocked her head. "Or are you planning to walk into an Engali camp with your sword out and go down swinging? I won't help you kill yourself like a coward."

Nico took a step, but Nettle said, "Let them fight."

Cordelia didn't know if she meant with words or swords, but it was past time for either.

Fajir's hand twitched again, her expression stony. But the flush creeping up her neck and around her ears spoke volumes. She was moments from a meltdown.

"I lost people," Cordelia said. "And I couldn't get revenge in the moment because others were depending on me, but no one needed you, Fajir. Am I right, and you didn't want this to be over?" She leaned forward. "Or maybe you never really loved Halaan at all."

Fajir drew her sword and lunged, putting her shoulder behind the blow. Cordelia drew and blocked, but the effort sent tremors through her wrists.

"Finally!" Cordelia yelled. The whole world could change, and she'd still appreciate a good fight, though the look on Fajir's face said it wasn't anywhere near good-natured. That was okay. Cordelia wanted her mad, worn out. Then she might listen.

Fajir came on again, one swing after another. As Cordelia blocked but didn't counterattack, Fajir's face contorted, her lips open in a snarl. She huffed and panted, her blows still precise for all their madness.

Cordelia stayed ahead and slowly began to counter, hitting as hard as Fajir, forcing her to give ground. With one massive swing, Cordelia forced Fajir's arms to the side and stepped forward, punching her hard in the gut.

Fajir staggered, gasping. She kept her sword up and pressed her free hand to her stomach, using wild swings to keep Cordelia at bay. And when Cordelia blocked and stepped to the side, Fajir kicked, catching Cordelia's thigh with bruising force. Cordelia rolled before she could drop. She came up on one knee and slashed. When Fajir dipped her sword to block, Cordelia caught her blade and turned it to the side and out, tearing Fajir's sword from her grasp and flinging it into the grass.

"Finished?" Cordelia asked, standing.

Fajir leaned on her knees and breathed hard.

Cordelia gestured to the plains with her blade. "I only—"

Fajir leapt, one hand grabbing for Cordelia's hip, and the other reaching for her wrist. Cordelia staggered, and Fajir kicked, sending them both to the ground with bone-shaking force. Fajir knocked Cordelia's wrist against a stone, sending pain spiking through her fingers, but her blade remained in her grasp, held by tiny wooden tendrils.

Fajir gawked. "What is this?"

With a laugh, Cordelia released the tendrils and tossed the blade away. "Now we're talking."

Fajir punched her in the chin, and stars danced in Cordelia's eyes, her teeth rattling as pain ricocheted through her jaw. She wrapped her legs around Fajir and rolled. With a yelp, Fajir pummeled Cordelia's back and shoulders but couldn't stop the momentum as Cordelia rolled on top.

"My turn." Cordelia jabbed her hard in the face, making her head rock back and splitting her lip. Fajir's eyelids fluttered, but she still tried to swing. Cordelia reared slightly and dropped on Fajir's chest, making the air whoosh from her lungs a second time.

With a gasp, Fajir went limp. Cordelia stood. She heard movement behind her and held up a hand. "I won't hit her while she's down." She trusted Nettle to stop Nico if it came to it; she didn't want this to turn into a full-scale battle.

Fajir struggled into a sitting position, one hand on her belly, the other on her face.

"Finished?" Cordelia asked.

She nodded.

"Feel better?"

Fajir glared before wiping her bloody lip on one sleeve, leaving a smear of red. "You provoked me to make me feel better?"

Cordelia shrugged and retrieved both their blades. "There are only two good cures for relieving tension, or so Liam always says. And you're cute, but I didn't want to suggest the second way."

Fajir frowned, either not getting the joke or not caring for it. "I love Halaan."

Cordelia knelt in front of her. Nico and Nettle had returned to the ossors, leaving them alone. "I know."

"You can't know. I love him as if he was here now and not a memory."

Cordelia sighed and sat, laying Fajir's sword across her knees. "And if you kill his murderer, he's really dead. I get it."

She looked at Cordelia with tears standing in her gray eyes, mirroring the tattoos on her cheeks.

"So don't do it," Cordelia said with a shrug. "Do what you're supposed to: patrol the villages, keep the raiders away, and make sure no one else dies like he did. Then you'd be honoring his memory."

Fajir took a shuddering breath. "Halaan's killer will never murder another if he is dead."

"If you're going to stop all the accidental deaths in the world, you're going to be very busy." She shook her head, remembering how she'd felt after the Storm Lord had been killed. She'd thought she'd be happy, but she'd been tired of all the violence and ready for a nap.

"That's the thing about revenge," Cordelia said. "The satisfaction doesn't last. You have to keep living for the sake of the living, not the dead. Halaan is gone. Killing his killer won't make you happy. It'll just remind you of what you've lost."

"It is the way of my people." She looked into the grassland, her face full of sorrow.

Cordelia sighed, knowing Liam would call her crazy, but… "Come with us. To Gale. People might wonder about your tattoos, but you can tell them whatever you want or glare at them until they fuck off. You wouldn't have to worry about this revenge cycle or what your people might think. You could be happy. I'm sure Halaan would want you to be."

Fajir stared, expression unreadable. Cordelia felt as if they were standing on a cliff, and the slightest breeze could push them to safety or death. She thought of climbing the palace in Celeste and barely held in a shiver.

"I have to see him." Fajir ripped several blades of grass out at the root. "The murderer. I have to see."

With a sigh, Cordelia nodded, wondering if that meant they were safe or if they'd gone over. She stood and offered Fajir a hand. With a snort, Fajir ignored it and climbed to her feet, reclaiming her sword before marching back to the ossors.

All through the ride that day and later that night, Cordelia tried to be subtle with her hints, but tact had never come easy for her. If she pushed too hard, Fajir might defy her out of principle. Cordelia would have done the same. Or maybe that was the way to go: push Fajir until she ended their partnership and fled into the plains. Then at least Cordelia could go home.

That idea left her with a sour feeling and not just because Fajir might continue on with Nico in the hopes of murdering someone. She wanted to save Fajir, wanted to turn her around, wanted her to look past her rage and turn into…

Cordelia herself? Was she doomed to try to rehabilitate every revenge-driven lost cause, or was there something special about Fajir? Cordelia didn't know, but she didn't think she could be satisfied until she saw this through. Liam would accuse her of having a fucking hero complex.

The next day, they planned to repeat their pregnancy ruse to find Halaan's killer, but the group they found camped beside a river seemed far smaller than the one before. The plains sloped sharply to the river's edge, and a few hide tents gathered between the slope and the water. They hadn't bothered to post sentries.

Cordelia lay on the ridge and watched the plains dwellers go to and fro, doing chores or simply laughing and talking. Fajir had an intense look, and Cordelia wondered if she was seeing an enemy or if she was beginning to see something of herself in these people. Cordelia was about to ask, maybe push a little more for Fajir to come to Gale when Fajir stiffened, digging her fingers into the dirt and hissing like a drushka. She eased one hand over to Nico and took the shortbow from his grasp.

Cordelia's stomach lurched sideways. "Is it him?" She searched the camp and spotted a man coming out of one of the tents. He fit Fajir's description exactly, except he didn't seem like a cold-hearted killer. He knelt, smiling, and held out his arms. A toddler, a little girl, tottered from someone else's embrace and into his, screeching in happiness.

Cordelia looked to Fajir, to the bow. "You can't kill him in front of his child."

In the camp below, the man lifted the child and swung her around.

"Let us go," Nettle said. "We will wait for another time."

Nico glared at them. "If she kills him, her dead partner can rest. The child won't even remember."

"The dead do not wander," Nettle said. "They do not want."

Fajir's grip on the bow tightened, and she glanced at Cordelia. "You're right."

Cordelia nearly held her breath. "Good." She got ready to crawl backward and away and then tensed. Fajir's expression hadn't changed. This couldn't be so easy.

Fajir eased to her knees, the grass still hiding her. Cordelia followed suit, every muscle in her body telling her to act, but she had to give Fajir a chance. In the camp, Halaan's killer passed his child a rag doll.

A few tears dribbled down Fajir's cheeks, but she didn't wipe them away.

"Come on," Cordelia said.

Fajir nodded but paused. The whole world seemed to wait as she said, "I want him to suffer as I have suffered."

Cordelia reached for her, but she reared up and away. Nico lunged into Cordelia, knocking her into Nettle. Cordelia fought to rise, seeing the bow lift, knowing what Fajir meant to do. There was only one way Halaan's killer could suffer Fajir's fate: if someone he loved died, and he had to live with that pain.

Fajir nocked an arrow and drew.

Cordelia shoved Nico, giving Nettle room to leap. Nettle's slashing hand caught Fajir's arm just as she loosed.

Silence descended below them before the shouts of surprise started. Cordelia shoved Nico away and chanced a look, her heart in her mouth.

The man was alive, the child alive, her little hand bloody where Fajir's arrow had torn the rag doll from her grip. She was shrieking, but she was alive. Nettle had spoiled the shot.

But Cordelia didn't have time to rejoice. The plains dwellers were charging the slope. Fajir fell, and Cordelia knew Nettle had scratched her. Nettle staggered as an arrow from the plains dwellers stabbed into her stomach.

"No!" Cordelia ran to help, but another arrow punched into her own thigh, sending a line of fire through her leg, almost making her collapse.

Nico grabbed Fajir and lifted her across his wide shoulders to carry her toward the ossors. Cordelia and Nettle leaned on one another and followed. The arrows said the Engali wouldn't listen even if Cordelia tried to talk, not after someone had wounded a child. Nico hefted Fajir onto one of the ossors and fled south, toward Celeste.

The arrow burned in Cordelia's leg, but she kept hobbling, helping Nettle stagger. She grunted as she lifted Nettle into one saddle then climbed into her own, her leg screaming at her.

"Come on!" she told it. She wouldn't take any shit from it now, not when she needed it to work. She grabbed Nettle's reins and her own and sent the animals thundering west toward Gale.

In the morning air, Patricia Dué stood on a hillside and stared at miles of glorious, wind-tossed grass and nature. The sun was bright, and the air was clean. In the distance, an animal keened, and the breeze lifted her hair with gentle fingers. She smiled so hard her cheeks hurt. She had a body to herself, a mind to herself. To be in her own head after years of sharing Naos's babbling funhouse, it was bliss.

"Happy, Mistress?" Jonah asked.

She looked into his handsome face and reveled in the kindness of his gray eyes. He was something else that was hers alone. Jonah lived for her; she'd seen to that. It nearly made her laugh, but he'd never understand her mirth, and she wanted to be kind to him, too.

"I was thinking about how good it feels to be free," she said.

He rested a hand on her shoulder. It was a strong hand; every inch of him was just as strong. The thought made her shiver. When she'd first met him as Colonel Dillon Tracey—over two hundred years ago— she'd thought him strong then, too. She'd liked the play of muscles under his uniform. But he'd also been arrogant, demanding, and a bit of a megalomaniac. When she'd come into power, she'd stripped all of that away, leaving only her dedicated servant Jonah in Dillon's body. Even his people wouldn't come looking for him, not after she'd implanted the telepathic suggestion that he'd flown away into space.

Now that did make her laugh. When Jonah stared, she grabbed his hand and led him into the future.

After days of walking, they were close to the mine north of Gale. Since Patricia had absorbed Dillon's memories, she knew all about Gale's assets. She could keep herself and Jonah alive and well with her powers, but after spending so many years imprisoned in her own mind, she wanted more than that. She was free, she had the body of a sixteen-year-old since Naos had killed the mind of its original occupant, and she had the whole world of Calamity to explore.

But first, she needed supplies, capital, and allies. Overconfidence had brought Naos down. Patricia did not intend to share that fate. If she ever met Simon Lazlo, his drushka, or their allies again, she wanted to be someone, a force to be reckoned with. She wouldn't pick a fight like Naos, but she wanted to be ready in case one came calling.

She'd already started. The memory she'd given Jonah identified her as the sole survivor of a plains dwelling clan who'd been wiped out. Her mother had been a chafa, making her something of a princess, a person worthy of respect. But she could have told Jonah she was the queen of the universe, and he would have believed it. She hoped it would matter when they encountered someone else. She didn't want to use her powers to change minds, but she supposed she might have to, just at the beginning, to get the ball of respect rolling.

But more than company, she wanted some food! She didn't need to eat, but she craved it. Naos had rarely eaten anything, and it had been ages since Patricia herself had taken a bite. They had to have food at Gale's mine. Plus, Dillon Tracey had never gone there in the flesh. Hopefully, no one would recognize him in Jonah.

She squeezed his hand as they walked. The mine would also have shelters, and those shelters would have beds. She shivered at the thought of so many of her former fantasies coming true. The future, for once, was hers to take.

They reached the mine later that afternoon. Set above the foothills and against one of the mountains, the mining town was a scattering of wooden buildings, most big enough for large groups to share. A few smaller structures littered the area; they had a ramshackle feel, as if the people who lived there were consistently too tired to improve their surroundings. Patricia frowned. She didn't want to live in squalor. Well, she'd just have to do something about it. Her mother would have told her to look at it as a canvas ready for paint.

As she and Jonah came closer, she saw one man standing at a well, getting a drink from a wooden bucket. He stared, and she let her power play over him, detecting an injury in his foot. It was headed toward infection. Dillon's memories said the mining town had a couple yafanai, but evidently no healers. Probably no telepaths, either. That would make tampering with minds easier.

If she had to, she reminded herself. Only if she had to.

Jonah glared at the wounded man until he looked away. Everyone else was probably working the mine. Patricia stared at the towering mountains with their snow-capped peaks. A few black holes dotted the area, exploratory or tapped-out mines. They were dwarfed by the closest hole into the mountain, its entrance shored up by wooden beams.

Patricia headed toward the only building with smoke curling from the chimney. Jonah held the door while he scanned the room inside. A mess or canteen, she guessed by the long tables and the bar along one wall. She had a flash of going to a nightclub on Earth with her fiancé Jack, remembering the pulsing lights and holographic dancers working oiled muscles with undying stamina. It had been sleek and sophisticated. This looked like something out of an Old West vid.

Patricia moved toward the massive fireplace. The stones were stained black with soot, and a large pot hung above the fire. Near the back of the room, a stack of kegs sat beside an open doorway. No one occupied the tables or tended the bar, but as she watched, a spindly man wandered into the dining room, wiping his hands on a greasy apron.

He stopped when he saw them, eyes wide in surprise. "Travelers!" He passed one hand through thinning hair and grinned at them with a mouth only half full of teeth. "What brings you to the mine?"

"She is Mistress Patricia Dué, chafa's daughter," Jonah said. "You will refer to her as Mistress and treat her with respect."

The spindly man's eyes widened. "Is that so?" Sarcasm peppered his tone, dragging out the words. "Well, we've had plains dwellers in here before looking to make a ruckus. You take that tone with the miners, and we'll see whose side the respect is on."

Patricia frowned. Maybe Jonah had come on a little strong, but she'd hoped the first person she'd truly met on Calamity would at least be polite. She sighed. "I hoped I wouldn't have to do this."

The spindly man stared, and she sensed his confusion, but that was all right. He wouldn't be confused for long. "You—" he started.

Patricia cut off his voice with her power. He staggered and reached for his throat, mouth working, eyes bulging. He looked to them in panic.

Jonah smiled, knowing what she could do. "Shall I hold him for you, Mistress?"

"No need. Pleased to meet you." She sorted through the spindly man's memories. "Bert," she said with a smile. "As you can see, there's no need to be rude."

He stepped back, eyes so wide she could see white all the way around. It reminded her too much of the *Atlas*, the accident. Her eye throbbed, the black pit that Naos had filled, and panic reared within her, threatening to crush her.

"No," she said, curling her hands into fists. Fear fluttered through her like a caged bird. "Stop."

"Deep breaths," Jonah said.

"I know what to do!" she barked.

He blinked at her, surprised. "Mistress?"

She took deep breaths, still holding Bert with her power as she closed her eyes. "I have two eyes. I can see. I am myself."

"Could have fooled me," Jonah said.

Her eyes flew open, and she gawked at him. "What did you say?"

"I said nothing, Mistress."

She looked to Bert, but no, she still had his voice. She shook her head. She could not start imagining things, not now. Another deep breath, and she was in control, smiling at Bert again. "Good ol' Bert," she said, taking that from his memories. "Our man Bert, the man who can get you what you need. I need safe haven, Bert, somewhere to stay, somewhere I'm in control." She filled his mind with respect for her, with reverence.

Bert smiled, and she let go of his voice. "Mistress," he said, "welcome! Any seat you like, of course!"

She took a bench near the fire, gesturing for Jonah to sit across from her. "Food," she said. "And something to drink."

"The best you have," Jonah added.

"Of course," Bert said, bobbing like a floating apple. "The best I have."

Patricia watched him scurry to the back. He came out with bread and cheese before ladling stew from the large pot above the fire. The smell made her stomach rumble, and she dug in without waiting for Jonah. She barely waited for the wooden cutlery Bert supplied. She was ravenous as she tried hard to remember the last thing she'd eaten. It would have been before the launch of the *Atlas*, before the accident. She wouldn't count anything Naos had done. Thick and meaty, the stew was the best thing she'd ever tasted, and the bread was pure heaven.

"I'd kill for a cheeseburger," Jonah said.

Patricia dropped her spoon and stared at him, her belly knotting. "What?"

He looked up from his stew. "Mistress?"

"What did you say?"

He glanced around as if looking for someone else. "Me, Mistress? I said nothing."

He wasn't lying, radiated sincerity. But he couldn't know about cheeseburgers. She'd taken all of Dillon's memories, hadn't she?

Yes; she scanned him now and found only what she'd put there. He was still looking at her, waiting. She scanned him again. Only her work.

"Never mind," she said woodenly. "My imagination." Or maybe it was Naos. She could easily talk in Dillon's voice. She'd probably get a kick out of it. Patricia drew her considerable shields around herself, cutting off even the chance of telepathy. She'd have to be more careful.

CHAPTER FOUR

Cordelia and Nettle rode hard, and their pursuers faded into the distance. The first Engali to charge them had been on foot. Cordelia hoped they hadn't gone back for mounts, or they might keep up the chase. Or maybe they'd follow Fajir and Nico, two people who actually deserved their vengeance.

After another look over her shoulder, Cordelia pulled on the reins of both ossors and stopped them. She slipped down from the saddle, her leg aching, the arrow jutting out. Nettle had one hand pressed to her abdomen as she slumped in the saddle. Golden blood streamed around her fingers and the arrow shaft, darkening her leather shirt and trousers.

"Nettle," Cordelia said gently. "Let me look."

Nettle's eyes seemed heavy-lidded and dull, but she dropped her hand and tried to climb down.

"No, stay there." Cordelia cut Nettle's shirt open, evoking a hiss of pain.

Instead of head-on, the arrow had gone into her belly at an angle, and the motion of the ossors had probably moved it around, widening the hole and doing who knew what to her insides. They had to get it out. Cordelia put a hand to her forehead and tried to think. She looked to her leg. She needed to get that arrow out, too, but she only had a couple of spare shirts for bandages.

"I can't do anything while you're mounted," she said, half to Nettle but mostly to herself. "But after I take it out, you won't be fit to ride for a while, and the Engali might be following us." She looked back the way they'd come and saw nothing, but the plains dwellers would know how to track someone. Maybe they'd let her explain?

More likely, they'd shoot first. "Fucking Fajir! What the fuck did I ever see in her?"

While the anger still pulsed through her, she looked down, braced herself, and snapped the shaft protruding from her leg. "Fuck!" she yelled as the pain raced up and down her spine. But now only four inches of wood stuck out of her thigh. Progress.

"Sa?" Nettle asked weakly.

Cordelia took several deep breaths. "If I break your arrow, do you think you can ride easier?"

"I do not know."

She thought it best not to touch it, then, not until they had more time. Cordelia mounted her ossor again, gritting her teeth through the pain. "The best thing we can do is get to Pool before we pass out or get an infection."

"Infection?"

"Yeah, the wound itself gets…sick." She dug in her pack and passed Nettle a spare shirt. "Put this around the arrow. Maybe you can staunch the bleeding."

Nettle did so while Cordelia ripped her other shirt and tied some around her leg, trying to keep her own arrow from moving around.

"I know nothing of this wound sickness," Nettle said as they rode again. "Can one die of it, Sa?"

Cordelia nodded. If Nettle hadn't heard of infection, that probably meant she couldn't get one; a bit of good news, at least. Cordelia took Nettle's reins but didn't push the ossors as hard. She tried to look for the easiest, most level ground so the ossors wouldn't have to jump or trip, but the plains were rife with rocks and ditches. Even as slow as they were going, every step seemed to make Nettle slump farther.

They couldn't keep riding after dark, so as the sun began to set, Cordelia headed toward the faint sound of water. They reached a creek just before the light disappeared.

"Do we risk a fire?" Nettle asked as Cordelia helped her down. "Will it keep your wound sickness away?"

"I don't think so, but it can't hurt." She sat Nettle in front of a boulder that would shield her from the wind. Cordelia made a fire quickly; the air was chilly, and they could both use the warmth. Once she was done, she took the packs off the ossors and eased Nettle onto one of their bedrolls so she could look at the wound again. She didn't remember seeing barbed arrows among the plains dwellers or Sun-Moon worshipers. The tips she remembered were perfect ovals. If she could get the angle right, the arrow might slide right out, and then she could bandage the wound as best she could.

"Do drushka cauterize wounds?" she asked. "Burn the opening so it can't bleed?"

Nettle sucked her teeth. "The shawnessi pack the wounds with moss and sing."

Cordelia looked to the fire, wondering if she should experiment, but she didn't know if it would help. She certainly didn't want to risk injuring Nettle further or setting her dry skin on fire. "I think we should pull this out, for starters. The hole seems wider than before, and I don't want it tearing you up." Cordelia kissed her cheeks. "It's going to hurt. I'm sorry."

Nettle closed her eyes. "Be quick." She gripped Cordelia's thigh, her claw tucked away into her palm. Even injured, she was still mindful. Cordelia blinked away a few tears. Nettle was not going to die. Cordelia wouldn't fucking let her.

She wrapped some cloth around the sticky arrow, trying to get as much purchase as she could. With one quick yank, she drew it out. Nettle arched, her head thrown back, eyes wide. She didn't cry out, but her breath came in short, panting gasps. Cordelia pressed her body flat, held the wadded shirt against the wound, and used another strip of fabric to hold the makeshift bandage in place. Sticky, golden blood covered her hands, but she pressed them to Nettle's cheeks and brought their faces close together.

"Little breaths," Cordelia said. "Just keep breathing, love."

Nettle was looking at nothing, the nictitating membranes across half her eyes. Finally, she focused on Cordelia, her gaze going back to normal.

"Hello again," Cordelia said, nearly sobbing. She'd feared a drushkan version of shock.

"And your wound?" Nettle asked.

Cordelia looked to her leg. She could yank the rest of the arrow out, but it didn't seem to be doing as much damage as Nettle's, though when she moved, she could feel her muscles clenching painfully around it. But she feared unplugging a bleeding artery or something she couldn't see. She'd heard that arrows could sometimes do less damage if they were pushed through a limb, but she didn't think she could do that by herself, and Nettle was in no condition to help. "I think we leave it for now. We can't have two streaming wounds to care for." She stroked Nettle's hair. "When we catch up to Pool, the healers will have an easier time with my leg than they'll have with you." She kissed Nettle's soft, narrow lips. "Thanks for making me the easier one to deal with."

Nettle grinned weakly. Cordelia laid a blanket over her and curled up at her side. She wondered if she should slip free of her body and try to warn Pool, but she didn't want to leave Nettle with no one to defend her. The ossors were tethered nearby, and she hoped the rocks would shield them from anyone who came looking. She stared at the flames and rested her head near Nettle's shoulder as the last of her adrenaline left her, and sleep came easier than expected.

In the dark of night, Cordelia woke up, hearing her stomach growl loudly. Nettle could probably hear it, too. She chuckled, glad some things never changed. She should have made them both eat something before she'd drifted off. Now it was nearly pitch-black. The fire had burned to embers. She sat up, reaching for her pack when she heard the growl again. She froze. It came from the grass nearby.

The ossors shifted; she could just make them out in the dim light. Cordelia caught a harsh scent, one she'd smelled once before, when she'd volunteered to sit up with a member of Wuran's clan and watch for the predator that had been stalking their campsite.

She shook Nettle gently and leaned toward her ear. "Grelcat."

Nettle stiffened and began to stir. Cordelia helped her sit. "Weapons out. Stay here."

Nettle didn't argue, but Cordelia felt her shift as she drew her daggers. Cordelia eased toward the fire and drew her blade. She didn't want to go stumbling after the predator in the dark. Maybe if she got the fire going again, the grelcat would spook. She prodded the coals. The Svenal had given her some dried geaver dung to use as firewood, but she didn't have much left. Still, a little flame bloomed. She could see the legs of the ossors clearly as they pulled against their tethers. Behind them, she caught a flash of silver fur.

Cordelia pushed to her feet, trying to ignore the pulsing pain in her leg. When she blinked, the grelcat had disappeared. She limped toward the ossors. The meager light reflected off their bulbous, multifaceted eyes. She touched the thick, rubbery neck of one, and it calmed. The vestigial wings of the other flared, making a fast, flapping sound. It clicked its mandibles as if it could sense the grelcat watching.

Cordelia could still smell it, too. She hoped it wasn't circling around to get to Nettle, but she was even closer to the fire than the ossors. Maybe that was the key: keep everything closer. Cordelia undid the first tether and led one ossor toward the fire. She turned for the other when it keened and jerked backward into the dark as if yanked by a giant hand.

The tether pulled taut, still caught on the ground. The ossor screamed, and there came an answering growl. Cordelia shuffled forward as fast as she could, shouting, but the keens of the ossor ended in a massive crunch that made Cordelia's insides go cold. She took another cautious step and saw eyes that shined back at her as if glowing with green fire. She could just see the glossy fur on its snout, the peculiar tufts of hair to the sides of its wide mouth, and the gleam of its teeth, two sharp rows bared at her. It seemed larger than the one she'd seen before, but now that it had what it wanted, it didn't seem interested in a fight.

It dipped its head and tugged at the ossor again, pulling against the tether. Cordelia considered taking it on, but it was night, she was injured, and it could see in the dark. She swiped her sword down and cut the tether, letting the grelcat take its prize before she limped back to the fire.

Nettle was looking anxiously into the dark. She relaxed slightly as Cordelia sat. At least she'd thought to take the packs off both animals before she'd fallen asleep. "We were raided by a grelcat."

Nettle sighed, looked relieved but still pained. The whorls in her skin seemed more like cracks in the dim light. "Will it return?"

"Nah." Once they'd eaten, they lost interest in hunting, or so Wuran said, but she bet it would return to this spot tomorrow night, hoping someone else had caught it a tasty meal. "Are you hungry?"

"No, Sa," Nettle said, sounding tired more than anything.

Cordelia made her drink some water. "Sleep. I'll stay awake just in case." She helped Nettle ease down again before she dug in the pack and pulled out some rations. At dawn, they would set out again, and Cordelia would let Nettle ride. Nettle would object, but if it came to it, Cordelia would pick her up and tie her in the saddle.

She leaned her head back and tried to focus on what it would be like when she got back to Gale. First thing she'd do after getting Nettle healed: drink the Pickled Prog dry. Everything else that had to happen: meetings or briefings or bullshit could wait.

Second thing... Killing Fajir sounded nice. That was a vengeance quest she could get behind.

❖

Fajir awoke to a ceiling over her head. She frowned, remembering the plains, the camp. Was she dreaming or dead? Captured? After Nettle had scratched her, making fire run through her veins and freeze her muscles, she couldn't recall anything. Wouldn't the vermin rather kill her then capture her? After all, she'd attacked one of their children.

In the moment, it had seemed so right. After Cordelia had spoken of finding peace, Fajir feared the future, feared what she would do after Halaan's killer was dead. What reason would she have to keep breathing? No, she'd decided, better to kill the child, make the murderer suffer as she had suffered, and then the vermin would kill her, and she would go to Halaan while the murderer lived in anguish. It would have been perfect.

Nico leaned over her, healthy, unbound, and she knew what had happened. Nettle had foiled her shot, but Nico had rescued her, and now the cycle would start again. It left her sad and empty, but she would keep going. Halaan needed her.

"How do you feel?" Nico asked.

Fajir tried to speak but found her throat too dry. She swallowed, licked her lips, and tried again. "Where are we?"

"Home." Nico put a hand under her and helped her sit up in a narrow cot. She recognized the small clay house: a table with two chairs, sealed barrels and pots in the corner, the remains of dried herbs hanging from the ceiling along with a lone lantern. It was Nico's old house, where he'd helped lost travelers. He'd brought her here after finding her on the plains, just after Halaan had died.

Her throat caught. Ah well, if she had to start again, she supposed it was only fitting she start here. Or maybe she'd gone back in time, and Halaan had just died again. Maybe she could get her revenge sooner this time. Or when they burned Halaan's body, perhaps she could evade Nico's grasp and cast herself into the flames.

But she would never be so fortunate.

Nico passed her a clay mug, and she sipped water, swirling it in her mouth before swallowing. "How long?"

"A few hours. She scratched you deeply. It's nearly dark out." He sat at the foot of the cot and stared at his feet, despair hanging over him like a cloud.

She squeezed his hand, happy that he always shared her moods. "Don't worry. Next time, I won't miss."

The sadness in his dark blue eyes didn't lift. "You weren't aiming at the man. You wanted to shoot the little girl."

He looked so pained, she shook her head. "I thought you'd understand." She started to explain and stopped. Maybe he *couldn't* understand. He had no target for his grief. "If he suffers as I have suffered…" She stopped. The words didn't sound right outside of her head.

Nico smiled, and a few tears fell, but he wiped them away. He seemed smaller as he leaned against the clay wall. As a dual child, a man born in a female body, she'd always thought of him as male, but the light of the single flame softened his face.

"I…haven't been honest with you, Seren." He chuckled and swallowed. "Do you know why I call you that, even after you gave me permission to use your name?"

"You've always been respectful of rank."

"No. I cannot call you Fajir because…" He took a deep breath. "My heart always wanted to shorten your name as if we were lovers. Faja." He closed his eyes and exhaled as if the word lifted a weight from his chest. "My Faja."

She blinked in surprise and fought the urge to squirm. Part of her had sensed his attraction, but she thought it more like admiration for a leader than lust for a mate. She didn't know what to say.

"But that's not the dishonest part," Nico said. "When the storm took Shira from me, I could never put her to rest, not truly. I could only guide the lost, could only guide you, Faja. After I came to know you, I hoped that when we honored Halaan, we could find some peace together. I loved you, and even if you never loved me, I still wanted to help. We could always be friends."

She couldn't meet his gaze; the words were too bold, the emotion in his eyes too raw. "I…" And what could she say? She didn't love him, didn't know if she could love anyone again.

"Faja," he said, leaning forward and making her look at him. "You had a chance to lay Halaan to rest. So few of us have a single target, and *you didn't take it.* You chose instead to make the circle of violence wider." He bit his lip as if he'd witnessed a great tragedy and was holding in the urge to weep. "Faja, you…don't want to be found. Ever."

She stared hard, her own sadness welling. Was it true? Something in her wanted to lean into his arms and weep, wanted to beg him to understand, to beg him to help, perhaps. Pride demanded she lean away and snarl. "You only helped me because you wanted me for yourself!"

He sighed and looked to the ceiling. "Perhaps that's true. I might be guilty of selfishness even as I thought I was doing good. But now I know I can't do anything for you. No one can." He stood and moved to the door where his pack waited. "The other ossor is tethered outside. I hope you find your peace. I love you, Faja."

Before she could ask him to wait, he was gone. Fajir stared at the door and breathed hard, part of her wanting to run after him and the other half saying it was good that he was gone. Now she could go on the killing rampage she'd always desired in her heart.

Alone? She'd never been truly alone in her life. She staggered to the door, her muscles still heavy. She threw it open in time to watch Nico disappear into the fading light. The wind howled through the grass, and she could see the faint lights of Celeste through the gloom, but there wasn't a soul around. She sank to her knees in the doorway. He was wrong. She *wanted* peace. Didn't she? It was so hard to know anymore. The need for vengeance still burned within her, but now there was something else, too. She was tired, body and spirit. She'd been tired for a long time. Maybe that was another reason she'd fired at the child. She wanted to make sure the Engali would kill her quickly.

She looked to the north. They might still be searching for her. She could ride that way, hope to run into them. Maybe they'd grant her wish.

Or she could follow Nico to Celeste and ask his forgiveness. He'd give it to her eventually. She cared for him. Even if they never became lovers, they could be friends, as he said. They could laugh together, share wine, take a house with other widows and just…live.

And Halaan? Nico had been right about him, at least. She'd had an opportunity for true vengeance and hadn't taken it. And from the world beyond, Halaan would know that. If her people were to be believed, that meant he still suffered, his death not paid for.

She couldn't let that continue.

Fajir stiffened and stood. If Nico abandoned her, so be it. The idea of death didn't frighten her nearly as much as being alone, but then, she wouldn't be alive to be alone much longer. She would ride north and confront every Engali she met until she found Halaan's killer again. If he managed to overcome her, so be it. But if she killed him, then his family would kill her. Either way, she and Halaan would be together again.

She went back inside the house. First, she would sleep, then she would set her feet on the path to her destiny, and no one would stop her, not Nico, not Cordelia, and not another vermin.

❖

Simon felt Gale before he saw it. The palisade was only a haze in the distance, but after what the drushkan spy had said, Simon had been stretching his powers as far as they would reach, using Pool's tree like an antenna. The entire population of Gale hovered on the edge of death, poisoned. He pictured them lying in their beds, in doorways, in the streets. He clasped Horace's hand and tried to stretch their powers beyond sensing to healing, but there were limits.

"Easy," Horace said. "We're almost there."

Simon shut his eyes tightly. "Hurry, Pool."

The tree picked up speed, but Simon didn't know how much faster it could go without toppling. They'd be there soon, but not enough for some. He felt two people die, even at this distance. More would follow.

"Pool," Simon said, "set Horace and me down just inside the palisade. Can your people spread through the city, gathering everyone they find, and bring them to us?" He turned to where Pakesh rode beside them. "We won't be able to cover you with our power while we're healing so many."

Pakesh nodded, his face pinched with anxiety. "I'll stay outside the wall."

"Be ready, shawness," Pool said in Simon's mind.

He nodded, and when they reached Gale, the long branches reached over the palisade and lowered Simon and Horace inside. They clasped hands and ran for a person lying in the street. When they knelt beside her, Simon repaired all the systems the poison had damaged then looked for the contaminant itself, but the woman's body was laced with it. He sensed the same wrongness Horace had detected in the captured Galeans, but this person had ingested something else, too. Her nervous system was shot, but this poison was easier to cure than the Svenal's disease. He supposed he should be grateful he'd had so much practice healing recently.

He and Horace went cell by cell, cleaning the woman's systems with the efficiency of a street sweeper. One last nudge, one last check, and she was done. Simon waved at a nearby drushka. "She's done. Next one."

The woman disappeared and was replaced by someone else. Simon felt more coming, carried by drushka in an endless parade. He and Horace worked as fast as they could, their powers as one. Simon kept muttering, "Done, done, done," as he healed, and patients were replaced as fast as the drushka could move them.

Still, some died before they reached him.

The ground seemed to fall away as Simon stretched his powers. Pool lifted him and Horace, moving them farther into the city. As soon as the tree set him down, the parade of patients began again, and Simon cast his power over them all.

"Done, done, done."

Pool moved them again. Simon was dimly aware of the drushka breaking into houses to drag out sick and injured people. There were a few cries of alarm quickly calmed by other human voices: the renegades, paladins, and yafanai working to help.

Horace directed a few of the yafanai, and Simon sensed his frustration. His voice sounded weak, and Simon turned some power in his direction.

"No, don't worry about me," Horace said.

A hard thing to ask, but Simon forced himself to obey. Horace played triage, his power finding those most in need. He guided Simon's power where it was needed most, reaching for the patients before they even arrived.

The rhythms of the human body surrounded Simon, and he sank

into the pulse of the city. It would have repelled him once. It had once terrified Horace, but they had no choice. Simon soon lost track of where they were, of the feel of the sun or the wind. Sounds faded into dim irritants and then to nothing. His lips moved, but he could no longer hear himself.

"Done, done, done."

At last, he reached and found no one to fix.

Simon blinked. His eyes felt gummy and sore. The palisade was in front of him again. Had he gone all around the city or all the way across? His left fingers cramped, but he couldn't remember what to do about that. Someone was holding his hand, and he followed the line of an arm to see Horace passed out next to him. Simon tried to heal him, but his power moved sluggishly, and his body felt like a wet sponge. His skull ached, and he couldn't quite get the power together to heal it. Funny, he'd always wondered what his true limits were.

"More?" he asked, his throat raw. He burst into coughing.

Reach held a waterskin to his lips. "Drink, and rest."

He sipped the water gratefully. "Are there more?"

"No, shawness. Your work is done."

He looked up at her, and pain stabbed through his neck. Her face was in torchlight, and her orange hair seemed to glow. Darkness surrounded them. "What time is it? Is Horace all right?"

"Shawness Horace is sleeping," she said with a frown. "As you should be. It is past midnight." She waved a hand, and several drushka appeared, lifting Horace away from him. He tried to stand but couldn't. Two drushka put their arms around him and lifted him, too. He could barely feel their touch, but he wanted to sink into it.

Still, he had his pride. "I can walk!" His eyelids betrayed him by slipping closed. They'd arrived in Gale at midday. How the hell could it be after midnight? No wonder he was exhausted, and Horace had passed out.

"Rest in our hands, shawness," Reach said. "We will watch over you, your mate, and the boy Pakesh." She began to hum, and the melody spread through Simon's limbs, soothing him in drushkan arms. "Let the world fall away." The sound of her song carried him into darkness.

When Simon finally awoke, it was to the gentle creaking of Pool's branches, a sound he'd become comfortably familiar with in a very short time. The feeling of the drushka surrounded him, and shifting shadows and light drifted across the large branch outside one of Pool's sleeping cubbies.

Horace was snuggled next to him, forehead pressed against his arm, one hand on his chest. Blankets had been tucked around them, but as usual, Horace had shrugged them off, and Simon had pulled them to his chin. The bliss of Reach's song had stayed with him, and safe in the rhythms of Pool's tree, he could have stayed there forever, never mind how far they were off the ground.

"Shawness," Pool said in his mind. "I sense you are awake. We have need of you."

Simon suppressed a groan. "Now?" he whispered.

"Humans are awake in Gale. Most are weak, though none seem in danger. They want answers, shawness. Liam is with them. Our captives have been returned, but they wish to hear from their healer, from you."

Horace stirred. "When Pool talks in your mind, it sounds like a buzzing swarm," he mumbled.

Simon smiled. Horace couldn't share in drushkan telepathy. Simon supposed a human either had to become one with them like he'd done in the birthing pod or had to leave their body, as Cordelia could.

"The people we healed want to talk to us," Simon said.

"Will you come?" Pool asked.

He smiled, liking that she always asked, never demanded. He wondered if that was one reason her drushka obeyed her without question. From what she'd said, the old queens subjugated the minds of their drushka, but Pool would never do something like that, not when she admired freedom as much as she did.

He felt her amusement and realized they were still linked. The idea didn't bother him nearly as much as it would have nine months ago, when he'd first come to Calamity. "We're on our way."

He and Horace struggled upright. A drushka waited outside with water and dried meat. They chewed thoughtfully while the tree lowered them to the ground.

"Travel rations?" Horace asked as he gnawed.

The drushka spread his hands. "The queen thought it best, shawness. We do not know the source of the poison in this city. Food will be a problem. If we are to hunt, we will need to travel into the swamp."

"Where the old queens are," Simon said with a sigh. "Or venture out into the plains again."

"Oh good," Horace said. "I don't know what I'd do without a load of problems."

Simon snorted a laugh that he bottled when they reached the crowd inside the gates of Gale. When it became clear who he was, word spread, and people pressed into the streets to gawk at him.

Liam pushed through to Simon, Jon Lea at his side. The horde of people closed after them, more joining the crowd until it reached both sides of the street.

"We've set patrols," Jon Lea said, "to watch for looting or anyone trying to take advantage of the broken doors."

Simon thought that might be a jibe at the drushka for breaking in when they had to, but the man said it with his usual lack of expression. No doubt he was just stating the facts.

Pool joined them. "Your soldiers should also watch for members of the old people."

"How will we know them from you?" Lea asked.

Pool gestured to her green hair. "My drushka have shorn hair. The old drushka wear theirs long, braided. I will keep watch for them, too."

Lea nodded. "I'll spread that around. And maybe you should keep your drushka outside the palisade for now, as much as possible, anyway, until we know the situation."

Simon shook his head, offended by the very idea that Gale would ban its saviors. Before he could launch into a tirade, Horace touched his arm.

"I'm not sensing fear from the crowd when they look at Pool," Horace said. "Some might even feel safer with her here."

"Right now," Lea said. "Later? Who knows?"

Pool rested her long fingers on Simon's and Horace's shoulders, her claw prominent for Lea to see, but she couldn't very well help that. "Perhaps it is better to be cautious," she said. "If you find drushka who are not mine, please, do not kill them. Bring them to me, and I will see them dealt with."

Children of the Healer

"You got it." Lea jerked a thumb at the crowd and looked to Simon. "You ready to talk?"

"Just a sec." Simon leaned close to Liam as Lea turned back to the crowd. "Well, he seems to have accepted our return readily enough. Think the others will follow?"

"Lea's always been practical," Liam said. "You can count on him to do what needs to be done."

"Like finding the source of the poison," Horace said. "Now that I know what I'm looking for, I can detect it in a living creature."

Liam nodded. "Water's a likely source, too."

"Take Reach with you to search, shawness," Pool said to Horace. "Then you can sniff the poison out."

Horace gave Simon's hand a squeeze before he walked back toward the tree. Without his presence, the crowd seemed to loom. Simon breathed deep and tried to summon the confidence he'd felt when he'd first emerged from the drushkan pod. Pool was still with him, and that brought him some comfort. He moved closer to the crowd and raised a hand for their attention.

People wanted answers, so he gave them what he knew, starting with finding the lone drushka on the plains and hearing that Gale was in trouble. He also told them the Storm Lord was dead, but it seemed most had already heard that from the returned paladins and yafanai, though versions of what had happened differed. The crowd had a decidedly mixed reaction to the news, everything from tears to smiles. Simon didn't even know how to begin to help them heal from that.

"We're trying to find the source of the poison now," Simon said. "But—"

"What about the missing?" someone asked.

Simon stuttered to a halt. "Missing what?"

One of the soldiers stepped forward, and he recognized her from the tree, one of Cordelia's renegades. "We've been sorting through everyone," she said. "Living and, um, dead. There are two hundred people unaccounted for."

Simon fell silent, stunned. How could he have missed them?

"We didn't miss anyone," Horace thought to him. Even when they weren't side by side, Horace was still with him. "They must not have been here."

The crowd began to murmur, and the soldier spoke again. "We searched the fields and sent some people into the plains in case they tried to run from the illness. Some people say they remember drushka in the city after everyone was already sick."

"What's your name?" Simon asked, impressed by her efficiency.

"Jacobs, sir."

He waved the sir away. "Simon, please, everyone. I'm not a god, and I'm not in charge." Though standing at the head of a crowd making speeches, it sure felt as if he was. Double damn. "I'm only a doctor, a healer, I guess." He was about to babble on about being a botanist and biologist as he used to, but he bit his lip, suddenly missing Samira. "I'm only here to help." He turned to Pool. "Do you think the old drushka could have something to do with these missing people?"

"It is possible, shawness."

Simon looked to Liam. He'd been about to ask why the drushka hadn't finished everyone off, but the poison would have done that without major healing. The old drushka might not know about him, might have assumed Pool would find a town of dead humans and two hundred missing ones.

But why take people at all?

"Oh God," Simon said, covering his mouth. "They're bait."

Liam's eyes widened as if he'd reached the same conclusion. Pool seemed grim and looked to the swamp. Two hundred humans held captive in there? How the hell would Gale get them back?

"We'll keep searching," Liam said as the crowd erupted in murmurs again. "We'll double-check lists of the missing. If anyone's been taken by the drushka, we'll find them."

Someone shouted, "How?" and angry mutterings were peppered with pleas for the return of family or loved ones. Some asked what they were going to do for food and water. Simon sent out some soothing waves, and the crowd quieted, but those were all good questions.

"You don't have a mayor," Simon said. "And right now there is no paladin captain, no god." Some shuffled their feet, but they had to face the truth. "So we'll have to work together. You have to trust each other and help each other. I won't hide anything from you, and neither will Liam or Pool." And bang, he realized he'd just set up the three of them as leaders. Double, triple, quadruple damn.

He rushed ahead, trying to quash that idea before it could take hold. "Leaders…will emerge. Right now, take stock of what you have. Ask the drushka to inspect any food or water before you try it. Their noses are better than ours." That got a few smiles. "If you have any concerns about violence or someone breaking the law, please direct those questions to Lieutenant Jon Lea."

"Is he the acting captain?" Jacobs asked.

Simon looked to Liam, who shrugged. "I'm not a paladin anymore," Liam said. And Lea had already gone.

"That's up to the paladins," Simon said. "I suggest you work out for yourselves who's in charge of what, who's a paladin anymore and who's not."

The crowd murmured again. It seemed as if the idea of working together to solve their problems might be more daunting than being told what to do. If they were all working together, they'd have no one to complain to, after all.

Simon stared at them for a few more moments, waiting for other questions, but they stared at him just as expectantly. He froze, every bit of stage fright he'd ever had creeping within him. Liam cleared his throat awkwardly, but when Simon turned to him, he smiled.

Liam faced the crowd. "Let's get to work!"

Some of them moved; others didn't. They watched Simon with forlorn expressions. Tired of being stared at, he wondered what he should do until he noticed how messy the street was. Acting on his natural tidying impulses, he moved to a tipped rickshaw and righted it. He then picked up a piece of broken crockery and a wooden spoon. When he dared another look at what was left of the crowd, they were dispersing, some randomly tidying like him. Another group had gathered near a mess of spoiled fruit and were discussing how to handle it. Some still seemed purposeless or worried, but at least they were moving.

"You did well, shawness," Pool said.

"I do *not* want to be a leader."

"Sometimes, want and need intersect; sometimes, they do not." She spread her hands and wrinkled her narrow nose.

He picked up another bit of trash. If he acted quickly, maybe they'd put him in charge of cleanup. At least it was one job he knew he could handle.

CHAPTER FIVE

Cordelia limped through the plains, leading the ossor with Nettle atop it. Nettle had already tried to fall out of the saddle, so Cordelia tied her aboard with pieces of shredded shirt. Now Nettle's head lolled against her chest most of the time, her eyes rheumy and unfocused. Her skin had faded from dark brown to ashy gray. Cordelia had to force herself not to watch for every labored breath.

She didn't want to stop, not even to change the pathetic excuse for bandages tied around the wound in Nettle's stomach. Whenever new blood leaked through, Cordelia just pressed new cloth against the old. Why the fuck hadn't she paid more attention to the medics when she'd seen them work? She'd always thought of injuries as someone else's problem.

Maybe Nettle needed a distraction. Cordelia chattered about nothing, trying to summon some of Liam's drunken, carefree spirit, but she had to stop and gulp for air as her leg throbbed. Though the air was cool, the sun beating on her head had soaked her in sweat, and the occasional breeze took her from boiling hot to shivering cold within moments.

"Your people believe in a life after dying, do they not?" Nettle asked when Cordelia paused for breath. "Where you are reunited with those lost?"

"Some do. They think the Storm Lord will care for them, that he cares for all the dead." She shook her head violently. "No, we're not talking about that. No one's dying today."

Nettle stared ahead as if not seeing or hearing. "A pleasant idea. I would like to see my son again."

Cordelia stumbled as she turned. "Your…"

"My son Nush. He died…" She shook her head. "Long ago. I did not have many summers at the time. And I do not like to think on it. Perhaps if we drushka thought there might be life beyond death, we would think on the past more often." She frowned. "Would that make us more human?"

Cordelia blinked a few times, her mind whirling. Nettle had a child? And he'd died? And this was the first Cordelia was hearing about it? On the spot, she couldn't think of any secrets she'd kept, but Nettle was more than seventy years old. And she'd already said she didn't like to think about the past. Cordelia couldn't be angry about something so painful.

But it wasn't anger, not really. It hurt. What if Nettle didn't trust her?

"Nush was always eating," Nettle said. "Never stopped. His father named him after a fish that behaves in the same way."

"His father," Cordelia whispered. She shivered and thought of something her mother had once said about the living reminiscing about the dead. It meant they were soon to follow. Cordelia tugged the ossor's reins until Nettle was within reach. "I'm here, Nettle. Now. Please, stay with me."

Nettle blinked and looked down at her, smiling. "I am here, too, Sa. I thought telling you of Nush would take your mind from the pain of your leg."

Well, it had certainly done that. Cordelia limped forward again, staying at the ossor's side. "What…happened to him?" She swallowed. "You don't have to answer if you don't want."

"We had a summer of storms, and there was hardly any dry ground after the floods. Many of the larger saleska, the progs, were washed into our territory, but there was not enough food for them. We tried to drive them away before they began hunting us. I and a few others caught one saleska alone, starving. I told Nush to stay clear, to use his sling from afar." She wrinkled her nose. "He was young but obedient. When the saleska's long tail lashed at him, he leapt into a tree, but the blow from the tail shook loose a dead branch. He must not have heard it falling above the creature's roars, and it landed atop him." She spoke without sorrow, as if the grief of the past was as dead and buried as her son. Cordelia felt it for her instead, a hollow opening in her chest.

Nettle touched her shoulder. "There is no need for sadness, Sa. Nush has been dead for fifty summers or more, and life continues."

Cordelia supposed that people as long-lived as the drushka had to be able to forget their pain. "And his father?"

"Living. He has other children now. We knew ours would not be a long mating." Her touch grazed Cordelia's shoulder as if saying they had something different.

Cordelia nodded, happy to think that. Nettle was her first real, mature love. She wanted to believe she fit that bill for Nettle, too, but Nettle had been alive over forty years longer than her. "And he was a long time ago, too?"

"Just so," Nettle said.

"So, who is he?"

Nettle gave her a flat look and said nothing.

"What? I'm not going to do anything to him."

"I will not say."

"Why? Is he so badass that he'd kill me if I tried to start shit?"

Nettle spread her hands. "Think on it and try to guess his name. Perhaps that will carry you through this trial."

As if to echo that thought, Cordelia's leg throbbed, and she hissed through her teeth. Nettle watched her carefully, but Cordelia didn't complain. There was nothing to be said. The ossor wasn't big enough for both of them, and Nettle was more injured. Cordelia shivered again as the wind gusted, making her sodden clothes stick to her side. A feeling of light-headedness swept over her, and she shook her head, trying to balance. She ate a little dried fruit and limped on.

"Do you have the name yet?" Nettle asked.

Cordelia forced herself to think through the drushka. "It isn't Smile, is it? He's a little too carefree for you."

"Ahya, too carefree by far. And too young to be the one."

Cordelia ticked him off the list. One down. Several hundred to go.

They walked for hours as the sun crawled across the sky. Cordelia named drushka. Nettle dismissed some and wouldn't respond to others as she faded in and out of consciousness. The sun continued to pummel them, but Cordelia only got colder. She ripped her trousers open to look at her own wound. The flesh around the arrow was red and swollen, hot to the touch. Her mouth was as dry as geaver hide, but she feared drinking her fill because she knew she'd take all they had.

"Just a little farther," she said as she walked. How many hours had it been? The sun seemed to crawl across the sky, but they'd started before dawn. They had to be close. "A few more feet. They can't be far now. Just over that ridge, probably."

"Sa," Nettle said, doubt thick in her voice.

"We're almost there. Your old lover isn't that short scout, is he? What's his name? With the really long nose? He is the most unattractive drushka I've ever seen."

"Sa."

"If that's him, I'm going to be embarrassed for you."

"Sa." Nettle leaned closer, and Cordelia heard her bonds straining to keep her in the saddle. "You must leave me and ride for help."

"No." She patted Nettle's leg and made her straighten. "Don't worry. We're almost there."

"No, Sa. No."

"What do you know?" Cordelia felt more than a little drunk. Maybe she'd summoned too much of Liam's spirit. Somewhere inside, she knew that line of thinking should have alarmed her, but the woozy feeling was a welcome respite. "You've been asleep most of the day, and I say we're nearly there!" Her leg burned like fire, but that didn't bother her much either. "One limp in front of the other."

"You must go, Sa. Bring help."

"I'd never find you again."

"Sa—"

"No!" The shout threw her off balance, and she fell to her knees, jarring her leg and making her swear. She heard Nettle trying to undo the bonds. "Stay there. I'll prove we're almost there." She pictured their route in her mind and tried to slip from her body. They'd ridden east with Fajir and then north, but from the Engali camp, she'd headed straight west, angling slightly south, a much more direct route to Gale.

Cordelia strained but stayed inside her body. She couldn't concentrate, but she pushed and called for Pool. She felt Nettle doing the same. She'd been doing it all day, but now Cordelia joined in desperation.

When it didn't work, Cordelia looked down at her legs and frowned. What the fuck was she doing on the ground? "Get up." She smacked her uninjured thigh. "Get the fuck up." When her legs obeyed at last, pushing her to her feet, she hobbled forward again. "Good leg. Legs. Medals for the both of you."

"Sa?"

"I'm fine." She went back to naming names but couldn't remember who she'd already said. Nettle fell silent, head against her chest. She breathed, so Cordelia didn't stop, knowing she couldn't help. She just kept limping, following the line of the sun as it continued to ease across the sky, free as a bird. Maybe she should sing. Liam always sang when he was drunk, and it seemed to—

When the grass rushed toward Cordelia's face, she thought she must be imagining things. She'd drunk *way* too much.

The air left her in a rush as her face connected with the ground. It didn't hurt. Her arms were under her, her cheek pressed against a rock. It should have hurt. It should have worried her that it didn't. "Get up," she told her body.

It told her to go fuck herself.

"Is that so?" she mumbled. She spit out a few blades of grass and pushed up on her elbows. "Come on, you lazy fucker. Get up!"

"Cordelia?"

"Coming! I'm coming. Hang on." She couldn't help slurring her words. That was a bit worrying. How much had she had? She remembered drinking…nothing. And Liam wasn't there. It was her and Nettle, and Nettle was…hurt. Right, she was hurt, and Nettle was hurt, and…

"Cordelia Ross?"

Nettle wanted her to leave. To get help. "I'm not gonna leave you here!" Cordelia shouted.

A hand helped pull her up. That wasn't right. Nettle should be in the saddle. Cordelia stumbled in a circle. "Get back on that ossor, Nettle! Right now!"

But it wasn't Nettle. A man in a broad-brimmed leather hat stood behind her. His face was as brown and lined as an old boot, and he was grinning. "It is you!"

"The fuck?" She peered at him, but his face kept swimming in and out of focus. Then she had a crystal clear memory of sitting with this man at a campfire, passing around scuppi, a plains dweller liquor that would knock the unsuspecting flat on their asses. "Wuran?"

He nodded. He was the chafa of the Uri, the clan Cordelia had spent the most time with on the plains, but what was he doing here? Maybe she *had* been drinking.

No, his clan was near Gale, and she was going to Gale. She grinned and swayed. "I made it!"

He grabbed her shoulders, steadying her and looking into her face. He pressed a hand to her forehead and frowned. "You're burning up."

Right. She was hurt. She gestured toward her leg and then looked to the ossor, but a group of plains dwellers were already taking Nettle gently from the saddle. "We need help." She licked her lips. "Water?"

"Of course." He fumbled with a water skin, but when the sky started to tilt, he grabbed hold of her again and shouted for someone to help.

"I told you it was just a little farther," she said as a group of hands lowered her to the ground. Her vision was fading around the edges, but she was happy. "Now who can go fuck herself, huh?"

Horace leaned over the well, Reach beside him. They'd hurried through the streets of Gale with the drushka, and Horace had kept his micro-psychokinetic abilities open for any more sick or injured people. So far, they'd been lucky. The marathon of healing the day before had saved everyone who could be saved.

Even though people were still missing, it was hard not to beam with pride. Horace had never worked as hard as he had with Simon; he'd lent his power until darkness had fallen over him like a blanket, but the exhaustion had been worth it. Even now, he sent a little telepathic tendril Simon's way, just to make sure everything was all right.

When he got a happy, loving feeling in return, he focused on the task at hand. They'd done a lot for Gale, but they weren't done yet. He hauled on the rope that led into the well, bringing up a bucket.

Reach sniffed the water carefully. "It smells off, shawness, not quite like the captives, but…" She stared into nothing, thinking. "The drushka we took on the plains said the people were poisoned, and you sensed a poison in two parts." She pointed at the water. "This must be one."

Horace shook his head, his pride drowning in a tide of worry. "We need to check the other wells, but if the old drushka got to one, they probably poisoned all of them."

"And the second part of the poison?"

"Maybe in the food?"

Reach spread her hands. "Plants would be difficult to tamper with undetectably."

Horace let the bucket go. He put his hands to his back and stretched as he considered all the food sources in Gale. "We need to check the grain silos to make sure. And the food stored in the warehouses."

Reach sent some of her fellow drushka to check the silos and the other wells. She and Horace headed for the warehouse district, stopping at any food stores so Reach could poke her head inside.

At one, she paused and breathed deep. "Here, shawness. Something is not right."

Horace glanced at the mounds of dried grass in the warehouse's dark interior. They were at the edge of the district, near the hoshpi pens. "This isn't people food. It's for the hoshpis."

She crept closer to the dried grass, eyes roaming the floor. At one pile, she knelt and dug until she found a stalk with a few leaves attached. "These are spyralotus leaves." She shifted more grass out of the way. "And here are more. The hoshpis do not normally eat so many. It grows high beyond their reach."

Horace watched her think. Simon was the plant expert, not him. He wouldn't know spyralotus from any other leaf if it bit him. But even Simon didn't know all the plants of the swamp.

"Helpful for some ailments," Reach said, turning the leaves over. "But if you were to eat it raw…" She glanced at the door. "A hoshpi might tolerate it, but a human? Shawness, I believe we have our answer."

She marched out the door and toward the hoshpi pens. Horace followed, eyeing the pen full of the large, bumbling insects. A few lay in heaps, still as brown boulders. More tottered, mewling, on their six legs.

Reach pointed at the downed hoshpis. "See there, shawness? They have eaten enough spyralotus to affect them, but this behavior comes too late for the humans to notice. Their meat is no doubt saturated with poison, and the humans who ate it would be as well. But still that would not kill them." She crushed the leaf in her hand. "The old drushka must have laced the wells with veira pollen, and that mixed with the spyralotus was enough to kill. A nasty trick indeed. The Shi must have consulted her shawnessi to think of an agent so insidious."

Horace looked to the hoshpis and focused. He'd helped heal one of the insects before, when traditional methods hadn't been enough. He tried to remember how their bodies worked when they were healthy, the better to pinpoint the differences now. He worked slowly, methodically, until each hoshpi seemed healthy again.

When he opened his eyes, they were all up and moving, rumbling and bumping into one another. And they'd all secreted several mounds of pinkish goo. Horace knew that the distillers would normally take those secretions and make mead, but he called to one of the drovers and told him to throw this goo out and to take care handling it.

The hoshpis bumbled over to him, staring with watery brown eyes. Horace chuckled nervously, hoping he hadn't just acquired his own devoted herd. Where in the world would he put them? "You're welcome."

Reach inhaled deeply. "They smell right, shawness." She clapped him on the shoulder. "And now we have some food."

He turned away. He couldn't look at them any longer if they were going to be eaten. "There aren't many."

"Enough to feed those in desperate need. The queen tells me she will go into the field and dig a clean well."

He nodded, trying to let pride reconquer his uneasy feelings. They could deal with this crisis. And maybe this would make all the Galeans welcome Pool's drushka with open arms, though some were still angry. He couldn't really blame them. They'd been poisoned, a few kidnapped, and many killed. They were looking for someone to blame. He'd heard muttering about how humans would be better off splitting from the drushka entirely. After all, the drushkan dispute was an internal one, and some thought they should work it out without bringing humans into it. Horace would argue they were already in it, had been in it since they'd first encountered drushka on Calamity. And the Shi wasn't attacking humans just because they were Pool's allies. According to the drushka, the Shi wanted to see all humans wiped out.

Reach grabbed his arm. "Pool senses something in the plains, a call for help. We must go to her, shawness." She started moving, keeping hold of him.

"But we—"

Reach made a slashing motion in the air, cutting him off. "Have your mouth speak to your legs and teach them to move!" She started running, and Horace had to give himself a boost to keep up. He sent out a telepathic call to Simon and found him being similarly dragged toward Pool's massive tree with only the knowledge that they were needed.

❖

By morning, everyone in the mining town called her Mistress Dué, and she didn't have to bully anyone, not as Dillon would have done.

Well, she didn't have to bully them physically, anyway. Bert, the man in charge of the cookhouse and all its supplies, told everyone about her, and she'd hoped the conversion to her way of doing things would spread naturally. But people were more stubborn than she remembered, and she had flashbacks of trying to talk her way into places or positions on Earth. It had never worked right. Even when she'd been the right choice for a job, her words never seemed to be enough. She could never master charm. She had to work quickly, and hard, just to be noticed.

So, even though she didn't care for it, she tweaked the people of the mine with her power, making tiny alterations in their minds. She made herself keep it simple, and it turned out to be easier than she thought. Most people wanted to believe in someone grander than themselves; they wanted to worship. And she was powerful. This body was beautiful. Many of the miners considered her mismatched eyes exotic and her face radiant with the blush of youth, yet she had the wisdom of someone much older. How much better could a god be?

When she'd heard there were two yafanai currently working in the mine, she knew she had to use her power there and quickly. But as she pounced on their minds, they proved as easy to twist. They were both macros, here to poke holes in the mountains, and they had no defense against telepathy. Easy peasy.

Now Patricia had her pick of tables in the cookhouse; she had the best food. The mine foreman gave her his little house while he moved into a bunkhouse with the others. She made sure to thank him where everyone could see. She never wanted it said that she took her worshipers for granted. Not that anyone would say it, especially with Jonah watching them like a hawk.

Wonderful, attentive Jonah. With Dillon Tracey's expertise in the bedroom, he made a fabulous lover, and even if he didn't have the inexhaustible energy of her young body, she could always help him with her power. Even thinking about his strong touch on her skin made her weak in the knees. She had to put off her tour of the mine to spend another hour alone with him in their little house.

What could be better? Even if she had to use a little power to get it, she was having the best time of her life since she'd been with Jack on Earth. As she lay beside Jonah in their bed, both of them breathing hard and spent, she promised herself that from now on, she'd only use her powers when she had to.

"Mistress," Jonah said, voice filled with love. "You are a wonder."

She laughed. "You're not so bad yourself." His admiration felt good, even if it had been put there by her. Naos had always craved linear emotions, cause and effect, but Patricia was happy to experience anything that was wholly her own. She glanced at Jonah, wondering if she'd ever tire of him.

That question would break his heart if she said it. What would his face look like marred by that much pain? Would he weep? Beg her to keep him? She tried to shake the thought away. It didn't matter. For now, she was happy. If she had to walk away from him someday, she'd deal with that when it happened.

"Nah, you'll never get over me," he said.

She sat up sharply, looking at him. He stared with confused eyes and tried a hesitant smile. "You desire more, Mistress?"

He acted as if he hadn't spoken, but she'd heard his voice clearly, just as she'd heard it in the cookhouse. But before he'd said anything, he'd worn a satisfied, Jonah-like expression. That other voice, though it sounded the same, carried an undercurrent of self-assuredness that she'd stripped from Jonah, a cocksure abrasiveness that had belonged to the body's former owner.

When Jonah tried to speak again, Patricia laid a finger over his lips.

"Naos?" she whispered.

Masculine laughter echoed through her mind, Dillon's laughter.

But she'd erased him. She'd taken his memories and his power, then put him down. Nothing existed of Dillon anymore except his body.

Someone thought they were clever.

"Lieutenant Christian?" she asked. But that didn't make sense. He wouldn't contact her without his counterpart, Marlowe. You didn't get the Sun without the Moon. She put her hands to her head, searching for a telepathic signal.

"Mistress?" Jonah asked. "Is it a mind attack?"

She waved to quiet him and sent her telepathic power out in a spiral, reading minds and then passing them by, searching. She sensed some of the breachies from the *Atlas* in the hills, those who had elected to get far away from the rest of the satellite pantheon. None seemed focused on her, and she left them behind with barely a whisper of power. She didn't want to send her power to Celeste or Gale. Not yet, not when she wasn't sure.

Patricia opened her eyes and slapped the covers. This couldn't keep happening. Someone was poking around in her brain at will, and she wouldn't allow that!

Or she was going crazy. Again.

It came back with a flash: the boom of the crash, the shriek as the bulkhead collapsed, the pain of the shrapnel tearing through her eye, and then the universe pouring inside, driving her out of her skull until she had to become something else just to keep breathing, her real self shut away like a rat in a cage.

"No!" She put her head in her hands, feeling the tears trying to come but denying them. The world was becoming a tunnel again, a long black hall with no way out, her surroundings something she could see but never touch.

Jonah's arms went around her, his warmth pressing tight to her body. "It's all right, Mistress. I won't let anyone hurt you."

She hugged him fiercely and slowed her breathing. She didn't have to be that lost again. She wouldn't. She had to get a fucking grip!

Jonah's hand moved to the small of her back, caressing, and a wave of lust hit her so hard she gasped. Yes, she needed a distraction. She pushed him down to the bed, needed him now. His eyes widened, and she heard herself growl.

"That's right, baby," Dillon's voice said in her mind. "Come and get it."

Jonah's lips didn't move. That was an old trick of Naos's, but Patricia's terror was lost in another haze of lust: primal, animal, with a masculine energy she'd never felt before. She couldn't resist it any more than she could resist breathing.

She had him and came almost instantly. When she rolled off, the lust faded, but the fear remained. "Who are you?" she said in her mind.

No one answered, and she didn't know which scared her more: that she was alone in her head to fight this opponent or that she wasn't alone and had no one to fight but herself.

Jonah wasn't moving, but he still breathed. He was probably waiting to see what she would do. She sat up and looked at him timidly, ashamed she'd simply used him even though that was what he was for. She hadn't even bothered to see if he enjoyed it.

He gave her a hesitant smile. Bright red welts ran across his chest where she'd clawed him. She healed them with a thought. "I'm sorry, Jonah."

He cupped her cheek. "You never need to apologize to me, Mistress."

In her mind, Patricia thought she heard a derisive snort. She climbed out of bed. "Let's clean up and get some clothes on. I want some food, something to drink." A further distraction. "Then we'll take a tour of the mine."

They walked to the cookhouse together. "I wonder if we'll see anyone from Gale," Jonah said. "Unless they've heard that you've come and are afraid to face you."

She chuckled and breathed deep. Right, they had to think about the future. "No, if Gale finds out we're here, they'll probably send Simon Lazlo. He's the only one who knew me before."

"Before when, Mistress?"

"It doesn't matter, Jonah. I'm not afraid of him or anyone else." She gave his arm a hug. "Not with you to protect me."

He smiled, clearly pleased with the compliment. Another lust-flash arced through her, and she gasped, fighting it. What the hell was wrong with her today? She took a few deep breaths and waved away Jonah's concern. She didn't want him to touch her again if he was going to be irresistible. Maybe this was just what two hundred and fifty years of celibacy did to a body.

"I suppose we should get ready for when Gale does come calling," she said, walking again. "Some defenses." She could take on quite a few opponents with her power, but Simon Lazlo had led the charge that defeated Naos. He could pull enough power to win, and she couldn't fight him and worry about mundane threats at the same time. She looked to the edge of the town, to a shadow of a wall only big enough to keep out pests, maybe a few predators. She'd have to do better than that.

First things first. After refreshments at the cookhouse, Patricia and Jonah walked to the mine. She summoned the foreman with a telepathic call, and he met her in front of the black pit leading into the mountain.

The foreman offered her a smile and a hard hat made from a hoshpi shell. Patricia tapped Dillon's memories and tracked the word to an animal in Gale, an insect with a leathery hide. She donned the hat. Though she could protect herself with her power, she'd been too distracted lately and wanted a backup. Jonah took one, too, as the foreman prattled on. She'd already snagged his name the morning before.

"How long have you worked here, Wendel?" she asked.

"Going on four years, Mistress," he said, "though not just at this camp. We've moved now and again, chasing ore."

The two yafanai wandered out of the dark, lanterns in hand, and walked with her into the darkness. The rock was held aloft with the aid of timber, solid around her, and she could feel the comforting weight of the mountain. Dark spaces were good for hiding, especially if whoever was pursuing you was too big to fit inside.

The end of this mine shaft stood rough and ragged. Kelly, the younger of the macros, laid a hand on a bulging hunk of rock. This deep, the air had a wet, metallic tang. "This is where Rich and I have been working, blasting chunks out of the walls."

Patricia nodded. Calamity didn't want to yield its ore easily. Iron, bronze, even gold was hard to come by. The Galeans had to resort to random searches in order to find scraps. Patricia passed a hand over the wall, sending her senses into it. "This could use the touch of a micro and macro: one to find the ore, one to get it out."

The yafanai glanced at each other. "Who has that much fine control, Mistress?"

She smiled. There wasn't a yafanai alive who could do it. She could get them started, but she didn't want to stay down here in the dark all day, not when she had defenses to build. She thought of the breachies she'd sensed before and sent her power looking for them again.

Three were clustered together, but Patricia reached for the strongest, a spokesperson. Raquel had claimed a little clan in the foothills, people who'd once been plains dwellers but were now hill people; hillbillies, Patricia supposed, and the thought made her laugh. From their minds, she saw that they called themselves the Kiri, and Raquel stood out among them like a beacon.

Panic flared in her at the first touch of Patricia's mind. "Who is that?" Raquel thought, her shields coming up hard.

"It's Patricia Dué."

Raquel's mind raced, and Patricia wondered if she knew how easily her thoughts leaked, even through her shields. "Naos?"

"That's not what I said, is it?" Patricia pushed down her irritation. "I'm at Gale's mine. Come and meet me." She put power behind the words, not much, just a little carrot dangling before the donkey. Raquel was curious. She'd always been a bit of a gossip, and no doubt she was bored living on Calamity among the plebs.

"I'd…I'd love to!" Raquel thought back.

"Bring any others from the *Atlas* that you have nearby."

Raquel signaled assent, and Patricia cut contact. The others were watching her expectantly. "I've called in some help, but I'll get you started. Lend me your power."

They nodded, and she used the little trick she'd learned from Simon Lazlo, merging powers for greater effect. Teamwork, so foreign aboard the *Atlas*.

She sent her senses through the rock, using the expertise of Kelly and Rich to find the right signals. She called the ore forth, filling the air with a harsh, grinding sound as she shifted other rock aside. Instead of blasting outward, ripping the rock from the wall, she coaxed it, and the wall swirled like a whirlpool. The watchers gasped as the ore wandered to the forefront of the churning rock and thumped to the ground in large chunks.

"Get someone to carry this," Jonah said. The foreman hurried away, yelling. The regular miners were working in a different shaft. Patricia continued pulling ore from the stone.

Her head began to throb at the delicate work, and even with her healing powers, the feeling wouldn't leave her. After half an hour, she stopped. "See? Like that."

Kelly and Rich were wide-eyed. They broke into applause. Patricia laughed as she waved it away. "I'll be outside if you need me."

The miners looked upon her with reverence, whispering her name as she walked out. She healed their fatigue, but her power flowed sluggishly. She was out of practice. She'd have to work on that.

Out in the fresh air, she put her hands to her hips, leaning backward until her back popped. She felt Jonah stop behind her.

"The friends I called can help us build defenses, too," she said. "Where do you think we should start?"

"The wall," he said. "And a ditch. The paladins' armor might still have a charge."

She nodded. "Good thinking." Then she frowned. How did he know about— She turned slowly. "You didn't say that, did you?"

"I said the wall, Mistress."

She stepped to him and cupped his face. "And the armor?"

His confusion read as genuine, and she put a hand to his lips before he could speak again. Every time she let her guard down... She needed to do some mental exercises; that was all. Then she could keep out this telepathic interloper, whoever it was. And once she could keep them out, she'd take the fight to them.

CHAPTER SIX

Cordelia blazed with pain as she floated among the stars. Was she back with Naos again, being drawn into that titanic force and smothered? Or was she dead? At the edges of her vision, she thought she glimpsed her parents and Uncle Paul. Maybe they were welcoming her to the afterlife. But she sensed the silver cord still stubbornly connected to her body. And her family would never want her to give up. They'd tell her to fight.

Captain Carmichael appeared before her like an annoying ghost and told her to get the hell up. Cordelia groaned, torn between the desire to hug Carmichael and to tell her to fuck off, but she couldn't move to do either.

The stars swayed, an infinite dance. They'd never felt so close, so easy to touch, to be part of. Joining with Naos wasn't the only way to become one with the universe.

A scent drifted past her nose, greenery and life, the swamp after a storm. Water sprinkled over her, warm and soothing. Was it raining? The Storm Lord's revenge? If she had died, maybe her loved ones wouldn't be the only ones waiting for her. She could kick the asses of her enemies for all eternity while Captain Carmichael howled with laughter.

Cordelia smelled green again, something in the rain. She breathed deeply, and the water rolled into her, tasting like serenity, cold and sharp. She couldn't rest yet. There was always so much shit to do. She turned, and the stars retreated, falling away. Or was she falling instead? A chorus of voices called out, and she turned to the bright green jewel of Calamity. Pool shone from its surface as if a star herself. The drushka called out in one voice. "Sa," they said, the drushkan word for rain. As Cordelia came closer, drawn to the brightness, another light mingled with theirs, burning orange as flame.

"Cordelia?" it asked.

Simon Lazlo's voice. She tried to reply but couldn't. A cooling feeling washed over her, and she hadn't realized how warm she'd been. The rain lessened, too, and the ground faded, hazy. Was she going up again? Cordelia shivered. She didn't want to return to the stars, tried to fight for the ground again, for the drushka. She wasn't ready to die!

"You won't. You're all right. Just breathe."

Light flickered around the edges of her vision, and her eyes opened slowly. Simon leaned over her, smiling. He put a hand on her forehead. "See? Good as new."

Overstatement of the millennium. She blinked, trying to remember what had happened. A brown leather wall rose above Simon's head. A tent? She tried to say, "Nettle," but her voice came out as a croak. Simon's power tingled through her, and she swallowed. "Nettle?"

"Alive and here. Horace and Reach are with her."

She wanted to tell him to go help them, but all it took was a little push, and she could *feel* him helping them. They were all in the same tent.

"Sa," Pool's voice said in her mind. Worry and relief flowed through the connection. "Stay in your body."

"Agreed," Simon said. "Stay put for now."

She wheezed a laugh, and he helped her sit in a nest of blankets. She was down to her shirt and underpants. She supposed they'd had to take the rest in order to see the arrow wound, which was gone, not even a scar to mark it.

Simon handed her a leather cup with water. She sipped it slowly. His power still played over her, and she could feel him sitting there, their connection to the drushka connecting them as well. "I'm good now? Fully healed?"

He nodded. "But nothing will make up for genuine rest."

She snorted. "Who has time for that?"

With a chuckle, he gave her knee a pat. "Truer words were never spoken."

She looked past him, to the other side of the tent. Horace and

Reach were helping Nettle sit, and Nettle gave a tired smile that Cordelia returned. She mouthed the words, "I love you," and Nettle wrinkled her nose.

"What foolishness brought you to this state?" Reach asked.

"Why do you assume it was *our* foolishness?" Cordelia said.

Reach spread her hands as if to say the situation spoke for itself. Cordelia tried to be offended, but she was too tired. As the healing finished, she told them what had happened. Reach made a disgusted noise, and Simon and Horace shook their heads. Cordelia supposed they'd seen Fajir's actions coming, but she'd let herself hope. Maybe that was the foolishness Reach was talking about.

By the time she was done talking, Cordelia felt strong enough to stand. Nettle met her halfway across the tent, and they hugged for a long moment, witnesses and lack of trousers be damned. Simon told her that Wuran found them on the plains, that Nettle had managed a weak contact with Pool, and she'd come running.

"Liam will be satisfied," Reach said. "He predicted a bad end for Fajir."

"We don't know that she's dead," Cordelia said.

"We can hope," Horace said.

Everyone gave him a surprised look, the man who normally liked everybody. He wilted a little under their stares and gave a shrug. Out of all of them, next to Mamet, Fajir had treated him the worst.

"So," Cordelia said after she'd dressed and thanked Wuran. They'd left him and the plains behind as they boarded Pool's tree and headed back toward Gale. "Tell us the bad news."

Simon tried to feign surprise, but Cordelia saw right through him. Horace took a sudden interest in looking anywhere but at her, and Reach tilted her head.

Cordelia rolled her eyes. "Not one of you has mentioned what happened in Gale since you got there, which tells me there's bad news you didn't want the two sick people to hear before they'd been healed."

"Ahya," Nettle said. "I noticed this also."

Cordelia nodded. "So, what happened?"

Reach nudged Horace. "I said this would happen."

He sighed. "I'd buy you a drink if I knew where to get one."

"Enough stalling," Cordelia said.

Her stomach shrank as Simon told her about the mass poisoning by the old drushka. Two hundred people were still missing, and now Gale had a food and water shortage along with all its other problems.

Fucking fantastic. She almost wanted to claim she had to ride after Fajir for some much needed revenge rather than deal with this mess. So much for all her plans to drink the Pickled Prog dry. She only hoped it was still standing.

Two hundred missing people, though. Something had to be done. Maybe there was a way to get out of the rebuilding and replanting and politics. If those people had been taken by the drushka, someone needed to go after them. In her head, she started planning.

When they reached Gale, Pool set them down by the Paladin Keep. A crowd gathered quickly, Most of the paladins seemed relieved to see Cordelia, but other members of the populace seemed more grateful that Simon was back. After what he'd done for them, she wasn't surprised.

Liam pushed his way through and hugged Cordelia tightly. "I told you going with Fajir was a bad idea," he mumbled in her ear.

She laughed even as she wanted to slug him. "Yeah, yeah. Well, she's not our problem anymore. Not with people to find."

Liam's lips pressed into a thin line as if he would argue that point, but he let it go. "Come on. I'll give you the tour."

He led her through the city, telling her of its problems. She breathed deeply as she walked through the streets. Everything had changed just a little in the nine months since she'd been gone. The Storm Lord had changed it with boggins and progs. Several buildings she remembered were gone, and the warehouse district seemed completely new, but that was where the fire had started during the boggin attack. She was happy to see that the town had been rebuilding. And she grinned like a fool when she saw that the Pickled Prog was still standing and that its owner Edwina was still alive, though the bar wasn't open for business yet.

Everyone in Gale seemed busy cleaning up the mess the drushka left. Cordelia frowned as she watched them, feeling responsible for all this destruction. She'd fallen for the drushka she'd met in the swamp, Pool and Nettle and Shiv; she couldn't help but feel as if she'd led the old drushka here because they were chasing the drushka she loved.

On the other hand, a conflict like this seemed inevitable. Cordelia had taken a few things with her when she'd left Gale, including a journal written by her ancestor, Jania, whom the drushka called Roshkikan.

She'd been somewhat responsible for the drushkan schism, along with a first contact snafu where a band of drushka died in a skirmish with early paladins. The details of the schism itself were fuzzy, but Pool had told Cordelia that some drushka had wanted to trade with the humans, even after their initial conflict. Other drushkan queens had wanted to annihilate all humans. Still others had wanted to absorb the humans and make them into drushka, at least figuratively. Maybe they'd figured that if they spread the humans out and paired them with drushka, they wouldn't be able to have children.

Jania had found out about that last plan. She'd gotten to know Pool, had been almost friends before Pool was even a queen, and Pool had adopted some of Jania's rebellious nature. She'd ended up splitting from the drushka in order to trade with the humans, though Pool wouldn't say exactly how that split had come about. And Jania hadn't written about any of it, taking all her knowledge about drushkan queens and their plots to her grave.

And now the old drushka wanted Pool back, and it was clear they'd use the humans to get her.

The whole situation made Cordelia long for someone to punch. "Any word on the missing two hundred?"

"As far as people can remember, they were taken by the drushka." Liam shook his head slowly. "Our drushkan scouts tell us there's a trail into the swamp that's easy to follow."

"We'd better move as soon as we can get our gear together."

He gave her a grin. "I knew you'd say that. But I was hoping you'd stay the night and rest."

She nodded. "Only packing today. I like that idea better than cleanup duty."

"You always were a slob," he said, but the teasing didn't seem to have much heart behind it. Now that they weren't walking and talking about Gale's problems, a pall seemed to settle over him.

And after the way he'd spoken about her resting before leaving, she knew he wouldn't be coming with her. He'd never been as interested in combat as her, and he had too much to do here. But even with all the progress he'd made in Gale, he still had this pinched, worried look in his eyes.

"Tell me what's wrong," she said, leaving no room for denial. "Besides the obvious."

"It's Shiv."

"Ah." He got a lovelorn look she'd seen often enough. She wondered if part of him saw Shiv as he'd seen every other lover: only temporary.

"She's been distant, and Pool told me…"

She waited, trying not to be impatient even as she thought of everything she had to put together for a swamp expedition.

"When she healed Simon, Pool had to…deliver a drushkan baby early." Liam ran a hand through his hair. "That's exactly the way she said it, and since the drushka pause before they leave something out of a story, it's really easy to know when they're doing it."

Cordelia laughed. And Pool was the only one who could lie almost effectively. She told half-truths; most of the drushka couldn't even manage that. Even those as old as Nettle had trouble omitting facts. Lying went against who they were.

But Cordelia knew what Pool meant. She'd drifted through the drushkan birthing place in spirit form. They didn't bear children in their own bodies, but surrendered them to the tree, to little pods that made them grow. She'd never seen how the babies got *into* the pods, but she'd seen Simon after he'd emerged from one.

"So the baby's not right or something?" she asked. "What's that got to do with Shiv?"

He spread his hands before he lifted and dropped them, a drushkan gesture crossed with a human one. "Pool usually helps with this delivery, but Shiv had to do it, and now the baby is…bonded to her, a drushka to a queen. He doesn't have a bond with Pool at all, so…"

"She can't hear his thoughts, but Shiv can?"

"I guess." He sighed loudly. "She said a tribe of one is a really unique thing to the drushka, and it's occupying a lot of Shiv's mind."

Cordelia nodded slowly. The pull of the drushka was powerful, bathed in emotion, but it was regulated by Pool, who was well used to it, and the flood of thoughts kept Pool from being too close to just one person. If Shiv and this child were experiencing it with just the two of them, it had to feel powerful indeed, probably something like the Sun-Moon felt. "And let me guess, since she's Shiv, she's not letting her mother help her?"

Liam gave a sad smile. "Or anyone else."

Cordelia didn't say it, but she wondered how much help Liam

would be. He *was* very attached to Shiv. He probably couldn't help but be jealous of this little intruder.

"What if some of Pool's drushka switch allegiance to Shiv?" Cordelia asked.

"Pool thought of that. But her drushka haven't had another queen for generations. They won't go. We met one of the old drushka in the plains, and he switched to Pool without question. I think the old drushka want new leadership, so maybe they can help Shiv." He sighed. "If Pool could talk to them."

Cordelia nodded again, filing that information away. She patted Liam on the shoulder. "I'm sorry."

"I have it easier than the boy's parents. He keeps running from them to be with Shiv, and they can't communicate with him through Pool. It must feel as if they have a doll instead of a child."

She shuddered at the thought and tried to turn him back to the city, to something he was comfortable with. "How are the paladins and the yafanai we took from Celeste settling in?"

Liam perked up. "Lea's a rock, but he's always been. He's the leader of what we've started calling the unfaithful, those who thought the Storm Lord had overstayed his welcome. But there are others holding on to the thought that he might return."

"Are they causing problems?"

"Just mutters of dissent. Simon's been talking to everyone who will listen. He doesn't want to use his power to change people's minds, which is good."

She grinned. It had been a hard road to forgiveness for Liam, but he seemed to have gotten there. Simon had healed the Storm Lord after Liam had shot him the first time. If that hadn't happened, a lot of their misery over the last few months could have been avoided, but Liam's mother and Cordelia's uncle would still have been dead. And as the drushka said, you couldn't blame a shawness for healing someone. It was just what they did.

"Simon's too useful to stay mad at," she said, giving Liam a nudge.

He rolled his eyes. "I've never held grudges like you."

She wanted to say bullshit, but she only smirked.

He chuckled. "If mutters of dissent turn to violence, we'll have to do something about it, but we can't stop people talking. Simon and I both agree on that."

"Well, you have an open invitation to come with us to the swamp if you want to avoid your responsibilities."

He turned to her with raised eyebrows. "'Can't talk now, got a fight to win' is your battle cry, not mine."

"Damn straight. But I always need someone who can take a punch."

He tried to kick her, but she dodged. "Asshole. I would think you'd be more interested in someone who can throw a punch."

"As long as they're not better than me!"

A low rumble sounded in the distance, and Cordelia looked to where dark clouds had gathered, billowing toward them fast. She and Liam broke into a jog, but the clouds opened before they reached the Paladin Keep again, and the rain came down in sheets, drenching them. Cordelia wondered how many Galeans would be interpreting the rain as a message from the Storm Lord. Then she had another thought: If Simon was right, and the Storm Lord had been tinkering with the weather for years, shielding Gale from the worst of Calamity's storms, what were they going to do with him gone?

As the thunder boomed loud enough to rattle the windows, she tried to shake off the thought. It was the one thing she could truly do nothing about.

❖

Simon had been walking the city with Horace and Pakesh when the sky opened around them. They ran and hid under an awning, Pakesh and Horace laughing. Simon had let go of all of Gale's problems, all of the work that waited in their future. Something as mundane as getting caught out in the rain had cured him of worrying.

For a moment. Then he watched the torrent turn into lashing winds. An awning across the street came loose from its hooks and blew away. He hadn't seen such a storm since Dillon had first come to Gale and whipped something up to impress them. And even though he was dead, this weather was no doubt still his doing. Without his power, Calamity's weather would right itself, but the populace might have to suffer while it did so.

Horace's hand tightened in his as the wind picked up enough for the rain to come in at them sideways. Pakesh shivered, and Simon felt his fear. He also felt a dim call. Pool was headed toward the Paladin Keep, and she was worried, too. She'd laid her tree down so it wouldn't be hit by the lightning that burned across the sky. She didn't like doing it, didn't like the tree to be so vulnerable. He sensed her pulling back her drushka to watch over it.

"We need to get to the keep," Simon yelled above the wind.

"In this?" Pakesh asked.

Horace took both their hands. "Pool?"

Simon nodded, knowing it had to be frustrating for Horace to know Pool was communicating but not being able to hear what she was saying. "At least it's indoors," Simon said.

Horace shouted, "One, two, three!" Then he ran into the rain, tugging Simon and Pakesh with him. They ran as one, their strength buoyed by Simon's and Horace's power. Simon headed for Pool rather than trying to see through the rain. He caught a glimpse of the keep in the sudden gloom but kept his head down, hoping Horace was paying enough attention to their surroundings to keep them from running into anything. By the time they reached the keep, they were all soaked to the skin. They ran under the bailey and slid through the heavy keep doors, which stood open just enough to admit visitors and keep out most of the rain.

The inside of the keep was a flurry of activity, people hurrying through the rooms and making piles of equipment on the floor. Simon tried to shake his arms dry, but more water just rolled off his sleeves, his hair. Cordelia appeared out of one of the side rooms with three towels. "Pool told me you were on your way. I thought I'd better be ready."

Simon thanked her as he toweled off as best he could. "What's going on?"

"We're going after the people the drushka took."

"So soon?" But he could feel Cordelia's anticipation: proof that Pool must be near. He supposed he should have expected that they'd want to rescue the captives as soon as they could. Neither was the type to let grass grow under her feet.

So to speak.

The earth churned near the keep doors, and roots punched through the soil, lifting Pool into the doorway. She was nearly dry, but Simon didn't know if the rain would have bothered her at all. She stopped inside the gloom and lifted her nose as if scenting the air. "I have never been inside a human dwelling. It seems close and dark."

"This isn't typical," Simon said, gesturing at the enormous stone and metal walls. "They cobbled this together from some of the Chrysalis pods the original colonists used to descend to Calamity. Most homes are much smaller."

Cordelia rubbed her hands together, eagerness wafting off her. "Some of the armor still has a charge, and we're divvying up the suits. There's enough ammo for Lea and me to carry railguns. We'll see if we can spare enough for the other two."

"They've put you in charge, then?" Simon asked, a bit of teasing in his voice.

She grinned. "Lea said I was the best person for the job, and I can't argue with that."

Simon suspected she wouldn't be so eager if they weren't on a rescue mission. Part of her seemed to have lost the taste for mindless violence.

Pool frowned at the stacks of arms and armament. "I do not care for these railguns, Sa, The queens are not themselves. They do not deserve annihilation."

"We've got to do something, Pool. The old drushka aren't going to hand our people over, and it's clear they'll never stop chasing you."

"But it's the Shi who's the problem," Horace said. "Maybe if Pool can talk to her directly?"

Pool rested a long-fingered hand on his shoulder. "I do not think she will listen to my words, shawness, but I also do not wish my people to die. Perhaps if I offered—"

Cordelia held up a hand, and Simon knew what she was getting from Pool: a dash of pain, an air of resignation. "We won't give you to the Shi, Pool," Cordelia said.

Simon nodded. "No way."

Pool touched all of them but Pakesh, bending to press her forehead to Cordelia's and Simon's as if they were drushka. "Leave the queens to me," she said. "You need only get me close enough to reach their minds."

"With all their drushka attacking you?"

She spread her hands. "Sest has shown me the way. The drushka want to be free. To rob the Shi of power, we must first rob her of her drushka. She sees them now only as weapons. So we will disarm her."

"You think it'll be that easy?" Cordelia asked.

"It is a path we must try. We will rescue your people, Sa, but not at the cost of my species. The old drushka wish to be free. I will free them, and then perhaps there can be peace."

Simon nodded even if Cordelia still seemed skeptical. "All right. We'll try it your way." She looked at Simon and Horace. "A healer would be nice on this trip, but Liam will need one of you here." She grinned. "Talk amongst yourselves."

Simon opened his mouth to argue, but she was already gone. After a wrinkle of her nose, Pool departed, too. They turned to each other. Simon's stomach shrank at the idea of parting again, and he wanted to say so, but Pakesh was still there, listening.

Simon gave him a pointed look. He was glancing around the keep, oblivious. When he finally caught their looks, realization seemed to dawn. "Oh, you want…" He smiled awkwardly, cleared his throat, and went to examine the piles of equipment.

"Well—" Horace started.

"I'm going with them," Simon said. If they were going to have a fight about who was doing what, he wanted to get it over with.

Horace chuckled. "Think of the Galeans. First, some of their paladins left when the Storm Lord kicked them out. Then their god left, and the drushka came and poisoned them. Then you came, their almighty healer, and brought everyone back together. Minus God, of course. If you leave again, they'll panic. I'm going to the swamp."

"First of all, no one is almighty. Second, you were healing them, too. Third…" He groped for another reason. "I'd miss you!"

"And I'll miss you, too, but you have to stay for the city's sake. You showed up with the Storm Lord in the first place. You're much more mystical than I am." Horace smiled, his emotions loving rather than resentful, proving he truly believed what he was saying.

"I… You…" Simon cast about for arguments. He didn't want them to part at all, but if they had to, he could at least take the more dangerous mission. "You can't communicate with Pool like I can."

"I won't need to with her drushka all around me. I've lived with them for almost nine months. I know how they work, how to heal them." He winked. "And I could never soothe a human crowd like you can. And I don't have your skill with plants, which the Galeans will need if they're going to harvest early and feed everyone."

Simon didn't know how to respond, so he let his fear and worry and love come to the surface for Horace to feel.

Horace clasped his hands. "I don't want to leave you either, but the Galeans need you, and for more than just healing and plants. You're a symbol now."

"Don't wanna be a symbol," Simon muttered. "Unless it's a big sign that says Keep Out."

Horace beamed and hugged him, speaking into his ear. "Are we going to keep talking, or are you going to come with me so we can have a proper, mushy good-bye?"

Simon thought it funny how his heart could lift and sink at the same time. "You're just trying to distract me."

"And you know I'm right."

Simon sighed and sent a request that Pool look after Pakesh. She agreed, and Horace sent a similar message to Pakesh. But as they began to leave the keep, Simon wondered where they could go.

"The tree," Horace sent to him. "It might be lying down, but there are still plenty of places to hide in its branches."

The rain had let up slightly, and Horace and Simon ran to Pool's tree, to the little cubby they'd slept in before. As the storm ebbed and flowed outside, Horace and Simon said good-bye as they were certain many of the soldiers were doing, should be doing. Simon tried not to think of the morning to come, putting everything he had into making love, wanting to record every moan, every caress. Maybe if he wore Horace out completely, neither of them could leave.

Horace laughed at that thought and gave as good as he got.

But the night passed, and the morning came all too soon. The rain had subsided to the occasional gust as everyone gathered at the base of Pool's tree. Simon kissed Horace again, not wanting to let him go in spite of Pool's assurances that he would be safe in her branches. Cordelia gave him the same speech, but neither made parting any easier.

"Bring me a souvenir!" Liam called to Cordelia.

Cordelia grinned as Pool lifted her into the branches. "How's two hundred Galeans sound?"

"Perfect!"

Simon wished he could be as blithe, but as Pool's tree walked away, eventually disappearing among the trees in the distance, too far away for Simon to feel them, he had to turn back to Gale, wondering, among all the other things, where he was going to sleep now.

"Come on, Pakesh," Simon said over his shoulder. Pakesh seemed as if he might say something, then closed his mouth, his attention wandering once they were in Gale, and he clapped eyes on several young women.

"Come *on*, Pakesh," Simon said with a smile, part of him hoping Pakesh would never change.

Liam was ahead of them, calling people to bring in rain barrels and other containers they'd used to catch clean water. It was a good thought, and Simon was a little embarrassed he hadn't thought of it in the first place. He sped up until he reached Liam's side.

"What's the word on the food stores?" Simon asked.

"A bit empty. It's still a while until harvest, and we usually got through the season eating hoshpi meat. I'm posting guards on what we do have in case anyone tries to steal it. We're already rationing."

Simon nodded, though the need to ration chilled him. It didn't matter how thankful the population was, hunger could turn anyone into a monster. "I'm headed to the fields now to bolster the plants. That way we can harvest them early."

Liam nodded. "You should take a leather with you."

It took him a moment to realize what a leather was: a paladin who hadn't yet been promoted to metal armor. "Oh, I don't think that will be necessary."

"Do it anyway. Please. If you're healing the plants, you might not see an attack coming."

Who would want to attack him? But he could tell Liam wasn't going to back down. Simon tried not to think of it as the sort of control Dillon would insist upon and took it in the spirit with which it was given. Liam wanted to keep him safe. It might simply be because Simon was valuable, but he supposed he should be grateful anyone was looking out for him. And he always had Pakesh by his side. He was an extra pair of eyes if he could keep them off every woman he saw.

As they passed the keep, Liam asked Private Jacobs, the same woman who'd had a lot of questions when he'd first arrived in Gale, to follow Simon around. She kept to his side as he headed for the fields to the east. Bolstering the plants was the work of moments. He helped them process the excess water they'd gotten the night before, turning it into fuel for their growth. He couldn't do anything about the soil erosion from the heavy rains and told the few farmers he passed that it might be a problem.

After that was done, Simon wandered back toward Gale, watching as people cleaned their streets and homes. They'd already gathered the dead and carted them to the northern cemetery. Some people stopped what they were doing and watched him. Simon didn't know if people recognized him or if the escort gave him away as someone important. Either way, he could have done without the attention. It made him think too much about Horace calling him mystical.

One woman dropped a broom and trotted over, wiping the sweat off her face. "Was it raining because the Storm Lord's angry?" she asked. "That some of us lost faith?"

"He's dead," Simon started to say, but she wasn't listening. She looked around wildly, tears mingling with the sweat. She grabbed his arm, and he resisted the urge to yank it away.

Jacobs gently pried her off and sent her back to work.

"It's just a storm!" Simon called after her. "There were storms before we came here, before humans came here." And they might get worse, but he didn't want to mention that. She didn't seem to hear anyway. Simon hurried on.

"I was dying," a man called, "and you brought me back! Thank you."

A couple came forward, hands over their hearts. "I saw a white light," one said, "and then you called me." The other added, "We thought our little Iris was going to die, and you gave her back to us. Thank you!" He grabbed Simon's hand and squeezed.

As more came forward, Simon took a deep breath and tried to recall everything Samira had taught him about accepting gratitude, about how not to be afraid of touch, but the people were getting too close, and he couldn't hear one of them over the other. He sent out a calming wave, but they were pressing in, the feeling of their bodies overwhelming. He couldn't breathe. "Stop...stop."

Pakesh eased up beside him, creating a pocket of air. "Are you all right, Simon?"

"I'm...too many." His chest constricted, and he tried to turn his power on himself. He could move these people, but he didn't want to do that, didn't want to be Dillon. His heart pounded in his ears. He could interrupt their bodies, freeze them in place, but then they'd be locked around him like a cage. He tried to moderate their emotions, but he couldn't even control his own.

"Make way, please!" Jacobs called beyond the press. She took hold of Simon's arm and muscled a path forward. "The doctor has urgent business elsewhere."

As she peeled Simon away from the group, he took a closer look at her, focusing on her to keep the people out. Her strawberry-blond hair was pulled back from her face in a ponytail, exposing rounded cheeks and a dimpled chin. Acne scars ran down the sides of her jaw, but they were barely visible unless one came close, and she glared at the crowd with blue eyes hard as ice chips.

"Clear the road," she kept barking, reminding Simon of Cordelia, though she wasn't as tall, was the same height as his five foot nine. Still, her confidence kept people away, and Pakesh was able to go back to gawking at every teenage girl he saw.

Simon let his shoulders relax, let himself breathe. "Thank you, Jacobs."

"We headed to the temple, Doc?" she asked.

Simon nearly snorted a laugh. Most of his life he'd been Lazlo or Dr. Lazlo, but no one had called him Doc. It had an easy familiarity that both charmed and alarmed him. "I suppose we could."

He should check in on the yafanai, see how they were feeling. Many of them were Horace's friends, so they couldn't all be bad. And he did need somewhere to stay. He didn't fancy bunking down in the Paladin Keep. It seemed like a cold, forbidding place. Even Dillon had chosen the temple as his home.

"I'll wait here," Jacobs said as he approached the doors to the Yafanai Temple, and he wondered if the soldiers and the yafanai had some unspoken agreement about not intruding into one another's space. Pakesh stayed with Simon, and just inside the entrance, they stopped.

Fourteen women stood in a line as if waiting for someone. A quick scan revealed a multitude of powers as well as the fact that they were all pregnant. He remembered some from when he healed them of the poison. These were the lucky ones. They'd all survived.

"Um, I'm Simon Lazlo," he said. "Were you waiting—"

"We know who you are," one said. She was the tallest, looked the furthest along, but she already held a baby in her arms. Fine, wispy dark hair drifted around her head like a cloud. "My name is Miriam, and we were wondering what you intend on doing with us."

"Doing with you?" He had a wild thought that they were asking to be his harem, something Dillon had probably had. It nearly made him laugh until he scanned them again. They were nervous, angry. More than a few had protective hands on their bellies. He took another look at the baby. He knew this child, had been there for his birth. He sucked in a deep breath. He hadn't allowed himself to think too hard about when Dillon had kidnapped him, altered his mind, and used him as if he were a machine. He'd delivered this baby. He'd killed Caroline, the baby's mother.

"That's Evan," he said softly. He looked to the women. "Then you're…"

"Bearing the Storm Lord's other children," Miriam said.

"We heard about Caroline," another said.

On the end, one of them frowned. "We won't let you harm us or our children." They all nodded, though some were very frightened. The one who'd mentioned Caroline bit her lip and seemed as if she might bolt, but they all held their ground.

"I'm not going to kill anyone!" he said, far louder than he meant to. He took a deep breath. "I only…Caroline." He licked his lips. "How many of you know what she was doing to me?" One or two looked sheepish. Simon nodded. "She was altering my mind so I would be the Storm Lord's puppet. I was getting away on the plains, and she was trying to stop me, hurt me." The memory was hazy, but it still brought tears to his eyes. Just after that, he'd been shot, and there hadn't been time to think about Caroline at all. "I didn't mean to kill her. I just wanted her to stop."

They glanced at one another, and he felt a few tendrils of power looking for confirmation, for truth. Hard as it was, he let them in. None of them were as powerful as Caroline, and he felt some of them confirming what he had to say and sending that to the others. The tension in the air went down a few notches.

"Look," he said. "If you leave me alone, I'll leave you alone." It sounded lame to his ears, but the sentiment was there, and many of the women looked relieved.

Still, they didn't move.

"Um…" he said.

Miriam took a step forward and held Evan out to him.

Simon backed up. "What are you doing?"

"Caroline is dead," she said, "and she had no family. The Storm Lord is dead, too, so…" She took another step, baby first.

Simon sputtered, his mind whirling. "You can't expect me to—"

"Actions have consequences," Miriam said. "Whether you meant to kill Evan's parents or not, you're responsible for him now." She gave him a look that brought back librarians staring over their glasses.

He looked to the other women in terror. "But surely one of you—"

"We have our own to worry about," one of them said.

"If you can't care for him, find someone who will." Miriam had nearly reached him, almost pushed Evan into his chest. Evan squirmed, his face scrunching up as if he might cry. Surely Miriam wouldn't drop him?

Pakesh stepped around Simon and plucked the baby from Miriam's grasp. He held the boy close and bounced him softly. "Who's a sweet boy? You are!"

Simon gawked. Miriam had a satisfied smile, and Evan calmed in Pakesh's arms.

"What?" Pakesh asked to their stares. "My parents had five children, and I'm the oldest. Babies are just…life." He smiled down at the boy, his expression turning sad. "Before I got my powers, I cared for my youngest siblings all the time."

Simon rested a hand on Pakesh's shoulder and marveled at himself. When had someone else's sadness made him want to reach out rather than pull back? It must have been Samira's and Horace's teachings. "You'll master your powers, then you can do whatever you want."

Pakesh smiled. "I'll help you with this baby, then. I think he's hungry. And he doesn't smell very nice."

Simon cleared his throat. "Well, since you're used to babies, maybe you can take care of the smell. But the food…" He glanced at Miriam again. She stared at him, and he resisted the urge to put his hands on his hips. "Responsibility is all fine and well, but there are some things I just can't do."

She gestured over her shoulder. "Someone ask Mila if she's willing to be Evan's wet nurse."

One of the other women hurried away. Miriam turned her icy black stare back on Simon. "You'll have to find a way to pay for Mila's time. I, for one, am sick of being taken advantage of. Most of us are."

Some of the women nodded; others seemed less sure. Maybe Miriam had found out what kind of man Dillon was before he'd even left. Simon could sympathize. "Understood."

She turned and led the other women away. Another came from down the hall, smiling. With a quick scan, Simon could tell she'd given birth recently, though her child wasn't with her. She seemed more relaxed than the others. Her curly, graying hair had been pulled back in a simple twist, and her teeth were bright in her dark brown face as she smiled.

"I'm Mila," she said, and before Simon could make introductions, she waved for him to follow. "I'll show you where we keep the diapers and supplies."

Pakesh followed her shyly. With a heavy sigh, Simon followed to a storeroom and then to Dillon's old rooms, one of the only unoccupied suites in the temple, according to Mila. She fed Evan while Pakesh helped Simon rearrange the furniture in the study, bedroom, and living room; anything to get some of Dillon's stamp off the place.

Mila had long since departed before Simon was done taking down drapes and wading through mounds of cushions. He sat with Pakesh and wondered what in the hell they were going to do with a baby. Miriam had sent them a wooden crib, and Evan slept peacefully in the bedroom. Simon sat at a small table, staring into space and trying hard not to think about the man who'd lived here before, failing not to think of Dillon's face as he died. His last words had been about his son, willing Simon to care for him. Simon hadn't really thought about it before saying yes. He supposed part of him assumed that someone else would do it for him.

When a knock came at the door, he was relieved. Unless they'd come to blame him for Dillon's death, he was happy to have a distraction.

He didn't expect to see Shiv standing there, a sapling in one hand and a drushkan child clinging from her shoulders, hanging down her back. A human toddler hung on to her other hand, and Simon recognized Reach's adopted son Little Paul.

"Shiv?" Simon asked stupidly. He didn't know her well, but he knew her on sight by the green Mohawk. "What are you doing here?"

She lifted the hand that held the sapling. "Shi'a'na worried that the Shi would try to invade my mind now that I have a tree. She bade me stay, follow you, and reveal myself once you were alone." She glanced at Pakesh. "As alone as you will be." She frowned and suddenly seemed very young. "Please, shawness, may we be close to you? I know I threatened you once, but you and shawness Horace have made peace now, so you and I are at peace also. And you feel more drushka than any human."

Simon blinked before he waved her inside. "Of...of course." She walked past him, and the drushkan boy dropped from her shoulders and padded around the room. The drushka called him a baby, but he seemed nearly as large and dexterous as Little Paul, who was three, if Simon remembered correctly.

Little Paul went straight into the bedroom and crawled onto the bed to look into the crib. Simon started to scold him, then thought, "What the hell, as long as he's occupied." The drushkan child followed, and both stared at Evan.

After a look at Simon's face, Pakesh followed the boys. "His name is Evan," he said softly. "What are your names?"

Little Paul answered with his fingers stuck in his mouth so that it sounded like, "Lil Paw." Simon wondered if he'd forever have the "little" in front of his name or if people would allow him to one day grow out of it. The drushkan boy only stared.

"He does not yet have speech," Shiv said. "He is called Lyshus."

"What does it mean?" Simon asked.

"You would say new day, but I wish him to be called by his drushkan name." She lifted her chin.

Simon couldn't resist prying, always fascinated by the drushka. "Why?"

She slapped her thighs, a sign of frustration. "Because I wish it!"

Simon raised his hands as he'd seen drushka do when they wanted to avoid a fight. "Okay, have it your way."

"Thank you, shawness." She dropped into a chair as if she had the weight of the world on her shoulders.

Pakesh was staring at her as if he'd just noticed her after the children. His mouth was slightly open, face shining with admiration.

"Pakesh?" Simon asked.

Pakesh jumped, color making his brown cheeks even darker. "Yes?"

"Would you find some water, please? I'll keep an eye on your powers." He followed Pakesh to the door. "And I wouldn't even think about it, if I were you. As my dad used to say, she's out of your league."

Pakesh frowned. "Huh?"

"Never mind." He hustled Pakesh out the door. Shiv glanced at him and then leaned back in her chair. "He's young," Simon said to her. "And a little obsessed with...people. I'm sorry if he stares."

"His eyes cannot harm me."

Lyshus climbed into her lap and sank his teeth into the armrest of the chair. Simon was about to protest, but Shiv squeezed his cheeks until he opened his mouth. She offered him a wooden cylinder that was threaded through a cord around his waist. He bit down and gnawed, teeth grinding against the wood.

Simon knew he was staring but couldn't help it.

Shiv smiled, some of her former liveliness coming back into her expression. "It is called a nini. All children his age have them. That way they will not bite holes in everything and everyone."

"Great," Simon said. "A biter."

"Ahya, shawness, at his age, everything is food." She wrinkled her nose. "Even you."

"Good to know."

"In a year or so, the desire to bite will fade."

"Fabulous." Simon pressed the heel of one hand to his forehead, wondering where the hell all these kids had come from. Even Shiv was a teenager. "Why didn't Little Paul stay with Reach? Aren't there drushkan children aboard the tree?"

"Ahya, but Reach worried that he cannot hide as they can. He is not as dexterous, and the swamp holds many dangers."

Great, another reason to worry about Horace. Simon tried not to sigh.

Pakesh returned with a jug of water and poured for them while sneaking glances at Shiv. When he handed her one, she wrinkled her nose. "My thanks, young one."

Pakesh blushed harder, but Shiv had already turned her attention to Lyshus and Little Paul, helping them drink before taking one herself. When Pakesh sat, Little Paul climbed into his lap, clearly sensing someone who liked children.

For a moment, they all drank in silence. "Well," Simon said. He couldn't think of anything else. Even if he made an "I brought you all here to name the murderer" joke, none of them would get it.

Lyshus leapt down from Shiv's lap and stared at Simon. Simon froze, horrified that the boy might climb him next, but then Lyshus began to run around the room, grinning, his arms out for balance. He managed not to hit anything, and Little Paul giggled, hurrying to catch him. They peeked at Evan now and again but didn't try to touch, something to be glad of, what with the biting.

"What about something to eat?" Simon said above the laughing children. "Then maybe…a nap? We're going to have some long days ahead of us." One of the children skidded on a cushion, sending it spinning into a bookshelf and knocking over a clay pot. Simon sighed as he picked it up. He thought of Horace out in the swamp and wondered which of them was going to have a rougher time.

CHAPTER SEVEN

From her perch aboard Pool's moving tree, Cordelia peered into the gloom of the swamp, watching the endless, ropy branches and great swaths of water surrounding tiny islands of firm ground. Far above, the canopy blocked out nearly all the sunlight. Large flocks of birds, merely dark specks in the distance, swooped between the swaying leaves, their cries faint on the wind.

The light had been fading for hours, and before it grew too dark to see, Pool came to a halt. The hiss of her roots slithering over the bark of the swamp trees fell silent. Stillness surrounded them, making Cordelia's ears ring. No one spoke, human or drushka, and slowly, the natural sounds of the swamp returned: the chirp of insects, stray breezes ruffling the water, and the slurp of creatures diving to safety.

Pool stood in her cupola of bark, her eyes unfocused.

"Are we stopping for the night?" Cordelia asked softly. "Or do you sense something?"

"The sixth queen, Yunshi, bars our path."

Cordelia gestured for her fellow paladins to fan out among Pool's branches. Lea strayed far to the right, his railgun strapped around his chest. Cordelia hefted her own gun, but Pool's words about not harming the queens came back to her.

"How do you want to do this, Pool?"

"I call to her, but she does not answer." Pool sucked her teeth, frowning. "All I hear from her is an echo of the Shi, cursing my name, demanding I submit."

"So the sixth is going to fight you?"

"She will do whatever she is commanded, it would seem." Pool glanced at the railgun and frowned harder.

Cordelia sighed. "We won't use the railguns unless we have to, okay?"

"Thank you, Sa. That makes my mind easier."

Cordelia passed on the orders. Lea seemed skeptical, but he'd do as he was told. Everyone else was a chorus of "Yes, Captain" or "You got it, Cap." She grinned. Instant obedience from the lieutenants was pretty fucking sweet. Of course, if this plan went ass up, all the blame would rest on her shoulders, too.

At least the armor and weapons still had a charge. "Visors down," Cordelia said, and then they were on comms instead of having to gesture or pass the word from person to person. There were several mutters in Cordelia's ear until she barked, "Muzzle that chatter."

Pool advanced slowly. Cordelia scattered her paladins through the low branches. Drushka waited all around. With the help of her helmet, Cordelia saw the sixth waiting in the gloom. Smaller than the swamp trees but still massive, the sixth tree loomed far over Pool's. Drushka crawled along it, waiting, and Cordelia began to fidget. Maybe all they needed was a little prompting to attack.

Well, she could give them that. "Aim to wound," she said. "Use your targeting sensors."

She took the first shot; the soft crack of the bullet leaving the muzzle sounded louder than normal in the stillness. As the other paladins took their shots, the whine of streaking bullets echoed all around. Cordelia aimed to clip the legs of several drushka and dropped them into the water. The old drushka howled and leapt as their comrades went down, and the uninjured hurled themselves toward Pool's branches.

"Blades," Cordelia ordered. This didn't have the thrill of any other combat she'd known, but she didn't carry the despair she'd had when she'd first fought the old drushka. Lives were at stake, and she carried a sense of urgency coupled with the desire to see this job done, to put the threat of the Shi to bed at last. She drew the wooden sword that hung around her waist, but it was only a precaution. Drushkan weapons and claws couldn't penetrate her armor, so she flung enemies into the swamp or used her powered fist to wound.

Something whipped out of the darkness toward her. An alarm

sounded inside her helmet, and she leaned far to the side. Her stabilizers whined, trying to keep her on her feet.

"What the fuck?"

It came again, reaching out of the dark, and she dropped flat, getting a good look at a massive root. More of the huge, cable-like roots wrapped around Pool's tree, knocking drushka and several paladins into the swamp. The trunk of the sixth rushed forward, and the two trees collided in a massive boom, shaking the branch under Cordelia's feet.

Hordes of drushka poured into Pool's branches, swamping the paladins. Cordelia darted for one human who'd gone under a pack of drushka. Others cried out in her comm that they'd fallen into the water and couldn't find their way out.

"Try to breathe normally," Cordelia said as she punched a long-haired drushka in the face. "Use your lights to see and climb the nearest trunk." Their helmets would keep out the water, but they didn't have an air supply. "I'm sending help."

She dove into a pack of drushka, kicking and punching and throwing until she unearthed the paladin who'd gone down at their center. "Get to the low branches and look for the lights," she said to him. "Help guide them out of the water!"

Cordelia slashed at more drushka with her blade. "Everyone, keep on the move so you won't be overwhelmed." She'd lost track of Pool, of Nettle and everyone she cared about. There were too many enemies, and fear was quickly replacing her anger. She had to end this, but Pool didn't want to kill the sixth, and Cordelia didn't think that would help anyway.

But what if they captured her?

Cordelia rested a hand against Pool's bark and reached for their connection. "I'm going to knock the sixth queen out, take her prisoner."

Pool sent an acknowledgment, her mind distracted. Cordelia sensed the Shi attacking through the sixth, trying to subdue Pool's mind. The sixth was far older than Pool, yet the Shi had overwhelmed her, used her almost as a puppet. Still, Pool searched for her mind and pointed Cordelia in the right direction.

She leaped between the trees, landing in the branches of the sixth and knocking drushka out of her way, shooting where she had to, still trying to wound, though she didn't know how much longer that would be an option. Calls for help still rang in her ears.

"Hang in there," she shouted. "Just a little longer."

A burst of feelings came from Pool. She was headed for the sixth queen, too, surrounded by a cadre of her drushka.

Cordelia ran faster, meeting Pool on the upper branches. Nettle and several others were with her. Cordelia took point, bowling drushka out of the way. The glow of her armor washed over Pool, and their enemies stumbled back from the sight of Pool's green hair, her obvious status.

Pool muttered in drushkan, angry words spitting from her mouth. "Up!" she said in Galean. "There!"

The sixth queen had a cupola of bark like Pool's, but the bark had grown over her where she stood flush against the trunk, leaving one eye and half her mouth exposed. A handful of drushka barred the way. They bared their teeth at Cordelia, then stared at Pool, eyes going wide with wonder.

Pool spoke to them in drushkan, pleading. Cordelia paused, catching several words, enough to know Pool wanted to free the sixth rather than knock her out. The drushka looked to each other, bodies tense as if they didn't know what to do. Pool stepped closer, repeating her words.

The air seemed to still, everyone waiting. Cordelia gripped her sword, wishing someone would do something. At last, the old drushka stepped aside, leaving the way clear to their queen. The sixth's eye was glazed over, and her mouth moved, though she didn't speak.

Pool strode forward and slammed a fist against the sixth's bark. "She is barely aware." She rested her head against the trunk over the sixth queen's chest and went silent. Cordelia fought the urge to attack someone, to do something. Her paladins still yelled in her ears, and the sounds of combat hadn't died.

At last, Pool drew a deep breath. "Ansha was her birth name," she said haltingly. "You would call her Sky." Pool twisted her head, grinding into the bark. "She has nearly forgotten her name as she has forgotten all things."

A scream ripped through Pool's mind, cascading into Cordelia. Her legs nearly buckled, and Pool's drushka cried out. The Shi. The sixth queen's drushka tottered toward Pool, but Cordelia staggered forward, knocking them away.

Pool ignored them. "Come out, sister. Come to me."

Sky's eye closed, and all the drushka screamed again. In Cordelia's ear, the paladins reported that their enemies were collapsing.

"I know you are afraid," Pool said. "I will shield you from the Shi. These humans are not your enemy."

Cordelia felt traces of Sky's emotions, those that weren't swallowed by the rage of the Shi. Sky didn't want to become human; she was certain Pool had already done so.

"No," Pool said. "We are strong drushka, generations of us. Independent from the Shi, ahya, but still drushka."

Sky recoiled from that. Drushka were not meant to be alone.

Pool fed memories into their connection, truths. "It is growth I offer, not loneliness. Drushka can be together and still free."

Sky whispered something, her voice a ghost.

"Come, sister." Pool dug her fingers into the bark, cracking it, peeling it away. After a moment's hesitation, it yielded. She tore it open, revealing Sky's tall, naked body. She fell forward, and Pool caught her, laying her along the branch.

Around them, the drushka stilled. "Hold your fire," Cordelia said through her comm. "Don't attack unless someone attacks you."

"Gather the wounded," Pool said.

Nettle ran to do her bidding. Cordelia felt the Shi calling to Sky, cursing, but Pool blocked her voice.

Pool chuckled softly, a sad sound. "She is trying to give her mind to me." She laid a hand on Sky's forehead. "No, sister. You are your own now. Awaken."

Sky stirred and touched Pool's face with hesitant fingers. Pool helped her stand, though she was almost a foot taller. Light bloomed around them as drushka lit candles, the better to see the two queens walking together. Cordelia felt it as Pool kept her mind wide open to her drushka, letting them feel Sky, letting them reach out to another tribe. Sky followed her lead. At the sight of their queen walking free, touching their minds as she probably hadn't in a long time, the old drushka drooped in relief.

Cordelia trailed along behind the queens, her blade still out and ready.

"Will you call Horace, Sa?" Pool asked.

Cordelia passed that over her comm. When Horace joined them, Lea at his side, Sky regarded them curiously. Cordelia lifted her visor but stood close to Horace, guarding him. Even with the chummy feelings flowing from Pool and the drushka, she wasn't up to trusting just yet. Sky stepped toward her, staring at Cordelia's armor, the wooden sword.

"Can you heal her, shawness?" Pool asked.

Horace glanced at Cordelia, and she nodded, catching on. The drushka didn't trust the humans, but if one of their healers healed the queen...

Horace lifted a hand, palm up as if asking Sky to dance. She stared before placing her long hand on top of Horace's, her clawed finger twitching but not striking. Her hand was nearly twice the size of his, and her fingers engulfed him. Cordelia felt a tingle as he used his power, and Sky's eyes widened. She straightened slowly and breathed deep, smiling. Other drushka gathered behind her, shawnessi by the long bags around their waist. They watched the healing with surprise and wonder.

Sky said something in drushkan, and Cordelia caught a few words: healing, thanking, human. She knew she should have paid more attention to Reach's lessons.

Still, she understood the sentiment. "She's thanking you, Horace."

"I know," he said. "Some of us paid attention to Reach." He smiled and winked. "And she called us Pool's humans." He said something in drushkan. "I told her that we're allies, but we're our own people."

Sky tilted her head and turned to Pool, and the two started talking. Cordelia waited until Pool left Sky to stand on her own before asking, "What was that about?"

"She remembers me differently," Pool said. "I told her the years have changed many of us. She asked if I was coming back to the drushka, and I told her not while the Shi is as she is. I have told her I will free the other queens. She asked me if I intend to be Shi."

"Do you?" Cordelia asked. "And what about the captives?"

"She knew nothing of the captive humans. As for being Shi, I suppose we shall see when I meet her."

Cordelia took a deep breath and let it out slowly. She'd been hoping the captives would be close, but now she might have to go all the way to the Shi to get them? Just her fucking luck.

When Pool went back to her own tree, Cordelia went with her, taking Lea and Horace. No humans had died in the battle, and Cordelia called for them to regroup, telling them to stay away from the old drushka for the time being. There was no sense in risking a fight, but the tension seemed over for the time being. They could relax, at least for a little while.

In one of Pool's cubbies, Cordelia shucked her armor. Soon after, Nettle crawled inside with her, and they shared a long embrace.

"Is everyone getting along?" Cordelia asked.

"Well enough, Sa. It is good you did not show Sky your spirit form. She has had enough surprises for today."

"Do you think she'll come with us to fight the Shi?"

Nettle spread her hands. "I do not think so. I believe she fears falling under the will of the Shi again. Her drushka will stay out of our path and tend any wounded we happen to leave behind."

Cordelia snorted, wondering if humans were included in that tending. Probably not quite yet. "Any mingling between old and new drushka?"

"Ahya, very much so. All the sixth's drushka seem curious about new faces. So far, they stay away from this part of the tree, the human branch, so they call it. Jon Lea has set up guards."

"I told him to. I didn't want any misunderstandings."

Nettle snuggled against her. "Wise. We move at dawn." Her fingers trailed down Cordelia's stomach. "There is not much to do until dawn."

Cordelia grinned. "Sleep?"

"Ah, but we are trying to show these old drushka that humans and drushka can, what was your word, mingle."

Cordelia chuckled and gave her a long kiss. "I don't want an audience, thanks."

"Then you are lucky, Sa, for we are safe from prying eyes in here." She nipped Cordelia's earlobe. "We will simply spread the story of our love, and tomorrow, the sixth's drushka will see the truth of it by the happiness in our eyes."

Cordelia laughed, wrapped her arms around Nettle, and kissed her deeply. She couldn't argue with that.

❖

Lydia was tempted to use her prophetic powers, something she hadn't done since she'd become the ex-prophet of Gale. But the sun was setting, and she was nowhere near finding all the purple starflowers she needed. She only wanted to know if she'd *ever* find them. But she couldn't start down that path, even for something as trivial as gathering flowers. Seeing the future brought nothing but trouble.

She looked through the grass around a hummock, wishing she and Samira could give up and go back to the Engali encampment, but her friend Samira's pride had been nicked by a challenge from Mamet. Lydia knew her well enough to know that she wouldn't be bested.

As she parted two blades of grass, Lydia finally found a perfect starflower, not missing a single petal. She plucked the blossom and held it up. "Got one!"

Samira stood from the tall grass where she'd been searching. "That brings us to five. We're going to win!"

"How many do we need?" Lydia asked, already knowing the answer. She hoped saying it out loud would convince Samira to pack this in.

"Thirteen if we're going to beat Mamet and her cousin."

"We're not even halfway," Lydia muttered. It was a stupid bet. Lydia had already guessed that Mamet had only proposed it to get Samira away from the camp for a little blessed privacy. But then Mamet hinted that no one could find so many starflowers, that it was beyond even someone with mental powers like Samira's and Lydia's. Lydia saw the boast for what it was: Mamet wanted Samira to go with her, and she was trying to goad her cousin into taking Lydia.

Samira, however, had heard it another way. She took it as a challenge to the yafanai and dragged Lydia off with her. After all the trials of the past few months—rescuing Simon Lazlo, reuniting with old friends, and besting the Storm Lord and Naos—Samira overreacted to anything she saw as a challenge.

Lydia leaned on the hummock and winked. "I heard the Engali give each other wreaths made of starflowers when they're going to propose."

Samira gave her a wry look. "No one's marrying anyone. We haven't known each other long enough."

"She's smitten."

Samira smiled a little as she searched. "When Simon told me to take a chance, I went for a little romance, not a marriage."

"And the romance is going well?"

"Yes," Samira said with a sigh. She glanced around as if afraid the Engali might be spying on them. "She's very tender."

Lydia suddenly missed Freddie, killed nearly nine months ago in the siege at Gale. Still, her heart warmed for Samira and Mamet. "Ah, love."

"And you?" Samira asked. "I've seen the way you look at Mamet's cousin."

"Amelia is taciturn and broody." And she had a sexy, athletic figure, a rare smile, and soulful brown eyes. But Lydia didn't know if she was ready for a new relationship.

"She's shy, but she only has eyes for you. All Engali have a little poetry in their souls. Maybe Amelia's trying to think of the right words."

"When she does, I might hear them."

Samira sat next to her. "I'm sorry if I'm pushing. If you're not ready—"

Lydia patted her knee and leaned close as if for a secret. "I'll tell you what I'm ready for."

"What? Tell!"

"To give up this damn bet and go back to camp."

Samira sat back with a disappointed look. "We can't give up now."

"Mamet wasn't even goading you! She was trying to get you alone."

"That's your opinion."

Lydia rolled her eyes. "You're not avoiding her, are you?"

"Nope." Samira bent to comb through the grass. As someone who read people very well, she still projected her own feelings bright and clear.

Lydia knelt next to her. "Weren't you always pushing Simon to talk about his feelings?"

"No, not really."

"Samira."

Samira gave her a look and sighed. "When you said engagement wreath, well… I think Mamet is leaning that way, and I'm not ready."

Lydia's heart went out to her. She'd been lucky that she and Freddie were always on the same level, relationship-wise, but she knew the opposite happened more often. "Maybe you should tell her how you feel before she asks, give her a chance to save face, and take a weight off your mind."

Samira leaned against her, always so easy with touching people.

It delighted Lydia, but she tried not to show it. When she'd been a prophet, most people had gone out of their way to avoid her, as if her power made her different from other yafanai, as if she made the future instead of just seeing it. In a way, it was true. What she saw couldn't be changed. She'd heard some yafanai theorizing that it was the act of looking into the future that fixed it. As long as no one looked, anything could happen. Lydia didn't know about that, but just like seeing the future, speculating didn't change anything.

"I don't want to break her heart," Samira said.

"If she's not in love with you already, she's nearly there. Make it clear you're not breaking up with her, and explain you're not ready for bonding. It may dampen some of her romantic dreams, but she'll get over that."

"You're right. I know you are. It's just..." She straightened and stared into the grass. "Did you see that?"

Lydia turned, but in the fading light, she saw nothing. The grass waved, and the sunset was turning the sky purple. As the wind gusted, a chill traveled down Lydia's spine, and her skin crawled. Maybe someone *was* watching them.

She shook off the foreboding and grinned. It could only be one person. "I think your dashing lover is spying on us." She strode a few feet into the grass. "Come out, Mamet." She watched again, but nothing moved. Her smile faded, and she felt someone's gaze slide like oil over her skin. The wind gusted, and she smelled something sharp and musky, someone who hadn't bathed in a while.

A dark-haired woman rushed from the grass, pale sword held high and murder in her gray eyes.

"Samira!" Lydia cried.

Without thinking, Lydia fell into her power just as she had during the boggin attack. She looked seconds into the future and saw how the woman would stab from the right. She snapped to the present and dodged out of reach. The woman's eyes widened above tattooed cheeks. She darted to her left. Lydia kept her hold on the future and dropped as the tattooed woman came on again. Tall and lean, she was far more skilled than a sick boggin. Even with her power, Lydia didn't know how long she could stay ahead of the strikes.

The tattooed woman flew backward, rolling through the grass, a victim of Samira's power. She leapt again, then launched backward to smack against a large boulder. She struggled as if pinned, cursing and wriggling against invisible bonds.

Samira marched to Lydia's side, glaring at the tattooed woman. A sheen of sweat broke out on her forehead, a sign of the incredible control it took to hold the tattooed woman in place. Macros were often called hurlers in Gale; they lacked fine control, but maybe all they needed was rage.

The tattooed woman yelped and cried out as she writhed.

"We haven't actually been introduced," Samira called, serious and deadly. "My name is Samira Zaidi. You might remember me from the time you stabbed me in the back and left me to die. Right before you kidnapped my friend and long before you tortured the woman I'm falling in love with." She frowned, and the tattooed woman cried out again.

"Samira," Lydia whispered. "Who is she?"

"Mamet called her Fajir, some leader among the Sun-Moons." A bead of blood seeped from her left nostril, a sign of yafanai strain.

Fajir coughed a laugh, and Samira frowned again. Fajir began to bend backward over the boulder, stretching, arms and legs straightening past the point of comfort. She howled in pain.

"Samira, that's enough," Lydia said.

"She tortured Mamet!"

Lydia could almost hear the grinding of Fajir's joints as she stretched. "Bring her to Chafa Yuve and the elders." Lydia stepped in front of her. "I know you hate her, but you can't become like her."

Samira took a deep breath, and Fajir dropped to the ground, gasping. Samira rubbed the sweat from her forehead and the blood from her nose.

Lydia put an arm around her shoulders. "Breathe."

Samira glared at Fajir again. "As long as they make her pay."

Fajir began to laugh, a rusty sound. She continued even as it seemed to pain her, as she curled into a ball.

Samira barked at her to get up, to precede them as they marched into camp. Lydia kept her eyes pinned on the long line of Fajir's back, even when people began to call out to them, asking what was happening.

"Stay back. Don't touch her," Samira said.

"Get the chafa," Lydia added. "This woman tried to kill us."

Expressions turned confused before that news sank in, then brows darkened, and frowns started. Lydia and Samira hadn't been with the Engali long, but they'd made more than a few friends. And since everyone seemed to like Mamet, they liked the woman she'd chosen as a lover, too.

Speaking of Mamet... Lydia glanced around and saw her walking toward them from the edge of camp, a purple starflower in one hand. She raised a hand to wave, but when her eyes fell on Fajir, she froze. Her lips moved, and it seemed as if she was saying, "No," over and over. The flower fell from her hands.

Mamet stumbled as she came closer, her eyes going wide. Samira had told Lydia a little about Mamet's torture, and Lydia bet she was seeing that dark basement under the Sun-Moon's palace, feeling the whips, the kicks, and punches. Fajir and her widows had cursed Mamet and spat on her, told her that her entire family had been killed. All lies, but while Mamet was alone in the dark, it had no doubt added to her pain.

If not for Horace's healing power, Samira had said, she'd be covered in scars.

Chafa Yuve strode toward Fajir. Lydia met him and gave him Fajir's bone sword. "She attacked us."

"Don't let her in here!" Mamet said as she reached them.

Fajir turned pitiless gray eyes on Mamet, an almost inhuman gaze. Yuve watched them both.

Samira went to Mamet, arms out. "It's all right, all right. We caught her."

Mamet seemed to struggle not to fall into her arms. She looked as if she might cry, then stared at Fajir and drew herself up. "Get rid of her!"

"She's our prisoner," Samira said. "Not our guest. But if you want..." She stared deeply into Mamet's eyes, her gaze one of utter conviction. "I'll kill her."

Lydia gasped. Killing could never be so easy.

Mamet cupped Samira's face. "I'd never ask you to."

Fajir was watching with a smirk. Lydia wanted to kick her.

"That's one of the reasons I'd do it," Samira said. "Because you'd never ask."

Yuve took Fajir, bound her hands, and led her away. Several others fell in with them.

"They'll find out why she's come," Lydia said. "What she wants." Mamet turned her head and spat. "She came to kill Engali. It's what she lives for. Was she alone?"

Lydia nodded, and Mamet frowned. "Sun-Moons are never alone, even the widows. In the Sun-Moon palace, Cordelia pledged to hunt down Fajir's dead partner, but maybe she refused in the end, and Fajir has come herself."

"But no one here has killed a Sun-Moon, have they?" Samira asked.

Mamet shook her head. "She probably wants to kill every Engali she can. Who knows how many she's killed already?"

Lydia shook her head. "She's gaunt and dirty. She seems half dead already."

Samira put an arm around Mamet's waist. "Not dead enough."

The words made Lydia frown, and she tried to see the killer Mamet and Samira saw, but Fajir didn't seem anything but defeated. Maybe she'd come looking for death.

CHAPTER EIGHT

Cordelia awoke at dawn with the drushka. She thought she might have to bellow for her fellow humans to get out of bed, but the paladins didn't need a lot of prompting to muster. They were nervous, many of them casting glances toward where the sixth queen's tree waited in the swamp. No humans had been killed the day before, but the paladins had been knocked around enough to get a good mad on.

When Cordelia ascended to the cupola, Pool sucked her teeth and stared into the swamp. "I feel the second and third queens nearby."

Cordelia craned her neck but saw nothing in the distance. "Any thoughts from them?"

"These queens were born after my departure, and so they are far younger than Sky or myself. Their minds have crumbled before the will of the Shi. I do not even sense separate personalities."

Cordelia sighed. "Sounds like another fight."

Pool spread her hands. "Ahya. And I doubt the captured humans are with the second or third queens. No doubt the Shi holds them close." She slapped her hands against her thighs. "The Shi is frustrated by how we freed Sky. She knows she cannot defeat human weapons and armor, so she uses the second and third queens as sacrifices to slow us."

"In order to do what? You told me she's too big to move, so she's not going anywhere."

Pool didn't answer, and Cordelia resisted speculating wildly. According to what Pool had learned from Sky, the Shi had pulled many drushka in close. The Shi might be buying time in order to shore up her defenses. As long as they weren't building a wall made of humans.

"With two trees, we might have to use the railguns. If you threaten the second and third queens with heavy firepower, will they surrender?"

"I would need to be close in order to reach them as I did Sky. And telling the Shi would do nothing. She does not care for drushkan lives." Pool frowned hard, and her eyes focused on Cordelia, on the railgun. "These queens may not have enough minds left to reach."

She sounded so forlorn, Cordelia couldn't help patting her shoulder as the drushka did when they wanted to comfort someone. Pool smiled, but her eyes didn't lose their sadness.

"If you free them one at a time," Cordelia said, "we'll keep the other one off you. And we won't kill anyone we don't have to." She sincerely hoped she could keep that promise, but she wouldn't let her people die if she could help it.

Pool's tree didn't have to venture far before they saw the two queens in the distance. Their trees stood only slightly larger than Pool's, and as before, Cordelia ordered her paladins to wound where they could. As soon as the enemy drushka closed, Cordelia went hand-to-hand again. She kept on the move, trying not to get buried under drushkan bodies, and she shouted for her soldiers to do the same. Pool's tree darted through the swamp, using the swamp trees to maneuver around. The other queens couldn't seem to catch her. They tangled easily with water roots, hanging vines, or each other.

Pool's tree dodged sharply to the left, branches swaying crazily. Cordelia's stabilizers kept her upright, and she tossed another wounded drushka into the water below. Fights raged all around her, but so far, she hadn't seen a clear path to either queen. Maybe if they could push one back, Pool could close with the other without wrestling with them both.

"Lea," Cordelia said through her comm. "Give the smaller tree a few bursts with the railgun."

"Roger that."

Cordelia swung her own gun around. "I'm sorry, Pool." She aimed, using her targeting sensors, but as she curled one finger over the trigger, the display in her visor flickered and died.

The weight of unpowered armor and the heavy railgun brought her to her knees. She grunted, trying to get upright again, but it was clear that her fucking battery had died. The tree moved, and Cordelia dropped to her belly, grasping the branch so she wouldn't be flung over the side. Her comm had gone down with everything else, and she sent a desperate thought to Pool. If anyone else's battery had decided it was time to sputter out, paladins could be dropping from the branches in droves.

The enemy drushka were still coming, used to navigating in a moving tree. Cordelia tossed the railgun toward one of Pool's cubbies, and it slid to safety. As she reached to jettison the heavy battery, a drushka crashed into her, knocking her flat.

His wooden blade screeched along her armor as he looked for gaps. She flailed, hitting him in the stomach. Even with no power behind the swing, the drushka arched upward, crying out. Cordelia kicked and drove him back while fumbling for her battery.

She hit the release as the drushka lunged again. Much lighter than before, she sat up to meet him. It'd been a long time since she'd fought in unpowered armor, but her body remembered. Without the battery, it was almost easy.

She brought her blade around to catch the drushka's swing. He reared back to strike again, and she stabbed him in the gut before throwing him from the tree. If everyone's batteries were as drained as hers, the time for wounding was over. She kept her visor down. She could see through the ultra-thin material, and it lessened the risk of being stabbed in the face.

All around her, paladins could be buried under piles of drushka. Some still leapt and whirled, their batteries live. Others struggled just to rise. Cordelia ran for the nearest, hauling him up and jettisoning his battery. Some of these paladins had never worn unpowered armor. She barked at them to get deeper into Pool's branches and stay there. She drew her sidearm and fired into the drushka as she stayed low and struggled from one paladin to another, helping them ditch their heavy batteries and sending them to gather with the others.

When she'd helped everyone nearby, Cordelia searched for a way to climb to the others. Pool's tree whipped to the right, and Cordelia teetered, waving her arms for balance, but without the stabilizers, it wasn't enough. She fell hard and hit the branch below in a rattle of armor plates. Gasping for breath, fighting her fear, she scrambled for purchase, but the branch slid out from under her as if she was covered in grease.

"Shit!" Airborne, she flipped, trying to see where she was headed just as she smashed into the ropy branch of a swamp tree. The wind rushed from her lungs, but the armor absorbed some of the shock.

Coughing, she stood, resisting the urge to go slow, to check herself for injuries. Pool's tree was getting away. Before it got far, its branches hooked with another queen. Finally, some luck! Cordelia picked up speed, not wanting to miss her chance to catch up. Before she'd gone far, she spotted an armored form fall from Pool's branches and splash into the water.

"Shit, shit, shit!" Cordelia changed direction, heading for where the paladin had already disappeared. She blocked out thoughts of her own time underwater, when a prog had tried to eat her. She jumped in after the sunken paladin, not knowing if they'd be able to get themselves out without power but unable to stop herself.

Her helmet's seal held. She had a little air, and she tried to breathe shallowly as she plummeted through the brown mire. A cloud of silt marked where the other paladin had hit bottom. When she landed, Cordelia trudged into the cloud as fast as she could. Even with the water helping to hold her, it was as hard to walk as she remembered. The armor wanted to pull her down. Speaking of, she spotted the other paladin on his back, writhing. She bent and went for his battery. He flailed at her, no doubt thinking she was a prog come to devour him.

"Hold fucking still!" Cordelia cried. Her comm was dead, but it felt good to yell. She fumbled for the battery again and finally found the release.

She could see into his visor, see his wide, panicked eyes, his open mouth. At least now he could see who she was. She grabbed his hands and pulled him toward a mass of brown: the trunk of a swamp tree. A tinny taste filled her mouth, and her body felt heavier with every step. Pain built in her head; she was running out of air, but she had to keep putting one foot in front of the other.

When she grasped the trunk, the paladin finally seemed to get in the groove. He climbed beside her, and when her sluggish limbs tried to fail her, he helped pull her up. Her vision was growing dark around the edges when her head finally broke the water's surface. She reached for her helmet, and took huge gulps of air when she'd finally pried the visor open.

The scent of brackish water and floating algae almost made her gag. Her fellow paladin was coughing alongside her. Water trickled in through the open visor, and Cordelia hauled herself up again, trying to get clear. She didn't recognize the man beside her—one of the new recruits—but she wanted to promote him on the spot.

They clambered onto a branch together and went for Pool. Cordelia drew her sidearm and fired at every long-haired drushka in range. They fled from the gun, and she yelled for any other paladins who'd fallen.

They found one along the branches near the water, unmoving. His shoulder plate had been peeled away, and a drushka had scratched him. Cordelia grabbed his top half, while her fellow grabbed his bottom, and they hustled toward where Pool waited, more paladins joining them from the surrounding trees.

At the base of Pool's tree, Cordelia pushed for her tie to the drushka, asking to come back aboard. The tree lifted them and put them near the trunk where they could fire from cover.

Cordelia really wanted to stay somewhere she could hang on, but she ventured forth again, looking for others who might need help. She bent low, nearly crawling as she sought to stay on board. She heard the thump of a railgun firing into one of the queen's trees and made her way toward the sound.

Jon Lea stood tall, proving that his battery still worked, at least. He fired into the mass of drushka, some of his shots hitting the tree, but most scattering drushka to the wind, freeing groups of paladins to struggle toward Cordelia. She sent them back to the others who hung on near the trunk or had taken shelter in the cubbies.

Cordelia gasped as Pool leaped between the trees, Nettle at her side. Lea had cleared the way for her.

"Oh fuck!" Cordelia would never be able to catch up with them. But she had more than one way to help. She left Lea to his work and went back to the paladins near the trunk. "Watch my body," she said to Carter, one of her fellow exiles.

He nodded. As she lay down on the branch, he stood over her. It took a moment to relax since she knew her people might be wounded or floundering, waiting to become prog chow. She focused on her breathing, thinking about how to help Pool, help Nettle. With a desperate shove, she pushed free from her body.

She hung motionless, blinded by the lights of three queens together. Quickly, she flew toward the closest and headed upward, searching for Pool. Still on the move, she was easier to spot than if she'd been standing still. Drushka barred her path at every turn, but Nettle and her warriors made quick work of most. Some caught sight of Pool, but instead of hesitating as the sixth queen's drushka had, these fell at Pool's feet. Cordelia thought they were bowing at first, but they sought to block the way with their bodies. Either the Shi didn't want Pool hurt, or she couldn't overcome the drushkan resistance to hurting a queen. They piled in Pool's way, and her party slowed to a crawl. Cordelia spotted the tendrils of light connecting Pool to her drushka, just as the drushka in her way were connected to someone in the distance. And from these trees, another light stretched into the swamp, probably the connection of these queens to the Shi. That light was mottled with ugly gray spots, infected by the hatred of the Shi.

Cordelia flew to Pool. "My armor lost its charge. Some of the others are unpowered, too. We need to end this."

Pool glanced to the side as she clambered over a pile of drushka. "Go to the second tree, Sa, and find the queen. Touch her. I will merge with the third myself and the second through you."

"Right." Cordelia streaked away. She didn't relish the idea of being a conduit again. Her fight with Naos hadn't exactly been pleasant, and she didn't really want to get in a mind fight with the Shi. Her spirit didn't need any new scars, but if that was the only way forward...

The second's tree had gotten tangled in a swamp tree, but she'd be free soon enough. Cordelia headed for the light of the queen herself even as she wanted to run. Maybe all she needed was some human backup. She called as loudly as she could for Horace and felt the tingle as he answered.

"Are you hurt?" he asked in her mind.

"I'm going to help Pool fight the queens. I might need your help."

"There are so many wounded!"

"The faster I do this, the faster you can see to them."

He sent his frustration, but she shook it off. He could be as frustrated as he wanted as long as he stayed with her. Cordelia threaded through the branches and finally found the second queen.

She stood hidden, fully encased in bark; only her light shone through. After a deep breath she wished she could feel, Cordelia dove inside.

❖

Pool felt her drushka dying, felt the deaths of the old drushka as they succumbed to wooden blades or metal bullets. So much death, and none of it necessary. The humans could no longer afford to be merciful, not with the drushkan hordes and the attacking queens. She had to stop this.

As more drushka sought to bar her path, she snarled in frustration. Even Nettle and the fiercest warriors could not cut their way through so many. Reach ran at Pool's side, crying out for the drushka to give way, promising that they would be free.

"Up," Pool cried, leaping to a branch above. She sensed Cordelia flying closer to the second queen; the third was close. She ran faster, leaving her protectors behind, but these drushka sought only to slow her. One leapt at Pool's legs, but she jumped, swinging to another branch before dropping again.

She rolled as she landed and saw the trunk just ahead. The third queen stood encased just as the sixth had been. Only a hint of her body showed through her trunk. A host of drushka stood before her, faces contorted into feral snarls.

Pool screamed, putting all her rage as a queen into the cry. The host before her shrank, but she heard an answering scream from the mind of the Shi.

Pool hurled herself into the press of drushka, pushing through. They grabbed and sought to pull her down, but she persisted, taking one shaking step after another. They hung from her arms and clutched her legs, but she stumbled onward, a wordless cry on her lips. She stretched an arm toward the third and closed one fist over a lock of green hair.

She did not have time for niceties, for the careful extraction she had done with Sky. She dove into the third's mind, a queen far younger than her whom she had never met. The Shi had dominated the third's mind with ease. There was almost nothing left. But even as the Shi battered her with anger, Pool gained a foothold, taking what was left of the third in a firm, savage grip.

Pool reached for Cordelia's unique mind and found her connected to the second queen. Another wounded mind. Though the Shi was connected to both, she was also connected to the other queens, all but Pool and the sixth. Her attention was divided, and she did not have Cordelia's formidable will spurring her on.

"We must wake her, Sa," Pool said. "Show her what it is to lead." Cordelia assailed the second's mind with stories about leading her people, of what it meant to sacrifice oneself. She layered on recriminations. The drushka were dying, could she not see it? Did she not feel anything for them? Her duty was to them, not to the Shi.

It was not completely true, but now was not the time to point that out. The Shi focused on this interloping mind, trying to push it out, but it was clear she did not want to touch it, did not know what to do. Pool used her confusion to gain more ground with the second and third, to try to pull their true selves out. Every time the Shi turned her attention to the third, Cordelia made a thorn of herself again with the second. Then as the Shi looked that way, Pool would make headway with the third, and the Shi howled in frustration. The second was beginning to feel the mind of Cordelia, too, was wondering what to make of her, and her curiosity pushed her further from the Shi's grasp.

"Come out, sister," Pool said, keeping hold of the third's hair, trying to use that pain to wake her. The drushka around her had gone still, as if they could no longer move without orders. "Your name," Pool said, digging. "Your name is…" She dug until the third cried out in pain, her drushka crying with her. "Your name is Nau." Pool opened herself to this queen, this stranger, hoping the action would free her more. "Come out, sister."

But Nau was too afraid, and the second seemed the same. Pool wrested more control from them and sought the connection to their drushka, commanding the attack to stop. They hesitated but went still. She sensed them muttering in confusion, stumbling, hands to their heads as the Shi fought to regain control.

Pool dug her hands into the bark and began to rip it away, the sharp pieces cutting her fingers with stinging slices. The queen inside was breathing hard, gasping, face creased in pain. Pool reached in and tore her loose from her birthright-turned-prison.

Nau's eyes rolled upward as she shuddered in Pool's arms. Pool called for Reach and felt her near. "Stay with me." She lifted Nau and hurried toward where Cordelia's spirit waited with the second. As they ran, Reach sang, keeping Nau alive.

"Sa, make the second queen angry."

"You got it." Cordelia cursed the second, calling her a coward, claiming she was not worthy of being a queen, that whatever trick of birth that made her a queen had been a mistake.

Pool would have answered such a challenge in a moment. The mind of the second shuddered, seeking to attack what it could not. Pool picked up speed, whispering to the third's mind, trying to bring her drushka to peace. The Shi continued to push in with brutal force, and her rage beat at Pool like thrashing wings. All around them, drushka fell and screamed in agony, rolling from the branches and plummeting to the swamp below. How many would die from this? How many would be forever broken?

"Stop this!" Pool called to the Shi.

"Traitor! Rebel! Murderer!" the Shi screamed. "I will not let you corrupt them!"

The third's lips trembled as she tried to speak along with the mind words. Pool staggered, but Reach's arm pulled her upright, and now someone joined Pool's other side: Nettle, helping to carry her and Nau.

Inside the Shi's rage, Pool caught memories of dead drushka. The Shi was still scarred by the murders among her tribe two hundred and fifty years ago, one of the first meetings between humans and drushka. She had been the seventh queen then, but she still hungered for the humans' death. She saw herself as rescuing the rest of the drushka from the same fate. Anything that was not drushka was the enemy. She did not understand the shortness of human lives, and she could not see her way past the ancient loss. Pool grieved for her, but the Shi rejected the feeling.

When Pool reached the second, the bark had already opened, and the second lay along the branch, struggling to get to where Cordelia's spirit hovered, trying to answer the challenge. Kneeling, Pool gathered both queens into her arms. "Stay with me, Sa. Help me keep the Shi at bay."

"She doesn't know who she's fucking with," Cordelia said.

Pool laughed at the thought, and it helped her focus. Humor was no longer part of the Shi, so it was not part of the second or third. Pool shared the humor with them along with all the joys of life. She showed them Cordelia's courage, her loyalty.

"That is human," Pool said. "Knock them down and watch them

rise. Like pests, ahya, but does the pest not survive? It can swarm. Better to be their allies than their enemies."

The two queens pondered this, and that thinking gave them room to think about other things, so much of life that had been denied them for so long.

"Speak your name again, sister," Pool said to the third.

"Nau," the third said, her eyelids fluttering.

"And you, sister?"

The answer was weak, breathed more than spoken. "Lasa."

Their names opened their minds further, and Pool slackened her grip, letting the queens become themselves again. She held their hands as they shared so many memories: mothers and fathers, mates long dead, the image of a floating flower, a saleska, and a thunderstorm that fascinated a young queen-to-be. Their thoughts swirled like leaves in a high wind.

Pool shared some of her own memories, only a few, not wanting to overwhelm them. She sprinkled in humans: the slings, the feel of their smooth skin, their bright smiles, and easy laughs. The Shi tried to fight against the thoughts, but Cordelia repulsed her with human taunts. As Nau's and Lasa's minds expanded, the voice of the Shi quieted to nothing.

"Nau," Pool said. "The humans would call you Leaf Fall, but Lasa, yours is not so easy. Spirited, is how I think they would say it."

The two queens tasted the names in their minds, identities they had not been aware of before. Their hair dangled down Pool's back as they rested their heads on her shoulders. Reach sang to them, comforting them, and Pool felt Sky, the sixth queen, coming closer, her shawnessi spreading through the wounded drushka. Sky came to them aboard the second tree and knelt with her fellow queens. Shawnessi from all four tribes surrounded them, singing in concert. Leaf Fall and Spirited raised their heads and blinked at the sun-streaked swamp as if they had never seen it before. They touched Pool, the tree, their drushka, caressing all like newborns.

When Cordelia approached in her body, Horace at her side, the queens ran their hands over her metal skin. Cordelia stood and bore it with a scowl. Pool smiled, hoping the shawnessi could grant Cordelia some serenity. Horace let his powers play over all of them, and the queens reached to touch him, too. With a smile, he hugged each one, so free with his embrace for those who needed it. They wrapped their long arms around him and pressed his forehead to theirs before moving through their drushka, needing touch, craving it.

Pool moved away with Cordelia and Horace. "They will reconnect with their drushka," Pool said. "It must seem as if they do not know them at all."

"And when they've recovered?" Cordelia asked. "Will they help us or stay back like the sixth?"

"We will speak of it later." She kept a connection with the queens as they wandered among their drushka and looked out among the humans. Leaf Fall gave Pool a memory, and she stopped, her heart wrenching.

Nettle and Reach looked at her sharply. Cordelia turned, too, and Pool felt her curiosity.

"What is it?" Horace asked as he looked between them.

Pool hurried through the limbs, heading for the image Leaf Fall had given her. Cordelia would be angry, but better she see it herself than be told.

"Where are we going?" Cordelia asked as she followed. "Is there…" Her voice faded as she looked into the swamp.

A row of bodies swung from trees in the distance. Cordelia stepped to the edge of the branch as if trying to get a better look. Nettle took her arm to keep her back, but her eyes were locked on the bodies, too. The image Leaf Fall had fed to Pool, a row of murdered humans, swung lazily, fifteen of the captives. Their bodies were slack, heads tilted down or to the side, away from the vines that circled their necks and led to the limb above.

"Fifteen," Cordelia mumbled.

Horace had his hands to his mouth. "Why in the world—"

"It is a warning," Pool said. "Done by the Shi." She touched Cordelia's and Horace's shoulders. "The other queens did not do this, Sa. They have told me that the captives are held by the Shi."

"What's left of them," Cordelia said, her face tight with anger. By the way she clenched her fists, Pool knew all mercy had deserted her. As she stared at the swinging bodies, Pool could not help but agree.

CHAPTER NINE

Simon was happy he didn't have to worry about space, at least. Dillon had had three large rooms all to himself in the Yafanai Temple. Simon put Pakesh, Little Paul, and Evan in the bedroom to sleep. Shiv and Lyshus went into the study along with the sapling. The view of a large tree in the courtyard seemed to make Shiv happy, surrounded as she was in a human city.

That left the sitting room for Simon, with the only door into the hallway. The kids couldn't escape without alerting him, and anyone who came knocking was probably looking for him anyway.

Late at night, Mila came to feed Evan again. Simon set up a schedule with her and paid the only way he knew how, by soothing her aches and pains. Now he stayed up even later, going through Dillon's papers by lantern light. He hadn't found anything about food production or distribution. Dillon had no doubt fobbed that responsibility off on others, much as he did every task he didn't enjoy. Simon found one bizarre paper titled "People Who Want to Kill Me" and stared at it, wondering what exactly had prompted it.

He couldn't help but think of Dillon's face slack in death. The man who'd killed him had run away after the deed was done, and Simon had never seen him again, never knew the reason why. Maybe he'd been a servant who'd had enough of Dillon's shit. That seemed likely.

Simon read the list of possible killers again. The servants weren't listed unless they counted as "Renegades." He peered at a crossed-out name that might be his, but it seemed Dillon had changed his mind.

Simon rolled his eyes. Dillon probably thought Simon didn't have the stones to kill anyone.

But, a little voice inside him reminded, he hadn't killed Dillon. He'd merely held Dillon still so someone else could kill him. On the one hand, he was a little ashamed he hadn't done it himself. On the other, he was relieved. His hands were cleaner, never mind what Miriam said about responsibility.

Simon folded the paper and put it aside with others he intended to throw away. He turned to the next when Shiv wandered out of the study and flopped onto a pile of cushions. Simon didn't need to read her to see the sadness in her body, the way she drooped and couldn't seem to focus. He stayed silent, letting her decide when to speak.

"Before Lyshus," she said at last, "I wanted to explore this city."

He set the papers aside. "Taking care of a child is hard work."

She slapped her thighs. "Ahwa, it is not that. My feeling is..." She spread her hands. "Unexplainable. Stronger than motherhood, perhaps, or motherhood multiplied? I do not know. I am not simply myself. I am a queen." She rested her chin in one long-fingered hand. "I did not know what that meant before. How can my mother, my shi'a'na, stand it? How did she care for me when I was an infant while being queen to the tribe?"

Simon nodded, though he was certain Pool had help when Shiv was a baby. "It must be hard to have to do it on your own."

With a ghost of a smile, she glanced at him. "Overwhelming, but then, I wonder how I ever lived without Lyshus. When my tribe grows, maybe I will change. Maybe once Shi'a'na frees the old drushka, some will come to me." She stared at the ceiling, eyes half-lidded. "The idea pleases me. It is my purpose, but then I think..." A thread of irritation and fear wafted from her like a sour smell.

"So what's wrong?"

She stared at nothing. "My mother rebelled against our people. I am more rebellious than her, a queen born of a queen. What if Lyshus is more rebellious still? What if everyone who joins my tribe..." She trailed off, worry and fear roiling off her.

They were interesting questions. Simon leaned back and thought about it. He was still getting to know the drushka; they were endlessly fascinating, mixing his love of botany with his skill in biology. "I guess

Lyshus is an unknown, sort of like you. Since queens don't usually have their own children, no one knows what the tribe of a queen's queen will be like. Since you're both unique, I guess you'll have to wait and see what happens."

She wrinkled her nose. "Ahya, you are also unique, shawness."

He smiled back, thinking of Horace, someone to be unique with. God, he wished they could be here together now, safe, with nothing to ponder but a couple of unique drushka. "Your little tree seems to be growing fast, too."

"Ahya. Now that I have a tribe, it wants to fit my needs."

That was probably some kind of evolutionary tag being triggered through the telepathic connection. He wondered if she'd let him scan the tree, wondered if it was polite to ask. "When Pool comes back, do you think you'll stay with her, with your old tribe, or strike out on your own?"

She spread her hands, the gesture that meant anything was possible.

And it was late, with more work ahead of them in the morning. "Well, the one piece of advice I remember from new parents is: rest when you're able. I think it applies to new drushkan queens, too." He rose and patted her shoulder. "You're not alone, Shiv, and I don't just mean Lyshus."

She rose and wrapped her arms around him, burying her head in his chest. He stiffened, then tried to relax, awkwardly patting her back. When he stopped, she didn't step away. Her anxiety peaked.

He floundered, thoughts racing. "Shiv?"

"I have been…lying, shawness," she said, voice muffled against him. "My people do not lie, but I have done it, and I am sorry!"

He patted her again, his own anxiety wrenching up. He tried to push it down, letting his power soothe them both. "About what?"

"With my hands, not my mouth, but it is the same. I have hidden the truth, and now I will be alone with only Lyshus. Shi'a'na will hate me!"

He held her tighter, feeling again how very young she was. "She won't. She couldn't. Tell me what you did, and I'll help you fix it."

"I dyed his hair with berries and ash."

He tried to make sense of that and failed. "What?"

She leaned back and stared before taking his hand and leading him into the study, grabbing the lantern on her way. Lyshus had curled up on the floor, on the roots of the sapling, his feet resting on the rug. The branches leaned over him, shielding his small body. Shiv dipped her fingers in the water jug on the desk before crouching and rubbing Lyshus's head. She held up her hand, fingers colored reddish brown.

Simon knelt and peered at the sleeping boy, eyes widening at the sight of short, vibrant green hair under the brown dye. "A drushkan… king? Is that possible?"

Shiv curled her hands into fists and led the way back into the sitting room. "It should not be. Perhaps this is another reason queens do not bear their own children. Their every tribe member will be a queen!"

"Or a king."

"I do not know that word! Males are not queens!"

He didn't argue, trying to think what this meant. Drushkan queens had awesome telepathic powers but were only connected to their tribes or each other. They were hubs of communication. An entire race of queens? What could that mean?

Shiv ran her hands over her short hair. She'd grown it out some from when he'd first seen her, maybe so she'd look more like Pool. She seemed to have grown a bit taller, too. "If this happens to all who become my tribe, I cannot accept anyone! But drushka are not meant to be a tribe of one. And we cannot rejoin Shi'a'na's tribe. She will not accept Lyshus as a queen. No one will! He will be as doomed as I to never have a tribe!"

Simon sent another calming wave, but she seemed to be brushing them off. "You can stay here with us," he said. "With humans, I mean. Me and Horace, Cordelia, Liam."

At the mention of that name, her face turned down in sorrow. When she glanced at Simon again, she seemed desperate. "Can you change Lyshus, shawness? Make him normal? Even if I lose him as my tribe of one, he can return to Shi'a'na. He can forget me and be happy."

Leaving her all alone. Like he'd been on the *Atlas*, when there was no choice but Dillon. He couldn't help embracing her again and thinking about what she'd said, what she was willing to sacrifice, her very purpose. "I…can try, but if I do, I could hurt him, maybe even kill him. Messing with biology like that is what caused the smarter boggins, and you know how that turned out."

She planted her forehead against him again. "What shall I do, shawness?"

She couldn't hide Lyshus forever, but Simon was too far out of his depth to give good advice. They needed Pool. "We need to tell your mother when she gets back. Maybe she can figure out what to do." He held her close. "I don't think she'll try to hurt you, but if anyone does, I'll help you both."

She raised her head and smiled. "Thank you, shawness, for offering the safety of your hands. Perhaps the humans will be my new tribe. Or perhaps someday, I will make a tree for Lyshus as Shi'a'na made for me, and we will live in the swamp together." She leaned against the table and stared at nothing.

Simon wondered if she was thinking about how long queens—and probably kings—lived, about how long she and Lyshus would be alone together. Even if they stayed with the humans, they'd lose friends to their long lives.

But not him, not Horace. With their powers, they'd also live a long, long time. He tried not to think about it, preferring to focus on the now even with its host of problems. "You won't be alone, no matter what. Remember that. Now, try to get some sleep."

She wrinkled her nose. "Only if you sleep as well."

As if prompted by her words, he yawned. It had to be getting close to daybreak. "Good idea."

She went back into the study. As Simon went to bed on the pile of cushions, he knew he'd still be tired when morning came. That was all right. He'd just sleep a little later. The crops could wait. With that happy thought, he drifted off.

Around dawn, when Evan began to cry for breakfast, Simon remembered that children didn't care what his plans were. He pulled a blanket over his head, wishing someone else would take care of the problem, but Mila hadn't arrived yet.

The bedroom door creaked open. "Simon?" Pakesh whispered.

With a sigh, Simon sat up, rubbing his eyes. "The crying baby annihilated the need to whisper, Pakesh." He used a bit of power to cleanse his fatigue. It helped, but after a hard day, his body wanted rest.

Pakesh moved into the room, a sheepish grin on his face. "Should I take Evan to Mila?"

"I will." Since Pakesh was used to babies, he was no doubt used to seeing breastfeeding, but Simon didn't want to take the chance that he'd gawk at Mila and make her so uncomfortable she never wanted to come back.

Simon stumbled into the bedroom. Little Paul was sitting up in the bed, pointing at the crib and sucking his fingers. "Baby crying."

"Yes, thank you." Simon picked up Evan, grabbed the candle Pakesh had lit, and headed into the hall, trying to soothe Evan as he went, though he didn't much care if he woke the whole temple. They'd soon be swimming in babies; they should get used to it.

He found the right room after only one wrong turn. Simon cleansed some of Mila's fatigue, too, and eased the pain in her breasts. She fed Evan as quickly as he would eat, then handed him back, giving Simon a grateful smile before turning back to her bed.

Simon changed the baby's diaper before leaving, shutting Mila's door behind him. He took the long walk to the outbuilding where the temple residents left their laundry and put the dirty diaper there. When he shuffled outside again, he breathed deep in the morning air of the courtyard.

Evan had already fallen asleep, and Simon took a moment to listen to a quiet Gale. The sky was a featureless gray, and he couldn't see the horizon from inside the walls. The only people who'd be up at this hour would be bakers, maybe farmers…and people with small children. With a sigh, he wandered inside again, picking up some food from the kitchen before going back to Dillon's room. Dillon probably hadn't known where the kitchen or laundry was. Would he have taken care of a crying baby so early in the morning? Would fatherhood have changed him at all? Probably not. Even with an armload of offspring, Dillon would have depended entirely upon everyone else to do the dirty work.

Everyone was awake by the time he got back. Pakesh and Shiv were probably used to getting up early, living outdoors. And if he remembered correctly, all children woke up at dawn because they always did whatever was horribly inconvenient for everyone else.

"Morning," Simon said as he entered. He handed the baby to Pakesh and set out the fruit and rolls he'd snagged from the kitchen. The bread was at least a day old but hadn't been thrown away. He imagined everyone was going to be stretching food as far as it would go.

Lyshus stared at the rolls. When Little Paul nibbled on one, Lyshus grabbed another and crammed the entire thing in his mouth. Shiv sat forward and fished it out, replacing it with a piece of fruit.

She handed the bread to Simon. "These I do not think we should eat, shawness, but I thank you for the fruit."

He nodded and set the damp roll to the side. Maybe Little Paul would eat it.

"Will you take Evan as your son, shawness?" Shiv asked.

Simon looked to where Pakesh was putting Evan in the crib and fought down a wave of panic. "I don't…I'm not really the fatherly type. At least, I never thought so."

Shiv spread her hands. "I never thought I would have a tribe."

He sighed and thought about months of nightly feedings and breathing the dawn air. Surely *someone* in Gale wanted a baby. "What happens to a drushkan child if all his relatives die?"

"The tribe cares for him unless he bonds closely with someone."

By the dim light leaking around the shuttered windows, Simon watched Pakesh soothing Evan. He pictured himself or Horace doing the same. And Dillon *had* asked him to care for the boy. It didn't really matter what Simon had been thinking when he'd said yes. He'd still said it.

Plus, Evan was the child of Gale's ex-god. People might want to use him for their own ends. He needed protection. "I guess we're stuck with each other for the time being." But being a father? Guardian, maybe. Friend? One day. That was much easier to think about.

And he didn't have to think about any of it right away. "I have to reexamine the fields around Gale, and Pakesh has to come with me. Can you watch Evan, Lyshus, and Little Paul alone?"

Shiv slapped her thighs. "I have never cared for a human infant. They seem fragile." When Pakesh walked back into the room, she smiled. "Perhaps Pakesh can stay?"

Pakesh beamed at her until Simon cleared his throat. "Sorry, he has to stay close to me until we can get his powers fully under control."

Pakesh's smile faded, and he rubbed the back of his head. "Um, there's probably someone here in the temple who's cared for babies, someone who could help."

"I'll let Mila know you'll be alone," Simon said. "We'll come check on you as often as we can. And I'll try to find you some meat. I think Liam mentioned a hunting party."

Shiv mumbled something about wishing she was going with them. Simon had to pretend not to hear. He and Pakesh took turns doing a light wash in the bedroom, but the only clothes they had to change into were Dillon's. Simon ignored the ridiculous gold robes Dillon had once worn; his shirts and trousers were baggy on both Simon and Pakesh. And that wasn't the only problem. Dillon's scent clung to them as it clung to everything, even after washing. Simon only managed to wear Dillon's shirt for five minutes before he banged on their neighbor's door, begging for clothing. He had enough to deal with at the moment. He did not need to be reminded of Dillon every time he drew breath.

When Simon and Pakesh were finally ready, they strode through the temple. Once outside, Simon breathed the morning air again, letting it calm him.

"Look," Pakesh said.

Simon followed his pointing finger to a high wall nearby. He blinked at the graffiti scrawled there, and it took a minute before the words came into focus.

"The Storm Lord lives!" it read, each letter at least four feet high. "The pretenders will burn!"

He read the words again, frowning. "What the hell?"

Something hanging above the graffiti shifted in the breeze. Simon gaped at the remains of a scorched effigy dangling from a gutter. It had no features left, but after another look at the words, he knew who it was supposed to be. There was only one pretend god in Gale these days, mending crops and telling people the Storm Lord was dead.

Simon was so glad he'd decided not to wear Dillon's clothes. He would have ripped them off at the moment. And the sight of them would have made the graffiti artists even angrier, a pretend god in the real god's clothes.

"What does it mean?" Pakesh asked.

Simon took a deep breath, fighting the rage that spread through him like cancer. He pointed. "Pull that…dummy down, will you, Pakesh?"

"I don't think I can climb—"

"With your power, please." He tried to keep his voice calm, but threats got his blood up. He wasn't *pretending* to be anything. He hadn't done anything wrong. Dillon had done plenty of wrong, *and* he'd been a prick while doing it, but it seemed some people were still loyal. "Focus on where the dummy meets the rope and give it a yank." He tightened his hold on Pakesh's power, helping to focus the force. Even so, when Pakesh narrowed his eyes and flexed his power, he snapped the rope and hurled the effigy at the ground so hard it splashed mud up the wall.

"I did it!" Pakesh cried before he clapped a hand over his mouth. The sound echoed in the quiet morning air.

Simon clapped his shoulder. "Well done." He focused on the graffiti. It'd been a long time since he'd used his power on anything that wasn't alive, but he'd once shaped tiny metal needles with his mind. He could do this. He focused on the paint, let himself feel the wood behind it. The paint didn't belong, so all he had to do was warp the wood so...

Bits of paint rained down like snowflakes. Simon exhaled and felt sweat stand out on his forehead. Precision took more concentration than he remembered.

"Amazing!" Pakesh said.

"Thanks, but I'll stick to healing in the future."

"Who did this?" Pakesh picked up the effigy and frowned at it before putting it in a nearby rubbish pile. "What did it say?"

"A vague threat about me, not important." He wondered what more they could do. Pakesh could thumb through nearby minds, but the culprits were probably long gone. And such prying would not only be illegal in Gale; it would test Pakesh's control to the limit.

Simon tried to focus on other things instead. "Come on. We've got work to do."

With one more worried look at the wall, Pakesh followed.

Simon stopped first at the temporary well Pool had dug outside of town. To his surprise, Private Jacobs was already there, speaking to the workers who shored up the well's sides.

She smiled when she saw him. "I was just on my way to see if you were up, Doc. Off to see the plants?"

"You can call me Simon, you know."

She shrugged. "I've been calling people by their last names or titles for a long time, and I like it that way." She leaned close. "My unfortunate first name is Meriwether. Even my last girlfriend called me Jacobs."

He snorted a laugh. "Meriwether has a certain ring."

"Yeah, one that says 'playground punching bag.'" She turned and gestured one of the workers forward. "This is Clem. He's been helping clean up the water."

A ruddy-faced man put two fingers to his forehead as if in salute. "The water's still cloudy, Doc, but we're straining it before passing it out. I wish the queen drushka could have stayed longer." He looked up at the bright blue sky. "Or that we'd get some more rain." He gave Simon a sideways glance. "With a little less force, please."

Simon grinned. It sounded like a restaurant order. "I can't help you there, Clem." He watched the work for a few seconds. Clem waited, watching him, and Simon wondered if something else was expected. "Seems as if you've got a good system going here."

"The workers are good'uns." He beamed. "By the time people come looking for their morning water, we should have it."

Simon nodded but couldn't help doubting. As the sun was rising, the moisture had become trapped against the ground, stifling them in humidity. Simon supposed that was good because the water they'd collected wouldn't evaporate, but it was going to turn Gale into a pressure cooker. People would need to drink more to stay cool.

But there was nothing he could do about the weather, as he'd said. He wondered briefly if any of the workers had been doing any nighttime effigy burning, but most of them paid him no mind, focused on their task.

He said his good-byes, and Jacobs followed him to the fields. Once he was among the dirt and plants, Simon kicked his shoes off and sank his toes into the soil. He sent his power out among the plants, bolstering, maturing, shooing away insects and any hints of disease. His happiest times on the *Atlas* had been among plants, and he sighed now, relaxing in the feel of them. They didn't thank him, but they also didn't argue or have demands.

And they didn't hang effigies. With another sigh, Simon came back to himself and looked at Jacobs. She scanned the area around them, one hand to her forehead. Her blond hair was matted by sweat. Simon sent a cooling wave over them all before he called her over.

She smiled, her eyes kind before they turned hard as he told her about the effigy and graffiti. At last, she rubbed her chin. "I was afraid of something like this. I've heard grumbling."

Simon's stomach turned over. He'd hoped it had been an isolated incident. "Maybe the grumblers did the deed."

"Maybe. You need to keep both eyes open, Doc."

He sensed genuine concern, and it made him shift uncomfortably.

"Not to offend you," he said carefully, "but I have to ask, why do you care about me at all?"

She blinked. "I was there when you healed the whole town."

"But you seem to take my safety...personally." When she stared, he cleared his throat. "Like I said, no offense. I'm just curious."

She shrugged. "When I heard about some of the bad things the Storm Lord did, I..." She glanced around, and even though no one stood near them, she lowered her voice. "I hated the bastard. I wasted a lot of time and energy worshiping him. I thought he stood for everything I stood for, but the fact that he killed anyone who disagreed with him, good people, well..." She sighed. "Someone needed to take him out, someone who cared about other people." She nodded to Simon.

He fought a blush and cleared his throat. "Happy to help." He gestured toward town. "Shall we?"

As they walked, Pakesh cleared his throat, and Simon detected a surge of nervousness. "You said something about your last girlfriend?" Pakesh asked, gaze darting to Jacobs. "Do you have one now?"

Simon tried to give him a warning glance, one that said it was rude to ask people about their personal lives, but Pakesh wasn't looking anywhere near him.

Jacobs raised an eyebrow. "Nope, not a girlfriend or a boyfriend. Why? You got an older friend who's looking?"

It was a graceful way to say that Pakesh was too young for her, and Simon coughed to hide a chuckle.

Pakesh frowned before he seemed to get it. "I'll...ask around."

Jacobs winked at Simon, and he smiled. They continued chatting as they walked. More people in Gale were stirring, hustling through the streets on morning business. Simon stepped to the side of the road, out of the way of a rickshaw.

"Look out!" Jacobs shouted.

He looked to the rickshaw, but it wasn't coming near them. Before he could ask, she shoved him hard. He collided with Pakesh, both of them crying out as Pakesh slipped, and they fell. Jacobs stepped in front of them, truncheon drawn. The rickshaw rumbled away, but she didn't move.

Heart racing, Simon scanned the sparse crowd who'd stopped to watch the show. A few other heart rates were up, but that could be from the excitement of a paladin shoving people around. "What is it?"

"I lost sight of him," Jacobs said.

"Who?"

"You didn't see that?" When he only blinked, she hauled him and Pakesh upright, then strode a few steps away and picked up a clay bottle. "Someone hurled this at your head."

He stared. No, he hadn't seen a thing, had been talking to Pakesh. He would have noticed a person coming for him, would have sensed it, but a random person throwing things? He took the bottle, turning the smooth surface over in his hands. It had landed on a pile of straw and hadn't broken. Would it have broken against his head? Someone wanted to knock him out first—the same tactics Dillon had used—the quickest way to get around his power. It made his blood run cold.

"It could be the same people who did the graffiti." Jacobs stalked into the crowd, barking questions. She kept looking back to Simon, clearly torn between staying to guard him and chasing whoever had thrown the bottle. But they'd probably already gone to ground.

Still, Simon couldn't just wait here, hampering her movements. Anger pushed the fear away. He didn't want to be anyone's problem or anyone's target. "I'll go to the temple, Jacobs. It's time we ate something more anyway, and…" His nerves jangled, and he nearly swore, hating feeling this helpless, feeling his anxieties come rushing back. He tried to beef up his anger. "Then you can investigate. Or maybe I can."

She shook her head. "Leave this to the paladins, Doc, but keep a careful watch. I'll take you to the temple, then round up a guard for you." She rested a hand on his shoulder. "We'll find them."

On the way to the temple, Simon kept turning the bottle over in his hands. He tried to watch the crowd, but everyone seemed to be staring, and the rhythms of their bodies felt as if they were closing in. He kept his shields tight around himself and Pakesh, who was scanning the crowd with his own worried look.

Simon sensed a semi-familiar pattern as they rounded a corner. Liam stood speaking to a group of people outside a large building. He had one foot propped up on a bucket and laughed easily as he spoke, his green eyes twinkling. His clothes fit a little tighter than they needed to, showing off his muscular body. Pretty, but Simon had had enough of showy types.

The people of Gale disagreed, it seemed. The men and women listening to Liam stared at him with lustful gazes, and as he spoke, many of them blushed and stuttered and giggled. Simon chuckled, the sight easing some of his tension. No matter what was happening between Liam and Shiv, it seemed Liam couldn't resist being a flirt. It was good to know some things didn't change.

Simon nudged Pakesh. "You'll want to take notes from him."

Pakesh and Jacobs snorted at the same time, and the pall seemed to lift from all three of them, at least a little.

"We should all be so lucky," Jacobs said.

When Liam caught sight of Simon, he sauntered over. "Reports from the granaries are in. With rationing, we should be okay for the time being. We'll need to hunt before winter's finally here."

Jacobs wiped her forehead. "Winter feels a long time away."

It might be longer than they thought. Who knew what the weather would do without Dillon? Before Simon could say anything, Jacobs told Liam about the effigy and the bottle, much as she would do when reporting to a senior officer.

Liam frowned hard. "Cordelia would take a hard line with that."

Jacobs nodded. "I'm going to round up a guard from the keep."

"The plants are coming along," Simon said, wanting to talk about anything else. "I bolstered what I could and increased growth in some. They should be ready to harvest soon."

Some of the people Liam had been speaking to wandered closer, mouths open in surprise. "Ready to harvest?" one asked.

He nearly took a step back, wary. "Maybe in a few days."

They grinned. One whooped and several clapped, sending beaming smiles Simon's way. When Jacobs kept them back, Simon allowed himself a bit of pride and a soft smile. A few of them reached to shake his hand, and he returned the gesture.

"The doc has urgent business elsewhere," Jacobs said before Simon could be surrounded. They said good-bye to Liam, and Jacobs hustled Simon along, eyeing the crowd as she went. "Anyone who's got it in for you is a fucking ingrate, Doc."

He laughed, still pleased with the praise and feeling much better than he had a moment ago. In all the hand shaking, he'd dropped the clay bottle. Maybe that was for the best.

❖

Cordelia scowled into the swamp, in a hurry to be gone, but Pool was still speaking to the other three queens, lost in drushkan communion.

Better Pool than her. She kept seeing the bodies of the dead Galeans hanging from the trees, and she couldn't help wanting to punch anyone who might have been involved.

Pool's drushka had volunteered to cut the bodies down. The paladins had taken descriptions as best they could, but no one ever looked the same dead as alive. Then all that was left was to release the bodies into the swamp. Cordelia thought that the best solution; they didn't know how long they'd be gone from Gale, and they didn't want to carry bodies around. She kept remembering her first trip to the swamp and the bodies she hadn't been able to carry out then, either. But at least those poor souls had some mementoes to pass on. These people had nothing but the clothes on their backs. They'd been covered in cuts and bruises with a few broken bones, according to Horace. The drushka hadn't treated them well. And one hundred seventy-five were still out there suffering.

Cordelia rolled her shoulders until she heard a few pops. What the fuck was taking Pool so long? They had a huge battle still before them. Even if the second, third, and sixth queens joined the fight, it was still four queens to five. One of those five was the awesome mental power that was the Shi, and another was the eighth, the largest drushkan tree that could still move, one that could wrap her limbs around the Anushi tree and lift it from the ground. The swamp trees around them were taller than the Anushi, and Pool said the eighth rivaled them. Cordelia couldn't even imagine it.

With a groan, Cordelia finally sat and wrapped her hands around her knees. What the fuck were they going to do? The sight of those bodies had shaken her, brought home what was at stake, all they had to lose. The bullets were running low, and now most of the armor was unpowered. She'd taken hers off, didn't know if she'd put it on again. It could protect against drushkan weapons but was slower and clumsier and could more easily pull them to their deaths underwater. They were well and truly fucked.

Horace sat beside her, tucking his legs underneath him. "Your despair is leaking."

She smiled grimly. "Sorry."

"The drushka seem hopeful." He looked toward the queens. "What's the plan?"

She gave him a dark look.

"Right," he said. "No plan. Not good."

"Wishing you'd stayed in Gale?"

"I've been wishing everyone was home and safe, but it's not doing much good." He nudged her arm. "Here comes Pool."

"Finally." Cordelia stood, ready to hear what the queens had come up with.

Pool walked lightly along the branches. She seemed tired but determined. Her green eyes were bright, even if her long frame seemed to droop. "The time for your battle is done, Sa," Pool said as she reached them.

Cordelia's belly went cold. For all her dread, she'd never once considered quitting this field. "The Galeans need my help."

"Ahya, but only stealth will aid us now. I will sneak into the drushkan homeland alone and fight the Shi."

Cordelia tried to think of a crazier plan and couldn't. "You're going to sneak in—"

"The other queens have agreed to distract the Shi while I do so."

Cordelia rubbed the bridge of her nose. She didn't know whether to laugh in Pool's face, burst into tears, or slug someone. "The other queens are going to distract *every other drushka* and five *telepathic* queens?"

Pool slapped her thighs. "We have no other plan!"

Cordelia told herself not to yell. Horace glanced at her, and she felt a wave of calm flow over her. "Thanks," she muttered.

"Anytime."

She took a deep breath. "Look, Pool, you and your people, you're not used to…guile. I get that. But the other queens can't just wave their arms and hope the enemy drushka will come running. They need a way to keep the enemy guessing. And you can't go in alone unless your plan is to die immediately!" She took another breath. The image of Pool lying dead hurt more than she expected.

Pool tossed her head, a rebellious gesture Cordelia had often seen from Shiv. "We will do what we must to free the other drushka and your people."

Horace cleared his throat. "Then let's keep going as we have been: free the queens one by one. Then we'll have more allies, or at least more drushka who will stay out of the way. If we free all the queens, you can walk right up to the Shi."

"According to my sister queens, the rest wait together under the Shi's branches," Pool said. "We will not find more alone. That is why the humans' part in this fight is done."

"No, there has to be a way we can help." Cordelia pictured armored bodies falling like rain. But even unarmored, her people were good. She tried to think of something the drushka wouldn't expect, a trick. "The Shi is really pissed at humans. Maybe she'll come after us if she thinks we're vulnerable. The paladins can draw them, maybe with guns. Let them get close."

And then what? Without powered armor, the paladins couldn't get away quickly. And they couldn't stand around and be pummeled. Given time, the drushka could find a way into the armor.

Unless they couldn't get at it. "Even without power, the armor holds a little air, enough for a quick dive." She grinned as the plan solidified in her mind. "The paladins lure the drushka, then jump in the water, walk along the bottom, and come up yards away. Open the visors, refill the air, and bait the drushka again. They can lead the drushka along, reduce the risk of bloodshed on both sides."

It sounded good in theory. If the swamp's denizens steered clear. She had a flash of memory: a prog's teeth squealing along her armor.

Pool frowned. "Are you certain your paladins will do this, Sa?"

"I'll ask for volunteers. They'll need to scout the area ahead of time. With the way the Shi hates us, nothing's going to distract her like a pack of ornery humans."

"I know Lea would do it," Horace said.

Cordelia nodded. "I'll put him in charge."

"And you, Sa?" Pool asked.

"I'm coming with you."

Pool's eyes widened. "You cannot!"

"Can and will. I know we have at least one battery with some juice. You'll need someone to block for you." It made her smile just thinking of it. She wouldn't have to worry how the fight was going because she'd be in the heart of it.

"Sa—"

"Here are your choices," Cordelia said. "You can either take me with you or bury me in a hole; that's the only way you'll stop me."

Pool barked a laugh and lifted her hands. "I do not believe we could find enough ground to hold you, Sa."

Cordelia nodded. It was still an impossible plan, but it felt better now that she was at the middle. The only sticking point was breaking it to Nettle. Cordelia could already hear the conversation in her mind. Nettle would insist on going. Reach probably would, too. Cordelia would want to argue but didn't know if she could. If she was going to risk her life on a crazy plan, how could she deny anyone else the privilege?

She gestured around her at the waiting swamp. "When do we leave?"

CHAPTER TEN

Patricia perched on the roof of the bunkhouse and watched the workers in the late-afternoon sun. Jonah stood among them, directing them. She'd left him some of Dillon's knowledge about defenses and turned the construction of the wall over to him. A good leader had to know when to delegate, after all.

The base of the wall was made of stone, but the rest consisted of trees scavenged from the hills, more like the palisade of Gale, from what Dillon's memories said. Jonah had others digging a ditch and planting sharpened stakes designed to hamper attackers and give archers along the palisade time to fire. It seemed like a good plan. Jonah was perfect, and Patricia smiled at the thought of him.

Off to the side of the camp, another group of miners practiced archery with bows purchased from plains dweller clans. Dillon hadn't known how to use a bow and arrow, but the plains dwellers had offered to teach.

Well, offered was the wrong word. They'd had a little telepathic prompting. Patricia frowned, a tad guilty. She'd hoped she wouldn't have to use her power on everyone she met, but convincing them the old-fashioned way was just so…time consuming.

And difficult. She tried to remember if she'd ever talked anyone into doing something they weren't inclined to do in her former life. For the most part, Jack had been a pushover. That was one of the traits she loved about him. He was the emotional one, the one who understood people.

She'd disliked most people on Earth. She didn't know what had made her think she could talk to them now. Distance? All the wisdom of spending hundreds of years as an observer in Naos's mind?

She sighed, supposing she simply had to accept the fact that she would be forever using her power as a...jumping-off point. After all, that was better than manipulating people with verbal trickery. At least her way, everyone enjoyed themselves. She could make sure of that.

She looked back to Jonah as he barked at the workers. People didn't seem to enjoy themselves in his company. Maybe she should have left him a bit of Dillon's charm for when situations got tense.

"Aw, thanks, sweets. I do try."

Patricia fought the urge to freeze. She breathed slowly, listening to the wind, to the sounds of work, the calls of the miners, and the thump of arrows hitting their targets. She made herself look around even though she knew there'd be no one nearby. This voice wasn't coming from Jonah. It never had been. It was in her head. An *intruder*. She tightened her shields and sent out a probe, looking for the source of the telepathic message. Even if it was Naos, she needed to know.

Nothing. No tendrils of power, no telepathic signals, not even a tingle. Because it wasn't telepathy? Maybe power wasn't the only thing she'd taken from Naos. Maybe insanity had hitched a ride.

Patricia's heartbeat quickened, the sounds around her fading. She flashed back to being a watcher behind her own eyes, a mere flea in Naos's mind. The world pressed down, blackness creeping into her vision as her senses went haywire. She could feel the gravity around her, hear the call of the stars, and feel the sensations of every single goddamn organism on the planet.

Maybe once a mind had been Naos, it couldn't go back to being alone.

"No, no, no!" Patricia forced her breathing to slow. She pulled back the reach of her senses and focused on her own body: slowing the pulse, hearing only the closest sounds, and feeling only the nearest people. She could be alone in her head, voice or no voice. She would not surrender. The roaring in her ears calmed, making the blackness recede. The voice would be gone now. As long as she kept her mind in check—

"Keep telling yourself that."

Patricia ground her teeth, her power whipping out. "Leave me alone!" This was someone fucking with her, had to be! She sent a telepathic tendril toward Celeste, not close enough that the Sun-Moon would sense her, just enough to see their telepathic network threading through their people, none of it reaching toward her. She checked with all the breachies. Nothing. She reached for Gale, careful here, too, not wanting to alarm Simon Lazlo. Most of the Galean powers were weak; nothing there could touch her.

That left only one direction: up.

No, she wouldn't reach up there. Couldn't. Naos might not be able to possess people anymore, but who knew what she would do if she got hold of a psychic tendril to her former prisoner. Patricia wouldn't risk it. There had to be another explanation.

Well, if it wasn't a telepath, and she wasn't going to entertain the idea of madness...

"Who are you?" she asked.

The voice didn't respond. Patricia waited, listening to the sounds of shouts and *thunks* as the wall took shape and arrows found their targets.

"I'm growing," the voice said, followed by a throaty, masculine chuckle. Dillon's laugh. The hair stood up on Patricia's arms. "You put me here, and I've been figuring things out, sweets, getting the lay of the land."

Her mind raced, and she tried to think of all the time she'd spent with Naos. Had someone else been trapped in there with her? No, she would have felt them. Then who?

Dillon's voice, Dillon's chuckle, Dillon's memories. Patricia pressed a hand to her mouth. "It can't be. You're...you're just a bunch of memories!"

"What else is a person? Or maybe you took more than you bargained for. You should have been paying more attention to Big Mama Naos when she taught you how this works."

Her breath came quicker. She forced herself to calm before the blackness could come again. She glanced at Jonah, and a wave of lust hit her hard. She mashed her lips together to keep from crying out as an orgasm tore through her, leaving her panting and sweating.

"Mmm," Dillon said, "feels good, no? Isn't that what you wanted, sweets? For me to be your little sex puppet? Well, now you have my mind as well as my bod. I can make you come inside and out."

Patricia bit her lip as another lust wave sliced through her, leaving her on the cusp of orgasm, aching. "How…how are you doing this?"

"Like I said, I'm figuring things out. Soon I'll have the whole kit and caboodle, and you'll be a voice in my mind. A woman's body might take some getting used to, but I can manage. Let's see what this does."

Pain flared in Patricia's left arm. She grabbed it, her power ready, but how the hell was she supposed to combat something in her own mind? How had Naos done it? Patricia used her micro powers in her brain, searching for him, but if what he said was true, he'd be…everywhere. If he truly had reconstituted himself, how was she supposed to untangle the synapses that were hers and those that were his?

"How in the *hell*?" She killed her pain with power and focused on his thoughts. Maybe telepathy held the key. And she was the one with that power here. She focused on his voice and felt around it as she would a telepathic signal, slowly building a wall to keep him in.

"That won't work forever!" he shouted, his voice growing fainter. "I can work on you all day and—"

She layered another wall, shutting him in. Silence. Patricia waited, searching for him, for signals inside herself that didn't make sense.

Nothing. She waited some more, probing her wall for weak spots. Nothing, not a hint of him. At last. She sighed. He seemed contained, but now she had telepathic blocks in her own damn mind. How often would she have to strengthen them, maintain them? He'd constantly be trying to break through, and she couldn't focus all the time!

The ladder to the top of the bunkhouse thumped, and Patricia shot to her feet. "Who's there?"

Jonah climbed up, smiling at her. "Mistress?" His smile faltered as he stared. "Is something wrong? You're very pale."

She breathed hard and searched him with her power, finding only Jonah. But Dillon was tricky. "No," she said, knowing she sounded breathless. When he stepped closer, she backed up. She didn't want to touch him, didn't want him touching her, and that made her even angrier.

"Mistress?"

Patricia took a deep breath and straightened her clothes. She was in charge; she had to remember that. "Was there something you needed, Jonah?"

He gestured toward the wall. "Do you want to take a closer look? I think it's going well."

"Of course." She climbed down on shaky legs. The miners would be happy to see her, and maybe that would improve her mood. She could do this. Dillon was behind a telepathic wall. It wasn't optimal, but she could maintain it for a while. It wouldn't be forever. She simply had to find a way to purge him, and she had an eternity to figure out how.

❖

Pool wanted to leave at first light. That left Cordelia one more night where she'd definitely be alive. She didn't want to waste it. And by the way Nettle returned her passionate kisses, they were of the same mind.

Even though they had all night ahead, their lovemaking was hurried and fiery. Cordelia didn't mind. Nettle didn't seem to mind, either. It just left time to do it again. And it was better than arguing. Nettle had insisted on going with Pool and Cordelia to fight the Shi. No amount of talk would dissuade her. Cordelia had eventually given up trying. Maybe it would be romantic if they died together.

Cordelia snorted a laugh as she had that thought. She and Nettle lay tangled together in their dark cubby, both breathing hard and still awake. "Maybe we should try to sleep." But she knew she wouldn't be able.

"You sound worried, Sa. What troubles you?"

"We could both die tomorrow. Pool could die." She sighed. "The humans we came to rescue might already be dead. You know, the usual."

Nettle chuckled, and her thin lips pressed to Cordelia's temple. "I have the solution. We will be quick and sure in our strikes, and we will not lose. Simple."

Cordelia grinned. "Right. Simple. Now I can sleep fully reassured." She turned and rested her forehead against Nettle's chin. "You could stay here."

"As could you."

"I feel like you're only going because I am."

"They are my people, Sa. And you have never forced me to do anything, except perhaps love you, and that you do by your sheer presence."

Cordelia kissed her soundly. "I love you, my drushka who says incredibly romantic things."

"And I you, my human who never knows what to say yet says the perfect words."

They kissed again, and Cordelia pulled Nettle on top of her.

"Are you awake?" Horace asked in Cordelia's mind.

Cordelia let her head drop, thumping against the bark. "Horace is talking in my head."

Nettle grumbled. "Liam would call him a specific word, but I cannot recall it."

"Cock-blocker."

"That is the one."

"I'm up, Horace," Cordelia thought back. "But you probably already knew that."

"Sorry to interrupt," he said, "but the paladins are restless. Lea told them about the underwater plan, but he's...not so good at rousing speeches. And now some of them are talking about trying to head back to Gale on their own, and some want to come with you." He sent her a sigh of frustration. "And someone brought some mead from Gale, and it's making the rounds, and the grumbling's following it."

"I get it. I'm on my way." She felt around for her clothes. "I've got to go soothe some human fears."

"While still feeling your own." She squeezed Cordelia's hand. "Ahya, that is the fate of the hunt leader. Would that they had a queen to calm them."

Cordelia snorted, not even wanting to picture how that would work. She was closely attached to Pool, and it freaked her out sometimes. She didn't want to think what that kind of contact would do to someone who wasn't used to drushka at all. "Get some sleep while I'm gone."

"Ahwa, no, Sa! I am coming with you. You may need the busting of heads, as you say, and I will assist you."

Cordelia had to laugh. At least most of the troops were familiar with Nettle, even if they didn't spend much time with Pool. They'd take a head busting from her better than any other drushka. Cordelia only hoped it wouldn't be necessary.

The paladins who hadn't initially gone rogue with Cordelia were grumbling loudest, all but Lea. Most of them still wore armor, even though they didn't have a charge. They stared into the darkness, at the drushka, and scowled, arguing about what they should do. They'd been fine when they'd had powered armor, but now that it had been taken away, they'd lost their mettle.

Cordelia bit down the urge to tell them to get over it. Lea barked at them to do one task or other—most seemed like busywork—but they didn't appreciate that, either. Cordelia plastered a smile on her face and moved through them, clapping backs, giving the armor-wearers shit until they took the damn suits off. She shamed them into cleaning the armor in order to keep it as functional as possible. She brought Nettle into her joking, and Nettle kept a relaxed, casual air that drew in the paladins familiar with her and helped ease those who weren't.

Some paladins had whispered questions or loud suggestions for Cordelia, and she deflected most until they'd settled into a happier mood, more willing to listen. She let the mead continue to flow, getting a cup herself and making several obscene toasts that might have made even Lea crack a smile.

Some of Pool's drushka joined in, and some had questions for Nettle, too. Cordelia grinned at that, glad she wasn't the only one who had uneasy troops.

"Hunt leader," one drushka asked, "how should we answer a challenge from the old drushka, should one come?"

Nettle stared into the distance before spreading her hands. "Very dangerous, ahya, to fight among ourselves with so much at stake. Even if the challenge is to rightful authority, better to say, 'Have your queen speak to mine,' and leave it to them to untangle."

The drushka seemed mollified, wrinkling his nose. Maybe having a queen wouldn't be so bad after all. But as it was, Cordelia circled through her troops again, reassuring them. They had to trust Lea and the other lieutenants, those who had worn unpowered armor and knew its limits. She thanked those who wanted to go with her to attack the Shi but stressed the fact that it would be a quick and dirty mission, better suited to a very small group. She tried to leave them with the impression that she'd have less to worry about if they weren't there.

As for those who simply wanted to go home, Cordelia resisted the urge to bark at them about duty. That was something Carmichael might have done. Cordelia said they didn't have to be paladins anymore if they didn't want to, told them that she wanted only those who were committed to the cause at her side. She told them how dangerous the swamp was to trek through alone, and as Pool's drushka agreed, they seemed to relax. She warned all the humans to steer clear of the old drushka, just in case. Good advice, as few old drushka spoke Galean anyway. In the end, she thought a few paladins might sit out the fight, while others seemed more motivated to earn her respect.

By the time everyone settled for the night, Cordelia felt lighter in her own thoughts and crawled into bed with Nettle, exhausted.

In the morning, she gave her paladins one last look-over. Lea had them up and dressed, and they knew the plan. Pool would park her tree close enough for the enemy queens to sense her presence. Without Pool aboard, the tree wouldn't be able to maneuver, but it could come if she called. The sixth and third queens would lure drushka into the swamp toward the humans. The paladins would fire at the enemy, leap into the water to avoid them, come up behind them, refill their helmets with air, and attack again. Meanwhile, the third and sixth queens would move farther into the swamp, leading as many enemy drushka as they could away from Pool's path. The second queen would move closer to the Shi, ready to aid Pool's party should they need her.

Pool put her forehead to her trunk as they prepared to leave. "I have not been so far from the Anushi tree in a great many years."

Cordelia didn't know what to say. She'd taken one of the remaining batteries that had a charge and plugged it into her armor, powering it up, hoping it would last through the day. "If you want to call this off, Pool, you'd better tell me now."

Pool straightened and turned. "No. The tree will be well. No drushka would harm it, and none can control it while I live."

Cordelia nodded and lowered her visor. "We'll keep them off you, Pool, no matter what."

"Always, we must keep running," Nettle said.

Reach climbed up to join them. After much debate, Pool had decided to bring a shawness along, just as Cordelia thought. She only wished Pool had picked someone else, someone Cordelia didn't care as much about. She probably should have been guilty about that thought, but her eagerness was creeping up, rivaling her worry. She slung her railgun around her shoulders. Today, no matter what, she'd see an end to at least one problem. She just had to make sure it was the Shi's end and not her own.

Or Pool's or Reach's or Nettle's. Easy.

"The tribe is ready," Reach said.

Pool turned to the swamp, gaze fixed and intense.

Cordelia took a deep breath and sent a thought to Horace. "We're leaving."

"Be safe. We'll be waiting."

She didn't even have time to respond before Pool's tree grabbed the four of them and flung them into the swamp. Cordelia's stomach lurched as she flew, but she held in a terrified, exhilarated cry. Pool, Nettle, and Reach stretched like birds who'd taken wing, but Cordelia had to depend on the armor to absorb the shock of landing on a faraway branch. She rolled when she hit, pushing to her feet and running before leaping again. She spared a few looks for the others, moderating her speed to keep just in front of Pool, who directed them with her thoughts. Cordelia grinned at the wild charge. Even when she'd fought the boggins in her armor, she'd never flown through the swamp like this.

The four of them ran and leapt again and again, the brown trunks of the swamp trees flying past. For a moment, Cordelia thought their plan had worked better than imagined, and the old drushka had been thoroughly distracted. Maybe they wouldn't encounter any resistance at all. Cordelia nearly let out a joyful whoop, then she saw them, waiting.

"Here we go," she muttered.

Drushka crouched along the branches ahead. Not many, but there would be more. Pool had warned her that the bulk of them would be protecting the Shi, even if many were lured out by the promise of combat. Cordelia ran straight into them, bowling them over. She barely slowed and felt Pool pull up close, using Cordelia as a shield.

As more drushka leapt from the trees to slow her charge, Cordelia drew her sidearm and fired. Some ran from the shot, and others fell, wounded. More came from the surrounding swamp, drawn by the noise. As the press before them grew, Pool shouted, "Down!"

Cordelia leapt off the branch, carried by her faith in Pool. The swampy water had given way to solid earth, and as Cordelia plummeted—Pool, Nettle, and Reach around her—her fear peaked. She wondered just how much shock her armor could absorb if no one caught them.

As if summoned, the second queen's roots broke the ground and snagged Cordelia out of the air. She kept her arms to the side as they drew her under, flinging her through the earth and around the roots of the swamp trees. She hated this mode of transport, but at least she didn't have to feel the dirt sliding over her skin, bruising her. Instead, it rattled over her armor in a deafening din.

Sunlight bloomed as the roots threw her into the light. They flung her toward a swamp tree's branch, the world tilting crazily. Cordelia scrambled for purchase, her stabilizers whining. Pool's shove on her back got her going in the right direction again, and a quick glance revealed that they were still together, though far from where they'd been. Together, they skirted another tree, heading for what looked like a wall of foliage: trees and vines twisted so closely that it seemed impassable, but Pool urged them through.

Cordelia crashed through the foliage to find she was closer to the ground than she'd thought. The branch beneath her tapered and ended, leaving a short fall to solid, grassy earth and the bright sunlight of a valley amidst the swamp. She blinked in the light and nearly stumbled to a halt. If Pool hadn't been shoving, she would have simply stared at the tree before her.

Could she even call it a tree? It had to be a mountain. Brown branches and green leaves meant tree, but no tree had ever been this large. It stood in a bowl-shaped valley, spreading its boughs for a mile or more. Some branches grew straight down, supporting a massive canopy that sprouted out of a trunk so large, her brain kept wanting to make it into stone.

Two other trees moved beneath the canopy, dwarfed by the massive tree, though they would be much larger than even Pool's Anushi. The behemoth made them seem like matchsticks. It became easier to run than to stare, to simply pretend that what she was seeing couldn't be real. It was easier to look into the ocean of drushka that stood between them and the mountainous tree. Cordelia's stomach dropped out beneath her. This plan was never going to work. There was nothing in this valley but death.

Strangely, the idea rallied her. She ached at the thought of losing Pool, Reach, and Nettle, but…she'd seen the impossible now! Nothing would ever match this. Nothing could. And she'd go down fighting. She only hoped that one day, Liam would forgive her.

CHAPTER ELEVEN

Fajir knelt in the tent, eyes closed, and hands bound behind her. She smelled the scent of Engali vermin: the stink of ossors and bitter tea, of sweat and leather and too much time between washings. Her hands twitched as she imagined slaughtering them all.

After she'd recovered from Nico's abandonment, she'd ridden north, not caring which vermin she found as long as she found some. When she'd seen the two women alone, she thought it a perfect opportunity. But the redhead had avoided her strikes, and the dark-haired one had power like the Moon's. It wasn't until afterward that she'd realized she should have recognized the yafanai she'd once stabbed, but rage had clouded her eyes. Now she was a prisoner of the vermin. If Nico had been with her, he would have turned from her in shame.

Hadn't he already?

Fajir shook the thought away. After the vermin caught her, she'd hoped they would kill her so she wouldn't have to listen to them. But now she was sweating in this tent, and the vermin would not shut their mouths. She'd been questioned by an old man, but none of her answers seemed to satisfy him. He'd kept wanting to know why she hated his clan so much, even after she'd told him.

"But only one man killed your partner," he'd said. "Why hunt the rest of us?"

She hadn't been able to make him understand. In the end, she'd told him it didn't matter. If he let her live, she promised to kill him, his family, all of them. He'd only stared before leaving her alone with nothing but her thoughts.

She'd shrieked every obscenity she knew in his wake. They would either kill her, or she'd kill them all. Why was that so difficult to understand? She chafed against her bonds. She couldn't stand this. She was alone, and that wasn't right. She had to be killing, or she had to die. It was easy, simple. But vermin couldn't understand. She flashed back to Cordelia, of the offer to go to Gale. She could be there now. She still wouldn't have Nico, but she wouldn't be alone.

"Fool," she called herself. If solitude was the price of vengeance, she had to pay it. And she would only be alone until death. Then she could see Halaan again. But none of that would happen while she was tied up in this cursed tent!

They wouldn't let her go. They wouldn't kill her. There had to be another way. Her mind raced. She had no Nico, no Cordelia, no allies at all. Before despair could set in, a thought came to her. She had two of the strongest allies in the world. A Sun-Moon worshiper was never alone!

"Lords?" she asked quietly, pushing her thoughts toward her gods as she'd been taught to do since childhood. The Lords had touched all their followers in some way or another, a comforting presence throughout their lives. Now she felt a tingle as they sensed her plea and reached for her. "Free me," she said. "Free me, and I will kill them all for you!"

They shuffled through her memories and stopped on the face of the dark-haired woman. "Samira," they said in her mind. "Simon Lazlo's friend."

Her belly went cold, and she licked her lips. They feared Simon Lazlo, though he surely wasn't worthy of such feeling. He'd threatened the Lords before he'd left Celeste. He should have died for that, but the Lords were silent.

"I'm sorry, child," they said at last. "You're on your own."

Their presence retreated, and she gasped. They would not aid her? Because of Simon Lazlo? But she was their weapon. She had put off her quest for revenge for them. She had killed in their name! And now that she needed them, they abandoned her?

Now she was truly alone. No Lords, no Nico. No Cordelia. And no Halaan, never him again, not in this paltry life. Nothing left but her.

Her breath came hard. "Kill me!" she cried. "You must!" She

fought the urge to sob and lost. "I will kill you! Your children! I will…"
Speech became lost amid her tears, and she simply screamed.

❖

Lydia listened to the screaming coming from the tent and closed
her eyes, her heart filling with pity even after everything she'd heard
about Fajir.

"Why don't they just do it?" Samira asked from beside her.

Lydia glanced over, but even Samira's frown was fading. She
couldn't stop the way she cared about people, even if she loathed Fajir.
Or maybe she just wanted to put Fajir out of her misery. Lydia took her
hand and gave it a squeeze.

"Look." Lydia pointed to the center of camp. The elders and Chafa
Yuve were coming out of the tent where they'd been debating Fajir's
fate. "Here they come."

Samira hurried to where the elders gathered. Everyone in camp
went, too. The Engali hadn't taken a prisoner in a long time, especially
someone accused of murdering members of their clan. Mamet had
made it back from her Celestian raid alive, but some hadn't been so
lucky, and Fajir had confessed to killing them. Lydia thought she'd
confess to anything if it meant her death. She wondered if the elders
had come to the same conclusion.

Mamet followed behind the elders. They'd wanted to hear
everything she had to say; she was the only one who'd spent any time
with Fajir. She seemed shaken as she crossed to Samira and Lydia; her
forehead shone with sweat. Samira pulled her in for a hug. Lydia was
dying to ask what happened, but Yuve held up his hands for silence.

"The Sun-Moon worshiper Fajir has committed three crimes
which can be proven," Yuve said to the crowd. "She attempted to kill
Mamet in Celeste and tried to kill Samira and also Lydia outside the
camp. Since only Mamet is a member of our clan, the elders have
decided we must consider that crime only."

The crowd murmured and glanced at one another, frowning.
"What about the murders she confessed to?" someone called.

Yuve shook his head. "We have no proof. Fajir is clearly heartsick,
perhaps even sick in her brain. Those who have lost their minds say
many things which aren't true."

The crowd murmured again, sounding angry but not enough to revolt. Mamet's face tightened, and Samira hugged her harder, her own expression darkening.

"The elders have decided to put her fate in the hands of the wronged." Yuve looked to Mamet.

Now the crowd muttered approval. The woman who'd asked about the murders smiled and nodded. Lydia's chest went cold. What a load of shit! The elders were supposed to be the ones with all the wisdom, and yet they passed the judgment to a twenty-year-old? She fought the urge to speak up, not wanting to get thrown out of camp. Instead, she looked to Mamet, wondering how she could help.

Mamet licked her lips as everyone stared. "I have to think," she said quietly.

Murmurs and frowns erupted again. "What did she say?" someone asked.

"Give her a minute," Samira said, turning Mamet away from everyone.

Lydia stayed with them as they took a few steps. "I'm so sorry, Mamet. Is there anything I can do?"

Mamet glanced at her with a look of gratitude. "I don't know. I have no idea what to do."

"What do you mean?" Samira asked. "You know what you have to do." She gripped Mamet's arm. "And you won't have to be the one who kills her. I'll do it."

Lydia doubted it would be that easy, but if Samira was angry enough...

"No," Mamet said. "If I decide she should die, I must be the one to..." She wiped her lips and passed a hand through her short dark hair. "Do it."

"If?" Samira asked.

Lydia tugged on her arm. "Samira—"

"No! What do you mean 'if,' Mamet?"

"Taking a life isn't easy," Lydia said. "It shouldn't be." She knew Mamet had been in a battle for her life before, but this was different. This was execution, and it would haunt a soft soul like Mamet for the rest of her life. And for all Samira's anger, Lydia bet Samira couldn't just do it, either.

Mamet looked to Lydia. "Do you know what Fajir might do?"

For half a second, Lydia didn't understand, thought Mamet was asking her opinion, but no, this was about the power. She sighed. No matter what human group she stayed with, someone would always ask. Maybe she should have gone to live with the drushka. They didn't see the point of looking into the future since it would keep coming no matter what.

"It doesn't work like that," Lydia said. "I can't give you options. If I see that she lives, I won't be able to tell you why, but it will still happen. And if I see her killing people later, my looking won't stop her." She tried to think of another way to put it, a theory the yafanai had. "As long as I don't look, you have a choice." Or at least, the illusion of choice. She didn't add that people often blamed her if the future didn't turn out the way they wanted.

Mamet smiled weakly. "How about an opinion, then?"

Lydia let out a slow breath. "Well—"

"You're going to say we should spare her," Samira said, glowering.

Lydia frowned at her, not wanting to say it now.

"Lydia has a forgiving heart." Mamet laid a palm on Samira's cheek. "And you have a protective heart. I wonder what Nettle and Cordelia would say."

Samira snorted, and Lydia had to chuckle. Samira had never really forgiven Cordelia for hitting Simon Lazlo in the fields outside of Gale. After that, they'd never had much time to get to know each other, not like Mamet had.

Still, Samira shrugged. "They're both fighters. They'd vote kill."

"I don't know. They surprised me with how far they went to prevent killing." Mamet looked to the tent that held Fajir. "She wants to die. Perhaps a more fitting punishment would be to make her live."

Samira frowned harder. Lydia thought of Fajir's screams. She'd only ever met one suicidal person before, a shopkeeper who'd visited the temple and wondered if he was going to go through with a plan to kill himself. Lydia had paused before looking, doubting her own assuredness that the future could not be changed. If she looked, and she saw him kill himself, she told herself she would grab hold of him and not let go. She'd demand he be restrained and watched.

But if that were true, her vision of the future would *start* with her leaping from her cushion, and there would be no way he could kill himself. She considered just grabbing him without looking, making the future for a change instead of seeing it. But she'd surprised herself by taking his hands and saying, "Gale would be sadder without you. You...make the world better."

He'd seemed surprised, then he'd brightened and paid her for her trouble before hurrying out of the temple. She'd sat there stunned, realizing that he thought she *had* looked into the future and seen a bleaker time that didn't have him in it. He was just another person who didn't understand how her power worked. After that, she hadn't had the heart to follow his future, but a few days later, shopping with Freddie, she'd seen him selling his wares. She always wondered after that if he'd tried harder to make Gale a better place, thinking that was his destiny.

"Can I talk to Fajir?" Lydia asked.

"Why?" Mamet and Samira said at the same time.

Lydia didn't really know, save that she was now involved in the whole affair. She'd been there when Fajir first attacked, when she'd been captured, and when her fate had been laid on Mamet. She thought she should know all the facts before she gave her opinion, but she didn't want to set Samira off again.

"Curiosity," she said, hoping that would satisfy.

Samira seemed skeptical, but at least Mamet nodded.

When Lydia first stuck her head inside the tent, Fajir leaned well back, frowning as if Lydia was the worst thing she'd ever smelled. Lydia couldn't help a snort of laughter. With the way Fajir herself smelled, Lydia doubted she could detect anything else.

"I'm not going to hurt you," Lydia said. "If that's what you're worried about."

Fajir sneered. "Then go away, vermin."

"Charming." Lydia sat just inside the tent and let the flap shut behind her. Enough light came through that she could still see, but she'd brought a candle anyway, trying to make the air even brighter.

"What do you want?" Fajir asked.

That was the question, wasn't it? "I'm Lydia."

Fajir simply stared.

"I'm from Gale, originally." Lydia put her hands in her lap, then dropped them to her sides before clasping them again. Where was all the serenity she'd learned at the temple? Maybe it had simply been too long ago.

Fajir offered nothing, so Lydia blurted, "Why do you want to die?"

Fajir eyed her warily.

"Those marks on your cheeks mean you're a widow, right?" Lydia asked. "A Sun-Moon worshiper whose partner died? By an Engali? Is that right?" Fajir still said nothing. Lydia fought the urge to sigh. "So, you came here to kill other Engali?"

"Yes," Fajir said, leaning forward, her bonds creaking. "Now set me loose so I can continue, or kill me where I sit."

"Your fate is up to Mamet."

Fajir smiled. "I remember the smell of her blood. Will she face me in combat, or is she too much the coward?"

Lydia smiled back. People had tried to goad her before in the temple, and it hadn't worked then, either. "You talk about killing and dying in the same tone. You don't care which you do?"

"Tell them I have killed many of their vermin cousins: young, old, fit or not. I've killed some in combat and some as they slept. I won't stop. Ever."

Now Lydia smiled wider. "You do care, or you wouldn't be pushing me so hard. You want them to kill you, and you can't stand being toothless." She put a hand to Fajir's forehead and pushed, sending her off-balance. She fell sideways with a curse, wriggling against her bonds.

A stab of pity wandered through Lydia, but as she watched Fajir struggle and glare, the pity changed to something else. Perhaps they should let her die. That was what she wanted, and she wasn't helping anyone by being alive.

But then Lydia thought of Mamet again, of what executing someone would do to her: sleepless nights, bad memories. Lydia had enough of those for everyone. She thought of Freddie's beautiful face and sighed. The more time passed, the more the image faded, but Lydia still missed her keenly. A pain like that never fully disappeared. And though it wasn't the same feeling, Mamet was too young to be seeing Fajir's face for the rest of her life.

And Mamet might challenge Fajir to single combat. A fair fight would appeal to her. And Mamet might lose, might die. She was too young for that, too.

Lydia hauled Fajir upright before leaving the tent. Fajir hollered after her, the same litany: kill her or let her kill again. And to the Engali, those might be the only choices. They didn't keep prisoners for long.

Those who committed crimes were punished in other ways. The plains didn't have jails.

"What did she say?" Samira demanded.

"You mean you didn't have your ear pressed to the tent?" Samira flushed slightly. "Mamet wouldn't let me."

Lydia's thoughts were too grim for her to chuckle. "She tried to goad me into either killing her or demanding someone else do it. I agree with Mamet that leaving her alive in captivity would be a more fitting punishment, but…" She sighed. "Maybe she could be rehabilitated?"

Samira barked a humorless laugh. "Not likely. And it's too risky to keep her tied up forever. If she got loose—"

"You're right." Mamet ran a hand through her hair. "The first time I saw her after the torture, I wanted to kill her. But I was…"

Samira took her hand. Lydia wanted to hug her. Samira had told her of Mamet's crushing fear of Fajir as well as her rage. According to Samira, Mamet had woken up in a cold sweat every night they'd been together. But Samira had shared that in confidence, and Lydia didn't know if Mamet knew that. Lydia didn't want to shame her by bringing it up. It could be that Mamet was simply too afraid to face Fajir again, even to kill her. Understandable.

Mamet glanced at Samira and then at Lydia as if she wanted to say something but didn't know how.

"I'm going to take a walk," Lydia said, wanting to leave them alone to talk. "If you need me, I won't be far." She squeezed both their hands before wandering to the edge of the tents, but not beyond. Not yet.

In the valley of the Shi, Pool's stagger shook Cordelia out of her shock. She tore her eyes off the mammoth tree as Pool groaned in pain. The Shi was attacking her again. Nettle and Reach hissed in kind as the pain passed through them all. Cordelia shrugged it off, grabbed Pool, and shook her until her sharp teeth rattled together.

With a gasp, Pool opened her eyes. "Sa?"

"We have to move." Drushka were pouring from the Shi's branches like ants, adding to the horde in the valley, and there were more coming from the wall of foliage. Cordelia tried to think of a plan. Her worry wanted to drown out the thrill of battle, but she couldn't let it. She reminded herself that she didn't matter, and right now, she couldn't let herself think about Nettle and Reach. All that mattered was getting Pool close enough to make the Shi angry. They had to prompt her to grab Pool and fight one-on-one.

Cordelia ran, dragging Pool into a stumbling jog. If Pool won, the Galean captives would be saved; she had to keep her mind on that. Reach ran along behind them, singing to heal Pool's mind and help shield her from the Shi's attack.

Nettle grabbed Pool's other arm and helped her run. "Into the beast's mouth!" she shouted. "Ahya, Sa, my love?"

Cordelia barked a laugh that had more fear than humor behind it. "I love you! I love all you crazy bastards!"

Nettle gave her a look filled with love and fear. Cordelia summoned her anger. She remembered the Galean bodies swinging in the swamp and thought about all the shit the Shi had put them through when all they wanted to do was live their lives.

And she had one last card up her sleeve.

Cordelia let go of Pool's arm and swung the railgun in front of her, carrying the last of Calamity's heavy artillery. Without a word, she pulled the trigger, and the railgun's battery whined as the bullets pounded forth. She swept it side to side, and drushka fell in waves as if reaped with a giant scythe. Many staggered back or ran, tripping those behind and getting caught in a spray of bullets that tore through body after body. A path opened, and Cordelia ran into it, Pool behind her.

"Nettle, Reach, run for the swamp!" Cordelia called. They couldn't help past this point, could only be killed, and she was suddenly consumed with the fear of watching them die. Still, she didn't look back, didn't pause to see if they obeyed. Part of her knew they wouldn't. She kept firing and running until the bullets ran out.

She cast the empty railgun aside and drew her wooden blade. The drushka surrounded them, howling with the rage of the Shi. Cordelia swung wildly, hanging on to Pool with one hand as she kept pressing forward. She didn't see Reach or Nettle in the press of clawing, shrieking bodies. Some drushka veered away from Pool, and none were armed, perhaps too scared of killing a queen. Cordelia lifted Pool and staggered on, but too many bodies dragged on her shoulders, and her armor whined under the strain. Even if these drushka knew nothing of armor, they'd find a way inside soon enough. She only hoped they clawed her to death before they ripped her apart.

"Down, Sa!" Pool cried in Cordelia's mind.

Cordelia dropped among the bodies, kicking them out of the way until she spotted a patch of soil. Drushka piled on, blocking out the light, flattening her. Cordelia activated her armor's glow as Pool plunged a hand into the dirt.

A challenge went out, queen-to-queen. It couldn't go unanswered.

But no answer came through the howling, squirming press. Cordelia heaved herself into a push-up and tried to cover Pool. How long could she keep that up? How long before her battery ran out? The Shi couldn't refuse a direct fucking challenge, could she?

"Coward!" Cordelia yelled. The noise of the drushka drowned out her voice even inside her helmet. The lights in her visor flickered as the armor tried to withstand the strain of holding up what must have been every damn drushka in the universe. "Pool, we have to—"

Rumbling surrounded them, the sound growing until it overwhelmed the voices of the drushka. Roots as large as tree trunks erupted from the ground ahead, scattering drushka like seeds. One whipped forward and grabbed Pool from Cordelia's arms, dragging her underground.

"Kick her ass, Pool!" Cordelia shouted.

Then they were on her again. She tried to turn around, to struggle through and get out, but the drushka seemed limitless. She couldn't tell direction, could barely tell up from down. She swung and punched with abandon, gouging and kicking into the mass. Fear abandoned her. She'd done what she set out to do, and now she could lose herself in the force of armored swings. She summoned every drunken street brawl she'd ever had, every wrestling match; all had been preparing her for this. She had a vision of sharing war stories when she was old, boring countless people with the time she beat all the fucking drushka on the planet.

But that wasn't how this would end. She wondered if any god would listen if she prayed for Nettle and Reach to get out alive. As she slammed her helmet into more than a few faces, she wondered if she should leave her body. That way, she might not feel it when she died.

No, no fucking way. She howled into this sea of faces, wanting to hold on to this moment. If there was life beyond this one, she was taking a lot of fucking company with her.

The drushka parted, and a brown branch snaked inside, surrounding her, lifting her. Cordelia whooped. She'd reached the tree line after all, and her allies had rescued her! She looked down at the mass of drushka and gave them the finger.

Then she looked up. The tree line—and safety—stood far in the distance. Her stomach shrank, but she bared her teeth inside her helmet. She still had her blade. She could still fight.

The branch squeezed, and even inside the armor, she gasped as the pressure built. The branch turned her, and she peered into the unfamiliar face of another drushkan queen. This one had to be over seven feet tall, close to eight, and her long, whorled face stayed expressionless as she stared. Green hair dangled nearly to her knees, and her green eyes were as bright as floating algae.

She said something in drushkan, her voice a low bass rumble. Cordelia shook her head, and her armor squealed as the branch tightened its grip. "I…do not understand much," she said in drushkan.

The queen cocked her head. "I remember your people," she said in Galean, her accent thick, voice slow. "From what you would call long ago. I am the Sirinshi, the eighth queen." She tapped Cordelia's visor with one long finger. "Will you shed your metal skin, or must I tear it apart? I would speak with you bare-faced."

Even with everything Cordelia had learned about tech not being nearly as important as lives, the image of her armor being mangled hurt nearly as much as the idea of having it torn off her body. "I'll come out."

The eighth set her on a branch and let go. As her stabilizers corrected her balance, she had a wild idea about launching herself at the queen and continuing the fight. But drushka eyed her from every branch, their faces tense and expectant. Even the branches seemed to vibrate with suppressed energy. The eighth could have killed her or let the drushka kill her. They wanted something, and she didn't think it was just an easier kill. She unbuckled her armor and shed it into a pile.

The eighth leaned against a branch. Cordelia noted a slump in her shoulders; her eyes drooped slightly. She seemed tired, exhausted even, if Cordelia was reading her right. Without the armor, Cordelia was feeling a little battered herself. As the breeze cooled her, sticking her sweat-slicked clothes to her body, she took a deep breath and decided to press her luck.

"Are my friends all right?" she asked. "The drushka who came in with me and the Anushi queen?"

"Alive but caught."

Cordelia let out a breath as that weight lifted from her shoulders. "And the humans you took from Gale?" Her throat burned at the thought of the hanging bodies. She swallowed. "Those still alive?"

"Frightened only. The Shi wished to kill them when you first appeared, but I convinced her otherwise."

"Good. Thanks." She wanted to ask why but thought that might be risky.

"You care for the drushka who came with you?" the eighth asked. "For the Anushi queen?"

"Deeply."

"Strange." She took a step closer, looming over Cordelia by two feet or more. "Have they become human? You are certainly not drushka."

Cordelia thought fast, swallowing the urge to use sarcasm. She remembered what Pool had said about Cordelia's ancestor Jania. She had lived with the drushka and discovered that their plan at the time had been to absorb humanity and make them as drushkan as possible. If they spread the humans thin enough, their breeding would slow. One day, they might even die out. It would have been the slowest genocide on record, but then, drushkan queens lived for hundreds of years. They could afford to think long-term.

"No," Cordelia said. "Some of the humans are allies with Pool, the Anushi queen. We...complement each other. Humans think each unique person adds to the whole." She waved a hand, wishing she were her uncle Paul or Reach, someone with the right words. "We don't want to become one another. Then we wouldn't be...different." She hoped it didn't come off as lame as it sounded.

The eighth sucked her teeth. "No queen, no point of connection. The Anushi queen is still connected to her drushka?"

"She is. But humans form attachments as we grow; we aren't born telepathically attached to anyone. Most of us can't hear each other's thoughts. We feel loyalty. We fall in love, make friendships that last forever. Emotions keep us together." She didn't add that she was connected to Pool. Best not to confuse the issue.

The eighth considered. "The Shi believes that to know a human, to form these human attachments, is to become human. Pool, as you call her, is unlike any other drushka."

Cordelia had never been more aware of that fact. "She's still her own creature."

"That is her difference. Each queen is tied to the whole, all but your Pool."

"You don't seem as…tied to the Shi as the other queens I've met." For one, she wasn't encased in her tree, and her words didn't have the dominating anger of the Shi behind them.

"I fulfill my purpose. I guard the Shi." She leaned closer, and the scent of newly turned soil washed over Cordelia, making her flinch with its power. "But no one can dominate my mind."

Cordelia decided to press her luck still further. "But you let her do it to the other queens?"

"We need a Shi to survive; do you not see this? And unlike your Pool, we do not wish to be separate from the whole. We crave unity."

Something about the way her eyes shifted told Cordelia that the eighth wasn't sharing the whole truth. Drushka didn't like lying, even lies of omission. There was something else at work here, and Cordelia bet it was why she was still alive. But what use could the eighth have for a lone human and two renegade drushka? What use did she have for a bunch of kidnapped Galeans except as bait? And Pool was here now, so the only reason to keep all of them alive…

"You think Pool might win," Cordelia said. "She challenged the Shi, and instead of helping, you're waiting to see who wins."

"The Anushi queen will have her chance."

"And if the Shi…" She almost said "dies," but she didn't think any drushka who could understand her words would take too kindly to that thought. If the Shi died, this queen would take her place, and she clearly wanted Pool as an ally rather than an enemy. She wanted the drushka to be whole again, just as the Shi did, but Cordelia sensed she would rather be whole peacefully than risk everything in battle.

Cordelia only hoped that if Pool did win, she wouldn't want to leapfrog all the other queens and become Shi herself.

The eighth queen straightened, watching Cordelia closely as if to see how much she knew. "You seem different from the other humans. I sense something else in you."

Cordelia shrugged, not ready to blab about her abilities.

"Humans find it easy not to speak, find it easy to lie."

"Some of us. Some don't like it. Some can't bring themselves to do it."

"You spoke about caring deeply for your companions. Is one of them your lover?"

Cordelia spread her hands drushkan fashion. "Since I'm not connected to you, I can just say, none of your business."

A hint of a smile appeared on the queen's lips. "I think, perhaps, if the answer was no, you would have simply said so. Perhaps you decline to answer because you could not catch the lover you wanted."

"That's a good guess."

"And so?"

"It's still none of your business, but for the sake of drushkan-human relations, yes, one of them is my lover. But I won't tell you who caught whom."

"The hunt leader or the shawness? Or the Anushi herself?"

"You'll have to wait and see."

The eighth made a rumbling sound, and it took Cordelia a moment to realize it was laughter. She turned away. "Rest, human. When the challenge is done, I will tell you of the winner."

Cordelia was tempted to ask what it would mean if the Shi won, but she didn't want to know. She sat on a limb next to her armor pile and wondered how Pool was doing; she hated waiting.

But she could always get a good look, couldn't she? Maybe even offer a little help?

With a grin, Cordelia lay down, hoping to seem as if she was sleeping as she slipped from her body and went to find the fight happening underground.

CHAPTER TWELVE

Shiv lay on a pile of cushions inside the human temple, waiting for Simon Lazlo's return. The human baby Evan slept, having been fed by a woman who stared at Shiv but made no attempt at conversation. Little Paul tried to play with Lyshus. They were nearly the same size, though human Little Paul was older. But though Lyshus's body grew faster than a human child—faster than a normal drushka, even—he did not yet have the speech or the understanding to appreciate any of the games Little Paul proposed. Luckily, Little Paul did not seem to care as long as Lyshus watched him with an alert gaze.

When Little Paul smacked Lyshus with a cushion and ran from him, laughing, Lyshus seemed to understand. He let out a high-pitched keen and gave chase, tearing through the three rooms and knocking over furniture in their laughing haste. Good that they were occupied, Shiv supposed. She rose and looked in on Evan, but he slept through the noise. She wondered at him, at a child who remained immobile so long after birth. Drushkan children were toddling a day after they emerged from the birthing pods, but when they were born, they were larger than Evan was now. Simon said Evan would not walk until a year or more had passed. If he was attacked, he could not run or climb to safety. He could not cling to an adult. He would simply lie still and squall, an easy meal.

Shiv touched his chubby face, careful of her claw. Evan was soft, too, as if he had not finished forming before being born. She eyed the crib and frowned. If Simon had truly taken this child into his hands, perhaps he should have worn Evan on his back, as Reach once carried Little Paul.

Shiv rested her head on one hand and thought about Reach, about everyone fighting the old drushka in the swamp. She had wanted to go with them at first, but Shi'a'na had told her that the old Shi might try to take over her tree, and since she was young, the Shi might succeed. That had chilled Shiv to the core. And she did not want to risk Lyshus, either. He might try to run for her during battle, and she could not have that. Cooling her urge to fight was something else that acquiring a tribe had done for her.

Something smashed to the ground in the other room. Shiv gave it a glance: one of the clay baubles humans surrounded themselves with. It seemed of no consequence, and the children were still amusing themselves. Evan stirred slightly, then settled again.

Three hard knocks came from the door to the hall, echoing throughout the room. Shiv stepped into the sitting room and hissed loudly, gesturing for the children to be wary. Both boys, raised among drushka, dashed past her into Evan's room and shut the door, hiding.

Shiv opened the hall door slowly and saw a human female with tousled hair and reddened cheeks. Her belly stood out, marking her as a mother among humans. Such an uncomfortable-seeming body.

"What is it you wish?" Shiv asked.

"I have been awake all night," the woman said, one hand resting on her bulging belly. Her voice was tight, spoken nearly between her teeth.

Shiv spread her hands. "Shawness Simon is not here. Is there some cause I can help with?" When the woman gawked, Shiv blinked at her. "I have seen that humans often have a hard time speaking with others. Do you wish *me* to have words with someone in your stead?" That would make a fine distraction, at least.

"Yes, your children!"

Shiv sucked her teeth, not understanding. "What would you have me say?"

"I'm in the room across the hall. I was hoping for some *peace* so I can *rest*. Tell your children to be quiet!" Her eyes flashed, and Shiv had the brief hope that she was looking for a fight, but she was carrying her baby inside, and Shiv had no wish to hurt it. It was not the person making no sense.

"Children are not quiet," Shiv said. "Everyone knows this."

The woman drew herself up, face darkening further. Shiv grinned.

Maybe this woman sought a verbal fight to cleanse her mind. Sa often said that fighting put one in a state of peace.

"It's up to you to keep them quiet," the woman said.

Shiv spread her hands again. "Such a task seems impossible to my mind. Sleep elsewhere, ahya, and we will both have what we want."

The woman blinked before snarling and turning away. She marched down the hall, and Shiv supposed she was taking the advice. That was good. Maybe she would find her peace, though Shiv lamented that the verbal fight ended so quickly. But at least Shiv had managed to help her. Maybe she would return once she rested.

Shiv shut the door and let the children out. When another knock came a few minutes later, she grinned, hoping for more conversation, maybe even some light wrestling. Shiv could be careful of the belly, she was certain.

As she reached for the door, it leapt toward her, breaking free of its hinges. She lifted her arms to catch it, and it slammed into her, sending numbing pain through her hands and knocking her to the floor. Little Paul screamed, and Evan began to cry. Shiv pulled her legs under her and pushed the door upward. When someone stepped into the room, Shiv thrust the door toward them and heard them stagger back, muttering. She twisted into a crouch.

The intruder was wrapped in a long, thick shirt with a piece of cloth that flopped over their head, obscuring the face. Shiv thought her a female human by the scent, a different smell than the one who had come knocking before. Shiv leapt for her, leading with her claws, but an invisible force grabbed her from the air. A mind bender!

Shiv's insides lurched as she twisted and slammed against the wall. More numbing pain spread through her side, jarring her to her core. She fell to her knees, and a sharp hurt sliced into her knee. She had fallen onto a piece of clay bauble. Golden blood slid down her leg as she stood and kicked the remaining pieces out of the way.

The hooded woman ran into the room where Evan shrieked. Shiv ran after, snarling as the woman bent over the crib. Knowing how helpless Evan was, she would still attack him? Wretched creature.

But powerful. Shiv rolled across the floor, grabbed a water pitcher, and threw it. The woman looked up, and the pitcher bounced off an invisible shield. Shiv ducked, and the table that had held the pitcher flew into the wall hard enough to splinter. Shiv dived toward the crib as several pieces of the bed exploded into feathers.

Lyshus darted from a hiding place, headed for the hooded woman's back. "No!" Shiv cried.

Lyshus landed across the woman's shoulders and tore at her hood, revealing hints of blond hair. When she whirled and reached for him, he sank his teeth into her hand. She shrieked, and Shiv leapt for them, but the woman tore Lyshus loose and flung him in Shiv's direction.

Shiv caught him and twisted so he would land atop her. She rolled, trying to get both of them behind cover, but the woman cried out again. She fell to her knees, clutching her head. Shiv heard a step from the doorway.

The mother that Simon called Miriam stood there, glaring at the hooded woman with an intensity that Shiv recognized as mind bending power.

Miriam spared her a glance. "Come with me!"

Shiv swung Lyshus around to hang from her back. She scooped up Evan and ran around the hooded woman, going into the study to get her sapling. "Little Paul! Come now!"

Little Paul crawled out from under a table, his face wet and shiny. Shiv shifted her sapling to the crook of her arm and picked him up around the middle. He dangled facedown from her arm, but it would do for now. Evan had to be cradled carefully, or so Simon had said. So fragile!

The hooded woman shrieked as Shiv headed for Miriam. She would not be held for long. Shiv's leg ached more than her side or her arms, and she left golden footprints behind her. She would have to tend to that soon.

Miriam went into the hall. "This way."

"Who was she?" Shiv asked as she followed. "Why did you help us?"

Miriam did not answer, leading the way down the hall and occasionally looking over her shoulder. Simon had told her that Miriam would help if needed. She had saved them, and she bore a child that was Evan's kin. But Shiv did not know her. Best to seek out true allies.

Shiv waited until they reached an intersecting hallway, then ran. She resisted the urge to limp and ordered her sapling to cling to her so she could get a better grip on Little Paul. She would find Simon, and they could turn their attention to their enemies together.

Shiv barreled through the hall and dodged into the first room with an open window. Someone in the room cried out as she barreled through, but the window was tall and wide; she cleared it easily, even with all her charges. She hit the ground outside and ran, sprinting through an area covered in grass before charging down another hall, through a large room, and then into the open air just inside the gates of the temple. She ran through those, too, making the humans who had come to see the yafanai dive out of the way. She did not stop until she reached an abandoned street, the kind humans called an alley. Then she hid the children behind a stack of wooden boxes and rested her aching leg.

Little Paul was crying softly, but Evan seemed to disregard any need for secrecy. He wailed, and Shiv bounced him as she had seen Pakesh do. He quieted slightly, but she knew it would not be long before he needed food or grooming. All her charges were young, but they were heavy at the same time. She could not continue to carry them all and go as fast as she hoped.

What had she thought about Simon? He should have carried Evan on his back. Shiv put the sapling down and bade Little Paul and Lyshus sit on its roots. "You will remain here," she said sternly. Little Paul nodded, sniffling. Shiv commanded her tree to hold its branches forth, close as a basket, and she laid Evan within.

She crept to the end of the alley, to the busy street. No one had seemed to notice Evan's cries. That was good, but perhaps if she carried him close to her body, he would make less noise. She saw a swath of fabric hanging above a nearby doorway. A stack of boxes stood to the side. She kept to the shadows, her back to the street so no one could see her face, and sidled close to the boxes. She waited until there were only a few people passing then leapt atop the boxes and tore a strip from the fabric.

"Hey!" someone shouted, a man across the street.

She did not wait to see what he wanted but ran, heading for the alley. She tied the cloth around herself and was about to put Evan inside when the man ducked his head inside the alley's mouth. "You can't just—"

She turned to him and hissed, displaying her claws.

He staggered back, falling. "Drushka!" he cried. "The drushka are back!"

Shiv ignored him since he did not seem capable of a fight. She wanted to carry Evan on her back, but perhaps he would be better in the front. She situated him in the sling, and he quieted slightly.

"I want Shi'a'na," Little Paul said, sniffling again. Though Reach had not borne him, he seemed to accept her fully as his mother, even using the drushkan word.

"You will have her soon enough," Shiv said. Lyshus gnawed on his wooden nini, seemingly unconcerned. Shiv tore a ragged piece of the cloth and quickly tied it around her knee. She slung Lyshus over her shoulders before picking up the sapling and Little Paul.

As voices in the street grew behind her, she hurried away, threading through alleys. How to find shawness Simon amongst all these scents? She could not keep to the streets. There were mind benders who wanted to attack Evan and people who seemed afraid of drushka. She needed a safe haven. High ground?

She looked up to the tops of the buildings. An easy climb for her alone, but with all her charges? No, better to stay on the ground where they could not fall. She could run for the swamp or the plains, but that would be replacing human predators with animal ones. She cooed to Evan in drushkan and tried to think. If she could not find shawness Simon, she would think as he did. He would urge her to search for allies, someone she knew.

In a gap between buildings, she spied the Paladin Keep and grinned. Liam would be there. He would protect these children. But the idea also carried worrying thoughts. Shiv had avoided Liam these past weeks, not wanting to be distracted from her duties as a queen, but she needed somewhere to go. And he had fought to protect her and her family before. He would always be her ally.

She threaded her way in that direction, trying to keep to alleys and dashing across streets. At a street bustling with humans, she stole an enormous hooded shirt and slung it around all of them to disguise her and the children. She wondered how it made her look with all her charges: no doubt short and very squat. The idea made her chuckle, but still she hurried on. The sun grew harsh in the afternoon, becoming a friend as it drove the humans into their dwellings.

As she hurried past one storefront, someone called, "Hot enough for you in that jacket?"

She ignored him and went on. By the time she reached the keep, all her charges were whining, even Lyshus, and Evan had built to a harsher cry.

The front of the keep was largely deserted, so unlike the first time she had seen it, when she had come to warn the humans of the boggins. Now all the metal skins were gone. Shiv sprinted through the courtyard and into a massive central room. She caught Liam's scent and followed it up the stairs, but he was nowhere to be seen.

What to do? Evan would no longer be soothed, and she could not hide while he cried. People were already stirring in these halls. She ran for the office that smelled so much like Liam's mother and hid inside. She closed the door and arranged the children on the floor behind the furniture.

When someone pounded on the wood and demanded she come out, she yelled, "I will only speak to Liam!"

She readied herself for battle, just in case. She felt wound up inside, twisted like an old tree, but she would not give up her charges. The safety of her hands meant something. When she heard several people talking outside the door, she called, "Send Liam or risk the wrath of two queens and Simon Lazlo!" She felt safe adding the anger of Shi'a'na. Even if her mother never accepted Lyshus or never forgave Shiv her deception, she would not deal lightly with anyone who harmed her daughter.

The voices withdrew. Shiv tried to soothe Evan, but his cries were growing frantic, making Shiv feel even more twisted. By the time Liam's voice came tentatively through the door, she felt ready to burst. She flung the door open and nearly leapt into Liam's arms.

At the last moment, she stopped, stumbling to a halt. She had a tribe now; she could not go melting into the arms of her human lover over simple troubles. Liam stepped forward, his face shining with hope. When she backed away, he stopped and stared confusedly at the children.

"Um, hang on a sec." He turned and had a few words with someone outside before he leaned back in. "I'm sending for reinforcements."

So they were to be attacked. By whom? Shiv breathed deep. It did not matter. "I am ready." She had the sapling lean over the children.

"Stand by my side, Liam. We will strike as our attackers come through the door."

He frowned in confusion before his eyes widened. "Sorry, not those kinds of reinforcements." He ducked back out.

Shiv sucked her teeth. She had thought she knew that word. Humans could be so confusing. But she was here and safe. Evan was still crying, and Liam kept himself beyond the door, but everything would be well. Shiv picked up Evan again, promising him all he desired if only he would quiet.

At last Liam returned with a man and a woman who held a human baby of their own. "Who are they?" Shiv asked, holding Evan close. But then she looked from the one human baby to the other. Perhaps like could comfort like?

Liam gestured to Evan. "They can look after him while we talk."

Shiv thought of the mind bender looming over Evan's crib, but she had to do something to soothe him. She nodded to the back of the office, where these two could not escape with Evan without going through her. "There, where I can see."

The couple smiled, and that made Shiv happy. She seemed older than him, her hair graying as it did when humans aged. That meant she had more knowledge, and the way they linked fingers and held their baby close spoke of devotion. They sat at the desk with Evan. Little Paul and Lyshus stayed in the corner with the sapling, though Paul eyed the couple as if sensing someone who could care for his needs, too.

Shiv stood just outside the office with Liam. She crossed her arms over her chest, not trusting herself to keep her hands off his beautiful body or kiss his pliant lips.

"I missed you," he said.

Shiv ducked her head, cursing him for being exactly what she wanted. She glanced at Lyshus to find him watching her. Liam followed her gaze and frowned. Lyshus looked from one of them to the other as if trying to understand what was happening. He had to be sensing emotions from her, but he would not know what they meant, only that she was in turmoil. She sent him love, and he wrinkled his small nose.

"Your mother told me a little bit about what's going on," Liam said. "About you having a tribe now. That's why you've been avoiding me, right?"

"It is not…personal, as Sa would say."

"Yeah, I tried to think that way. But it feels as if you don't trust me to have room in my heart for you and Lyshus both. If you'd had a child when we met, that wouldn't have bothered me, either."

"He is more than a child to me." But how to explain? Even if he knew the pull of parenthood, she still did not know what she could say. "A tribe is…a bond. Like your telepaths, ahya, but for me and Lyshus, it is only we two, and it is powerful. And you cannot share it. You would always feel me pull away."

"So you thought it better to ignore me instead of trying to explain?"

He was angry, and her own anger flared in return. She thought back to their beginning, to her hunger for a lover. She had enjoyed him, but part of her had always known their time would not last forever. She had thought she felt that way because she was drushka and still had a very long life ahead, but now she knew it was because she was a queen and had a longer life still. And a tribe to care for.

She tried to think of what Shi'a'na would say and spread her hands. "We may still be lovers from time to time, if you wish it, but I cannot be yours alone. I am sorry if you ever thought I could."

His nostrils flared, and he seemed as if he might have angry words, but he bit them back and paced. She let him move alone, hoping it would ease his frustration.

When he leaned against the wall, he crossed his arms and glared at her. But instead of starting a fight, he said, "Tell me what happened."

She sighed and told him all. Speaking was far better than pining for his touch.

Simon heard a telepathic call on his way back to the temple with Jacobs and Pakesh. He froze, thinking it might be Horace, but no, this call was weak, far beneath Horace's ability.

And it was a call for help.

"I can feel it," Pakesh said. "Someone needs you."

Simon broke into a jog, and Pakesh filled in Jacobs as they ran.

Jacobs kept up with Simon easily, her stride loose as if she could jog for miles. "This could be a trap!"

"It's hard to lie in a telepathic call, especially one this urgent."

When the temple doors came into sight, he broke into a run, skidding to a stop as Miriam met him just inside. "What's the matter? Is Evan—"

"Last I saw him, he was fine." She pushed her hair off her forehead, the wispy strands slick with sweat. Her dark eyes were as unyielding as ever. "I tried to help your friend, but she ran."

"Who...Shiv?"

"Someone attacked her in the Storm Lord's rooms, and she ran from both of us."

Simon turned down the hall, heading for his room.

"She's not there!" Miriam called. "You're not listening, just like him!"

Simon spun around. "What the hell are you talking about?"

Miriam put her hands on her hips. "The Storm Lord never listened, either. He'd also bull into something before hearing everything I had to say."

Simon took a deep breath, trying not to snap at her, especially since she was right. Half-cocked was Dillon's forte. "All right."

"What happened?" Jacobs asked.

"Someone attacked your drushkan friend, a macro. She was standing over Evan's crib when I caught her."

"A kidnapper?" Simon asked, chilled at the thought.

"Evan is the Storm Lord's firstborn," Miriam said. "I suppose someone might find value in that." She shrugged. "The macro wasn't pregnant, but maybe one of the other mothers hired her because she wants her child to be the eldest."

The thought nearly made Simon throw up. "You can't be serious."

She gave him a hard look. "That's one of the reasons I gave him to you. I thought you'd protect him." She frowned hard. "I've heard rumors, and I didn't want him to be hurt. He's innocent, much more so than his father." When Simon gawked at her, she shrugged again. "I fell for the Storm Lord's words, his eyes, but I'm not blind. We were all taken in. And I'm the most powerful telepath in the temple now. Believe me when I say I know what's going on."

Simon shuddered as he remembered Caroline, the way she'd subdued his mind. He frowned, his suspicions rising. "Did you help Caroline control me?"

She shook her head quickly, looking almost as disgusted as he felt.

"I was on special assignment until very recently, helping people deal with their trauma and grief after the boggin attack."

He tried to picture her as a therapist and failed. Maybe her bedside manner was better in a professional setting. "I can't believe Dillon would let his second most powerful telepath *waste time* helping people."

She smirked. "He didn't know how powerful I am. If you don't want to be a tool for someone like the Storm Lord, don't broadcast the true depth of your ability."

"I see." And he was beginning to readjust his thinking as she surprised him yet again.

"And you can believe me when I say a lot of people will be looking to use Evan. You shouldn't have left him behind!"

He glared at her, fighting the urge to rant about how Evan wasn't his responsibility, but she didn't see it that way. And he was beginning to agree with her. "If you had told me all this in the beginning, I wouldn't have left him! Now, which way did Shiv go?"

Miriam frowned but seemed slightly mollified. "She ran outside. I don't know where. I can't track her mind."

"Don't try." Anytime a human had tried to break into drushka telepathy without an attachment to them, it went badly. Horace had told him that. Simon went back out and looked at the streets, trying to think like Shiv. Maybe she'd gone looking for him, but how would she have found him in such a large place? There weren't many people she knew, not many places to go to ground, but he could think of one.

"Liam," he said. "She'll head for the keep." Liam wasn't a paladin anymore, but Simon couldn't remember if Shiv knew that, and she'd met him at the keep before.

"I'll stay here in case she comes back," Miriam said. "Her attacker got away, but I'll ask some questions." Before he could thank her, she headed back inside.

Simon started toward the keep, hearing the others follow. He only took a few steps before he was running again, helping the others keep up. When he arrived at the keep, he barged inside and shouted, "Is there a drushka here?"

A private pointed him upstairs. When he saw Shiv standing in the hall with Liam, all the kids gathered in an office behind them, he couldn't help a smile. "Shiv!"

She turned, her own smile breaking over her narrow face.

"Shawness Simon!" She threw her arms around him. He hugged her back, and she buried her face in his chest, inhaling deeply as if she wanted to memorize his smell. He looked past her and saw the children being tended by a couple he didn't recognize and their own child. He didn't sense any animosity.

"You beauty!" Simon said as he held her. "You did wonderfully!" He sensed the wound in her knee and healed it with a thought, easing her aching back, too.

She wrinkled her nose away as she stepped back. Liam was glaring at them jealously, and Simon cleared his throat. Things must have gone truly rotten between them if Liam was envious of a hug.

For a moment, everyone stared at one another. Jacobs cleared her throat. "So…is everyone okay?"

"Shiv, what happened?" Simon asked.

"Perhaps elsewhere, shawness," Shiv said. "Evan has been fed, but the children need rest."

And by the slightly panicky look she gave him, she didn't want to rest in the keep…or maybe she didn't want to be anywhere near Liam. "Um, okay."

She nearly ran into the office and came out with the three children and her tree. Liam was scowling as Shiv pushed the sapling into Simon's arms, then handed Little Paul to Pakesh. She eyed Jacobs doubtfully and kept Evan in a sling while Lyshus clung to her back.

Simon sent his power over all of them: calming, relaxing waves. Evan fell asleep immediately, and Little Paul laid his head on Pakesh's shoulder.

"Thank you," Shiv said to Liam before she herded them down the stairs. Liam, to his credit, didn't try to follow. He only watched with a stricken, jealous look.

"Can I carry your…tree, Doc?" Jacobs asked.

"I've got it, thanks." He didn't think Shiv would appreciate him handing it off. He waited until they were outside before speaking again. "Well, now there's the question of where to go. The temple seems out, and the keep…" Shiv gave him another look. "Is not a good idea." For some reason. He searched through the places he knew in Gale, and one house in particular popped into mind: the most comfortable place he could think of, home of the former mayor, Paul Ross. He didn't think Cordelia would mind.

❖

Cordelia felt as if she was flying into a windy canyon as she passed into the ground. Drushkan telepathy buffeted her like a physical force. Even to her spirit eyes, the cavern was dim, but dots of phosphorescent light showed a mass of roots, so much larger than Pool's. They covered the ground in a writhing, boiling mass.

She looked for Pool or the Shi and saw nothing but roots. The rage of the Shi surrounded her, fought by the anger of Pool, warring emotions bouncing and careening invisibly through the cavern. Cordelia caught flashes of Pool's independence and rebellious nature, her stubbornness in the face of all odds. Pool was reliving the separation from the drushka long ago, when Pool had accompanied Jania, Cordelia's ancestor, back to the human homeland rather than stay with her kin.

The Shi countered with drushkan rage. She'd wanted to kill all the humans, every single one. At the time of the schism, the other queens thought it best to kill Jania and any other humans she might have told about the drushkan plan to absorb humanity. Then they could continue with their long game. A human race that was scattered among the drushka could not breed. They would die out soon enough.

Cordelia would have frowned if she could. Why hadn't they killed Jania and continued the plan? What stopped them? Jania had never written of drushkan queens or these secret bargains. Did she even know why she'd been spared?

"I lied!" Pool howled. "Lied to all of you!"

"Impossible!" the Shi said, her words translated through Pool.

Cordelia felt the Shi's outrage and Pool's shame as if someone was taking a hammer to her spirit. She groaned under the weight.

"I would do it again," Pool said. "For my freedom."

Cordelia gasped at a barrage of images: Pool, claiming that Jania had saved her life while she was still a queen-to-be. And such an act was not taken lightly. In exchange, Pool claimed that Jania asked to continue trading with the drushka. To do that, she needed a queen closer to the human home. Pool could not refuse someone who had saved her life.

But it was a lie, manufactured images crafted by Pool so she could get what she most desired: freedom from the other queens. The humans held the keys to the future, to evolution and progress. Even before the current Shi had taken control, the drushka were pulling farther into their homeland, seeking to stay away from the humans. Pool wanted independence. And she'd learned how to lie in order to get it.

The Shi howled at her. "Abomination!"

"Everything changes," Pool said. "Or it stagnates and dies."

"Fuck yeah," Cordelia whispered.

The Shi countered with the history of the drushka, each queen moving to the next largest tree once a Shi died; a new queen being born only if there was a need.

Pool responded with each queen roving far through her own territory, of bands of drushka happily wandering under no one's control, exploring, experimenting. Separate but still connected, not subjugated as they were under this Shi's rule. Pool shared flashes of her own history. No queen-to-be was supposed to rule before ascending to her tree, but Pool's hunt leader and several others had died in a prog attack before she became queen. Everyone left alive in the band had been younger than Pool, and they'd turned to her because there hadn't been a full queen nearby. For days, Pool had led them until they'd found their queen. She'd helped carry the wounded; she'd given orders, and it had been *right*. But as soon as they returned to a queen and her tree, that power had been taken away, not to be returned until Pool took her own tree. She'd burned inside as decisions were made without her, decisions she disagreed with, but she could not even suggest a different course.

And then came Jania, Roshkikan. Alone, autonomous, with nothing to make her different from other humans yet possessing free will and the power to make her own decisions. That life had been as seductive as a lover's touch. When the old Shi had died and Pool had taken the Anushi tree, Pool had thought herself finally free, that she could lead her tribe as she wished, and she wanted to be closer to the humans. She'd had plans. Cordelia admired that.

The Shi's mind lashed out. "I should have known! You were born disobedient, deformed."

Cordelia reeled as more images poured into her mind. The Shi showed the drushka being ripped asunder by Pool's leaving, but Pool countered with the mindless drones they'd become. They could have survived without Pool, but the Shi had chosen to enslave them instead.

"Liar!" the Shi howled. "You lied once, and now your tongue

is covered with them! You will know my mind, and it will bring the drushka peace!"

The mass lifted Pool's body out of the press. Several roots turned to spikes and drilled into her flesh. She cried out, and Cordelia flew toward her.

"Pool, don't give up!"

Pool's eyes opened, boring into Cordelia, pleading with her.

Cordelia hesitated for a moment, thinking of the force of Naos. "Fuck it." She dove into Pool, becoming one with that shining light. She felt Pool's strength and lent her own. Pool threw both into the mind of the Shi.

The roots parted again, lifting a drushkan queen even taller than the eighth. She hung suspended as the roots crawled over her naked body, clothing her in a wriggling mass. With a snarl like a feral animal, she cursed them.

Cordelia gave those taunts right back at her, hoping she could sense their meaning through Pool.

"The humans survive!" Pool cried. "As I will survive!"

The Shi sent another mental battering ram their way. Cordelia groaned under the assault but sensed it could be much worse. The Shi still didn't seem to know what to do with human thoughts. She snarled and flinched whenever their minds touched. She slashed at the air near Pool's body with her claws, but Cordelia had no body to attack.

"Human filth," the Shi called. "Leave this place or die!"

"No," Pool said. "She will not. She would share her strength with you if only you would be her ally. There are good humans, sister."

"As there are bad drushka," the Shi said. "You are no sister of mine." The Shi struck again, but Cordelia struck back, her mind entwined with Pool's.

The roots beneath Pool slumped, and she fell. Cordelia chased her downward as she smacked into the cavern floor. The roots withdrew from her flesh, and golden blood streamed from her wounds, but she staggered to her feet.

"Go on, Pool!" Cordelia said. An ache throbbed through her, as if her whole mind and body were afire, but she kept pushing. They could do this together, damn it, even if Cordelia didn't have enough strength left to float back to her body. She only wished this could have been a physical fight, but no, she seemed doomed to always be sucked into this telepathic bullshit. "Fight, Pool. Climb up there and give her hell!"

Pool climbed the roots, back to the top of the writhing pile. "I will not surrender, sister."

"You will die. The humans will die." But the Shi's voice was quieter, her gaze unfocused.

So they were winning? "We're not going anywhere, asshole!" Cordelia yelled.

"No." Pool's eyes went wide. "She reaches for the minds of the other queens who are still under her control. I cannot fight them all at once."

Not winning, then. Okay. Cordelia cast around for a weapon, but she was only a voice in Pool's head. She yelled at the Shi, trying to distract her, and felt Pool sending out a call.

"Sisters," Pool said. "I am sorry I failed you. Resist her if you can."

"We're not beaten yet." Cordelia's mind raced. If Pool went down, Cordelia had no doubt she'd be right behind. And the kidnapped Galeans would die. Nettle and Reach would die. "Fuck that! We're not going down without a fight!" She joined with Pool again, pictured herself bracing her feet, getting ready for the rush.

The presence of the other queens fell over them like a blanket, smothering Pool's thoughts. She bowed under the onslaught. Cordelia screamed as part of her spirit flew away in tatters, leaving her feeling hollow. It was hard to remember what she was even fighting for. It would be so much easier to submit, to sink into the drushkan telepathy as if it were a warm bath.

"No, no." She tried to push back as the ache built, and the silver cord that connected her to her body shivered, flickering. Well, it had broken once before, and she had survived. She tried to keep hold of her thoughts, but it felt like trying to keep a tornado from gobbling a bit of paper. The force of the queens wedged themselves between Cordelia and Pool, thousands of whispers. They began to unravel Cordelia's connection to Pool, to unravel the work Simon Lazlo had done to attach Cordelia more firmly to her body. She grabbed her silver cord and held on. She threw her memories, her fortitude into that force, shouting, "Fuck you, fuck you," over and over. But even her cries were fading before the rushing in her mind, the sound like waves swallowing her up. The Shi cackled in triumph.

On the edge of the tidal wave, Cordelia felt another presence watching them, curious. Cordelia had a flash of a long drushkan face. The eighth queen. "Please," Cordelia said. "Please don't kill them." She flung her love for Nettle into the air and hoped that somehow, Nettle felt it. If not… "I am so going to haunt you, motherf—"

As quickly as the minds of the other queens arrived, they faded, led by a mental hand that guided rather than demanded. Cordelia's awareness came back slowly, her thoughts and memories settling, her silver cord still intact.

The cavern went still. The Shi stared at nothing, mouth open in shock.

"Pool, what's happening?" Cordelia asked.

"The minds of the other queens," Pool said as she wheezed. The mass of roots ceased moving beneath her. "They withdraw, led by the eighth." She looked to the Shi. "The eighth's mind is still here, watching." Cordelia felt Pool focus, sending her mind into the Shi's again, but not to attack, merely to watch. With an expert touch, the eighth reached for the Shi's mental connection to the other queens.

And severed it.

The Shi choked, and the roots lowered her to stand atop them. "What is this?"

Cordelia whooped. "Yeah! It's a fair fight now."

Pool waved as if trying to quiet her. "Our people want change, sister. Accept it."

"No. I…keep them safe." But the Shi looked so flabbergasted, Cordelia nearly laughed.

"Let them decide how safe they need to be," Pool said. "Let them roam. Let each queen decide whom she will take for an ally. We can learn together."

"I…" The Shi went to her knees, her green hair cascading around her into a puddle. "I cannot."

Pool crossed to her over the roots. The Shi looked pathetic, but Cordelia could still feel her will, strong as iron. She wouldn't change even if her life demanded it.

Pool pressed their foreheads together. "I am sorry it has come to this. Do you wish to see the light once more?"

The Shi stared at her, and for a moment, Cordelia thought she might plead for her life. Then her gaze hardened, and she swung a hand, leading with her claw. Pool ducked. Cordelia grabbed for her sidearm, her blade, anything, but in her spirit form, she held nothing.

Pool reached under the waist of her trousers and brought forth a knife, Shiv's little homemade blade. With a leap, she thrust upward, burying the knife in the Shi's neck and tearing it across.

The Shi rocked backward, gurgling, her hand to her throat. Cordelia hovered closer, looking for any final tricks the Shi had planned. But Pool caught the taller drushka as best she could and laid her down, stroking her hair as she died, smiling sadly into her face. "Farewell, sister."

"Pool, I…" Cordelia didn't know what to say, wanted to celebrate, but it didn't seem the right moment. She felt a mental tug, as if someone was calling her name, perhaps moving her body.

"Go, Sa," Pool said, not looking up.

Cordelia rushed upward, back to her body, uncertain of exactly what she was going to find, but certain they'd finally found an ending, one way or another.

CHAPTER THIRTEEN

Patricia felt the arrival of the breachies before she saw them approaching the mining town. She strode to the wall, then made herself slow. She didn't want anyone to see her hurrying. She'd been meditating, and the fact that she had to do mental exercises of any kind put her out of sorts. Instead of helping with the wall and defenses, she had to focus on the mental blocks that held Dillon's consciousness captive in her mind.

She still caught a whiff of him from time to time, but now she'd have backup. Raquel had finally answered Patricia's summons, leading her clan of worshipers out of the foothills. And by the feel of her group, she'd brought two other breachies with her, Sophia and Kenneth. Patricia passed the wall and walked out to meet them. Maybe that seemed overeager, but she didn't care. Soon she'd be rid of Dillon's ghost for good, and Raquel would never even have to know about him.

Raquel marched at the front of her people. Her thick black hair had been twisted into a braid that hung over one shoulder, and she wore what probably passed for hill dweller finery: a long leather dress dyed maroon and covered with beads and fine stitching. Sophia and Kenneth walked just behind her, also dressed more elaborately than the mere mortals but slightly less than Raquel. On the *Atlas*, they'd all been sycophants of the Contessa, the now deceased Marie Martin. Now it appeared that Sophia and Kenneth had become lackeys to Raquel.

Raquel frowned when she saw Patricia, confusion wafting from her. She glanced at the mining camp, probably looking for Patricia's old body, Naos's body now. Raquel's micro-psychokinetic powers played over Patricia, and she let them, adding a powerful nudge of her own combined with a telepathic message: "It's me."

Raquel's jaw dropped, but she recovered quickly. "Of…of course. Nice to see you again, N—"

"Patricia Dué," Patricia said before she had to hear that name again.

They all glanced at one another. Patricia gave them a quick scan. Kenneth was a telepath of hardly any power, and Sophia was a macro of the same level, but it was Raquel she was interested in. She was a micro and macro. Her powers wouldn't come anywhere near to challenging Patricia's, Naos's, or Simon Lazlo's, but she'd do for mining work.

"As you can see, I got a new body," Patricia said.

"What happened to your old one?" Kenneth looked her up and down but with the curiosity of a scientist rather than the leer Dillon would have given.

Deep in Patricia's mind, she heard a snort of laughter.

Patricia warned him to shut up and strengthened the mental blocks. "That's a long story," she said aloud.

"Can we all get new bodies?" Sophia hugged her slender frame, and Patricia recalled that she'd always been uncomfortable in her own skin. What made her think she'd be happy in a new one?

Patricia shrugged. "If you can find the power, you can do whatever you want." Kenneth was still eyeing her, and she put up a hand to keep him from coming any closer. He backed off with a slightly embarrassed look. With ink-black hair and bright blue eyes, he had a handsome face, but she remembered him as standoffish and aloof. Naos used to enjoy spying on his flirtations with Simon Lazlo. Patricia once thought they'd make quite a couple, but Kenneth got bored with people too easily, and Naos argued that Simon would always have eyes for Dillon.

Patricia waited to see what Dillon would say to that, but he remained silent. Maybe her blocks were finally strong enough. "Come meet Jonah." They'd need to get used to seeing Dillon's old body with its new mind.

As Patricia turned, Raquel caught up, leaving her people to set up tents outside the wall. Raquel stood tall, looming over Patricia's new body. Patricia used to do the same thing to shorter people, and now it made her smile.

"So, what are you doing here?" Raquel asked.

"Setting up shop." She could see another question forming, but Raquel saw Jonah walking out to meet them and stopped, gawking. Even with the silver hair and the scar Patricia had given him, he was still very recognizable. Fear oozed from all three breachies like swamp gas.

"You've allied with the Storm Lord?" Raquel asked through a petrified smile.

Patricia chuckled. They were even more afraid of him than they might have been of Naos. At least she'd kept to herself most of the time. Dillon's sneering contempt had been hurled right in their faces, and he was too powerful to oppose directly.

Even through her shields, Patricia felt him preen.

Jonah stared at them without recognition, eyes flat.

"It's just his body," Patricia said. "The Storm Lord is dead."

"You wish," he said in her mind.

She layered blocks atop blocks in one angry burst, making him fade to a dull muttering. Raquel glanced at her, and she clenched a fist, trying to exude calm. Luckily, the other two were busy scanning Jonah, and their excitement caused Raquel to look at them again.

"This is Jonah, my servant," Patricia said.

Their awestruck gazes shifted to her. Jonah stood still under their scrutiny, even the sexually appraising glances they cast his way. If Patricia remembered correctly, Dillon had slept with Raquel and Sophia both. Maybe Kenneth was hoping for a chance as well.

A jolt of jealousy arced through Patricia, surprising her. Dillon's work? No, she didn't think so. Jonah was hers; that was all. They could keep their hands to themselves. Patricia put a bit of power behind her smile, inserting telepathic tags in the breachies' heads, miniscule but important. Now they'd leave Jonah alone. While she was in their heads, she added a subtle need to make her proud. They all turned smiles her way.

Patricia shifted, flushing, knowing she shouldn't throw power around that way, but this was where she'd stop. She wouldn't be pushy like Naos. One little telepathic nudge to start out with, and she was done.

Definitely. Maybe. Very probably.

Patricia found another private house for the three breachies to share. It had been for storage, but Patricia had some of the workers fit it with beds, making it more comfortable. The whole camp looked better since she'd arrived, more homey and permanent. Patricia put Raquel to work in the mine, and Sophia went to work on the defenses. With his telepathic abilities, Kenneth was perfect for keeping watch along with the hill dweller scouts. Everything was coming together.

As she laughed with everyone in the cookhouse that night, Patricia began to relax. She didn't need an army or thousands of worshipers. These people were enough. If a few more breachies were within shouting distance, maybe she'd invite them, too. For now, she had enough. She was content.

"Good for you, sweets," Dillon said.

Patricia slammed a hand on the table. "Shut up!"

The room silenced. Jonah stared with concern, the rest with something like fear. She scowled. "What are you looking at?"

When one of them gestured, she glanced down to see her fist embedded in the wooden table, covered in blood. Long cracks radiated from where she'd struck, and as she lifted free, the table splintered and collapsed.

Everyone leapt up. Patricia pushed the remains of the table away with her mind, staring at her bloody hand instead. Easy to heal. She hadn't even felt her bones break.

"Mistress?" Jonah asked. "Are you all right?"

In a snide voice, Dillon made fun of him, adding, "Did you have to turn me into such a douchebag?"

Patricia stood, her cheeks on fire. "I'm going for a walk. Alone." She marched from the cookhouse, knowing no one would follow. She stalked through the darkness, past the guards on the partially constructed wall and into the plains, wrapping herself in a telepathic cloak so she couldn't be seen.

"Why can't you be quiet?" She ground her teeth. Her muscles felt like cables under her skin. "Just shut the fuck up and be happy!"

She let down some of her blocks, wanting to hear what he had to say. Of course, he seemed to make his way through no matter what she did. She couldn't even touch Jonah without his pithy comments.

"How the fuck am I supposed to be happy trapped in your brain, Dué?" he asked. "You know what this feels like!"

"I can try eradicating you. Think that will help?"

"If you could do that, sweets, you'd have done it by now. You want me to stop fucking with you? Put me somewhere else."

Would that work? She clearly couldn't keep him quiet, and he didn't seem to need or want rest. He'd keep trying to take her over, to make her a stranger in her own body, and she wouldn't have that. Never again.

But where to put him? Jonah was the obvious choice, but she'd worked so hard to make him perfect. Besides, she didn't know what erasing a mind then putting it back might entail. It could cause some kind of brain damage that she couldn't fix. She didn't even know if she could sort out Dillon's memories from her own anymore.

And she wouldn't take the chance of damaging Jonah. Even if their history was fake, he cared about her. "Jonah's mine."

Dillon chuckled, low and sexy, seemingly pleased with the idea that his body was irresistible. "I could get used to somewhere new, someone younger. As long as he's fit. And reasonably good-looking."

"You'd be up to your old tricks in no time, and then Simon Lazlo would just kill you again."

A wave of his anger rushed through her. "Trust me," he said. "I don't want anything to do with him. Take one of your idiot followers, wipe him, and put me inside."

"Does it have to be a man?" she asked snidely.

"I could get used to being a lesbian."

She rolled her eyes. "Good to know you have your priorities. Would you go back to Gale?"

He didn't respond, and she wondered if he even knew. Maybe Dillon didn't have a plan. She focused a bit and sensed it was true. They *were* very closely connected. How could she ever make sure she got all of him? And how would she transfer one person to another? She'd taken his memories when he'd been near death but didn't really know how to put them anywhere else. And she hadn't used his power, but she had it tucked away in her head, too. Would she have to give that back? She thought of the Storm Lord walking Calamity again, younger, reborn. He'd find a way to get rid of Simon Lazlo eventually. Then he'd charge his paladins' armor and roust her out of the mine. Or he'd ally with Lazlo or maybe the Sun-Moon and make a bid for the entire world.

She couldn't allow that. Why was she even considering his feelings? Dillon wasn't a telepath; he couldn't beat her in her own brain. No matter how entrenched he'd become, she was in charge of her mind. She just needed one big push to shut him up for good. Patricia sat in the grass, closed her eyes, and focused. She would exorcise him, laser him out like a tumor. She just needed to focus!

She felt him shift in her mind, fleeing from her, hiding as she sometimes had from Naos. Patricia imagined her mindscape as a dark thicket, and Dillon's ghostly presence flitted through the trees. She stalked him like a hunter, but every time she thought him cornered, he disappeared. She snarled and willed the trees away, imagining her mind as an open plain. Dillon appeared before her, wearing the face he'd had in life, sneering.

"Got you," Patricia said.

He laughed. "This is my house now, sweets, and I've been exploring it a hell of a lot more than you have." A wall shot up between them, blocking her view. Patricia backed away, marveling at what he could do. She bumped into another wall and turned to run her hands over its smooth surface, trying to dispel it, but it wouldn't budge. Another wall sprang up under her feet and she jumped out of the way, turning in circles as a steel maze rose up around her.

"Find me now!" his voice called.

She tried to dismiss the wall, tried to return to her waking state in the plains, but her mind felt as stuck as if held by glue.

"It's your mind, Dué. Can't you find your way out? Maybe you'd have sensed me sooner if you did a little introspection once in a while."

"You wouldn't be much for self-analysis if you'd lived with Naos for centuries," she shouted. He laughed, but it was the truth. Introspection lost its appeal when it sent you spiraling into a mad state that took forever to escape. And Dillon knew nothing of being caught. Naos had pressed Patricia down so far, she could barely see and hear through her own body, let alone act.

Maybe that was the key. How had Naos trapped her so completely? Even in this mindscape, Patricia could still call out with her power. And Naos hated Dillon. Maybe there was some way to turn them on each other.

"What are you doing, Dué?" Dillon called. "Just going to lounge in here until some animal eats us on the plains?"

"Oh, I'm looking farther than the plains for something to eat you. You want another home? I'll give you one." She reached farther than before, pushing her power to the limit to find her old body, her old self, still in orbit where she'd left it on the *Atlas*. She couldn't see it, but she could feel Naos's presence turn her way.

"What do you want, traitor?" It was her old voice, but it belonged to Naos now.

Patricia couldn't help a shudder. "I've got something for you. A new playmate."

"No!" Dillon yelled. The walls tumbled, leaving Patricia and Dillon standing together against a field of stars. "Motherfucker, I'll make you kill me first!" He lunged at her, but she blinked out of the way. He was still too used to the physical world.

Patricia felt Naos look closer, drawn to Dillon's emotions like a bear to raw meat. "Aha."

"Take him," Patricia said. "He's all yours."

Dillon swore and turned in circles. Patricia held her own power ready to fight if Naos tried to collect them both. Naos couldn't possess anyone on the ground ever again, but Patricia had sent out a telepathic signal, and Naos had locked on.

Patricia smiled as Naos's presence drifted closer still, surrounding Dillon like a fog. All her problems were about to be over.

"Is that so?" Naos's presence turned to her. "Is that what you want?" The presence began a slow withdrawal. "I don't think so."

"What?" Patricia asked, breathless.

"I won't do it because you obviously want it, you little sneak."

Dillon laughed like a maniac. "Oh, this is too good!"

"I spite you," Naos said, her smugness drifting over Patricia, stinging her. "But now that you've got my attention, I'll be watching." Her telepathic grip settled over Patricia's mind like fingers boring into her skull. "The two of you can either get along, or so help me, I'll turn this space station around!" Her hideous laughter bounced around Patricia's mindscape, making both her and Dillon cringe. "Next time you call me, darlin', I'll take you both." Her power tossed them away with a shove.

Patricia gasped as she opened her eyes, surrounded by the real night. Her mouth filled with the taste of burnt metal, and her eyes felt gritty as pain beat behind her forehead. She spat and used her power to soothe her aching head before she stood. Some curious animal had come near her in the dark, and she shooed it away with power. From the mine, she could feel Jonah peering into the dark, worrying for her.

"Fucking asshole," Dillon muttered.

"Shut up," Patricia said.

"Happy now? Your former roommate wouldn't take me. Oh wait! She might take us both. Good work there."

"You started it. Stop attacking me. And stop talking so damn much."

"Fuck you! I never suggested involving Copilot Crazy in our little talks."

"Talks?" Patricia marched around in a circle. "You admitted you're trying to take over my body."

"You deserve it. You stole my mind. You're using my body. You're a fucking rapist!"

Patricia's mouth dropped open. "I am not! I would never!"

"If it walks like a duck and quacks like a duck…"

"You were *dead*." She tried to lower her voice, but his accusation hit like a wrecking ball. "I saved your body. You couldn't go on as you were before. Simon Lazlo would only have killed you again. Jonah was…the best option." But that story didn't hold up in the face of his anger.

"You only resurrected me to be your love slave. Seems to me there were a million other things you could have done to *save* me. But you didn't try any of them, just saw what you wanted and took it. *Rap*—"

"Don't you dare say that again!" She would use her power to bury him, to bury the shame he'd fostered inside her. She wasn't like that. She couldn't be. All she'd wanted was a new fucking life. Was that too much to ask for?

"Oh, boo hoo," Dillon said. "And I'm not the only one you fucked over. You haven't actually tried to convince anyone to go along with your plans. You fall back on your powers every single time and mind-fuck people until you get what you want."

She sputtered for a response. "That's better than telling them to do what you want or else. That's what you used to do."

"At least that gives them a choice."

She held her chin up, trying to summon any self-assuredness she had left. "My way, no one gets hurt."

"Yeah, baby," he said snidely, "fuck free will as long as no one gets hurt. If you mind-fuck someone into giving something to you, you're as guilty as if you beat them up and took it."

That wasn't true, couldn't be true! It was for their own good. She wasn't changing them that much. Some of them wanted to believe in…

She had a sudden flash of what she could have done on Earth if she'd had these powers. She could have made every boss give her a promotion, made every teacher see her worth. She could have made every man who'd ever rejected her want her more than anyone else. And to her horror, the idea appealed more than a little, sating some unrecognized need.

Patricia clapped a hand to her mouth, feeling the bile rise. "Oh God. I didn't want to be like her, like Naos."

He barked a laugh. "Don't you get it, yet? You *are* Naos, sweets." He sighed, sounding as emotionally drained as she felt. "I know you like to think she took you over, like an outside force possessing you, but it was just you split into different parts. Hell, even I could spot that."

Patricia had to sit, her mind reeling. She looked up at the blanket of stars overhead. Part of her was still up there. It was easy to see now. During the accident, her personality had split, and that part of her that had always wanted to be Naos had come tumbling out. Even the name was one she'd thought of before. Naos was a Greek word; some said it meant temple or spirit. Some used it as another term for god. Patricia had loved studying the classics in college, such a break from physics and engineering. One of her professors had said the word during class one day, and she'd thought it beautiful.

"I didn't want…" She wiped her eyes, torn between the desire to weep and throw up. "I don't want…please."

"At least we're saying please."

"I'm sorry." Sadness rose within her, a feeling all her own, and she sobbed, her whole body shaking until she couldn't speak, so she repeated the words in her mind, again and again. "I should have just brought you back. I'm so sorry."

He was quiet as she wept, and she wondered what that meant, what would happen when she went back to the mine and faced Jonah again. She had started something here, and she couldn't leave it half done, couldn't just create a mess that someone else would have to deal with. She dimly wondered if Dillon would let her sleep and felt his grudging assent before she headed back home, where Jonah waited.

❖

Cordelia floated back to her body and found the eighth queen bending over her, shaking her gently. Cordelia settled inside herself and opened her eyes, making the eighth lean back. Two drushka flanked her, frowning, hands on their weapons.

Cordelia tried a reassuring smile, but she felt too tired to be cheerful. "Hey. How's everyone doing?"

The eighth frowned. "I felt an alien mind in the Shi's cavern. Yours?"

"Guilty," Cordelia said as she scooted away. She was too tired to lie. Even with shaky legs, she managed to stand. "I wanted to see what was going on."

The eighth eyed her carefully. "That was a fight between two queens, on their own, as it should be."

"Definitely." Cordelia didn't know how much she should say, didn't want to give away that she hadn't simply been watching. "So, what now?"

The eighth sighed deeply and put a hand to her chest. "The Shi is dead." Her long face seemed even longer as she frowned sadly, though Cordelia suspected this was the outcome she wanted. Drushka all around them seemed grief-stricken, some staring at nothing, others glaring at Cordelia. She kept her smile contained.

At a churning sound, Cordelia looked over the branches. The roots of the eighth lifted Pool and the dead Shi into the light. Cordelia turned to ask if she could go to Pool, but the branches were already reaching for her and the eighth, ready to lower them to the ground. Another queen joined them, probably the seventh, and all three queens put their heads back and trilled. Cordelia jumped at the sound.

All around them, other drushka followed suit, and the sound filled the valley from end to end. Cordelia resisted the urge to clap her hands over her ears as the trill reached a crescendo.

From the distant tree line, more queens passed into the valley, friend and former foe. Though they were enormous, the branches of the

Shi were far over their heads, allowing all eight queens to gather near the Shi's trunk, making them nine once more. It was beautiful, a whole circle. Cordelia knew she'd never see the like again and couldn't help a jot of grief.

The eighth queen walked to the center of the circle where the body of the old Shi lay. Pool stepped back to Cordelia's side, one hand on her chest as she inclined her head to the new Shi, the former eighth. Roots broke the ground around the living and dead queen and drew them both slowly under the soil.

"She will never see the sun again until she is ready to die," Pool whispered.

"Good luck," Cordelia muttered.

A young girl then marched into the circle. Her green hair had been tied, unbraided, atop her head. The drushka began to hum, swaying, and the girl tugged on the leather string that held her hair, dropping the locks around her shoulders. A queen-to-be, but whose tree would she take? Cordelia nearly held her breath.

The queen-to-be looked to Pool, and Cordelia sensed Pool's hesitation. A new tree would mean a new tribe, though Cordelia thought all of Pool's drushka would follow her. But then who would be left for this new queen?

Pool's eyes flicked toward the second tree, as if sending this new queen in that direction, saying she would not yield her tree. The young queen-to-be cocked her head but moved toward the second tree.

All the queens but Pool shifted to a new tree. Each put her forehead to the trunk as if communing. Jagged edges sprouted from the bark, and they ran their arms over them, cutting their flesh. Cordelia grimaced, but the queens didn't seem to feel the pain as they smeared golden blood across their new trees.

The branches lifted each queen, and Cordelia supposed they'd finish this ritual above, each alone with her tree yet still connected to the whole. Maybe tonight there'd be a huge drushkan shift as each drushka selected who his or her queen would be.

But Pool would keep the same tribe. No one had come from her branches to mingle with the other tribes. Cordelia smiled, glad her people would stay intact. And no one else seemed intent on killing them at the moment; another plus.

Pool didn't move, bloody but unbowed. Cordelia touched her arm. "Hold on, Pool. We'll get you healed in no time."

"The eighth has passed your armor to my tree," she said, her eyes glazed. "And the kidnapped Galeans are aboard my branches. As are Reach and Nettle."

Cordelia grinned. "What are we waiting for?"

Pool gave her a tired smile. As the Anushi branches lifted them, Cordelia hugged Pool from the side. "I'm glad you won, and I'm glad you stayed in your tree. I would have missed you like crazy if you'd become the Shi."

"And I you, Sa. There are still decisions to be made, ahya, but we may rest awhile in the swamp and discuss them."

It sounded like the best suggestion Cordelia had ever heard.

Horace had never felt as if he'd had so much to do. The drushkan shawnessi had Pool well in hand, but Horace had to tend to the captured Galeans. They were injured, angry, and frightened and wanted nothing to do with the drushka even though Pool was their ticket home.

Not that Horace could blame them. He soothed them as they huddled in a mass near the heart of Pool's tree. Even surrounded by paladins, they hugged each other in worry; most were shaking. Some were staring at nothing, traumatized, and they would need more than soothing. But he didn't have time at the moment for any deep telepathic sessions that could help them process their trauma faster. Some dealt with the fear by shouting, demanding they go home immediately; a few even shrieked at the paladins to stop standing there and kill all the drushka.

Horace smiled gratefully at the Galeans who tried to help their injured brethren. He saw through their calm façade, but he appreciated the offer. All of them had seen some of their fellow captives be dragged away and not return, and no doubt the paladins had told them that those captives had been hanged. Another bad memory they'd have to deal with.

Horace healed the major physical injuries—large lacerations, broken bones, internal bleeding, one punctured lung—and kept exuding calm, but any soothing vibes he sent wore off almost immediately. He eased many of the captives into sleep, keeping up a steady telepathic litany assuring them that they were safe. They could rest. The presence of the paladins seemed to help with that, as well as the reassurances that Gale was fine, that everyone there had been healed. These captives hadn't succumbed to the sickness, perhaps because they hadn't ingested both parts of the poison, but they'd seen people dying in Gale. He reassured them that everyone there was all right and waiting for their return.

As he got a moment to rest, he sighed, trying to shake off the panicky feelings floating around. He took a long sip of water and wondered where Cordelia was, but he couldn't summon the energy to find her. He could only sit and stare at nothing, wishing Simon was beside him.

It hadn't been an easy fight in the swamp once Cordelia left. The paladins and Pool's drushka had fought as best they could, the paladins leaping into the water to lead the drushka away. They'd also carried some of their enemies to a watery grave, but some paladins hadn't returned either. Horace rubbed his belly as he remembered running to heal one when an enemy drushka came out of nowhere and buried a spear in his gut.

His core had burned in agony while the rest went numb. He'd curled around the pain, which made it worse, but he hadn't been able to focus. He remembered an arm catching him as he began to topple. He'd heard yelling, and then a drushka had tackled his savior, sending all of them into the water.

The cool feeling of the liquid had soothed him, and he'd wanted nothing more than to sink into oblivion, but he'd had a vision of Simon's face. He could still see Simon's lips curled into a smile, his blue eyes bright and welcoming as the sun turned his hair into gold.

Then, agony again. Hands had lifted Horace from the water, making the pain worse, but it had brought him back to himself. A female voice had told him something was going to hurt. He'd tried to laugh, to say he was already hurt, then the agony tripled, and he'd screamed as the spear left his flesh.

The woman had told him to heal himself. He'd thought it was Cordelia or maybe his old friend Natalya. But one wasn't there, and the other was dead. Maybe he was dead, too and hearing voices from beyond. He tried to tell Natalya he was sorry she'd died, but someone had smacked him in the face and shouted at him to heal himself.

It had to be Cordelia. He'd focused, catching the edge of his power. He remembered being on the plains with Mamet, trying to heal Simon and then getting shot. Maybe he'd never left there. Maybe this was the same battle.

But as the pain receded, he was able to draw on more power, heal more damage. He was in the swamp with the drushka, and one of the paladins was glaring at him, not Cordelia. One of the others. Several of them crowded round, watching the swamp. He'd healed himself and then felt someone else below him in the water, dying. Jon Lea. He wasn't breathing; he'd run out of air. But he wasn't dead, not yet. Horace had rolled over on the branch, staring into the water and reaching with is power. He'd squeezed Jon's heart and filled his lungs.

"Get him out," Horace had choked out. "Jon Lea." He couldn't let him die, had gotten used to his barking orders, his stoic face. He'd been a rock for all of them.

"Already being done," someone had said.

Pool's drushka had gone in after Jon and were hauling him, armor and all, out of the murky water, working with the paladins on land. Jon's body jerked as Horace squeezed his heart again, forcing his lungs to work. As the paladins laid Jon on the branch and yanked his helmet off, he took a deep, shuddering breath and locked eyes with Horace, his normally taciturn expression filled with wonder and a childlike beauty.

Horace had lain back, healing all of them, trying not to remember the pain, having a wild thought that he should find the spear that had gutted him and take it as a macabre keepsake. "What happened to the enemy drushka?" he'd asked.

They'd told him the drushka had run off as if summoned elsewhere. He'd later learned that was the moment the old Shi had died. Now, as he fingered the huge hole in the front of his shirt, he lamented that the call hadn't happened ten minutes before it did. Then he wouldn't have another awful memory to add to the rest.

And he wouldn't be down another shirt. He wondered if Cordelia would have found the spear and kept it, if it was still floating out there somewhere.

"Need a hand?"

Horace looked up to find Jon Lea watching him. He blinked,

thrown too quickly out of reverie. Jon smiled, but it looked a bit awkward, as if he was unused to smiling.

"Sure," Horace said. "Want to help me make the rounds again?"

Jon nodded and stayed at Horace's shoulder like a guard. Horace fought the urge to sigh. Whatever made the man happy.

"What did you think of the Shi's tree?" Horace asked. He'd taken a moment to look when they'd first arrived. When he'd seen a tree as big as a mountain, his brain had dismissed it as impossible, especially in light of all he had to do. But the image came to him again, following him around like Simon's dear face, and he knew that as small as his glimpse had been, he'd never forget it.

"It's big," Jon said.

Horace gawked at him. "That's it?"

Jon blinked. "Really big."

Horace chuckled, but any humor faded quickly as he scanned the freed captives again. All one hundred and sixty shaken humans would never forget the Shi either. With the fifteen dead in the swamp, that left twenty-five unaccounted for. Pool had assured him that all the captives had been returned. So the others had either died in captivity, or they'd gone missing from Gale in some other way. Now that the major damage was healed and most were sleeping, Horace healed small cuts, bruises, and sprains. He found a few dislocated limbs he'd missed. The old drushka had not been kind. He cleaned out any lingering poison, but there was a host of other ailments to worry about: infections, stomach bugs, and the like. The paladins were among some of those, and Horace healed them, too. Deep in Pool's tree, surrounded only by humans, it seemed many of them could finally relax, too. Maybe they could finally imagine they were somewhere else entirely.

Through it all, Jon stayed silent and at his side. Horace appreciated the company, but he'd been hoping for someone to talk to. At the edge of the gathering, he spotted Cordelia, unarmored, talking to a few of the former captives and assuring them they were going home. Horace caught her eye and smiled.

When she grinned, he nearly faltered, feeling his sadness and fatigue rising up to swamp him. What was it about kindness that made him want to sink into someone else and collapse?

"I'll be back, Jon." Without waiting for an answer, Horace crossed to Cordelia swiftly and hugged her tight, taking strength from her tall, muscular form. He felt her fatigue and bruises and healed those, too.

"I'm so glad you're okay," he said into her shoulder.

"Glad you're in one piece, too," she said as she hugged him back.

Night was falling around them, and as Cordelia stepped back, she held a lantern high, looking him up and down. She stuck a finger in the hole of his shirt, poking him lightly in the belly. "How bad?"

"Bad but over." He tried another grin but worried it looked sickly. "How goes it with the drushka?"

"Pool and the other queens are taking care of business." She glanced at the sleeping humans. "Let's talk over here." He followed her along the branches until they were among Pool's drushka. Out in the swamp, lights moved here and there: the old drushka keeping an eye on them.

"Pool's been healed," Cordelia said. "Now she's communing with some of the queens. She wants to spend more time here, but she realizes we have to take the captives back to Gale."

"Is she coming back here afterward?"

Cordelia shook her head, and Horace felt her relief. "Not right away. She's going to continue to be a go-between for us and the old drushka. The old ones want Shiv to come live with them with her sapling, though. They might want her to be the new Anushi and keep Pool separate."

Horace sighed heavily, missing Shiv, too. "How do you think that'll go over?"

"Honestly?" She shrugged. "I have no idea. No matter what they say, I bet half the reason they want Shiv is for insurance, to make sure Pool doesn't plot against them. Or maybe they want to see if she's become too human or to make sure she doesn't. I feel bad for Liam."

Horace nodded, but he bet Liam wouldn't be alone for long. Maybe after enough lovers, his heart would heal, too. It seemed trivial next to the host of problems that faced them, but Horace supposed it was comforting to think of little things.

CHAPTER FOURTEEN

L ydia dreamed the future. It happened sometimes whether she'd been using her power or not. Freddie had once compared it to a wet dream without the happy ending. Lydia had laughed, but there was nothing really happy about dreaming the future. It was always some tragedy, some huge devastation shared in many futures. The last time she'd dreamed, she'd seen flames destroying Gale. Now she saw an inferno devouring the plains.

Why fire again? Irritation mixed with fear, nearly enough to wake her, but the future spiraled on. A blaze roared across the plains, driving humans, animals, and insects before it. The scene played in fits and starts, like a vid being sped up then slowed. A pack of ossors fled with unnatural speed into an orange-tinted night. A rare, stubby tree exploded in the heat, and acres of grass and shrubs were consumed and obliterated. She had to imagine the shrieks of terror and the snarl of the flames. She could never hear the future when she saw it.

But who was she following? She needed a point of contact, usually one person, so she could see the skein of their life as it unspooled. The vision slowed on a single blade of grass caught by the wind. Fire had eaten into the side, leaving a bite-mark of sorts, and glittering orange embers continued to devour until they'd nearly cut it in two.

Long fingers caught the blade of grass, squeezing it, killing the embers. Lydia's vision pulled back to see Fajir's dark hair billowing in the hellish wind. Her gray eyes narrowed against the brightness of the blaze, making her tattooed cheeks swallow the rest of her face. She drew a bone sword from her hip and marched toward the blaze. A figure lingered in front of it, man or woman, Lydia couldn't tell, and Fajir moved to confront them as everything else fled.

Fajir held determination in her shoulders and no fear in her stance. She was going to stop the destruction, Lydia knew. It seemed certain. The future leapt forward, out of her grasp, and she saw great swaths of the plains burned to a crisp but still alive. The people, the animals, they'd found their way out of their destruction, back to their lives, and that was, in some part, thanks to Fajir.

Lydia awoke with a gasp and cried out at the crick in her neck. With bleary eyes, she stared at her surroundings, blinking in the sunshine that peeked over the horizon. Samira and Mamet had wanted to be alone in the tent, and Lydia had fallen asleep outside. Her head had fallen off her arm at one point, and she'd slept at an odd angle.

She sat up, massaging her neck, the dream future alive in her mind. "Storm Lord save us," she muttered, a plea from long ago. The plains were destined to have a massive fire, and only Fajir could save them?

Lydia looked around at the camp, not yet awake in the dawning sun. Who would believe her? But it wouldn't matter if they did. The future would happen, no matter what, but she pictured the fights in front of her, the arguments with Samira and Mamet. She put her head in her hands and moaned until Samira came out of the tent behind her.

"Lydia? We only wanted to be alone for a couple hours. You didn't need to sleep out here."

"It just happened," Lydia said, rubbing the sleep from her eyes.

Samira clucked her tongue and prodded the campfire back to life. "Poor thing. I'll make you some tea."

"Has Mamet made a decision about Fajir?" Lydia asked softly, hoping the decision was to let Fajir go. She was going to be free one way or another, and being released was far better than her killing everyone in camp in order to make her escape.

"A grim question for early in the morning, don't you think?"

"I dreamed the future." She couldn't help saying it. Better to get it over with.

Samira turned slowly. "By accident?"

"It happened all the time when I was a novice. Now it seems to wait for the really big events." She tried to laugh, but frustration rose within her, and a sob escaped instead.

Samira's arms went around her. "It's all right now. It was just a—"

"It wasn't just a dream! It was the future. There's a big fire, and only Fajir can stop it!" She was crying too hard for all the words to come through, and she didn't even know why she was so emotional. Why didn't her stupid powers just leave her be? Why did they only show her bad things? She had a vision of the darkened streets of Gale, of the prog's foot landing atop Freddie. She'd seen that future and hadn't been able to stop it. Her powers never helped anything!

By the way Samira stiffened, Lydia knew her point had gotten across. It said something about Samira that she didn't let go, only paused before her hands resumed making comforting circles across Lydia's back. "It's all right now. It's all right."

"Did she say something about Fajir?" Mamet's voice asked.

"No," Samira said.

Lydia pushed away. "There's a big fire, and she saves us all." Well, maybe that was laying it on a bit thick. She wiped her cheeks.

Mamet glanced around. "There's a fire?"

"Not now. I dreamed the stupid, shitty future in which stupid, shitty Fajir saves people. Or stops someone. Other people run, and she stands and fights. That's what I saw. The future isn't always clear, but what I see happens, so there'll be a fire, and she will work to stop it." She took a deep breath and gulped air, trying to calm down.

Mamet looked stunned. Samira frowned. "If we let her go…"

"There is no if!" Lydia shouted. Other people were stirring now, some calling to ask what the problem was. Lydia lowered her voice. "You don't get it. It's not a decision you have to make anymore, Mamet. She will be loose. I've seen it. It's fixed. It is *going to happen.*" She stood and paced in a tight circle. "Damn it!"

Samira and Mamet glanced at each other as if each wanted to call Lydia crazy but wasn't sure they should. She took several calming breaths. Dreaming the future was bringing back memories of Gale, of the boggins and Freddie, and she fought the urge to drown in them.

"It doesn't matter if you believe me or not," Lydia said, swallowing tears again. "I shouldn't expect anyone to understand, I know."

Samira shot to her feet. "We can't let her go."

Lydia sighed, but before she could argue, Mamet asked, "Did you see what I did in the future, Lydia?"

"I just know that Fajir will get loose one way or another."

Samira frowned hard. "Why don't I kill her and see if the future stops me?"

Lydia stepped aside, one hand toward Fajir's tent. "Go ahead."

Samira stalked past her. Mamet looked between them as if wondering what she should do.

"Relax," Lydia said. "She's not going to kill anyone."

Mamet seemed as if she had a question but didn't ask. Lydia hoped she'd decide to ride far into the plains and release Fajir there so no one else got hurt. Maybe they'd let her go right before the fire started, and she'd have to deal with that rather than hunt anyone down. Lydia hadn't seen her kill any plains dwellers, so maybe there was a way to keep her from doing so.

Like follow her. Watch her. Lydia's stomach went cold, even as she felt a touch of hope. She'd dreamed the future. Maybe she could see it through, minimize any damage.

Freddie would have liked that.

Samira paused outside Fajir's tent and glared as if she could flay Fajir alive through the leather with just her gaze. She looked over her shoulder at where Mamet and Lydia waited. Her hands clenched and unclenched. Lydia couldn't help a smile. She'd always said that killing a person in battle was one thing, killing a captive was another.

Lydia pulled Mamet closer to Samira, trying to think of a way to follow Fajir once she was loose. Samira would be against it, might even go so far as to sit on Lydia if she tried to get caught in Fajir's wake.

Samira seemed as if she might speak but looked at the side of the tent instead. Lydia followed her gaze. One of the tent pegs had been pulled from the ground. Lydia looked to the other side. Another peg was loose, and it seemed as if the tent sagged a bit in the middle.

Lydia went still. Now; it was going to happen now. "Where's Fajir's bone sword?"

"Um." Mamet looked around. "Rene had it yesterday." He gestured to an ossor waiting outside a nearby tent. It carried a saddle and bags as well as the sword, packed for a hunt. Rene must have loaded it early and was now getting ready in his tent. He hadn't even bothered to secure the ossor to the ground. It stood docile, waiting.

Lydia smiled, not bothering to look into the future when she could see it this plainly in the present. "Perfect." She squeezed Mamet's hand. "Everything's going to be okay."

Mamet smiled. "Thanks, but I—"

Samira bent and picked up a tent peg. "Did you see this? Who knocked over—"

Lydia held her breath.

A shape lurched up from under the tent, throwing the heavy leather. It landed on Samira, and Fajir fled into the plains. Her hands were still bound, but now they were in front of her, and she ran like the wind.

The tent billowed as Samira thrashed inside. She cried out and fell. Mamet went to help, and Lydia ran for the supply-laden ossor. She climbed into the saddle, stuck her feet under the bug's vestigial wings, and prodded it after Fajir. People were wandering out of their tents, probably roused by the noise. Fajir disappeared over a rise. Lydia drew the bone sword as she rode. If anyone wanted to chase them, they'd have to dress and saddle more ossors.

Lydia wouldn't have thought Fajir would be so swift. She'd seemed haggard and weak when they caught her, but she'd clearly found her second wind. Or maybe she'd heard some of the talk about keeping her alive. Now she streaked through the grass, leaping over ditches and rocks. Lydia lost sight of her twice and had to change direction. Fajir slid down a steep slope, and Lydia pulled the ossor to a halt so it wouldn't fall.

A narrow gash led downward, hiding a deeper ravine cut by some ancient river. Lydia kicked her ossor again and followed from above as Fajir ran along the dry riverbed below. The riverbed forked, and Lydia was forced to pull up short as Fajir took the branch leading away from her. She cursed and sheathed the sword before kneeing her ossor harder. The ravine had to come up sometime, and she rode hard, following the track until the ground leveled again. No Fajir. Lydia stopped, turning in all directions.

Nothing. "Damn."

She didn't hear any other sounds of pursuit, but the Engali would track them. Maybe she should go back. If she could find her way. The ossor shied and keened. She wondered if it was as frustrated as she felt.

Lydia felt a rush of air behind her, but before she could turn or focus her power, Fajir collided with her, knocking the wind out of her. They fell in a tangle, and Lydia grunted as she hit the ground. Fajir's bound wrists ground her face into the dirt, and she squealed.

Lydia fought down panic. She twisted, sending an elbow back into Fajir's ribs. When Fajir grunted, the pressure on Lydia's head eased. Lydia bucked, managing a half turn. She threw a wild punch and scored a hit somewhere soft. Fajir's weight lifted, and Lydia scrambled up, running for the ossor.

Lydia drew the bone sword and turned, but Fajir hadn't moved from the ground. She breathed hard, and whatever energy she'd summoned seemed to have abandoned her. She probably hadn't slept at all in the Engali camp, and she'd refused all offers of food and water.

"Get up," Lydia said.

Fajir didn't respond except to glare. With the tattoos, her face seemed skeletal and dangerous, even when she was exhausted and starved.

"I said, get up!"

"Kill me," Fajir said.

Lydia frowned hard. "I was the prophet of Gale. Do you know what that means? I can see the future, and last night, I dreamed yours. You don't die here today. You have a future, a job to do, and I'm not going to let you hurt innocent people while you do it!"

Fajir's face scrunched up. "What?"

"You're going to save the plains."

Fajir stared before sputtering a laugh that turned into a guffaw, and then she was rolling on the ground, cackling away.

Heat rose in Lydia's cheeks. "Shut up! Do you want to be caught by the Engali again?"

Fajir only laughed harder.

Lydia sighed. No one ever believed her, but people didn't usually act like this. "The Engali don't keep prisoners. Usually. They were going to make an exception for you."

Fajir's laughter faded away, and she went back to glaring.

"Since you wanted to die so badly, they thought it would be a better punishment to keep you alive and haul you from camp to camp, force-feeding you if necessary. You'd live a long, unhappy life."

Fajir scrambled to her feet so fast, Lydia took a step back and held the sword out. "You lie!" Fajir cried.

"I can see the future, remember?" And she hadn't seen all that, but it had gotten Fajir to stand.

"Why should I believe you?" She sneered. "Are you my nemesis, born only to torture me? You can kill me now, or I can kill you. It makes no difference."

Even with her power, Lydia didn't think she could take on Fajir, but a little proof of power might be in order. She looked a bit into the future, saw herself leading with the sword, and saw how Fajir would react. Lydia lunged, and when Fajir darted to her right, Lydia stabbed into her path before she had even finished the move. Fajir avoided the strike. Barely. Her eyes widened.

Lydia fell into her power again and saw Fajir feint to the left. She thrust that way, nicking Fajir's arm.

"I told you," Lydia said. "I can look seconds into the future and see what you're going to do. You can't beat me." Again, probably not true, but she pretended with all her might.

Fajir went still as if considering. "How will I save the plains when my hands are bound, and you're holding my own sword to my throat?"

Lydia thought fast. She'd hadn't really believed she'd get Fajir to listen at all. Now she had to think of a plan? "First…we get away from the Engali." So Fajir couldn't kill them, but she didn't add that. She mounted the ossor and gestured with the sword. "March. You might want to die, but I don't think you want to be cut to ribbons first." She put a growl in her voice, even though the thought of torturing someone sickened her.

Fajir lifted one eyebrow as she began walking. "How fearsome you are, Nemesis. Tell me, do you know what a *shirka* is?"

"Less talking, more walking."

Fajir glanced over her shoulder, smirk in place. "They are dancers, and each month, they open their stages to amateurs. They do so on the half moon, so the Lady only has to watch with one eye. As I look at you, I know it must be the half moon tonight."

Lydia snorted a laugh. "That's fair. I am an amateur, and I don't want to torture you, but I will defend myself. And I *can* see the future. The question is, do you want to ride toward it with your eyes open or be dragged into it like a petrified *shirka* with stage fright?"

Fajir didn't respond, and Lydia hoped she'd gotten through a little bit. She'd have to keep her own eyes open, that was for damn sure.

❖

The mayor's house was easier to stretch out in, much larger than Dillon's apartment in the Yafanai Temple. Lyshus and Little Paul seemed interested in exploring, particularly the staircase that led to the second floor bedrooms. Simon left Pakesh in charge of watching them while he sought a place for Evan. There was no crib in the house, so he settled for pulling out a drawer from a cabinet, putting a blanket inside, and laying Evan there. Shiv and her little tree found a room with a window.

Jacobs had gone to speak to her fellow paladins about setting up guard shifts around the house. It seemed a quiet neighborhood, and Simon hoped it would stay that way. One of the neighbors had told him that the house had been vacant since Paul Ross was murdered nine months ago.

Simon wandered around, happy to see the place so tidy. Evidently, a group of neighbors had banded together to keep it clean. Maybe they'd been keeping it ready for a new mayor, but Dillon hadn't held elections. Rumor had it that he wanted to keep all the power for himself. In reality, he probably hadn't noticed there needed to be an election. As long as the city was running, Dillon didn't ask how it got done. Simon was just happy one of the neighbors had agreed to send a message to Mila so she could feed Evan. Gale was a gossipy town, and he had no doubt that everyone would soon know where he was, but he wanted to keep that information to as few people as possible for as long as possible.

The nosy neighbors seemed happy to have someone famous nearby. Their compliments had made him blush, but any words were better than effigies and someone chucking a bottle at his head. They also told him the house was haunted by the ghost of Paul Ross. He'd done his best not to laugh, but after they left, the idea seeped in enough to give him the creeps.

Almost against his will, Simon went toward the study, the place where Paul Ross had died. Dillon had killed him with electrokinesis, then stabbed the body to cover up the crime. Simon had lied about the cause of death to Cordelia, telling her only about the stabbing, helping Dillon out of misplaced loyalty. It wasn't until he'd accepted that Dillon had become a murderer that he knew he'd never help Dillon again.

At least not willingly. Bastard.

After Simon took a deep breath, he opened the study door slowly, expecting to see a bloodstain on the wall, but someone had cleaned that, too. They hadn't repaired the crack in the plaster, though. Maybe that was all the reminder anyone needed. Simon shut the door again, hoping that if any of Paul Ross's spirit did linger, he'd keep himself to the one room.

He only had to wait a little while before Miriam and Mila arrived in a rickshaw. In the meantime, a man named Private Hought arrived to guard his door, and several more neighbors dropped by. Simon was never so glad to see Miriam and asked her if she wouldn't mind answering the door while she was there. Maybe she was better at shooing people away.

She regarded him with her usual flat look, then turned to survey the street, smiling when several watchers waved. "Trouble already?" she asked.

"I never know how to put people off without coming off as either threatening or timid."

"Aim for disinterested," she said. "It's all in the eyes."

Mila barked a laugh. "Where's your lovely baby?"

Simon fetched him, and Mila sat at the kitchen table to feed him. Simon rooted around until he found some tea, then began brewing a pot. Miriam leaned against a counter and watched him with her dark, piercing eyes. She could look far from disinterested when she wanted.

"Can you find some mugs?" he asked, anything to get her gaze off him.

She turned to the cupboards. "Well, at least there won't be any random yafanai running around here. You'll be able to see them coming. Or the neighbors will."

He snorted a laugh. "Until the yafanai burrow into their minds and try to take their heads off."

"True."

He gave her a sharp look to see if she was joking, but she was still searching. She found and stacked some mugs on the counter, then rubbed her large belly as if even that small motion pained her.

Simon hung a kettle over the fire. "Can I help?" He turned and held a hand toward her but didn't touch her, not without permission.

After raising an eyebrow, she nodded. He put a hand on her lightly. He didn't need to touch her at all, but it seemed to startle people less if he touched them before using his power. As a yafanai, maybe Miriam was used to it. He soothed the fetus inside, then relieved the twinge in Miriam's back and the ache in her knees and feet.

She took a deep, satisfied breath. "Thank you."

"You're welcome." He kept from giving her a gratified smile. Instead, he took the mugs to the table.

Mila grinned. "I could use a shot of those healing hands if you don't mind."

"I'm sorry! I should have realized." He grazed her hand and soothed her aches. Breastfeeding never seemed like the easiest thing in the world, no matter what anyone said, and healing was easier than chitchat. "Better?"

She nodded and smiled at Evan. "I'll have to bring my Kena over for a playdate."

Simon sat, dumbfounded. Playdates. He was planning playdates for Dillon's children. He shook his head, trying to escape the absurdity of it all. He pictured all the yafanai mothers in this house with their children, Dillon's children, playing together. He supposed he could do worse than a cadre of yafanai as close friends. No one could sneak up on him then.

"And the rest of the mothers?" he asked.

"One died in childbirth while you and the renegades were gone for months," Miriam said. "Then Mila had her baby. The next is due any day now."

The first statement gutted him so hard, he couldn't really process the others. Died in childbirth? So long after humanity had solved that problem? But this wasn't Earth, and even with yafanai, things went wrong. Mila seemed sad, but Miriam didn't seem fazed. They must not have been close.

"Any…any day now?" he asked. "Who?" He could do nothing for the dead but grieve, though guilt would come looking for him later no matter the facts.

"Victoria," Miriam said. "She wasn't there when we confronted you. She's overdue now and doesn't move unless she has to."

"Why didn't she ask for help?" He tried to swallow his indignation.

Mila snorted. "Victoria doesn't ever ask for help. She's a pyrokinetic. Rare powers like hers think they're above it all."

Miriam chuckled. Simon nodded slowly, digesting that. Pyros and prophets were rare, followed by micro-psychokinetics. Macros were a little more common, but telepathy was the most common power. Maybe they were the yafanai who made friends easily. He looked to Miriam. Or not. But electrokinesis was the rarest power of them all. Only Dillon had it, and he loved talking to people. Well, as long as they kissed his ass. Or any other part of him.

Simon fetched the kettle and poured hot water into a ready teapot. The unnamed woman who'd died in childbirth kept rattling around in Simon's mind, and when they'd finished the tea, he asked if he could go with them to the temple.

Mila said, "Of course!" but Miriam gave him another strange look.

"To see Victoria?" she asked. "We still don't know who attacked you." She rolled her eyes. "Though I would have recognized Victoria. Still, you want to risk it?"

"I won't bring Evan this time," he said. "Pakesh will have to come, but Shiv will be here to watch Evan, not to mention the nosy neighbors." And the ghost of Paul Ross, but he didn't say that. The idea made him shudder, and he told himself not to be an idiot.

On the way out, they met Jacobs, and she tagged along. Once at the temple, Miriam led them straight to Victoria's door. Miriam knocked, and a weary voice called for them to come in before muttering something else.

"We'll wait out here, Doc," Jacobs said, nodding to Pakesh.

He nodded and followed Miriam inside. The room was nearly dark, and a tiny woman with an enormously round belly sat on a sofa, her feet up, and her head lolling over the sofa arm.

"What do you want, Miriam?" she asked. "I just got to sleep."

"I brought you some help, you ungrateful hoshpi." Miriam went to the shutters and opened them, letting in the light.

Victoria squinted. Her reddish brown hair was an untidy mess, and her eyes looked unfocused. "It's too bright!"

Miriam ignored her, and Victoria turned her half-hearted glare on Simon. He had a flash of the graffiti he'd seen about pretenders burning, but this woman didn't look as if she'd climbed any buildings with a can of paint lately.

"Well?" Victoria asked. "Are you going to tell me why you're disturbing me or linger until I explode under my own weight?"

"Oh, give it a rest, Victoria," Miriam said, entirely without malice.

"Stuff it, you old prog," Victoria said, still eyeing Simon.

"I'm…here to help you," he said.

"You already healed me when you healed everyone else."

"With your baby."

She eyed him skeptically and looked to her belly. "I'm starting to think no one can help me."

"Let him try, Vic," Miriam said. "He does wonders."

"Well." She brightened a bit and waved him forward. For two people who weren't rumored to spend time with each other, these two seemed very comfortable. Maybe they were the only two who could stand each other's company.

Simon sat, and Victoria's expression changed, becoming almost demure as she batted her eyelashes. Her bright green eyes were a pleasant contrast to the dark shadows underneath them. "I didn't know that I rated your personal attention."

"Save it, Vic," Miriam said. "He's not going to fall under your sway."

Victoria glared over Simon's shoulder. "Because he didn't fall under yours? That just proves he's *discerning*."

Miriam sat on the other edge of the sofa. "She could manipulate the Storm Lord with those hooded eyes. Gave me quite the laugh."

Simon had to smile, happy someone could do to Dillon what he often did to everyone else. "Well, that alone rates some assistance."

Victoria sighed deeply. "Oh good. I'm too tired to flirt anyway."

He held a hand over her. "May I?"

"Might as well. You can't make it any worse."

He sent his power easing through her, soothing the same pains he'd felt in Miriam, but he couldn't do anything to ease the pressure of the child except deaden the nerves. Victoria smiled at him gloriously, and he saw how a man like Dillon could be swayed by her. It nearly made him blush.

"Well…" He cleared his throat. "Want to deliver today? Completely painless, I guarantee it."

Her jaw dropped. His scans told him the child was healthy

and ready for the outside world. Fear came from Victoria as well as excitement, but whether it was the pain of childbirth or the lifetime of motherhood that scared her, he couldn't say.

Miriam was looking at him in wonder, too. "Do it, Vic," she said. "Why not?"

"You just want to see what he can do for you when it's your turn, greedy guts!"

Simon cleared his throat. "Do you want us to call your friends?"

"No." But her gaze flicked toward Miriam.

"I'll stay," Miriam said. "If she pees herself, I want to be the first to know so I can tell everyone."

Victoria snorted. "Then you should have been here the last time I waddled for the chamber pot and didn't make it." She turned and Miriam helped her up.

Simon looked around the room. It was as good a place as any. "The bed will probably be the most comfortable place. Caroline gave birth in a special room…"

Victoria waved that away. "Here's fine. What do you need me to do?"

He gestured to her clothing. "Well, taking off everything from the waist down is essential. Everything else is up to you."

She barked a laugh. "That's not the way the Storm Lord tempted me to bed, but it's compelling all the same."

Simon fought another blush. He turned away as Miriam helped Victoria undress and lie on the bed. Miriam got a few more blankets out of a closet and pulled them under her, no doubt hoping to save the mattress. Victoria arranged herself on the pillows.

"Going to stay for the whole show, Miriam?" Victoria's voice shook slightly as if she feared Miriam would say no. "Want to see how it's done?"

"Or what not to do. Though it's hard to ignore your odious personality."

Simon fought the urge to roll his eyes and tell them to get a room. He didn't even need to read their feelings to see their obvious admiration for each other. Samira would have laughed at their need to cover their feelings. He guided Victoria to the end of the bed, making it easier for himself as he knelt. He let his power play over her, calming her nerves before he started the contractions.

She took a deep breath. "I feel it, but…"

"It doesn't hurt?" Miriam asked, an anxious quality in her voice.

"No!"

Simon lifted the end of her long shirt, and she parted her legs. He began to dilate her slowly and spread the towels around her as he guided the amniotic fluid forth.

"Ready?" he asked.

"I…"

"She's ready," Miriam said.

"Push." He helped, and just as with Evan, the baby eased out under his power. He tried not to think of the woman who'd died, tried to keep his focus on the here and now. He remembered every moment of Evan's birth but tried not to think of Caroline and how she'd died, either, how he'd killed her.

Victoria grunted, and Simon cursed himself for the pain that came through. He focused all his attention on the baby girl sliding into his arms and thanked every deity that had ever been that this one wouldn't be his responsibility also.

He cleared the baby's nose and mouth, and she wailed. Victoria was staring as if she couldn't believe it. Simon wrapped the baby in towels and placed it on her chest before taking care of the afterbirth. Miriam helped Victoria sit farther back on the bed, and Simon wrapped up the soiled sheets and towels, pushing them to the side before he washed his hands in a nearby basin.

"I'm sorry, but I'm not available to babysit," he said.

Victoria laughed, and it had a little hysteria in it. He sent another calming wave her way.

"What's her name?" Miriam asked, a rare smile on her face.

"Evelyn," Victoria said. "I thought it might go with Evan."

Simon sighed. So she cared about Dillon enough to make sure his children's names matched. Or maybe that was just Simon being petty. "Keep a close eye on her."

"I already told her about the attack," Miriam said.

Victoria nodded, but she appeared unconcerned. Maybe she had a lot of faith in her power. "I might stay with some friends."

Miriam snorted.

Victoria gave her a look. "I have friends!" When Miriam didn't respond, Victoria caught Simon's arm, her expression intense. "Thank you for a taste of that pain, of seeing what I would've gone through if you hadn't been here."

"Sorry, I—"

She squeezed his arm. "If you need me, call."

He nodded and fought a rush of emotion. Maybe being the patron saint of pregnant women wouldn't be so bad.

CHAPTER FIFTEEN

Patricia sat on her bed with her head in her hands, trying to think. She'd sent Jonah away. She couldn't stand Dillon's muttering when his body was walking around without him. After Dillon urged her again to find a host for him, Patricia stood and paced.

"If I kill someone else's consciousness and let you have their body, I'll just be fucking someone over with my power again. Isn't that what you told me not to do?"

He was silent for a moment, and she knew he was trying to think of a way to weasel out of his former words. At last, he sighed. "So put me back in my old body. It wasn't perfect, but it was home."

Patricia sagged against the wall. "I can't do that! Jonah is his own person now. And he's the only one who..." She couldn't say it.

"Cares about you?" Dillon asked with a sneer. "Don't make me laugh, sweets."

She curled a hand into a fist but didn't bother to argue. He didn't understand. She'd made Jonah, true, but he'd become real since then. She'd created his memories and reinforced them so many times, it was hard not to believe them herself. She resisted the urge to cry and took a deep breath. "I'd have to wipe Jonah's brain, your body's brain, in order to put you back. I left some of your memories with him, about defenses and whatnot, but I don't know if I'd be able to tell between the memories that are yours and those that I made up." She sighed. "And I don't know what that much tinkering could do to a mind."

"Don't give me that shit. You can fix whatever you break."

"That's true only to a point. Something mended is never as good as something brand new. I might…break you, fix you, but then you might keep breaking after that. I'm guessing you're not going to want to stick around here so I can keep your brain running, right?"

He grumbled again, something about not wanting to be a vegetable.

"There has to be another way." She'd spoken the truth about fixing him, but she didn't want to lose Jonah, not if she could help it. "Maybe we can find someone who's lost their mind because of natural causes."

"However long that takes," Dillon said.

She grimaced. Waiting for an accident that caused brain death or irreparable psychological damage felt…repugnant.

Jonah banged through the door, and Patricia nearly lashed out with her power. She kept it in check, barely; she needed to find her calm again.

"Mistress." Jonah frowned, his expression taut and angry. "Some plains dwellers have arrived, demanding to speak with you. The miners are holding them outside the wall, but we can get rid of them if you wish."

Patricia brushed the hair out of her face and smiled, grateful for a distraction. "I'll take care of them."

He led her to the wall where a group of plains dwellers were making noise. Ten men and women, they stood surrounded by trading goods such as heaps of skins and leather. A geaver stood in the distance, held by another plains dweller. Raquel's hill dwellers gathered behind the rowdy ten, watching with stoic faces, but the miners were frowning at some of the taunts leveled their way.

"Where is this mighty mistress?" one of the new plains dwellers called. "Is she afraid to face us?"

The crowd opened for Patricia, and she smiled at the group of yahoos bellowing at her gate. This was going to be fun. "I hear you've come to speak with me."

The plains dwellers peered at her then laughed. A fellow with dark hair braided in two plaits stepped to the front. "I'm Chafa Neale," he said, eyeing her up and down with a smirk. "Are your parents about, little one?"

The rest laughed, slapping one another on the shoulder as if the question was the funniest thing they'd ever heard.

Patricia smiled wider. "They're dead. They left me in charge."

Chafa Neale's eyes widened, but he shook his head and stroked his thick beard. After another look at his fellows, he put a foot on top of a bundle of skins and leaned toward her. "Well, little chafa," he said slowly, "my clan has come to trade. Do you know what that is?"

Dillon barked a laugh in Patricia's mind. "He's showing you his crotch a bit early in the game, if you ask me. And the condescension is a classic asshole move. If you get angry or embarrassed, he automatically gets the upper hand."

"Lucky for us," Patricia thought. "I'm not as young as I look." She readied her power, eager to turn this grinning idiot's swagger into worship.

"Just a second," Dillon said. "Don't bull your way through this with telepathy. He's just some asshole trying to push your buttons. Find his and push back."

Patricia considered for half a second before putting on a smirk and looking pointedly at where Neale's trousers stretched tight across the front. "I don't deal with *small* timers."

"Nice," Dillon said.

Neale frowned, but some of his clan members sniggered. He put his foot down and crossed his arms. "Small-time trade is all a girl like you will get."

"He's defensive. Good," Dillon said. "Now you've got to prove you have the biggest dick out here."

"Yes," she thought. "He's sitting in my head."

Dillon laughed, and Patricia smiled wider. She gestured to her followers and the mountain behind her. "Everyone will want to trade with us soon enough." She nodded at one of the miners. "Show the man what we've got."

The crowd shuffled, and the miner brought forth a hunk of iron ore.

Chafa Neale stared. His tongue poked out but darted back quickly, as if he was going to lick his lips but thought better of it. Anticipation roiled off him like cheap cologne.

"Perfect," Dillon said.

Neale shrugged, pretending he wasn't impressed.

"Fine." Patricia waved again, and the miner took the ore back into the crowd.

Neale smiled awkwardly. "Now, now, young lady. Let's not put the goods away just yet."

"You will call her Mistress," Jonah said, his voice low and dangerous.

"Mistress." Neale's smile grew brittle. "What are you asking for the ore?"

"See, sweets," Dillon said. "He's baited and hooked, and you didn't have to use any power."

She reveled in a jolt of pride. "Didn't you hear Jonah?" she thought. "I'm called mistress. Or Patricia."

Dillon chuckled, low and deep, and she felt a shiver of lust, but it wasn't forced, just a natural reaction.

They negotiated for close to an hour. When Neale and his group left, they seemed happy enough, and word would spread. Maybe Neale would even tell people she wouldn't be fucked with when they came to buy her ore.

When another group showed up later that afternoon, Patricia nearly ran to the gate. She hadn't expected another visit so soon, but she was happy to have something to do, happy to be able to flex her negotiating muscles.

Jonah met her halfway. "It's a contingent from Gale, Mistress."

Patricia skidded to a halt. She knew someone from Gale would come sooner or later. This was their mine, after all. Her mind raced as she tried to think of what to do. She supposed a show of force was necessary.

"No," Dillon said. "Not yet. Leave them guessing. Tell them they can't come in. See what they do."

She frowned. "Are you trying to make them angry enough that they'll eventually defeat me for you?"

"You die, I die. Remember?"

As long as he remembered that, they'd have no trouble. While she and Jonah stayed hidden, her followers told the group from Gale that they couldn't come in, that the mine was under new management. She laughed a little at that. When the Galeans demanded to see the person in charge, the guards told them no. If they wanted metal, they'd have to trade like anyone else. After a bit of discussion, the group went away. They clearly hadn't expected to find resistance, but next time, she bet they'd be prepared.

"See?" Dillon said. "You didn't have to use your power, and they're still in the dark."

"I'll have to use it eventually."

"Like I said, you only have to convince them you have the biggest dick. You don't have to actually swing it around."

"Lovely image," Patricia muttered. She turned to the man who'd spoken to the Galeans. He'd repeated her words just as instructed and proved to be a good speaker. He seemed to know where to put the right inflections, the right tones of boredom or menace.

He smiled back at her. A handsome man, he was somewhere in his forties, though his grin made him seem younger.

"Well done," she said.

"Thank you, Mistress. I'm used to dealing with difficult, bullnecked people."

"Are you a foreman?" Though if he was, she should have already met him.

"No, not here! Everyone here is a picnic compared to my ex in Gale." He put a hand to his chest. "Wyn Gallway."

Patricia was about to introduce herself but stopped. He already knew who she was. She began walking back to camp, and Wyn fell in step beside her. Jonah gave him a frown, but Patricia laughed that off. Maybe it was time she had more normal conversations, more practice talking to people without using her power. "Did you come to the mine to get away from this ex?"

"I'd love to say no, but…" He shrugged. "We weren't getting along. And she'd become captain of the paladins when I left, so she could have made life really hard for me."

"Captain Brown or Carmichael?" Dillon asked in Patricia's mind, not sounding pleased by either idea.

"How long have you been here?" she asked aloud, thinking that a less suspicious way to get the answer.

"Oh, about twenty years now, I expect."

"Carmichael, then," Dillon said. "Good."

"Why do you care?" Patricia asked in her mind. "Didn't you kill both?"

"Yeah, but I was happy to kill Carmichael. Brown was…an accident."

She wondered why that mattered. Wyn clearly didn't care about his ex. Why should Dillon care how he felt? But she couldn't go poking around in Dillon's memories anymore, not without him knowing, at least, and that might lead to another battle of wills.

Wyn was still talking. "Shame I had to leave my baby boy," he said. "I hoped he'd come up to the mine someday, but I guess I wouldn't recognize him if he did." He smiled sadly. "Little Liam. I hope he turned out happy."

"Liam Carmichael!" Dillon said. "That bastard shot me in Gale *and* on the plains!"

Patricia winced at the volume. "Excuse me, Wyn. I have a headache."

He mumbled pleasantries as she hurried away. Jonah stayed with her and cast a glance at Wyn over his shoulder. "Would you like me to shut him up for good, Mistress?"

"No, Jonah," Patricia said, thinking about Dillon's "swinging dicks" comment. "Everything's fine." But Dillon was still grumbling about Liam Carmichael, and she knew nothing would stay fine forever.

❖

Shiv liked the big house much better than the group of three rooms. Here she could stretch, and there were many pieces of furniture to look through, many clothes and baubles to examine. Evan was safe in his little bed, and Lyshus and Little Paul were entertaining each other. As a bonus, several humans had stopped by and spoken with her, offering their aid. Many spoke of Reach with fondness. Even with the pungent odor of soap, the scent of her still lingered here and there, a comfort.

When Shiv asked the visiting humans for tales of the area, they were happy to oblige, and Shiv found many of them entertaining. Of particular interest were stories of who had taken whom for a lover and why. The humans never seemed to tire of speculating. To Shiv, it seemed they lived on a very busy street, and she wondered how anyone had time for anything but being a lover. If she had to settle with the humans, perhaps she should stay on a street like this. They seemed to find all lovers temporary, seemed content to share, perhaps. They might understand that a queen could never belong to any one person.

She tried to put such thoughts out of her mind. As Simon had said, she could not worry about her fate or that of Lyshus until Shi'a'na returned with the tribe. Perhaps Simon was right, and Shi'a'na could fix Lyshus, make him a regular drushka even if that meant she would be alone. But she would never be truly alone, as Simon said. She would have him and Cordelia, would have Liam if he agreed. She would become like Reach, ahya, and learn all about the humans so she could take that knowledge to the drushka. The idea did not make her entirely happy or sad, but such conflicted feelings seemed the heart of being a queen.

She sat on the staircase in the quiet house, wishing one of the neighboring humans would come speak with her again. As the day had worn on to evening, they had stopped, though some had brought food for the evening meal. Perhaps the humans were all settling down together. Shiv had hoped some would come to eat with her, but alas.

She remembered what some had said, that the spirits of the dead still roamed this house. It seemed a silly thing to her. The dead were… dead. They were not like Sa Cordelia, who could leave her body then return. They were at an end. But the idea seemed to frighten some of the neighbors and intrigued others. One, a man named Minh, had asked her for a "tour" of the house, and when she understood he simply wanted to wander around, she agreed. He had already passed under the scowl of Private Hought. When she let him in, Minh seemed frightened to wander alone. She had gone with him as he recounted how the former occupant, Reach's lover, had met a bloody end and still roamed the halls at night.

It had been difficult not to laugh, but she had managed. Sa would have praised her diplomacy. In the end, Minh had amused her so much that she had told him to call for her if anything else frightened him. He had said his downstairs neighbor was a "bully" who scared him from time to time. Shiv had promised to fight by his side if needed.

Minh had smiled widely at her before he left, seemingly touched by the promise. The encounter had stirred a feeling inside her, not unlike her attachment to Lyshus, though with a human, she could never complete the bonding ritual of tribe to queen. She could not communicate with him telepathically, but that did not stop this feeling in her chest, that they had pledged themselves to each other. As Shi'a'na had collected many humans into her tribe, so Shiv felt connected to Minh, as if he was her tribe.

She tried to shake the feeling away as she went through the house lighting candles and lanterns. She took Little Paul and Lyshus to a long table near the front of the house and bade them sit and eat. She brought Evan's bed to ensure all was well with him. Mila had already come to see him and told her Simon Lazlo was still at the temple. Shiv hoped he would be back before dark. His enemies could more easily hurt him in the night.

A worrisome thought. Shiv felt connected to him, too, but it seemed more personal than what she felt for Minh. Simon was connected to Shi'a'na, both in body and spirit. He was only a friend of Shiv's body, though he also eased her mind. If she did not have the human children to look after, she would meet him, and they could keep a watchful eye together.

But his enemies might come here, too. If she had been alone, the thought would have excited her, but she remembered her anger at someone attacking Evan, her worry for Lyshus and Little Paul, and how hard it had been to carry all of them and her sapling. The house suddenly seemed too large, too dark. There were too many corners to hide in.

Feeling nervous, she called to her sapling and felt it totter forth from a bedroom upstairs.

Lyshus lifted his head from his meal and stared at her. The food was meager. He could not eat the breads and grains humans thrived on. Simon had gotten them some meat and plants, but not many.

"Soon, Lyshus," she said. "There will be more meat."

He wrinkled his nose, not understanding the words but appreciating the sentiment.

"I like pie," Little Paul said. He had already eaten one of the sweet breads and reached for another.

She helped him take it. "It is good to be happy." When he smiled, she knew she had done the right thing for him. "I must help my sapling down the stairs. I will return."

Lyshus followed her, which meant Little Paul followed, too. Shiv sighed but thought on her earlier words. It was good to be happy, and if following her kept them happy, so be it. And Little Paul was human. Maybe thoughts of the wandering dead upset him as much as it did Minh, and he did not like to be alone. She mounted the steps to grasp the limbs of her tree. It slipped, and Shiv knelt to push it upright, not wanting it to fall. Lyshus darted under her, into the sapling's path, and laid a palm upon the trunk.

"Lyshus!" Shiv said. "Back away. If it falls…" The words choked off as a new feeling raced through her, a jolt of energy that careened through her tree. The very air seemed to pulse, and the tree swelled under her hands, growing. Its branches creaked as it gained a full foot in height, becoming taller than her. With longer roots and branches, it steadied itself on the staircase and did not need her aid.

Shiv stared in wonder. The power had not come from her. She looked to Lyshus as he stood back, a grin on his lips that he turned on her, wrinkling his nose away. A shawness? Possible, but they did not show their powers until they could talk, could sing, and then other shawnessi taught them. Lyshus had not spoken a word. And she had never seen a shawness make a tree grow. She looked to Lyshus's hair, still dyed, but she knew what lay underneath. He was a queen like her, but she could not make her tree grow through will alone.

But she was a queen born of another queen, and he was her tribe of one. There had to be a reason that even Shiv's existence was counted as forbidden. Who knew what Lyshus could do with his will?

❖

Simon had visited all the pregnant women in the temple again, making sure they were well. Thoughts of the one who'd died kept running through his head, but it hadn't seemed right to ask her name, not from any pregnant women. He bet she was on all of their minds.

Pakesh followed him, looking bored, though he chatted from time to time with Jacobs. He'd been practicing keeping his own shields tight, putting Simon's mind at ease while he focused on helping people. Night was beginning to fall, by the time Simon had checked on everyone; time to get home and relieve Shiv. He needed to look in on Victoria one more time.

Pakesh stopped him before he reached the door. "I smell smoke."

Simon turned, and the acrid scent drifted across his nose, too.

"Cooking?" Jacobs asked.

"We're a long way from the kitchen." Maybe someone's lantern had gotten away from them? Whatever the cause, Simon and the others knocked on everyone's door as they went down the hall and told them to move toward the nearest exit.

"I need to make sure Victoria is all right." Simon couldn't stop thinking of the mother who'd died in childbirth. None of the others could die, not as long as he could help it. "Jacobs, Pakesh, maybe you should go."

"Not leaving you, Doc," she said.

Pakesh shook his head. Whether he didn't want to abandon Simon or he was too afraid of his power getting loose, Simon couldn't say, but he appreciated the company.

As they rushed, the smoke thickened, threading through the hall like wandering spirits. Simon pushed his sleeve to his nose and tried to fight down panic. He called for Miriam in his head, as loudly as he could, but he had no idea if he was getting through. He cursed his lack of telepathy, and not for the first time.

Jacobs called, "Fire!" as they broke into a jog. "Where is it coming from?"

Everywhere seemed the answer. A group of people were coming up behind them, all of them chattering in panic.

"Not this way!" Jacobs yelled. "We're heading deeper in. Find a way out."

"The entrance is on fire!"

"Damn," Simon turned in a circle, trying to remember the way to the kitchens, the back door, but more people came down an intersecting hallway through a cloud of smoke.

"The kitchen is on fire!" someone yelled.

Both entrances blocked. Someone was trying to burn them alive. Simon's stomach cramped, and he remembered the graffiti, the bottle.

"Go out the windows!" Jacobs yelled. "Wherever you can!"

Simon's throat burned, and he coughed, using his powers to help himself, to help everyone. "Stay low!"

They opened doors and finally found a shuttered window. With a unified cry, a surge of people pressed toward it, but Simon spotted an orange glow around the edges and the smoke that billowed through the cracks. "Wait!"

Ignoring him, someone threw the shutters open, and fire billowed inside with a roar. The crowd staggered back, screaming. The courtyard was on fire, too.

"Enough!" Simon punched through the crowd with his power. Calming waves weren't going to do the trick anymore. He interrupted them almost as much as he once had a group of attacking paladins, nearly shutting down their ability to produce and process fear.

"Everyone into the hall," he shouted. "Macros, push away the smoke. Micros, use your power together to help everyone breathe. Telepaths, contact everyone you can find and tell them to look for a way out. If they can't find one, come to us."

Two people staggered out of the smoke ahead, Victoria and Miriam, supporting each other and a crying baby Evelyn. Simon cleansed their fatigue and the damage done from the smoke. They stood straighter and picked up speed, joining the crowd.

Simon breathed a sigh of relief. "Victoria, can you put this fire out?"

"All at once?" She shook her head. "But I can help as we go."

Simon heard the flames outside crackling up the walls, blistering the paint, creeping inside. The group moved slowly as everyone moved in a huddle with the macros parting the smoke. More people joined them, called by the telepaths. Simon couldn't see through the smoke, but he thought they were shuffling toward the front door. A tongue of flame crept across the ceiling ahead, coming through the wall. Someone screamed, but the flame shrank until it disappeared.

"There's more," Victoria said. "I can sense it."

With everyone sweating and panting, they kept moving. Simon pulled everyone away from the walls, not wanting anyone to get burned or lost in the tunnel of smoke. The air was flowing forward, away from them. They had to be getting close to the door.

They rounded a corner, and Simon had to hold in a cry. A sheet of flame clung to the wall like some great beast, as if they'd walked into a furnace. Several people staggered back, but Simon kept them from running down the hall, barely. Victoria narrowed her eyes and flexed her power. She moved her hands through the air as if she could guide the fire. The flames parted where she drew them and became two beasts, then three, then smaller and smaller until she could suffocate them one by one.

Simon bolstered her, though his power felt stretched in too many directions. This wasn't like healing the populace, where he only had to focus on one thing. The crowd kept threatening to break through his calm. The micros were helping keep people on their feet, but they weren't very powerful. At one point, Jacobs had taken Simon's arm to help steer him along, and he hadn't noticed. He spotted the door in the distance, but Victoria had to kill the flame slowly. The calm wouldn't hold. He had to think of a way…

The ceiling cracked, and bits of flaming plaster rained down. Pakesh cried out along with many others, breaking through the soothing waves. Pakesh's eyes were wide, terrified. His power strained against Simon's bonds, but Simon couldn't spare him anything else.

"Pakesh—"

Everyone pushed forward as the ceiling began to buckle. Pakesh's power burst through Simon's shields as easily as popping a balloon. Simon transferred more of his attention to Pakesh, and others cried out as their terror returned. Simon ignored them and tried to keep Pakesh from being caught up in the power. He helped focus a macro-psychokinetic blast that ripped down the hall, blowing the doors off their hinges and snuffing the flames like a fire extinguisher.

The crowd surged for the exit, carrying Simon along. He kept hold of Pakesh, trying to tamp down the power before Pakesh became lost in it. He'd lash out at everyone and everything if left unchecked and panicked. He could have blown them all back into the fire.

When everyone staggered free of the burning temple, breathing deep in the night air, Pakesh clutched Simon's arm. "I'm sorry, I'm sorry," he said. "I couldn't…I…"

"It's all right," Simon said as he coughed. "You did fine. You're all right."

"I couldn't stand it." Pakesh hugged himself tightly.

"It's all right. You did fine."

People had formed bucket brigades, but the temple stood engulfed in flames, lighting the dusk around them. Jacobs was shouting, organizing people.

Simon quickly found Victoria. "Is there anything you can do?"

"Keep it from spreading. That's all."

"I'll come with you," Miriam said. She looked to Simon. "I sensed this…overwhelming hatred, and then the wall was on fire."

He nodded. The fire wasn't strong enough to melt the ice in his stomach. Overwhelming hatred. For Dillon's children? For him? All pretenders would burn…

"Someone needs to check on Shiv," Simon said.

Jacobs nodded. "I'll send a patrol."

Simon wandered among the crowd, helping anyone who'd been hurt, helping the bucket brigades by soothing overtired muscles. There didn't seem to be many people unaccounted for. They might not have lost anyone. Jacobs soon reported that Shiv and the children were fine, and Simon's relief nearly got lost in everything he had to do, in the swirl of emotions within him. Overwhelming hatred. It made him sad more than anything.

When next he noticed, night had fallen, and the temple had burned almost to its frame. But it hadn't spread. Simon replenished Victoria and a fellow pyro who'd escaped. He healed Miriam, too, who looked as tired as everyone felt. Miriam and Victoria took turns holding little Evelyn, and Simon wondered if he'd see a firefighter hauling a newborn from flame to flame again.

"Looks like we're out of a home," Victoria said at last. She sounded as if the idea didn't really bother her. Some of the yafanai were weeping in one another's arms.

"Need a place to stay?" Miriam asked.

Victoria raised an eyebrow. "Are you offering one of the houses of your many friends?"

"I thought we could look together. I'm used to your smell by now."

Victoria snorted a laugh. "Sounds good. I was lying about having friends I could stay with."

"I know."

Simon sighed and knew he was going to regret it, but the words came forth anyway. "Come stay with me." When they both looked, he tried to seem nonchalant. "I just want free babysitting. I don't actually care about either of you."

When smiles broke out on their faces, he knew he'd taken the right tone.

"Are you going to put all of the yafanai up, or just we privileged two?" Miriam asked.

Simon turned to look at all the misplaced yafanai. Even the mayor's house wouldn't fit everyone. "I don't think—"

"Don't worry, Doc," Jacobs said. "We're working on it."

He could have kissed her, but they were all covered in soot.

"I'm putting additional people on your house detail," she said. "These assholes are more serious than I thought."

"It might not have been about me," he said. "The expectant mothers are going to need somewhere safe, too."

Jacobs rubbed her chin. "Maybe I can get them to come to the keep. They'll be safe, and it's made of stone, so no one's going to burn it down."

As she faded into the crowd, Simon sighed, looking over everyone. He hadn't set this fire, hadn't asked for any animosity, but he still felt responsible. He had to stop himself from telling everyone he was sorry. All those who met his eye and recognized him offered him a smile. Everyone he healed or rejuvenated looked on him with a kindly eye. They weren't bad people. All he had to do was convince whoever was against him that he wasn't bad, either, that he didn't want anything from them.

Or maybe once Horace returned, they should go somewhere else, take Evan with them so he'd be safe. They'd bring Pakesh and go see how Samira was getting on among the plains dwellers. He was pretty sure no one there would be upset about the fact that Dillon was dead.

But he couldn't leave the rest of the mothers. Even without him, someone clearly wanted Dillon's children for their own purpose. And he really wanted to see what Cordelia and Liam and all the rest would do with Gale now that it was free of Dillon. Once they stopped searching for a god to solve their problems, maybe everything could settle down.

He heard a nearby conversation wondering if it was drushka who set the fire. He started in that direction, hoping to quell that rumor, but someone punched him in the back. Simon turned.

Pakesh was a few steps away, staring at the fire. He hadn't seemed to notice anything wrong. Simon turned again slowly, and the pain turned with him, traveling from one point up and down his back. "What the hell?" It wasn't a punch. An ache spread through him, and he tried to heal it, but it resisted; something stuck in the wound.

A shadow moved and became a man with dark, frightened, angry eyes. "You shouldn't have killed him," the man whispered. He wiped at the spittle dotting his thin lips.

Simon felt behind him. Something trickled down his back. Blood? He tried to speak but suddenly couldn't. His fingers brushed a hard edge. A knife? He couldn't think straight, and the knife, if that was what it was, felt as if it was traveling through his torso, drilling through him. His knees went weak. He had to do something, had to call for help.

A host of telepaths stood nearby. Pakesh was one of them, a powerful one, and just how powerful didn't matter at the moment. Simon's vision began to go fuzzy. He dropped the shields around Pakesh and thought, "Help."

Pakesh whirled around. "Simon?"

The assassin took a step closer as Simon's legs gave way, and he fell forward. He heard Pakesh's yell, then felt a wave of air as the assassin went flying. Then everyone seemed to be crying out at once. He heard Jacob's roar for the assassin to stay where he was, but someone else yelled, "He stabbed the healer!" and the noise of the crowd rose to a crescendo.

"Get it out, get it out," Simon tried to say, but his breath had become a wheeze. His power flowed over the wound, but the feel of his flesh reknitting around the sharp blade was agony over and over, and he couldn't push the blade free. At last, someone pulled it out. Simon grunted and grabbed frantically for his power, healing himself as quick as a thought. He took deep breaths as he lay still, inhaling smoke and dust and a thousand scents that had been ground into the stones.

Hands pulled him up. Pakesh. People were yelling, but now Jacobs was calling for everyone to give way. Simon thought she was trying to get to him, but then he saw the crowd, a tight fist of people, and in their center...

"Stop!" Simon could feel the strikes against the man in the center, the pain radiating from that one point. He sent his power out again, engulfing the crowd, interrupting them so they fell; not even their synapses could fire without his permission, but they weren't what captured his attention.

The man who'd stabbed him was nothing more than a huddled, red-slicked lump. "Oh my God." Simon staggered forward and knelt at his side, feeling for a flicker of life. Broken arms and ribs, a fractured skull, damaged liver and kidneys and lungs, and a thousand cuts and bruises, but there was a spark at his core. Simon nurtured it gently, healing layer upon layer, all the way out, until the man breathed again. He was still covered in blood, but he would live. He peered up at Simon with wonder instead of anger or fright, his sharp features scrunched together as if trying to figure out how and why he still lived.

"You're alive," Simon said quietly. "We both are."

He let the crowd go, and they stood carefully, watching him, watching his would-be assassin.

Jacobs hauled the assassin to his feet. "You're under arrest." She gave him to another paladin before the crowd could turn ugly again.

Simon faced them, searching for what he could say. "You can't do that," he decided on, his anger growing. "If someone breaks a law, they get arrested. You don't beat them to death in the street!"

"He stabbed you!" someone yelled. "Maybe he set the fire!"

"I don't care!" Some of them took a step back. Simon took a deep breath. "Let the law handle it." He remembered when a crowd had beaten someone who tried to kill Dillon, but Dillon encouraged that kind of adoration. "I'm not your god. No matter what happens, I'll still help you, but please, don't ever kill anyone on my account or in my name. Please."

Some of them grumbled, but others nodded, and he felt their shame. Good. Maybe they'd think twice before becoming part of a mob again.

CHAPTER SIXTEEN

Lydia marched Fajir south, closer to Sun-Moon territory. The Engali might be less likely to pursue them there, but Lydia didn't know what she'd say if they ran into any Sun-Moon worshipers. She didn't think they'd take kindly to seeing a widow bound and prodded by a Galean.

But what else was she supposed to do? Fajir would turn on her if set loose. Maybe she should stay tied up until the fire started.

Lydia took a deep breath and told herself again that there was no use dwelling on what could or would happen. Fajir would be loose when the fire happened, then she would stop it. All Lydia had to do was find a way to keep her from killing anyone before that. Lydia supposed she could wander into the future and find out, but that had gotten her into this mess. She didn't want to follow one mistake with another.

"Can you see the future after your death?" Fajir asked.

Lydia blinked. The very idea gave her the creeps. She'd never tried. "Why?"

"Because I'm going to kill you, Nemesis. I just don't know if it will be before or after this fire you saw."

Strangely enough, the words made Lydia smile. It was good to know some things didn't change. Fajir might save the plains for purely selfish reasons, after all. Whatever. She could be contained after she took care of the problem.

Brave thoughts, but Lydia couldn't let herself doubt them at the moment. "I think that calls for a breakfast break." Lydia halted the ossor and dug through the packs, finding geaver jerky and some dried fruit. She tossed it over, and Fajir caught some even with her hands bound. She plonked down in the grass and began to eat. Lydia stood as she ate, sore from the saddle.

"In this future, were my hands tied?" Fajir asked.

"Nope. You'll get loose exactly when you're meant to."

"And when is that?"

Lydia shrugged.

Fajir sighed. "Can you not simply look?"

"It's…complicated. Most of the time, it's better not to know. If I hadn't dreamt of the future, I wouldn't be out here with a maniac."

Fajir frowned hard. "You are the strangest creature I have ever known."

"I'm not a creature," Lydia said, shifting uncomfortably. "Shut up and eat."

"With such great power, why not use it? You're like a swordswoman who trains night and day, then binds her arms."

Lydia tried to fight her irritation and lost. "If you won't eat, we can always walk." She mounted the ossor and prodded Fajir to move, but Fajir kept muttering until Lydia's temper boiled over.

"If I see something, there's a chance I'll cause it!" Lydia yelled. "Like with you. I knew you were going to get loose, but I didn't want to cause it, so I decided to wait, and sure enough, it happened. And I don't know why, but I feel as if I *did* something, as if my power shapes the future instead of just seeing it. That's probably untrue, but it's still awful and terrifying. I can't help how I feel, okay?"

Fajir walked backward for a moment, one eyebrow raised as if waiting for more. Outbursts didn't seem to faze her.

After another long sigh and nothing but uncertainty ahead of them, Lydia told Fajir about the boggins attacking Gale. She'd seen the soldiers gathered on one side of the city, so she'd told the Storm Lord that was what would happen. That had left the eastern side of Gale unprotected.

"But according to you," Fajir said, walking beside the ossor, "it would have happened that way no matter what you did."

"Yes, but I saw it happen that way in the future because I told him it would happen that way. If I'd already learned my lesson about not wanting to see the future, I never would have told him, and then it might not have happened."

Fajir's face scrunched up as she tried to process that. After a few moments, she nodded. "I understand."

Lydia was so shocked, she nearly reined the ossor in. "You can't. No one does."

Fajir shrugged. "You look, and you're caught, even if the looking made the future worse. And you can't change what you see, so it's better not to look."

Lydia's jaw dropped. Only Freddie had ever understood so clearly. No, she was not going to compare this murderer to Freddie. Not ever. "That's...close," she muttered.

Fajir gave her another lifted eyebrow, but Lydia didn't respond. They walked a few more steps in silence before a shout came from ahead, followed by the keening of ossors in peril. Lydia slowed, listening. Another person shouted, and Fajir broke into a run, headed for the sound.

"Wait!" Lydia cried, riding after. She crested a hill just behind Fajir and saw a group of plains dwellers fighting Sun-Moon pairs over a small ossor herd. As the groups clashed, Lydia caught sight of a symbol painted on the plains dwellers' clothes: a single red eye, the sign of Naos.

Lydia gasped. She hadn't been directly involved in that battle, but she'd seen some of the damage it had caused. Chafa Yuve had told them some plains dwellers still followed this goddess even though she'd abandoned them. And there were far more of them. The Sun-Moons didn't stand a chance.

"Free me." Fajir held out her hands, gaze locked on the battle.

Lydia looked back and forth, her anxiety building. If the Naos worshipers killed the Sun-Moons, she and Fajir might be next. "But—"

"You said I would save people. Well?" She held her hands farther out.

Lydia bit her lip. She couldn't save anyone on her own; she didn't think she could end this battle with words. She drew the sword, cut Fajir free, and tossed the sword to the ground in front of her.

Fajir scooped it up and raced toward the plains dwellers like silent death. She sliced one across the back, and he spun away with a cry. More turned in her direction, and Fajir took one across the chest before spinning and blocking the sword of another. She knocked his thrust to the side and slashed him across the face.

She'd kill them all before they even knew what ran among them.

"Run away!" Lydia cried. "Everyone! Go, go, before she kills you!"

A few obeyed as Fajir continued to tear into their ranks like a cyclone. The Sun-Moons grabbed the ossors and fled. Within moments, the battlefield was still, and Fajir bent over a Sun-Moon worshiper lying in the grass.

"Nemesis, bring water!" Fajir called.

"My name is Lydia," she grumbled. Quickly, she dismounted and hurried over with a water skin. "We can probably make some bandages from—"

Fajir lunged, knocking Lydia over and slamming her into the ground. Lydia struggled, but she couldn't catch her breath. Fajir's hands whipped around her neck and squeezed, flooding her with pain. Lydia clawed up Fajir's arm, but Fajir knelt, digging a knee into Lydia's thigh. Even that pain became lost in the pressure around her throat. She couldn't get air, and she felt as if her head would come off any moment.

Fajir bent close. "Shall I find my own future now, Nemesis?"

Spots of light danced in Lydia's vision. She couldn't find her power, could barely think. She swung for Fajir's face, but her limbs felt leaden, and Fajir nudged her clumsy attacks away. A rushing sound built in her ears, and her eyes slipped closed. Like a pop of lightning, she saw Freddie's face, smiling.

"Hello, love," she tried to say. If Freddie was there, everything was going to be all right.

Dimly, someone screeched. The horrible pressure on Lydia's throat eased. Still, she floated in darkness. She tried to look for Freddie, but her body wouldn't move.

"Lydia!" someone called.

"I'm here, Freddie," she tried again. Why wouldn't her mouth work?

"Lydia, breathe!"

Freddie lifted her, and she wanted to open her eyes, to look at Freddie as they kissed.

Someone pounded on her back. Lydia's eyes flew open as she sucked in a breath so hard it hurt. She coughed, gagging, and someone turned her to the side as her meager breakfast came up in a rush. She coughed again and again as someone rubbed circles on her back, and it damn sure wasn't Freddie. She looked through her tears and saw Mamet's worried face.

"How?" she tried to ask, but a coughing fit seized her again.

"Stay down!" Samira's voice, coming from the side.

Lydia tried to look, but her neck burned like fire when she moved.

"Easy." Mamet eased Lydia around.

Samira stood with her legs apart as if braced for a rush. Beyond her, Fajir rose from the grass, but an invisible force flung her to the ground. Her bone sword bounced away. When she lunged for it, she kept flying under Samira's power until she smacked into a rock. The bone sword tumbled through the grass and landed at Mamet's side. She scooped it up and helped Lydia stand.

"Lydia's all right," Mamet called.

Lydia squeezed her tightly and tried to stand on her own. Fajir had stopped moving. "Is she unconscious?" Lydia whispered, coming to Samira's side.

"I don't know." Samira pulled Lydia into a hug. "Idiot! What were you thinking? She nearly killed you."

"Sorry," Lydia said. "I thought…" She winced and rubbed her throat, feeling as if she was trying to swallow hot knives.

"Don't talk. I can guess. You saw the future, but you couldn't just let her go. It probably felt like the right decision at the time."

"Samira," Mamet said, "don't badger her. She's hurt." She walked a few steps closer to Fajir, sword at the ready. "She's still breathing."

"Of course she is," Samira said darkly. "We're going to tie you up," she called to Fajir's unmoving form. "And if you give us any trouble, I will crack your head against that rock again." She gave Lydia another hug from the side. "Since you saw it, I know that she lives. And you were right. I don't want her death on my conscience. But so help me, if she pisses me off, I will roll her around the plains until she behaves."

Lydia smiled and squeezed Samira again. Fajir seemed truly unconscious. She didn't move as they bound her hand and foot, then made a small camp so Lydia could recover. The rest of the Engali were far behind them, and they had a moment to think.

Until Fajir woke again, at least.

❖

Cordelia tilted her face up to the sun as Pool's tree broke out of the swamp, and she saw Gale in the distance. After two solid days of travel, they'd finally made it home. Just thinking the word "home" lifted her heart.

Morning mist covered the fields, giving the cool air a humid tinge. She couldn't see anyone at this distance, and she didn't want Gale to think they were being attacked by the drushka again. "Hold me out in front, Pool."

From her bark cupola, Pool glanced in her direction. "Why, Sa?"

"To say hello." Cordelia grinned as the branches lifted her out front. She took her sidearm and fired one shot in the air, just to let the people know their paladins had returned.

Or she was now giving someone the nightmare image of drushka using guns.

Ah well. She'd have to wait and see. As they came closer, people poured out of the gates, cheering. So, her message had gotten across. Pool set the humans down, and the rescued captives ran into the arms of the rest, everyone calling out names of those they'd thought lost. Everything dissolved into a weeping, laughing mass. Here and there, people looked for missing loved ones, and she knew they wouldn't find them. The other captives would have to tell them who had died.

Cordelia got lost in the people who slapped her on the shoulders or threw their arms around her. Others seemed angry, shouting, but their words were lost amidst the happiness, and all she could do was yell back that everything was all right for now. She moved too swiftly through the crowd for anything else.

A wave of people brought her up against Liam, and they hugged each other fiercely. He had bags beneath both eyes and lacked his normal swagger. Maybe he'd been too busy, or things with Shiv weren't going well. Probably both. She tried to ask him about it, but there was too much noise. Something must have shown in her frown. He waved a hand as if dismissing her concerns.

"I'm glad you're all right!" he shouted near her ear. "Everyone?"

Not quite, but she didn't really want to scream that in the midst of the celebrations. She gave him a thumbs-up. There'd be time for bad news later.

Soon, the crowd began to filter back inside the city, and Cordelia was swept up by well-wishers again. There didn't seem to be any immediate crisis, and the party atmosphere swelled when Pool's drushka produced a herd of hoshpi they'd caught on the way home. Some seemed leery of the drushka, but as the people thinned out enough for Cordelia to be able to hear, she caught several conversations stating that Pool wasn't like *those* drushka; she was different, more human. Cordelia thought of the eighth's fears about drushka becoming human. She tried to steer the conversations to other topics, but she knew nothing would change overnight.

And she was tired. And the mead had begun to flow.

When Cordelia looked through the crowd next, she spotted Simon Lazlo. He looked tired, too, but he managed a wave and a smile. Shiv stood behind him along with the plains dweller Pakesh. Each of them held a child by the hand, and Pakesh had a baby in the crook of his arm. Someone had gotten roped into big-time babysitting.

Reach jogged toward them and lifted Little Paul, planting a kiss on his cheek. He hugged her around the neck, and when Cordelia was close enough, she heard Reach say, "Thank you for keeping him, shawness."

"My pleasure," Simon said with a smile. "He…wasn't any trouble."

Reach barked a laugh. "This I doubt, but I know a kind human lie when I hear it."

Cordelia grinned at them both. "Well, I see the city's in one piece."

He winced.

She sighed. "What happened?"

"There was a fire. The temple. A few people were hurt." He held out a hand before she could head in that direction. "There's nothing more to do. Private Jacobs should be commended, though. She's been invaluable."

Cordelia shook her head as she tried to process that there'd been a tragedy, and she could do nothing about it. "The temple burned down?"

"Forget that for now," he said with a shaky laugh. "I'm sorry it was the first thing I said. Just remember the part about Jacobs."

Shiv pushed forward before Cordelia could ask more questions. She wrapped her arms around Cordelia and looked more downcast than Cordelia had ever seen. What the fuck had been happening since she'd been gone?

"I missed you, Sa," Shiv said.

Well, if that was all… Cordelia lifted her and swung her around. "I missed you, too!" Shiv laughed, and Cordelia was glad she could cheer one person up, at least. Maybe she should have swung Liam and Simon, too. "Were you in the temple when the fire started?"

"Ahwa, no! Better if I had been, perhaps. I would have smelled the smoke soonest." She bit her narrow lip with pointed teeth, dimpling the skin. "I have other thoughts crowding my mind." She glanced behind them at Pool's massive tree, then at her young charge, her tribe of one.

"Go say hello," Cordelia said, holding a hand toward the drushka.

Shiv seemed as if she might, but then shrank as if Cordelia was asking her to head into a nest of stinging insects.

Cordelia put her hands on her hips. "What's wrong?"

Shiv seemed torn. Finally, she walked away, gesturing for Cordelia to follow. Cordelia frowned but obliged. What could be so bad? Shiv had never been…hesitant with her words. But instead of speaking once they were alone, Shiv licked her fingers and rubbed them along Lyshus's hair, revealing green strands beneath the dirty brown color.

Cordelia straightened. She'd been around enough queens lately to know their hair color when she saw it. "What the fuck?"

"Indeed," Shiv said sadly. "I do not know what it means. Shawness Simon told me to ask Shi'a'na, but what will she say?"

That was the question, wasn't it? Cordelia had to shrug. She'd seen enough drushkan politics to know they weren't exactly straightforward. Sometimes, they seemed to feel their way through leadership disputes rather than think, using drushkan emotions and attachments that Cordelia knew little to nothing about.

But Pool did, and Cordelia trusted her. "She won't hurt him, Shiv."

Shiv spread her hands. "For something this new, we can know nothing. I do not like Lyshus's new appearance, and I am his queen. My people will not like it."

"Yeah, but maybe you're too close to the problem. Your mom is the master of change. She can handle anything."

Lyshus chewed on his wooden nini and crouched to watch an insect crawling across the ground. He put one finger in its path before guiding it back the same way. When it changed again, he laughed like a maniac and hopped from foot to foot, not squishing it. Not yet.

Cordelia had to smile. "He's a little weirdo."

Shiv sucked her teeth.

Cordelia waved a hand to say it didn't matter. "It's a term of affection."

"You will not let them hurt him, Sa?" Shiv asked. "Shawness Simon says he will help protect us, but I would prefer it if you would, too."

Cordelia's heart went out to her. She knew Pool wouldn't harm this child, but she also recognized the need in Shiv's eyes. "I won't let anyone hurt him. Now, let's go. Best to get all the serious conversations out of the way so we can do some serious drinking."

Lyshus swung up around Shiv's shoulders, and Cordelia walked with her to where Pool stood near the gates of Gale, talking to Liam. Shiv looked between them as if she didn't know who she was most afraid of talking to.

Cordelia put a hand on her back so she couldn't run. "Pool!"

Pool turned and wrinkled her nose at her daughter. Even Liam had a hopeful smile. Shiv didn't waste any words. She swung Lyshus around into her arms and swept a hand through his hair, shaking loose some of the dye and dirt until she'd revealed the green underneath.

Pool's face went still, her eyes wide. She stepped closer to peer at the child, her expression unreadable. Cordelia's belly went cold. No matter how sure she'd been of Lyshus's safety, she stiffened and took half a step closer. She wouldn't raise her hand to Pool, but she would grab Lyshus and run if Pool was overcome with some kind of drushkan instinct to kill a male queen.

"How?" Pool said at last.

"I had hoped you would know, Shi'a'na," Shiv said.

Pool sucked her teeth, scowling. Lyshus had gone very still, like a tiny animal caught out in the open. Nettle approached from Pool's other side and studied the child the same way, the same look of confusion on her face.

Cordelia looked between them. Everything seemed poised, just as when Fajir had decided to take a child's life. Cordelia didn't know which way to turn this time, and she really resented being this tense *after* her mission was over. She wanted to yell, "Say something or hit someone!"

Before Cordelia could snap, Nettle stepped closer and smiled. Cordelia had a flash of conversation she'd nearly forgotten: Nettle saying she'd lost her child fifty years ago. Cordelia grieved for her again. With a soft smile, Nettle lifted the child's nini and held it in front of his face. He sank his teeth into it without hesitation and chewed away, wrinkling his nose at them all.

"He seems a normal enough child, Queen," Nettle said. Cordelia grabbed her hand and squeezed it, loving her.

"Normal?" Pool said. "Nothing about him is normal."

Shiv took a step back. "The old drushka no doubt thought the same of you, Shi'a'na."

Pool stared her in the eye. "Did you feel it when the Shi died, daughter?"

"N…no, Shi'a'na."

"Curious. Is it because your tree is not connected to the whole, or is it for other reasons?" She looked to Lyshus again. "He was not a queen when he was born."

Shiv glanced at Cordelia as if wondering what to say. Cordelia gave her a reassuring smile even though she didn't know where Pool was going with this, either.

"No, Shi'a'na," Shiv said. "His hair fell out soon after and regrew as a queen's."

Pool frowned hard, but she didn't seem as if she might hurt anyone. "You will not be able to have a tribe if this happens to every child you bear. A tribe of queens? There will never be enough trees! And they would be able to invade one another's minds as well as speak to them? To fight as queens fight? An entire tribe?"

"Please, Shi'a'na!" Shiv said, a frightened wail. "Do not speak of such things! Can you help him? Make him normal? As normal as the rest of us, ahya?"

Pool's stony façade cracked. She smiled and reached out. Part of her had to know what her child was going through, how it felt to be considered strange by her own kind. "You would give him to me, daughter? Trust me to know the right course?"

Cordelia looked between them with no idea what advice to give. Shiv stared into Lyshus's trusting eyes. She could refuse, but would that mean turning her back on her people? She could live in Gale; Cordelia would see to that, but no drushka did well when separated from the whole, even with a sidekick. It had made Reach really grumpy, or so Cordelia remembered.

At last, Shiv drew herself up. "I trust you, Shi'a'na." But she stepped forward with Lyshus. "I will go with you. I am his queen, and he is in my hands. Also, I must learn what to do if ever this problem rises again."

It was a nice speech, and Pool seemed to appreciate it. Cordelia wanted to whoop when Pool led them to the tree.

Nettle wrapped an arm around Cordelia's shoulders. "You were worried, Sa."

"A little. Too much drushkan politics for one lifetime."

"You can say that again," Liam said. He'd watched Pool and Shiv together, and now he wandered away from the group. She expected to see even more sadness in his slumped shoulders, but he seemed thoughtful. Maybe he was just happy Shiv was finally getting help.

Nettle spread her hands. "The old drushka asked that Shiv go to them and learn. I wonder if she will go without argument. No matter what Pool is able to do for Lyshus, Pool may insist he stay here while Shiv visits the old people."

"You think they'd hurt him?"

"Who can say? Better to be cautious."

"Well, we can forget cautious for a little while," Cordelia said as she wrapped an arm around Nettle's waist. "For now, there's drinking to be done."

Nettle gestured down the street. "You have taken the words from Liam's lips. He has already started."

They headed for a barrel of mead someone had set up in the road. Liam waited in line. Simon and Horace stood nearby, Horace cooing over the baby in Pakesh's arms. When they had mead in hand, Liam and Nettle got pulled into conversation with Horace.

Cordelia found her way over to Simon and nodded toward the baby now in Horace's arms. "What's the story there?"

Simon took a long pull from his mug. "That is Evan, the Storm Lord's firstborn. He's got no other family, so…"

"You volunteered?"

"Got drafted."

"Yikes." She shuddered.

He chuckled. "I'm so glad I'm not the only one who thinks that way when it comes to children. I was beginning to think I might be the grumpiest man in Gale."

"Babies aren't for everyone."

"Hear, hear." He toasted her, and with a chuckle, she toasted him right back. Her shoulders had begun to relax already, and she wondered if that would be some cue for the universe to fuck with her again. Any minute now, Fajir would ride a flaming geaver into town, followed by a mad, armor-clad god shooting two railguns.

As she pictured that in her head, she only laughed harder, then went to fill her cup once again.

❖

Shiv sat cross-legged in her mother's tree, Shi'a'na across from her, and Lyshus between them. Someone had fetched her sapling, and it stood behind her, all of them connected through the trees to one another. Even though it went against Shiv's very nature, she allowed Shi'a'na into Lyshus's mind, desperate for any help.

His emotions were simple, and he did not seem to care who else could touch his mind as long as Shiv was there. He played with a few sticks and radiated happy contentment. Shiv heard nothing from her mother except watchful curiosity. Shiv fought the urge to frown. She kept her irritation inside, not wanting to flood her mother or her tribemate. She had hoped to be learning something about how to treat tribemates if needed, but so far, nothing.

At last, Shi'a'na opened her eyes. "His is like no mind I have encountered, even your mind as a child, unique as you are. His thoughts are simplistic, ahya, but there is something else."

Shiv bit her lip, the urge to tell all rising within her. She could not help but dislike lying, and leaving out facts seemed the same. Surrendering, she said, "He…touched my tree with his mind, made it grow. I have never seen the like."

Shiv felt her mother's confusion and disbelief. She stared at Lyshus, then at the sapling.

"The sapling was in danger of slipping down stairs," Shiv said. "When I went to aid it, Lyshus seemed to sense its need as well."

"Through you, no doubt, the same as when all attached to me feel any damage done to my tree. But to change it as Simon Lazlo can do?" She stood.

Not knowing what else to do, Shiv followed. Shi'a'na crossed to the sapling, then held her hand out to Lyshus, giving him a mental nudge to indicate what she wanted. He obeyed, laying his hand in hers. Shi'a'na was still a queen, even if she was not his queen. She knelt at his side.

"Did you make the tree grow, little one?" Shi'a'na asked softly. Though she bore all her tribe's children in her branches, she did not spend much time with any one of them. Through most of her childhood, Shiv had run free, tended by every adult. Shi'a'na had to worry for the entire tribe, something Shiv never understood until now.

Lyshus smiled at her soft tone. When Shi'a'na placed a hand against the sapling, he watched it carefully, waited a moment, then put his hand atop hers. Shiv felt her own connection to Lyshus, and her connection to Shi'a'na, tree to tree, queen to queen. Then she felt something else, small but there, a connection of Lyshus to the sapling that did not go through Shiv. It should not have been possible. Queens connected to trees one at a time. They could speak to one another through their trees, through the connections that bound them all, but this was different, like a tendril of ivy twisting where it did not belong.

And it was not the only one. Barely visible, but there for the looking, was a newly formed connection that led from Lyshus to the Anushi tree, Shi'a'na's tree.

Shi'a'na rose quickly, breaking the connection, and Shiv felt her mental defenses go up. She backed away from them, eyes wide. No emotions came from her now; her defenses were too tight, but Shiv knew she must be thinking of her recent fight with the Shi. She would not risk anyone who seemed as if they might try to control her.

"Can you sever it?" Shiv asked hurriedly, not liking the way Shi'a'na stared at Lyshus. He knew something was wrong, but had no idea what he had done.

Shi'a'na breathed deep, coming back to herself. She was silent for a few more moments before touching her forehead as if it pained her. "No, I cannot see a way, not without injury to Lyshus. Take him from my tree, daughter, and let me think on this."

Shiv obeyed hurriedly. When she reached the ground, she scooped up Lyshus and her sapling and hurried through the raucous crowd. Despair built within her. Her mother had tried to help and failed, and now she was sending Shiv away. It did not matter that Shi'a'na had offered to help, it still felt like a rejection. She headed toward the mayor's house, not knowing what else to do, where to go. She thought to look for Sa or shawness Simon, but the revelers made her scowl; their happiness mocked her despair.

"Shiv!" someone called.

She almost did not slow, but she felt a wave of happiness from Lyshus. She turned to see Reach approaching with Little Paul, and Lyshus reached for his friend.

"Shawness," Shiv said.

Reach tilted her head. "Your mother could not help you?"

But of course everyone would know. They were all connected. How many of them would shun her? "She…wishes to think on it."

"Wise." Reach rested a hand on Shiv's shoulder. "Do not despair. Answers are coming. Teach yourself patience."

"I am tired of patience!" Despair melted into anger, and she wanted to hit and kick and bite, wanted to be able to throw herself into something besides worry. She wanted to melt into someone. She wanted Liam.

Reach grabbed her chin and gave her head a little shake. "As a queen, you are far too serious."

"I have a duty!"

"And obeying it is admirable, but if you are heartsick, your tribe will be also. You still have yourself to care for."

Lyshus was looking at her. Little Paul was trying to get him to play, but he seemed caught up in Shiv's misery. "I know you are right, ahya. But…"

"Go," Reach said. "Rest, eat, or join the fun, perhaps. You must give the queen time to ponder, and nothing will be gained by spending that time in despair. Seek out new friends." Her glance shifted to the side. "Or old."

Shiv followed her gaze and caught sight of Liam on the edge of the crowd. She took a step in that direction without meaning to, caught up in visions of his body pressed against hers.

Reach leaned close. "I will watch the children, and Lyshus will come to no harm while in my hands. Even queens have lovers."

Shiv knew that was true. Queens could never belong to just one person, but one did not have to belong to be close. She squeezed Reach's hand and wrinkled her nose. Reach *did* owe her some time watching the children. And Shi'a'na *did* need time to ponder.

Shiv nearly ran to Liam, but as he turned, she hesitated. What if he did not welcome her anymore? What if his anger was too strong? When his green eyes lit up in a smile, she leapt for him. Though he seemed surprised, he caught her, stumbling. She wrapped her legs around his waist and kissed him deeply, finding his lips welcoming and pliable and as soft as she remembered.

His arms tightened around her, and he did not bother with words as he carried her away from the party. She did not care where they were going as long as it was private, and the two of them could find each other again.

CHAPTER SEVENTEEN

Simon's world was fuzzy. How long had it been since he'd gotten drunk? How many hundreds of years? He'd had so much mead with Cordelia that even his power couldn't keep up, and he had no desire to fight it. On the *Atlas*, he never would have been so vulnerable, but sitting across the table from Cordelia in a happy Gale, it seemed right to embrace life.

And alcohol.

"Havin' fun?" Cordelia asked, more than a little slurry herself.

Simon nodded too fast, and dizziness washed over him, making him laugh. "Oh yeah. Yep, yep, yep." He looked into his empty mug. "More?"

She drained hers, then grabbed his mug and strode to a nearby keg to fill them both. How could she still walk so steadily? He didn't know if he could even get up. She set his mug in front of him with a thud, and the red mead sloshed over his hand.

"Sorry," she said.

He tried to say it was okay, but the light glinted off the red, winking at him. "Looks like blood." The words made him sad, the feeling rising as if he had a pit of sorrow inside looking for an excuse to bubble over.

Cordelia leaned forward to peer at his hand. "Blood's brighter." She winked slowly. "I've seen it."

"Me, too. Too much." He waved around, but no one was bleeding anymore. He tried to cheer himself up, but the sadness wasn't done with him that easily. "What d'ya think happened to Dillon's body? The Storm Lord, I mean."

Cordelia shrugged. "Carrion birds?"

Simon sputtered a laugh. "They couldn't be so fast! I saw him die. He was right there, then he wasn't. What…what's up with that?"

"Dunno."

"He died." And that seemed really important at the moment.

"I know."

"But…you don't get it. He *died*."

"And so he's not here *now*." She slapped the table. "You're drunk. I'm drunk. We're happy. Relax. You sound like old me. Learn to let shit go, Simon, like new me."

"Old you?" She couldn't be much older than thirty. He shook his head, too tired to work out what she was saying. "We woulda never worked out anyway, as a couple, I mean."

She grinned crookedly. "You and me? You got that right."

He sputtered another laugh, and then they were laughing together, cackling. "No, me and Dillon. I loved him, but it never woulda worked."

She nodded, and some of her dark hair slipped loose from her ponytail, hiding one of her eyes. "If he didn't love you back, he wasn't right for you. You weren't compita…compada…thingy." She leaned forward and whispered loudly. "He was an *asshole*. And you're not. Well, maybe you were, but you're not now. You couldn't have ever made him a…non-asshole." She sat up and pointed an unsteady finger at him. "And now you're the most powerful person on the planet, and he's dead, and other people love you, so there." She drank her mead with a proud look, as if she'd proven a point.

Simon had no idea what that point might be, but he liked hearing that people loved him. "Yeah!"

"Fuck yeah!" They clanked their mugs together loudly and drank deep.

"Have you ever loved an asshole?" Simon asked. Then that mental picture washed over him, and he laughed until he felt sick. He coughed, and Cordelia crossed around the table to sit beside him and thump him on the back.

"Loved this girl once," she said, "long time ago, teenage love, ya know? But she didn't love me back. She liked this tiny little woman." She held her hand up, thumb and forefinger only an inch apart.

Simon pointed at her hand. "That's impossible."

She ignored him. "Dainty, that's what the asshole called her. Not like me, more…" She waved a hand.

"Cute?"

Cordelia blinked then stared, a frown building. "You callin' me ugly?"

Even through all the drink, his belly went cold. She could break him in half. "No! I think you're beautiful, stunning, lovely. If I liked women—"

Her frown cracked, and she burst out laughing. "Can't believe you fell for that!"

He had to watch for several seconds before he realized he'd been duped. "You're a prick!"

She only laughed harder. "Anyway, I only meant some people aren't right for other people." She frowned then shrugged. "Or something. Close enough."

"You're right. And anyway, I've got Horace."

"Fuck yeah!" She toasted him again. "Let's drink to love." They both tipped their glasses back, then she got them more.

Simon grinned, thinking about love, about Horace. He was happy, and Cordelia was happy because she had Nettle. His mind began to wander again. He'd never seen a naked drushka...

"How's that work?" he asked. "Sex?"

She spat her mead across the table. "Seriously? What've you and Horace been doing? Holding hands?"

"With a drushka!" He shoved her shoulder, but it felt like trying to move a rock.

She grinned. "I'll tell stories if you will."

He slapped the table. "Done!"

"Right." She glanced around and pulled over two condiment jars someone had left on the table. "Okay, say I'm the salt, and she's the spicy mustard."

He watched her maneuver the jars into position, both of them giggling away.

"Simon?" someone said behind him.

He turned too fast but managed to spot Horace through his hazy vision. "Hello, my love!"

Cordelia was still laughing, and now Simon started up again.

"Are you drunk?" Horace asked.

Simon nodded helplessly, trying to breathe. "Thank God you're here. You can tell me whether you want to be the salt or the spicy mustard." He lost it, and Cordelia followed suit.

"I'm sorry," Horace said loudly, "but I'm going to have to spoil your evening."

Simon gasped as Horace's power washed over him, cleansing the mead from his system and clearing his head with a snap.

"Oh, fuck yeah to that, too!" Cordelia said. She stood and seemed as sober as Simon felt. "That's it. You two are my permanent drinking buddies from now on!"

Horace was frowning, though, and that drove away the last of Simon's exuberance. "What's wrong?"

"The envoys we sent to the mine while you were gone have just returned, and they've got quite a story to tell. You should both come."

Lydia watched Fajir from across the fire. It had been a stressful couple of days, even after Samira and Mamet had joined them. When Fajir had regained consciousness, they'd ridden on, Lydia trying to get them to steer clear of the Engali who were no doubt following, and Samira arguing that they should go back.

But Lydia kept thinking of the fight she and Fajir had interrupted. The day after the initial attack, they'd seen another group of plains dwellers bearing the symbol of Naos while attacking a Sun-Moon farm. Even with their goddess cut off from them, it seemed some were still determined to fulfill the last command she'd given them: to destroy the Sun-Moon worshipers.

Samira and Mamet had handled that fight while Fajir watched, still bound. She'd railed at Lydia to let her go, but Lydia didn't want to risk that again. Her throat still ached, though Samira said the bruises had faded a little. They'd decided to keep Fajir tied up until they needed her.

From her place across the fire, Samira said, "We need to go back," for the hundredth time.

Lydia sighed. "We can't go anywhere while the plains dwellers are killing people out here, not while we can stop them."

"We're not responsible for the Sun-Moons!" Samira said.

Fajir sneered at her. "So much for all your talk about protecting innocents."

Samira sat forward as if she might lunge, but Mamet held her back. She jabbed a finger in Fajir's direction. "If you let this monster loose, Lydia, she'll kill you."

Lydia sighed again. "Is that true, Fajir?"

Fajir smiled, her teeth glinting in the light. "Of course not."

"The farmers we rescued will tell the guards in Celeste what happened," Samira said. "Then they'll send patrols. The three of us do not need to get involved."

"Four," Fajir said.

Samira glared at her, but Lydia ignored her. "The people being attacked are not the same ones you fought in Celeste. They're ranchers and farmers, not warriors. I can't just go home knowing they're in danger." And it was true. She'd come out here to guard people against Fajir, and now she'd seen that more of them needed help, and she couldn't simply turn her back on them.

"Okay," Samira said, a sigh in her voice. "I do feel bad about the farmers, but it's still not our problem. They have their own people to guard them! I mean, surely someone will get here soon." But as she said it, it seemed as if she didn't fully believe it.

"Would you kill these Naos followers?" Mamet asked Fajir. "They're not Engali."

"Oh, I'll kill them," Fajir said. "Set me loose, and I'll show you."

Lydia wanted to smack her for not helping. She was certain Fajir would defend her people, but the question was, how to keep her from going after everyone else? Well, having three people watch her was better than one.

"We know there are people out here being hurt, Samira," Lydia said. "And I believe that makes them our responsibility. I know you want to help them, too."

Samira frowned hard, almost comically so, a sign she was weakening. "For the Storm Lord's sake, Lydia! Stop trying to make me into a better person!"

They stared at each other before laughing. "You're already a good person," Lydia said. "And it's certainly not for the Storm Lord's sake. If we stay out here just a few more days, think of the lives we could save."

"You're right," Mamet said softly. "And there are more than

just the people out here to consider. Children might go hungry if their parents die."

"Ugh!" Samira cried. "Using imaginary starving children in your argument is not fair." But Lydia could see her weakening further. If Mamet had enough sympathy to care for a people who'd once tortured her, what argument could Samira have?

"All right," Samira said. "A few more days on the outskirts of Sun-Moon territory, but if we see an armed band from Celeste patrolling, we tell them what we know and go home. Deal?"

Mamet nodded happily. Lydia tried to do the same, but there was no telling what the future would bring.

"And we keep her on a leash," Samira said, pointing at Fajir.

That also seemed like a good idea, but what Fajir thought of it, Lydia didn't get to know. She stared into the fire, gaze inscrutable. But Lydia bet wheels were turning inside that murderous mind.

Fajir lay still and listened to the wind blowing through the grass. Every now and again, her nemesis would snore from across the fire. Fajir's temper flared every time she heard it. If they were going to leave her trussed up like solstice dinner, the least they could do was be quiet.

The other two had finally stopped gabbling. One was awake; Fajir heard someone shifting around, but she couldn't see anyone from where she lay. Nemesis snored again, and Fajir sighed, stretching as best she could against her bonds. What was she to do? She'd been so set on murdering as many Engali as possible before they killed her. Alone, it had seemed the best course. But when she'd seen her people being killed by plains dwellers, the exact thing she was supposed to protect them from as a widow, her heart had sung. That was a much better purpose, at least for the time being.

And if she could keep circling Celeste, killing the vermin, Nico might come back. Her Lords might take her to their bosoms again. She could forget her solitary days as a bad dream. But Nemesis and friends didn't trust her, wouldn't let her protect her people. They would wait and talk and talk and talk before dragging her back to the hated Engali, and her nightmare would start again.

And these three were so *bad* at killing. Nemesis didn't want to do it. The vermin was somewhat skilled but thought too hard about it, and though Samira grumbled like an angry geaver, she had yet to let her power loose and trample anyone. What good were they if they couldn't get the job done?

She would kill all three one day, but before that, she had to convince them to let her loose. And she had to do it soon. Perhaps if she convinced them to let her fight, then returned like an ossor to her bonds, they would let their guard down. She would not be able to fight all three while they watched her closely. She would ask to be their sword, protect her people, and when they had come to trust her a little, she would kill them all.

A comforting thought, but how was she to convince them of anything? She didn't have Cordelia's glibness or Nico's calm. She reached for the Lords again but felt no answering thoughts. Even this close to their city, they were ignoring her out of fear. She ground her teeth, trying to summon more rage to drown out the self-pity, but sorrow crept over her like fog. She bit her lip as hard as she could, trying to use the pain to center herself. She had to recall all the times she'd seen or heard one person trick another. There had to be some lesson she could use. Halaan had been able to charm people. Maybe there was a way to summon his spirit inside her and remember his words.

She opened her eyes, and he stood before her. His dark hair, just long enough to curl over his ears, ruffled in the wind, and his hazel eyes smiled at her.

Fajir gasped and tried to sit up, but her bonds were too tight. "How?" she whispered. Of all the times she'd imagined seeing him again, she'd never dreamed…

Her heart pounded, but her rational mind drowned out her awe. This couldn't be. It had to be a mind trick. Were the Lords so cruel?

"You must steer your captors west," Halaan said. "There you will find your destiny."

His lips didn't move in time with his words. Oh, she wanted this to be him, wanted this to be real, but life had taught her well. "Who are you?" she whispered. No one else came to see. Either they couldn't hear, or whoever had sent this apparition didn't want them to. "You are not my beloved."

The fake Halaan put his hands on his hips. "Look, just go west, okay?"

"You're a trick. The Lords didn't make you. Who did? Someone from Gale?" She sneered, looking at the facsimile up and down. It was a little faded around the edges, just like her memories of Halaan. Someone was reading her mind, thinking Halaan could sway her. Someday, she'd kill them for this dishonor. "You're not as clever as you think you are."

"Listen, asshole, I'm the best there is. I'm just a little...scattered, okay?" Halaan's form blurred and became that of a tall, wild-haired woman with a gaping hole where her right eye should be.

"Naos," Fajir said, impressed. She'd heard the goddess had been too wounded to use her powers. Or maybe that was just the power she'd used to possess one of the plains dwellers. She clearly retained the power to talk. That was all anyone did nowadays.

But maybe she retained other powers as well. "Free me," Fajir said, "and I will go west for you, killing as I go. I'll start with these three."

Naos laughed. "And look how quickly they jump ship when you offer them something! And it just so happens, I'm in need of a killer. So go west, find Patricia, and beat some sense into her. And if that won't work..." She drew a finger across her throat.

"All right." But once she was loose, maybe she'd go kill this Patricia, and maybe she wouldn't.

Naos darted forward, looming in front of her. "I caught that, sneaky! Don't want to be my sword, fine. See if I care! I'll do it myself." She sneered. "Have fun with the ropes and the morality gang." With a bark of a laugh, she faded, the afterimage lingering in front of Fajir's face.

Fajir struggled not to groan. She should have kept her thoughts quieter, should have been thinking of what Halaan would say before she said or thought anything. It wasn't fair! Talking wasn't her purpose! But talking would keep her imprisoned for the rest of her life, it seemed.

However long that might be.

❖

Cordelia leaned back in the captain's chair inside the Paladin Keep. Ever since she'd become a paladin, she'd thought of this office as Carmichael's, even though it didn't bear her stamp anymore. Brown had added her own touches: a clear desk, empty of Carmichael's ceramic inkwell; an extra chair against the wall. Now Cordelia supposed she'd have to do the same. Most of the paladins knew she'd been Carmichael's choice as successor. There had been a few grumbles, but she could sort those out. The new recruits seemed to accept it, and it occurred to her that for those who'd joined since she'd come back, she was the only captain they'd ever known.

Spooky.

The sounds of revelry had followed her inside the keep, slowing her steps. She couldn't drink herself into oblivion and wait for someone else to make decisions anymore. That was nearly as terrifying as what she was now hearing.

Ines, the stocky sergeant who regularly made trips to the mine to gather ore and check on the miners, stood in front of the desk. She'd already gone through her story twice. She'd gone to the mine and discovered a new wall, new defenses, and a usurper who'd taken over and claimed the loyalty of everyone.

The whole situation reeked of mind fuckery. Who could it be?

"And you didn't see this person who claimed to be in charge?" Simon asked from where he stood against the wall with Horace.

Ines shook her head. "I spoke to one person, and I didn't get a good look at him, either, but he referred to a mistress."

"This mysterious usurper might be fake," Liam said from where he sat on Ines's other side. He looked a little disheveled, and Cordelia couldn't help a small smile. His evening with Shiv must have gone well. She'd had to send someone to track him down for this meeting. "Maybe the miners have banded together and taken over."

"All of them?" Cordelia asked.

"They could have done away with any dissenters," Simon said quietly. "With the wall in the way, we have no idea what's going on."

"How big is the wall?" Cordelia asked.

"Six feet or so," Ines said. "Made of wood with metal bands. They used stone for the base. And there's a ditch in front of that."

Cordelia sat forward sharply. "A wall and a ditch around the whole damn town?"

"And every bit of it built since the last time I went," Ines said.

Horace whistled, and Cordelia had to fight to keep her mouth closed. There couldn't have been that many dissenters if they'd built that big a wall in a few weeks. Maybe there was more than mind powers at work. Someone with micro powers, who could augment strength and replenish the energy of the workers.

"It's got to be a yafanai," Cordelia said. "Or someone from the *Atlas*."

Simon stared at nothing and chewed on the end of his thumb. With Pool so near, Cordelia could feel hints of emotions from him, and she was certain he was getting a headful from all of them.

Liam crossed his arms and uncrossed them. "Could this mistress be a plains dweller chafa? There might be more people like Pakesh out there."

Ines shrugged. "I saw some plains dweller tents."

Cordelia stretched. She hoped it was just someone with too much ambition. That kind of fight she could handle, even if she didn't like fighting her own species. But an unknown power user? Either way, she supposed it didn't matter. She'd have to go look. "Get some rest," she said to Ines. It was already late. "Tomorrow we gather the gear and put together a team, then leave first thing the following morning."

Ines nodded sharply. "Captain." She left the room, and silence descended.

Liam was smiling at Cordelia, and when she glared at him, he winked. She knew he was proud of her, and she hoped it wasn't too hard to see her sitting in his mom's place. Of course, he'd never exactly had a fun time in this office.

"So, now I have to deal with this," Cordelia said. She pointed to Simon and Liam. "You two going to stay here and keep being co-mayors?"

They stared for a moment before they started babbling, each saying the other had done more for the city and waving away the other's compliments.

Cordelia groaned. "Would you two please stop jerking each other off and answer the question?"

Horace sputtered a laugh. The other two frowned. "We should hold an election," Liam said.

"You're running unopposed," Simon said. "I don't want to be mayor."

"You're living in his house," Liam said. It only sounded slightly petulant.

"Now that I don't have a hundred children to care for, I'd be happy to find somewhere else."

Liam waved that away with a bit of a blush, as if embarrassed he'd even brought it up. "We should still have a vote, but I'm all for being the new mayor if the people will have me."

"Good," Cordelia said. "Set it up."

"You can't boss me around if I'm the mayor," he said with a smile.

She snorted. "You're not the mayor yet." She nodded at Simon. "And you? The temple's always had an unofficial leader."

"As long as no one calls me God, and I don't have to wear robes of state, I don't care. Jacobs has been helping the yafanai find homes. We'll need to speak with the new mayor about building something."

"Already being planned," Liam said, looking smug.

Cordelia lifted her hands and dropped them on her desk. "Perfect. You two run the city, and I'll take care of the grunts. And the first thing I have to do is figure out what's going on at the damn mine."

"Going yourself?" Liam asked. "Sounds like a job for lieutenants, not the captain."

"Screw that! I'll take some paladins, but it's my show."

Everyone chuckled, and she grinned. Maybe this trip wouldn't be so bad after all.

Horace lifted a hand. "I'll go, too."

Everyone looked to him, Simon with a stricken expression.

Horace cleared his throat. "From what we heard, you might be looking at telepathy and micro-psychokinesis, and I have both. And the soldiers are used to me."

"Do you…" Simon trailed away and glanced at everyone. Cordelia bet there'd be more words between them later. "You're going to need other yafanai as backup."

Horace smiled softly. "I'll make some requests."

"What about the drushka?" Liam asked.

"I know Nettle will volunteer," Cordelia said. "I'm sure others will as well, but Pool should stay here since we don't know what we're dealing with."

"I'll give you descriptions of the breachies from the *Atlas*," Simon said. "That's what Dillon called the people whose pods broke open during the accident. They weren't as powerful as the bridge crew, but some of them are more powerful than yafanai."

Cordelia nodded. "Go, enjoy the rest of the night."

They left, Liam with a questioning look, but she nodded him out the door, then leaned back in the chair, her chair. She couldn't help a smile even as the problems of the future weighed on her. She was home, and she was the captain of the paladins, and everyone she cared about was alive and well. Tomorrow she'd sort out some minor problems and gather her gear. The day after, she'd sort out the mine, and then everything would be back on track.

She snorted. Or not. Whichever happened, she was going to go find Nettle and soak in as much comfort as she could.

CHAPTER EIGHTEEN

Once alone, Horace and Simon spent the night in each other's arms. After the partying, then the worrying, then the lovemaking, Horace thought he'd sleep the morning away, but when he opened his eyes, light was barely peeking around the curtains. He lay still, forgetting where he'd slept after so many days in Pool's tree. Then Simon made a noise beside him, and he remembered: the mayor's house. He was home.

Horace eased from the bed. Simon didn't stir, curled up as he was with his head on one arm. Horace wanted to climb back into bed and kiss him awake, but something had been bothering him ever since he'd returned to Gale. He couldn't put his finger on it. A sense of unease had followed him all throughout the celebration. Now it wouldn't let him sleep.

He dressed quietly, then tiptoed down the stairs. Pakesh was already up, messing about in the kitchen. Evan lay in his makeshift crib on the table, and Horace took a moment to touch the baby's sweet face and run his power over him, looking for any abnormalities.

Fit and healthy. Horace sighed, wishing he could say the same thing about his own turbulent thoughts. He went out into the morning air and breathed deeply. It was a bit too warm for the time of year. Another thing to worry about.

Even this early, many people were up and around. As he walked, he caught several conversations about the election that day. Liam was going to win by a landslide. He started to smile, but a jot of melancholy stopped him. Was that what was bothering him? No one had asked him if he wanted to run for mayor?

He didn't. But the day before, Cordelia hadn't bothered to ask what his role in Gale would be at all. Everyone thought of him as a helper, a sidekick. He frowned. Did he want to be something else? He'd always wanted to help people, and that was what he'd been doing. He didn't want to be in charge. Maybe he was just angry no one had thanked him.

He rolled his eyes at himself. Maybe being augmented in power had augmented his ego as well. It was probably just the idea of splitting up with Simon so soon after returning that was making him moody. But then, he'd volunteered to go. Why had his hand shot up so suddenly? When they'd gotten home the night before, Simon had asked that same question. Horace had given the answer he believed at the time: people needed him. And he truly wished Simon could go, too. Horace wasn't trying to run from the man he loved. Maybe he was craving adrenaline, like someone who was half yafanai and half paladin. In the thick of battle, there wasn't time to think about anything else.

He told himself to stop being silly, go back home, snuggle up with Simon, and not waste any of the precious time they had together, but he kept walking. He'd head for the market. Maybe seeing people with real problems would cure him.

As he turned around, someone else pulled up short as if they'd been following him. The man turned from side to side awkwardly before stepping to a display window and pretending to study the contents.

Horace didn't sense any sinister thoughts, merely a keen sense of embarrassment. He walked closer, recognizing Jon Lea. "Jon? Were you looking for me?"

Jon turned with a grimace. He was normally so stoic that his face and emotions were hard to read, but now he seemed in turmoil. But that could be because Horace had called him by his first name. No one else seemed to.

"Is something wrong?" Horace asked softly. They'd nearly died at the same time in the swamp. Maybe it was affecting Jon more than it was Horace. And Horace had used his telepathy to help traumatized people before. "Do you need help?"

"I…needed to make sure you were okay." Jon took a deep breath, and his face settled into something closely resembling his normal blankness.

"Okay." Horace resisted the urge to pry with his power, though he didn't sense any dishonesty. "Was there some reason you thought I wouldn't be?"

"You seemed worried last night shortly after sundown, when you received a report from Sergeant Ines Duncan. Then later, after you fetched Simon Lazlo and Captain Ross, you seemed calmer, so when I received notice of a mission to the mine, I thought I would...check on you." He frowned again. The report had been delivered calmly, but now he seemed confused, as if unused to the sort of relationships where he checked on someone.

"So you've been...checking up on me since I got back?" Following, more like. Horace hadn't even noticed. He looked for any hint of romantic feelings. He didn't find anything sexual, but he did notice Jon's keen admiration. Maybe that was as close to romantic as he got.

Horace didn't know whether to smile kindly or run away.

"You fixed me in the swamp," Jon said, voice soft.

"Oh!" Relief coursed through Horace. He could handle a bit of grateful hero worship. "You don't need to worry about thanking me. I was happy to help."

Jon smiled, an awkward look Horace remembered from the swamp, like someone trying out their face. "Well, I'll be going on the mission, so..." He gestured vaguely, and it took Horace a moment to realize he was trying to shoo Horace back toward the mayor's house.

"I was going to the market if you want to join me," Horace said, not in the mood to be herded by anyone, good intentions or not.

"I..." Jon hesitated as if no one ever invited him anywhere.

"Well, you can't follow me anymore," Horace said, "so you can either join me or find something else to do." He couldn't help the irritation that threaded into his tone. Even if Jon was simply worried about him, he could take care of himself. He'd proven that, or thought he had. Horace had saved both himself and Jon as well as many others.

With a sigh, Horace started walking again. When he reached the end of the street, he glanced back, but Jon was gone. Either he'd decided to go about his business, or he was following more clandestinely than before. Horace told himself not to care, but the whole exchange burned him. He wondered when he'd stopped thinking that someone caring for his safety was sweet.

Well, Simon caring was still sweet, but Simon also believed in him. How many others thought he needed a nursemaid? He'd told Cordelia that the paladins were used to him, but maybe they still didn't think much of him.

When he saw Cordelia walking toward him through the market, he pulled up short, wondering if he'd summoned her with his thoughts. Or was she looking out for him, too? But she didn't seem to have noticed him, and she'd never been very sneaky. He told himself not to be paranoid.

People got out of her way as she walked, even when she smiled. She was tall, three inches more than him, and even in street clothes, she was impressively muscular. Maybe that was what he needed, some outward sign of the power inside him. But he didn't want to invest the time it would take to get her impressive physique. And he didn't want to go back to wearing yafanai robes. Maybe he should just wear a sign.

She caught sight of him and grinned. "Hello, Horace. Shopping?"

"Just walking. You?"

"I went to see what's left of the temple." She shook her head sadly. "There's a lot of work to be done." She glanced around. "And Jacobs tells me there's a fledgling street gang cruising the market."

"A gang?" He couldn't believe it. The guilds usually took care of such things. "How?"

"Shit like that happens when a town is vulnerable."

"And you're going to stop them with no weapon and no armor?"

She grinned. "If they see weapons and armor, they won't show themselves." She clapped him on the shoulder. "And now that you're here, I've got backup."

He returned her smile. At least someone thought he could take care of himself, even though she'd cast him as backup and not the hero. He told himself to shut up and take the compliment.

They strolled together, and Horace scanned the surface thoughts of those around him, not going deeper, avoiding breaking the law. They stopped and spoke with the people selling wares. Even with all the work Simon had done on the plants, the offerings of fruit were a little meager. Both Horace and Cordelia tried to reassure people that the hard times would eventually pass.

While Cordelia was chatting with someone, Horace spotted a group of young people lounging in the shade. They were watching him and Cordelia and grinning. Horace wandered closer, wondering what they were smiling at. His surface scans revealed a bit of nastiness. Maybe he'd found the gang. Perfect. Just what he needed.

He sighed at the thought. Cordelia was really rubbing off on him.

"Hey," one of the gang called, a young man near the front with greasy blond hair hanging in his eyes. "That your girlfriend?" He nodded toward Cordelia.

The others snickered. Horace fought the urge to smile. He could knock all of them out with a snap. "Maybe."

"Aren't you a little small for her?" another asked, a sharp-faced woman.

"Maybe he's big where it counts," another said.

They all laughed. Horace waited for the part that was supposed to embarrass him. "She likes to pick me up and run around with me."

They blinked as if not knowing what to say. Cordelia came up beside him and wrapped an arm around his shoulders. She must have caught some of the conversation. "I do like my partners portable."

The greasy guy stood and hooked his thumbs in his belt. "Maybe having a better lover would cure you of that."

Horace frowned. As insults went, it was pretty terrible, but he figured it didn't matter. This group wanted a fight, so they'd do what they had to in order to get one. And Horace spotted more of them coming from the alley behind, adults. The real gang.

Cordelia no doubt noticed them, too. "I don't think you or your friends would know a good lover if they bit you on the ass." She grinned. "Or even after that. Why don't you go home and be a waste of oxygen there."

The adults came out of the alley, frowning. Cordelia took her arm from Horace's shoulders. Anticipation rolled off her.

"You're in the wrong part of town," the largest man said. He pushed past the teens. "We charge a toll for people like you."

"Snappy dressers?" Horace asked.

Cordelia snorted a laugh. "I think he means people who bathe."

The big man lunged forward, reaching for Horace.

Horace jumped back, taken off guard. He'd been certain they'd go for Cordelia first. Maybe they were hoping to use him as a shield.

Cordelia stepped into the big man's path and hit him in the chin with an open palm. He tottered, and the others leapt to help, coming for Cordelia. Horace turned to one who rushed around her. He swamped the gang member's mind with power, and she dropped. Cordelia swung one of her opponents onto her shoulders, then threw him into the street. When another launched a punch toward her face, she grabbed his arm and tossed him away, too, narrowly missing a cart stall.

"Mind the fruit!" Horace called.

"Right!" She punched her next opponent into the alley instead. Horace knocked out another with his powers. Those who'd been thrown squirmed where they'd landed, gasping for air. One tried to run, and Horace sabotaged her legs. He sent a telepathic call to the Paladin Keep. They'd need more people to haul this bunch away once Cordelia was done with them. She grabbed for another one, but Jon Lea stepped out from between two market stalls and stopped the runner with a punch to the gut.

Horace frowned, but he didn't have time to deal with Jon at the moment. He put another runner to sleep, then turned to Cordelia. She had the big man on the ground, one arm pulled up behind his back.

"Get off me!" he cried. "Motherfucker!"

"Want me to knock him out?" Horace asked.

Cordelia nodded.

"Try it, asshole!" the big man yelled.

Horace put him to sleep with a neat flick of power. "Nighty night."

Cordelia gave him a grin, then dragged all the gang members into a pile. She nodded to Jon as he added another. "Lucky you were close."

"I called for reinforcements," Horace said, not wanting her to know that Jon had been keeping an eye on him. "Just to haul them away," he added for Cordelia's ego.

The shopkeepers were clapping, some of them crying, "About time!"

Cordelia gave them a little wave, but some were clapping for Horace, too. He fought the urge to beam, wondering what in the world had gotten into him. He'd never craved applause, ever. He made a mental note to talk to Simon. Maybe something else was affecting his brain.

"Lea, wait here with the captives," Cordelia said. "Help's on the way."

He nodded. "Captain."

He didn't look at Horace, and Horace wondered if having Cordelia here put Jon's mind at ease.

Cordelia clapped Horace on the shoulder. "Come on, my portable paramour."

❖

Cordelia followed Horace back to her uncle's old house, but she wasn't up to going inside, not yet. Every time she thought about it, she saw his body on the floor. She shivered as she waited while Horace went inside. When Simon came out, they made plans to meet later, after Cordelia checked on a few things at the keep. She'd need a good drinking buddy that afternoon.

At the keep, preparations for the mine trip seemed to be going well. She kept thinking back to her days as a lieutenant, when she'd wandered the keep trying to avoid meetings with Carmichael. She wanted to be friendlier than that, but not so friendly that people felt as if they could waste her time. Of course, maybe that was how Carmichael started out, too.

With a sigh, she wandered out to the practice field for some fresh air, stopping when she spotted Liam watching the troops. Since he'd gotten back, Jon Lea had some of them running around the field; others were doing crunches or push-ups. Still others were working on the practice equipment the Storm Lord had constructed. Cordelia had ordered training to restart that morning. Too many of the new recruits had collapsed under the weight of unpowered armor in the swamp. Since she didn't have a way to charge it, they'd have to get stronger.

"Getting nostalgic?" Cordelia asked as she paused behind Liam.

"About having some lieutenant chew my ass until I run it off?" He breathed deep. "Kind of."

Cordelia chuckled. "I thought you'd be off doing mayor things. Word is, you've got the election in the bag."

"I was supposed to meet Shiv, but she's still with her mother." He kicked some dirt around and smiled almost shyly. "At least we're… talking again."

Cordelia snorted a laugh. "Good."

"Though she did warn me that she might have to leave soon and spend some time with the old drushka."

"Ah." She didn't know quite what to say. Life never seemed to stay good very long anymore. It made her wonder what would happen with Lyshus, what the drushka would do with a male queen.

Liam pointed to a soldier, her brown ponytail swinging behind her as she jogged. "Watch her."

When the joggers passed Lea, he barked at them to pick it up. Some groaned, already sagging, but the woman with the ponytail clenched her jaw and ran faster. Even from across the field, Cordelia saw pride in her eyes. "Who is that?"

"Not sure. I heard one of the others call her Baby Ross, but I don't think that's official."

Cordelia snorted. "Well, she's sure as shit not my kid. And if you say I look old enough to be her mom, I'll turn you inside out."

"She's tough and so eager Lea had to chase her off the equipment so others could use it."

Cordelia smiled. "Is this what you've been doing all morning? Gossiping?"

"I think that's primarily what a mayor does."

With another snort, Cordelia watched the field again, thoughts of her uncle rearing within. But the moves of the troops were hypnotic. No wonder Liam came to watch them when he was sad.

"Hey, Lea!" Cordelia called.

He jogged over. "Captain?"

"Who's the ponytail in the lead?"

Lea didn't even glance over his shoulder. "Private Sunny Swanson, Cap."

"Any good?"

Lea shrugged. "If you can call the best of a bunch of sorry-ass newbs good, Cap."

Cordelia had to laugh. "As you were, Lieutenant."

Lea strode back to his charges, bellowing and hollering at them to move their asses and push through the pain, though he didn't even sound angry as he did so, more like he was reading from a script. If he wanted the job of pushing the newcomers on a permanent basis, she was happy to give it to him.

She didn't need something else to worry about. "Come on, Liam." He followed her back through the keep and into the courtyard. "What else are you up to today?"

"I've got a few meetings." He grinned at her, then turned that smile to the street where Pakesh was fast approaching, Horace following far behind him. "Here's my first appointment."

"Pakesh?" she asked.

"After the party, I was able to give him some advice on dating. He's seeing someone this afternoon and wanted a few last-minute tips."

Cordelia laughed, but as the young man approached, a wide smile on his face, Cordelia tried her best to turn her laugh into a cough.

"You ready?" Liam asked.

Pakesh nodded. "She should be here any minute. Like you said, I had her meet me somewhere impressive."

"Good man. Remember the rules?"

Pakesh looked up for a moment, the pose of someone desperate to recall something important. "Everyone likes to be told they look and smell nice."

"But not too many times or else…"

"…it's creepy," Pakesh finished. Cordelia barked another coughing laugh.

"What shouldn't you do?" Liam asked.

"Interrupt her when she's trying to talk."

"And?"

Pakesh bit his lip and glanced at the ground before realization popped into his eyes. "No staring south of the neck!"

Cordelia had to press her lips together and pull them into her mouth. No cough would cover her next laugh if it got out.

"And if she catches you staring?" Liam asked, his face still serious.

"Tell her how nice her shirt looks."

Liam clapped him on the shoulder. "Remember, that won't work more than once, so keep your head up."

Cordelia's laugh came rushing out so hard she had to lean on Liam. "You…" She gasped for breath. "You forgot, always ask her what she wants to do next, then pretend to enjoy it!"

Pakesh's eyes widened, and he nodded fervently. "That's good. I like it."

Liam elbowed Cordelia off his side. "That's the advanced class. You said this girl is kind of shy, so she'll be relying on you for today's activities."

Pakesh nodded proudly. "A stroll through the market. We could buy some sweet rolls."

"Sounds good," Liam said.

Cordelia couldn't stop snickering. "Don't expect any tongue on the first date."

Pakesh's mouth dropped open, and his color deepened by several shades.

"Ignore her." Liam nodded toward the street. "Here she is. Off you go."

A young girl Pakesh's age stood at the gates to the keep. She smiled shyly, and Pakesh beamed at her. He nearly ran to her side, and they moved away together, Horace following a discreet distance behind. Cordelia gave him a wave.

Liam put a hand to his heart. "I love young love."

Cordelia pushed him gently. "Romantic ass."

"Where are you off to? Want to go to the Pickled Prog?"

"Good thought," she said. "Simon and I are already meeting there. Let's go."

Liam's expression turned stony as he crossed his arms. "He sure does make friends easily."

"What's the problem?"

"Nothing, nothing," Liam said, waving. "On your way. I can occupy myself."

Cordelia frowned, looking for the joke, but the way he wouldn't look at her spoke of genuine hurt. "What the fuck? Did he do something to you?"

"No."

"Say something?"

"He's fine. He's great. He's everyone's friend."

Cordelia tried to think of what could have happened since the party but came up empty. "You were singing his praises pretty hard last night."

He did look at her then, and she didn't like the anger in his eyes. "That's because he's Mr. Fucking Fantastic, and everyone loves him."

"Holy fuck, Liam, are you jealous?" She'd never known him to be jealous of anything save Cordelia's relationship with her uncle, and that was because his mom should have won an award for bad parenting.

Liam laughed so loudly it screamed overcompensation. "Of course not! After all, you only want to leave me in the lurch and—"

Cordelia's temper spiked. "Either stay here with your self-pity, or come get a drink with us, your choice." She started to turn away, but he mumbled something about everyone picking Simon over him. Cordelia threw her hands in the air. "Do you want me to go get him so you can compare dicks and decide whose is better?"

Liam gave her a nasty leer. "Seen his dick, have you?"

"Oh yeah," Cordelia said, drawing the words out. "You know it. That's why I like him. We're going to get plowed and then fuck until the sun goes down!"

Behind her, someone coughed, and she felt Simon standing there. "Um, if I'd known that," he said, "I'd have worn something nicer, maybe used some cologne."

Cordelia fought the urge to squirm. She cleared her throat. "Just a minor misunderstanding."

Simon fidgeted before he stepped forward. "Liam, I..." He sighed. "Samira is so much better at these kinds of talks than I am, but here goes. I know it must seem...significant that the people you love are becoming my friends, but..." He took a deep breath and smiled hesitantly, but Cordelia sensed impatience simmering below the surface. They were alike in a lot of ways. Maybe that was one of the reasons they connected so easily through Pool.

"Please, believe me," Simon said. "I'm not trying to take people away from you. I've never had many friends. I'll take all I can get." He offered Liam a hand. "One big dysfunctional family?"

Liam rolled his eyes but shook the hand. "Stop winning me over."

Simon grinned. "You got it."

Cordelia wound her arms through theirs. "Come on. We'll get good and tipsy, crawl under a blanket, and play a rousing game of 'Whose Hand Is That.' Then we'll be the best of friends. Or we'd better be. I don't have time for all this personal shit."

They had a quick drink, and Cordelia left them laughing and talking, glad to know they could get along in her absence. It left her time to wander around her city a bit more, taking it all in, promising she'd be back as soon as she could. Maybe one day, she'd even make it into her uncle's house.

Before she knew it, morning had come, and it was time to leave for the mine. When she met Horace and the rest who were going on the expedition, some of them seemed eager to go. Maybe they'd all had their fill of personal conflicts in Gale. Along with the handful of leathers and two armors was a pile of gear, including Cordelia's personal pack. One perk of being captain was that someone else always toted her stuff. Wearing armor that was now as heavy as she remembered, she was happy to have her burden lightened however it happened.

Nettle had insisted on coming, not that Cordelia minded one bit. A few other drushkan scouts were coming, too. Sergeant Ines was leading the way, and Horace had brought two other yafanai. Everyone geared up and said last-minute good-byes. They were standing just outside the eastern gate when Liam came out to join them.

"Come to see us off?" Cordelia called. He had a pack slung over his shoulders, and she pointed to it. "If that's a barrel of mead to take with us, you're getting a big sloppy kiss."

"Divine as that sounds, no, it isn't. I'm coming with you. You need someone from the government of Gale to speak with the people at the mine, and since the election yesterday, I'm it."

Cordelia nodded slowly. "Congratulations, but I've learned some diplomacy in my time, you know."

"I know, I know. You talk good now. I'm still coming."

She knew he trusted her, so she wasn't quite sure what was going on. Maybe Shiv had gone cold again. Whatever it was, if he wanted to avoid his own shit for a while, she didn't see how she could argue.

Ines approached, rubbing her hands. "We've got food and water for four days. If something happens and we need to stay longer, I've brought hunting gear."

"Hustle up!" Cordelia called. Lea and Porter, the two armors, bullied the leathers into line, Sunny Swanson among them. If they got into a fight, the leathers would be using truncheons, and the armors would use blades. They'd recovered some of their slugs from the swamp, but they hadn't had time to refashion them. If things got really hairy, they'd have to rely on the yafanai to help them out.

Cordelia walked up the line of paladins, nodding. Private Swanson was watching her intently. When she met Cordelia's eyes, she stood so tall, Cordelia thought she might be on tiptoe.

It was hard not to smile, but Cordelia kept it inside. Barely. "Ready, grunts?" she asked.

"Yes, Captain," they chorused, Swanson yelling louder than the others.

"Eyes wide. This isn't a pleasure hike."

After another affirmative, they were off. Cordelia stayed near the middle of the line, off to the side, letting Lea take point. Horace and Nettle walked beside her while Liam had gone up to talk with Ines. The scouts strayed far ahead and only came back to report.

"We should trade Wuran for some ossors," Horace said. "I'm spoiled."

Nettle made a face. "I prefer the queen's tree."

"If she wanted to lend it to us, I'd take it," Horace said.

"No whining." Cordelia lifted her arms, reveling in the pull of the armor, in its weight. She realized she'd missed it more than powered armor. "This is paradise!"

Nettle wrinkled her nose. "Not all revel in hardship, Sa."

"You can say that again," Porter mumbled. He'd dropped back to just within earshot.

Cordelia put on her best Carmichael face. "What was that, Lieutenant?"

He straightened, eyes wide. "Nothing...nothing, Captain."

"I didn't hear you, Lieutenant!"

"Nothing, Captain!"

Everyone's eyes were wide, and Cordelia chuckled. "It's all right. I'm just fucking with you."

Some chuckled, a little nervously to her ears. Liam turned and mouthed, "Bully."

She laughed, and it felt very good indeed.

They marched through the day and set up camp while the mine was just out of sight. Darkness was falling, but that wouldn't matter to the drushka. It was time for a little scouting. Cordelia stripped off her armor, determined to go with them. Hopefully, they wouldn't let her embarrass herself by falling in the dark.

"Be careful," Liam said. "Stay hidden."

Nettle grinned. "We will be as lizards among the reeds."

They hurried into the night, and Cordelia couldn't help thinking of being wounded with Nettle, of the close encounter with the grelcat in the darkness. She tried not to shiver at the thoughts. They were the past, done with, like the drushka were always saying. She couldn't afford to focus on such things now.

They paused when they saw torchlight glimmering atop the mine's new wall. It didn't seem as well-constructed as the palisade around Gale, but she'd expected something hurried and shoddy. She didn't see any walkways, but they could have been hidden. In the light of the torches, she saw two gates, a smaller one within a larger, but no other gaps. A ditch lay between them and the wall, filled with sharpened stakes, but that wouldn't stop their small scouting party.

With the drushka leading the way, they sneaked around the side. The wall met the hill beyond in an area too steep to climb. If someone went far enough into the mountains, they could probably double back and come at the town from above.

Where anyone would see them coming. Smart.

"I can climb the wall," Nettle whispered in Cordelia's ear.

She didn't like the sound of that and didn't bother to hide her frown. "A quick look. Keep your head down."

Nettle went with one other scout. They twisted easily through the ditch and stakes, then ran their hands over the wall before skittering upward. Cordelia bit her lip. She could hear voices from inside. People were awake and moving around; the drushka might be spotted at any moment. She tensed, ready to fight or run, whichever was needed.

Nettle and the other scout moved sideways as they peeked, staying far too long for comfort. A cramp began to form in Cordelia's calves, and she tried to stretch while remaining out of sight. She was thinking of ways to signal when Nettle and the other scout climbed down and hurried over. Together, they retreated into the darkness.

"Small structures interspersed with larger ones," Nettle whispered. "It seems a typical human place. There are indeed plains dwellers and tents." She gripped Cordelia's arm. "I saw someone I have seen before, a young human woman, the one who bore the consciousness of Naos."

Cordelia's belly went cold. What the fuck could that mean? "Come on. We need to talk to the others."

CHAPTER NINETEEN

At their camp in the plains, Horace shook his head as he listened to Nettle's report about the mining town. He could hardly believe it. What in the world was Kora doing there?

"If she's not possessed," Horace said, "I can't imagine why she'd take over a mine. Maybe she's just...staying there?" He related again what his old friend Natalya had told him. Kora had been a four-year-old trapped in a teenager's body when she'd been under Naos's control. He hoped like hell that she'd simply taken refuge in the mine, but he couldn't really believe that.

"What if Naos is still with her somehow?" Cordelia asked. "Or what if she's got some of Naos's power?"

Horace shook his head even as his stomach went cold. "No, no way. I was with Simon when we beat Naos. I felt what he felt. He broke Naos's link, the power that let her possess people."

"Could she still be guiding the girl telepathically?" Cordelia asked.

Horace rubbed the bridge of his nose. "Could she convince someone to take over a town with words alone?"

"Maybe everything Kora went through unhinged her," Liam said. "And now she can only do what Naos wanted her to do before."

"Well," Cordelia said as she stretched. "There's one way to find out. In the morning, we'll ask."

"Ahya," Nettle said. "That is the best way."

"First light?" Lea asked from where he'd been watching.

Nettle gestured at the night. "I could help us sneak over the wall now."

Horace shook his head. "If she has even a fraction of Naos's power, Kora will sense us."

Cordelia nodded. "Lea, set watches. Everyone else, get some sleep."

Inside his tent, Horace stared at the darkness. The little girl who'd become a pawn in Naos's games had broken his heart when he'd first seen her. He'd wanted to help her then. Hope fluttered at the thought that he might be able to help her now. He'd been unable to help Natalya, and looking after Kora had been her last wish. Now maybe Horace could fulfill it.

It felt as if he'd just closed his eyes when Cordelia bellowed a wake-up call. With a groan, Horace rolled out of his blanket and used his power to brush the cobwebs from his mind. He'd need real sleep the next night. Maybe once he'd helped Kora, she'd find a place for them in the town. It was a nice thought to keep in mind.

With a lighter heart, Horace fell in line with the others and marched to the wall. The morning daylight stretched out before them, but a chill settled over Horace. He kept flashing back to Natalya's face, her shattered body. He hadn't found it until after Pool had reached Celeste. Had Kora killed her? Or had it been Naos? Was it better to be a puppet or a madwoman?

Noise came from the mining town. They were already up, probably working. People wandered in and out of the tents that stretched before the wall, and several people caught sight of Cordelia's band. They ran to the wall, yelling for someone.

Cordelia kept marching even as a group of plains dwellers gathered, some of them with weapons ready. A group of archers lined the top of the wall by the time Cordelia called a halt.

"Easy does it," Cordelia said as her troops shifted from foot to foot. Horace sent them some calm, ready to change that to a jolt of adrenaline if they needed it.

"We're here to see the woman in charge," Cordelia yelled.

Soon after, the small door set inside the larger gate opened. A tall, willowy woman walked out. Her black hair stood out starkly against her red dress, and her air of superiority was clear even from this distance. "We told you not to come back," she called, with traces of an accent that wasn't Galean or from the plains.

Horace scanned her. "She has power," he whispered. "More than a yafanai."

"Looks like one of the breachies," Cordelia mumbled. "Our mystery puppeteer?"

"Maybe." But she didn't seem powerful enough to subdue a whole town.

"This mine belongs to Gale," Cordelia shouted. "Who are you?"

The woman snorted and crossed her arms. "I'm Raquel, and I'd watch how I talk to my elders if I were you."

"Well, I've faced the ultimate badass from the *Atlas* and lived. What have you got on Naos?"

Raquel dropped her arms. "What are you talking about?" Her head tilted as if listening to someone.

Horace swallowed as he detected a telepathic signal, but he didn't pry, remembering the way Naos had batted him away like an insect. When Raquel turned, and Kora stepped past her, he almost breathed a sigh of relief. He didn't try for a deep scan, but even a surface one revealed that there was no outside link. Whatever had happened, Kora wasn't tied to Naos. He sent a quick mental note to Cordelia, and she nodded over her shoulder.

"Mistress," Raquel said, "I can take care of this."

"I want to see her again." Kora seemed different, more confident and centered, though she still looked about sixteen. Her brown hair hung loosely over her shoulders, framing a thin face, though she didn't seem malnourished. As she came closer, he noticed her eyes were mismatched: one blue, one brown. He didn't remember that from before.

"Kora?" he asked. "Are you all right?"

She glanced at him and frowned. "Sorry, I don't remember you." She pointed at Cordelia and smiled. "But I know her. A little bee, wasn't that what she called you?"

Cordelia's hand rested on her wooden sword. "Naos. Is she speaking to you? Through you?"

The girl smiled wider. "Not anymore. I'm Patricia Dué. Nice to meet you in the flesh."

Cordelia glanced over her shoulder. Horace thought back to his conversations with Simon. "That was Naos's name before she came to this planet," he said in Cordelia's mind.

"Ah ah," Patricia said, wagging a finger. "It's rude to talk where people can't hear." She grinned, seemed genuinely happy to see them. "I separated from the rest of my body and left Naos up on the *Atlas*. I'm just Patricia now." Her smiled turned a bit wooden as if that might not be exactly true, and her gaze wandered upward as if she was listening to someone else.

Horace looked again but still didn't detect a link or a telepathic signal. What was going on?

Patricia took a deep breath. "I'm free." The words had a bit of an edge to them, as if she was trying to convince herself as well as them.

"What happened to Kora?" Horace asked, dreading the answer.

"Naos killed her mind before your battle. The body was empty, so I stepped inside." She shrugged as if such things happened every day.

Horace shut his eyes and mourned for her. For Natalya.

"Whatever your story is," Cordelia said, "it doesn't change the fact that this mine belongs to Gale."

"Not anymore."

Cordelia took a step forward.

Patricia laughed. "Let me save you some pain and suffering. When I left my body, I didn't go empty-handed."

Horace sensed it as she tapped her power, but she was faster than him. He froze under her psychokinetic grip, and he couldn't access his abilities. He saw his fellow yafanai sink to their knees just before he followed. Why had he ever wanted anyone to see him as the primary threat?

Cordelia whipped her blade free. The paladins charged, then flew backward. Horace tried to call a warning, but he struggled even to breathe. Ines and Liam dove for cover in the grass. The drushka tried to scatter, but they rolled away, battered by invisible force.

Patricia strode to Horace. She hadn't lost her smile.

He sucked in a deep breath as she let him breathe easier. "Stop," he said with a wheeze. "We can talk."

"I'll let you go this time," she said. "Tell the rest of the Galeans that if they want metal, they'll have to trade for it." She smirked. "This mine is...mine."

"Wait!" Liam stood, his hands raised. "Please. I'm the mayor of Gale. I only want to speak with you."

"You brought soldiers to my gate. That sends a different message."

"For protection. We needed to see what was happening. And now that we have, I'd really like to stay and talk it over. You want to trade? We'll have to sort out terms." His face and tone were calm, reasonable. Horace swallowed and looked between them.

Patricia cocked her head as if listening to an internal voice again. "Okay, but just you."

"Fuck that!" Cordelia yelled from where she lay.

Patricia grinned. "I do admire her spirit."

"It's okay, Delia," Liam said. "I want to stay and figure this out."

"Brave," Patricia said. "I'll let you have two bodyguards, just to show there's no hard feelings. But the bee can't stay. How about that one and that one?"

Raquel waved. Lieutenant Porter and Private Swanson slid through the grass as if dragged by a giant hand. They landed in a heap at Liam's side. Both climbed to their feet, rubbing their limbs and shaking their heads.

"There, one of each, armor and leather, male and female," Patricia said, "cozy as the ark." With a hearty laugh, she walked away, not releasing Horace's power or his limbs until she'd gone inside the gate.

Raquel stayed to watch, and the plains dwellers hadn't dispersed.

Horace healed everyone's minimal injuries as he stood. "She's too strong," he said as Cordelia gripped her blade. She had murder etched into every feature.

"Liam," she said, "you can't do this."

He cast a glance at Raquel and lowered his voice. "This is what I'm good at, Delia. Let me do my job. If she wants to do business, she's not going to kill me."

"If her telepathy is strong enough, she won't have to," Horace said. "Let me give you something to protect you." He put his hands on either side of Liam's head and focused. Liam gasped, but Horace didn't have time to be gentle. He built blocks and walls inside Liam's mind, the strongest he could make. It only took a moment. If Patricia tried to take him over or alter his mind, it wouldn't be easy. Maybe Liam would have time to strike or run.

Liam blinked when it was done, swaying a bit as if he'd stared at the sun. "Um, thanks."

"Now for your guards." Horace turned to them and quickly did the same. It wouldn't save them from her psychokinesis, but at least he felt as if he was doing something.

"Come if you're coming," Raquel called.

"Thanks." Liam gripped Cordelia's shoulders then started for the gate, Swanson and Porter with him.

"Keep him safe," Cordelia called to the paladins. "Do me proud." They saluted, then Liam was through the gate, the paladins on his heels.

"Come on," Cordelia said, her expression stony as she led them down the road until the wall was out of sight. "What the fuck was all that? Who the fuck is she?" She marched up and down, seemingly at a loss without someone to punch.

"We need to talk to Simon," Horace said.

"Ahya," Nettle said. "He can best tell us how to fight. If this woman has even a part of Naos's strength, we will need a solid plan."

Cordelia put her hands on top of her head. "Fuck!"

"We need to get back to Gale," Horace said, completely out of his depth. He couldn't help feeling as if they all were. He only hoped that what he'd done to Liam's mind was enough to keep him safe until they could figure out something else. He'd wanted more to do. Well, now he had it. He never should have wished for anything but a peaceful life.

Simon strolled through the empty warehouse behind Jacobs. All morning, they'd been searching for somewhere to house the yafanai until the temple was rebuilt. They'd tried putting some in the keep, but that hadn't gone well. The soldiers and the yafanai had never been the best of buddies. And with Miriam, Mila, and Victoria to add to the household, the mayor's house was full. Simon had taken Miriam with him today for an extra opinion, and she scanned the warehouse while Pakesh trailed after them.

"It's...sparse," Simon said, staring at the naked beams overhead. The dirt floor had been cleared, but he spotted a few scraps of grass, and the place smelled stale.

"After we divide it into rooms, it might look all right," Miriam said. "Some of the yafanai won't be happy, but it's better than a tent."

Jacobs put her hands on her hips and nodded. "It's the largest space available. There are some empty houses we can check out, but nothing this size. If the yafanai want to stay together, this is the best they're going to get."

"You'll never please all of them. Let them whine," Miriam said.

That was easy to say while she was staying in the mayor's house, but Simon didn't point that out. And maybe they'd all be out of there before too long if Liam decided to move in. They'd parted on good terms, but every now and again, Simon thought of his petulant face and wanted to frown. Hopefully, governmental power wouldn't go to his head.

Pakesh wandered to the rear of the warehouse and felt along the wall. "It seems sturdy. Maybe you can build a second story. Then people can spread out more."

Simon glanced up. Several slats were missing from the roof, letting daylight leak in, but that could be repaired. A shadow flitted by one of the holes; it might have been a bird, but his senses told him it was something larger. He didn't even need the following thump to convince him.

"Someone's on the roof." He held his power ready, an image of the man with the knife flashing in his memory.

Jacobs craned her head. "Maybe they're fixing it."

Something blocked out the light, and it took a moment to register that an object was falling, that he should move. Frantic, he tried to catch it with his power, but it proved too big.

Pakesh cried out, and Simon tried to duck. He'd barely moved when it smashed down, half on his head and half on his shoulder.

It didn't hurt. It should have. The world went dull and quiet. Dimly, he knew his legs had given out. He was on the floor, and it tilted crazily before his half-lidded eyes. Someone was shouting, but they sounded far away, underwater maybe. He couldn't bring himself to care. Emotions seemed as distant as voices. Even his power was a memory. He tried to blink, tried to get some thoughts in order. Someone was tugging on his arm. He tried to turn his head, but his body wouldn't work.

A bit of telepathy wormed into his skull, someone calling his name, their mental voice frantic. He tried to tell them to relax, to swim in this painless sea with him, but speech hid just out of reach. He rolled sideways, and Miriam's panicked face contorted in pain before him. She grasped her head and fell away.

"Doc!" Jacobs's voice. The world tilted again, and his stomach seemed to move through his body. Was he sick? His chin was wet. His whole face seemed wet. The smell of smoke filled his nostrils, and that wasn't right. There'd been too much fire lately.

He stood. How? His legs weren't working. No, Jacobs held him up. He could float away from her if he tried. All he had to do was let go. Miriam had fallen. Pakesh had fallen. A cloud of smoke rolled past Jacobs's face as she shouted. They needed help. He could help. Maybe then they'd be quiet. He searched inside for his power, fumbling for it. Nothing.

Wait. A spark. There, he could hear a little better. Pakesh had risen to help Miriam as she clutched her stomach. "The baby is coming!" Pakesh cried.

"Not here it isn't!" Jacobs shoved Simon into Pakesh's arms, and the world lurched. Simon tried to hold on, but his body wasn't quite his yet. Jacobs grabbed Miriam and helped her stagger.

Miriam grasped her head with one hand and her belly with another. Pakesh stumbled, and Simon felt telepathic needles stabbing them all, but they barely pained him. He felt a wave of heat from the doorway, could feel the trickle of liquid on his face. Blood? He grabbed for his power again, but it was as slippery as an eel. What the hell was wrong with him?

"Watch out!" Pakesh shouted.

Four people rushed through the smoke. Jacobs called out, and the newcomers streaked for her and Miriam, but one held something in his hands. Jacobs drew her truncheon, and Miriam slid to the ground. Two of the strangers lunged for Jacobs, deflecting her truncheon with a loud whack.

"Stop!" Pakesh yelled.

The other two strangers lifted Miriam and carried her away. "No," Simon tried to say. He tried to tell Pakesh to use his power, but the grip of an unseen telepath battered both their minds.

Simon needed his power. Anger began to seep through the haze. He could feel the telepath standing beyond the smoke. He tried to heal himself again, but that was too much work. He lashed out at the telepath clouding Pakesh's mind. Two could play dirty.

Pakesh cried out in rage as his power flowed free. The telepath blew away, taking the stabbing pains. Pakesh's power bloomed again, and bits of the warehouse wall exploded outward. Jacobs's attackers shot across the room, bodies bent unnaturally. Pakesh's power became a wild thing, stabbing, flinging, blindly grabbing whatever it could.

Simon turned his power on himself, trying to heal, but it felt like trying to find something hidden in a vat of taffy. "Pakesh, enough!"

Pakesh's power caught him up, carried him along on a tide of destruction. The power had engulfed Pakesh's mind, carrying him away to an infinite place filled with stars.

"No," Simon tried to say.

"Why do all the wounded birds flock to my door?" a new voice asked. Simon knew that voice, Naos's voice. They had to get out, to go back.

Pakesh couldn't answer, lost as he was in the forces within his own mind. Naos held him fast. Simon tried not to think of himself, tried not to be noticed. Maybe not being able to use his power at the moment was a good thing.

"You reached too far, little bird." She laughed. "But then, I'm closer than ever before." Her presence breezed past them. "Look up, and you will find me."

Simon jolted and opened his eyes. He'd collapsed on the warehouse floor with Pakesh. Jacobs lay nearby, face bloody, unmoving. Simon reached for his power again, but he'd never heal them before they were lost to the smoke. Why wouldn't his power work?

Brown roots broke the ground around them, and Simon nearly wept with joy. Pakesh's eyelids fluttered, and he struggled as the roots wrapped around him, shouting about snakes until the roots dragged them underground. Simon shut his eyes, trying to keep out the dirt that scratched over his skin. He felt Pakesh's power again and tried to calm him, but he'd soon see.

The roots brought them into sunlight. Drushka and humans were stomping out burning grass bundles, the source of all the smoke.

Reach knelt beside him. "Rest easy, shawness." She sang, and Simon leaned into the calm feelings that spread throughout him. He capped Pakesh's power, letting the song soothe them both. His head began to clear, and he could find his power more easily, repairing the damage to his brain before fixing the rest of him.

Brain damage. Horrifying. No wonder he'd felt like a wet sponge. At last, he could sit up. He healed Pakesh and looked over him to see Jacobs lying in the road. He healed her, too, before he asked, "Where's Miriam?"

Reach spread her hands. "I know not."

Pakesh stared with wide eyes. A few tears dribbled down his cheeks as he looked at Jacobs's and Simon's bloody faces. "Did I lose control? Did I hurt you?"

Reach put an arm around him, but Simon stood. "We're fine. We need to look for Miriam." He felt for her with his power, but there were too many people. He sent an image of her to Pool and felt it spread to the drushka. They split up, searching.

"It's okay, kid," Jacobs was saying to Pakesh. "You only hurt the bad guys."

Simon didn't know if that would be any comfort. He began to walk around the warehouse, looking for wounded, searching for Miriam. Pakesh and Jacobs stayed with him, Pakesh crying, clearly not listening to anything Jacobs or Reach had to say.

"It's all right, Pakesh," Simon said.

"I'm useless," he said. "I let them take Miriam and hurt you!" His face was so full of sorrow it seemed like a mask. "I forgot everything you taught me and went to the dark place."

"That wasn't your fault." He took a deep breath. "Help us find Miriam, and I promise, we'll work harder to master your power." He clutched Pakesh's shoulder. "Let's use your telepathy."

Pakesh nodded and scrubbed the tears from his cheeks. Before they could go farther, though, a group of drushka ran up to them. "We have found her, shawness. Just outside the gates."

But finding her didn't mean... "Alive?"

"Ahya, but without her child."

Simon's stomach dropped. "Oh God."

"Monsters," Reach said.

Simon ran, following the scouts. Beyond the gates, a group of drushka gathered. Simon pushed through them, his power already reaching out. Miriam lay on the ground, her wispy hair fluttering in the breeze. She wasn't moving, her mouth slack, but she was alive. Her belly had collapsed somewhat, empty.

Simon tried not to stare, anger building within him. He knelt and let his power play over her, healing the damage he'd found. Someone had accelerated the birth of her child, but they hadn't been gentle. She had bruises on her arms and blood under her nose. Someone was going to pay.

That wasn't the worst. Whoever had used telepathy on her had done some damage to her brain. Delicate work, and the repair went slowly. At last, Miriam sighed and opened her eyes.

She frowned in confusion before grabbing Simon's arm. "Did you find him? My son?"

"Not yet," Reach answered. "But soon."

Miriam's eyes widened as tears filled them. She tried to stand. Simon helped, not wanting to be on the receiving end of her rage. "I told him I'd see him soon." She swiped at her eyes. "I have to keep that promise."

Simon nodded. He'd forgotten that telepaths could commune with their unborn children. They must have had quite a bond already. He put his arms around her, and though she stiffened, she also patted his back as if saying she appreciated the gesture.

"We'll find him," Simon said. "I swear."

"Ahya," Reach said. "The queen knows. She is searching, too." She stiffened, and Simon caught a trill of alarm from Pool.

"Your house, shawness."

"Evan!" Simon took off at a run, leaving it to the others to follow or disperse. He saw the smoke rising above the line of buildings and felt himself growl. Had they tried to burn the block down? How many people would they kill in order to get at him?

But they hadn't just gotten at him this time. They'd come for Miriam's child. Surely they wouldn't risk Mila's and Victoria's children with another fire?

He turned the corner and spotted a burnt husk smoking in the street but no flames. Drushka littered the way, searching for someone to fight, helping the nearby humans out of the way. Some were inside the house along with several paladins, but Simon rushed past all of them.

"Mila? Victoria?" He turned in a circle and spotted Victoria shouldering through the crowd.

"Here," she said. "Bastards tried to take the kids."

"Evan?"

"He's fine." Victoria nodded over her shoulder.

Simon sighed as relief filled him. He found Mila sitting with three babies at the kitchen table. The rest of the house seemed a wreck, with furniture strewn everywhere and several scorch marks. Private Hought sat beside Mila, his face bloody and his arm in a sling.

Jacobs was talking to the paladins, and everyone was slowly filtering out of the house. Mila put an arm around Miriam when they found out her child was taken. Victoria frowned hard and cuddled Evelyn to her chest.

Simon searched everyone else for injuries and healed what he found. "What happened?"

"A group of people tried to get in, and Hought fought several," Victoria said. "Mila tossed them around, and I burned their asses. I don't think they expected to find both of us here."

Miriam slammed a hand on the table. All traces of sadness had gone from her face, and anger radiated from her in waves. Her dark eyes seemed to crackle. "What now?"

"The scouts are still searching," Jacobs said as she joined them. "The kidnappers can't have gotten far."

Simon looked to Evan, torn between guarding the children and helping Miriam search. As she stood, though, so did he. There were enough soldiers and drushka at the house now. He needed to be out there, looking. Pakesh stayed with him and Miriam as they went outside.

Before he went too far, Reach caught up and laid a hand on his arm. "Do you hear that rumble, shawness?"

Simon stopped and listened. Now that he focused, he did hear a bass growl, like heavy machinery.

"Thunder?" Pakesh asked. He looked to Simon with a confused frown. "Did we... Someone told us to look up."

Simon had nearly forgotten that. Anxiety built inside him, carrying the taste of bile to his mouth. Shouts erupted up and down the street as the rumbling grew louder. He looked up. South of Gale, the clouds were billowing like waves.

"Is it a storm?" Reach asked.

Simon shook his head. His anxiety peeked so hard he nearly trembled. The clouds weren't moving naturally but being pushed. A fireball broke through, and the shouts around them turned to screams. The fireball streaked through the sky, becoming a flat shape, rounded at the edges. The rumbling grew deafening as the fireball curved. The orange heat flared out, leaving the sun glinting off a curved metal surface that headed for the mountains in the north.

"Oh God," Simon whispered. Naos had converted the orbiting station back to a ship, even though the skip drive didn't work anymore.

But she didn't need the long-range engines in order to land.

"It's the *Atlas*. Naos is coming here in the flesh."

EPILOGUE

L iam sat on one of the narrow cots in the small house Patricia Dué had stuck him in. She'd shepherded him and the two paladins inside, then left them to sit untended for at least an hour. He rubbed his hands together and tried to think of what that might mean. He'd had good intentions when he'd volunteered to negotiate, and he tried not to let the delays sap his confidence. It wasn't easy, and he wished Patricia had let Cordelia come with him, though he couldn't admit that. Even Simon Lazlo would be a comfort. At least he was powerful.

Private Sunny Swanson sat cross-legged on the rug in the middle of the room, one arm resting on her knee, and her chin in that hand. She looked as bored as Cordelia would have been, only with far less cursing.

"How long do we wait?" Lieutenant Porter asked from where he leaned against the wall. He hadn't stripped his armor off, and Liam didn't know whether or not to ask him to. Liam knew how uncomfortable it was, but they needed all the shows of strength they could muster.

"Making you wait is a diplomatic tactic," Liam said. "My mom pulled it all the time."

Sunny sighed. She wasn't beautiful, but she had a glowing attitude that made her more attractive than she seemed at first glance, so much like Cordelia again. It was no wonder the recruits called her Baby Ross behind her back. Porter was much easier on the eyes with his dark skin and strong jaw.

Liam told himself not to go there. Things with Shiv were back on track but still left a sour taste in his mouth. She'd said she could never belong to him, that she'd always have to think of her tribe first. But why couldn't they think of the tribe together? Because he wasn't drushka? That had never mattered to her before. Maybe it meant they could each have multiple lovers. He let his gaze shift back to Porter then sighed, telling himself to keep his mind on the mission.

"If they don't come soon, we'll..." He trailed away as a low rumble filled the room. "What's that?"

Sunny jerked her thumb at the door. "Want me to go see?"

Liam stood and held out a hand, listening. "I'll look."

❖

Standing outside, Patricia heard the rumble, and she knew in her bones what it meant. "No."

She'd known the *Atlas* inside and out: the curve of the hull, the echo of its hallways, the ghosts that haunted it. Even now, she could summon the memory of the smooth console under her fingers. "She can't land it." Her insides had gone numb. "It wasn't made for an atmosphere; she can't land it."

But somehow, Naos was holding the ship together. It roared overhead, past the mine and to the east, to the mountains. Then it was out of sight, leaving a smoke trail and still rumbling. Then came the boom. The ground shook, and screams filled the air. A second boom came from the mine, and Patricia felt a wave of terror.

She swiveled toward the sound, her limbs wooden. Screaming people tottered from the shaft, all of them covered in dust and dirt. "Cave-in! Cave-in!"

When the dust cleared, the entrance to the shaft framed a pile of rubble; the hole into the mountain had disappeared. People were shouting her name, calling for help. Some were trapped, and their calls echoed in her brain.

Raquel stood in front of the mine, digging with her power, but the people needed their mistress, their leader.

Patricia's feet wouldn't move. Naos had come to Calamity.

"She'll kill us," Dillon said.

Kill or enslave. Patricia began to shake. She'd be trapped in her own mind again, forever this time, doomed to watch eternity play out in front of her eyes.

"I can't go back." The shaking wouldn't stop, threatened to tear her apart. "I can't, I can't, I can't." Her teeth began to chatter. "Dillon, Dillon, help me!"

He was silent for a moment, and then, "I can't do anything from in here."

Patricia's head snapped up. She needed a vessel, but everyone was running for the mine. Even Jonah.

A door opened on one of the houses, and a head poked out. It was the mayor of Gale, Liam Carmichael. His eyes locked on hers. "Are you okay?"

Patricia rushed him and pushed him inside the house. His guards stood, but Patricia hit them with a micro-psychokinetic jolt, knocking them out.

"What the fuck?" Liam cried.

Patricia grabbed him with telepathy, but something in his head blocked her. He had no powers of his own; this was someone else's work. He rushed her, his arm bent as if to bowl her over. Patricia hit him with power, bouncing him off a wall. She tried to gain entrance to his mind again, but those same blocks rejected her.

Naos trying to thwart her? Patricia grabbed her head and dimly heard an animal squeal coming from her own throat. She'd wanted to shove this man's consciousness aside, to give Dillon a temporary home, but the blocks prevented her, teased her. It had to be Naos.

"I won't go back!" She hit the blocks with everything she had. Her terror punched through them as if they were paper. She grabbed his mind and swept it away, taking his memories as she'd once taken Dillon's, but she scattered them, wouldn't let them coalesce as Dillon's had. She left his body an empty shell. Its eyes rolled to the whites as it slumped, and Patricia rushed forward, grabbing on to it as she dumped Dillon inside.

He slipped from her mind like oil, all of his thoughts and memories, all of his consciousness; she gave it all freely, desperately, even his power. Liam's body jerked, eyelids fluttering. The green eyes opened slowly, and he peered at her almost as if he didn't recognize her.

Then he smiled. Dillon's smile.

Before she could jerk away, he kissed her deeply. She pushed him back.

He grinned. "Let's go save some lives, sweets."

SELECTED CAST

Ansha—The sixth drushkan queen.

Caroline Gerard—Deceased telepathic yafanai, Dillon Tracey's lover, and Evan Tracey's mother. Killed by Simon Lazlo.

Cordelia Sa Ross—Former lieutenant in the paladins, Paul Ross's niece, Liam Carmichael's best friend, and Nettle's lover. Has the ability to astral project and can speak to Pool and Simon Lazlo in spirit form. Last seen leading a group of renegades back to Gale after the war with the Sun-Moon and Naos.

Dillon Tracey, aka the Storm Lord—Deceased colonel from the *Atlas*, god of Gale, electrokinetic, and father of Evan Tracey and many other children. Killed by Simon Lazlo and a worshiper of Marie Martin's.

Enka—A drushkan hunt leader for the Shi and the poisoner of Gale.

Evan Tracey—Dillon Tracey's firstborn with Caroline Gerard.

Fajir—A Sun-Moon worshiper, widow, and seren (captain) of the palace guard. Formerly bonded with the deceased Halaan. She once tortured Mamet.

Freddie—Deceased lover of Lydia Bauer. Killed by a prog in the siege of Gale.

Halaan—Deceased Sun-Moon worshiper, Fajir's lover and partner.

Horace Adair—Telepathic and micro-psychokinetic yafanai, Simon Lazlo's lover, and one of Cordelia Ross's renegades.

Jack—Patricia Dué's fiancé back on Earth.

Jacobs—Former private in the paladins and one of Cordelia Ross's renegades.

Jania Carruthers Ross, aka Roshkikan—Cordelia Ross's distant ancestor who was partly responsible for the drushkan schism.

Jen Brown—Deceased captain of the paladins. Killed by Dillon Tracey.

Jon Lea—Lieutenant in the paladins, now a guest of Cordelia Ross's renegades.

Jonah—The personality created by Patricia Dué to reside in the former body of Dillon Tracey.

Kora—Deceased plains dweller who was a vessel for Naos. After her mind was destroyed, her body was taken over by Patricia Dué.

Lasa—The second drushkan queen.

Liam Carmichael—Former lieutenant in the paladins, Linda Carmichael's son, Shiv's lover, and Cordelia Ross's best friend and fellow renegade.

Linda Carmichael—Deceased captain of the paladins and Liam Carmichael's mother. Killed by Dillon Tracey.

Little Paul—Reach's adopted human son, an orphan from Gale, and one of Cordelia Ross's renegades.

Lydia Bauer—Prophetic yafanai. Fled Gale after the death of her lover, Freddie. Now living with the plains dwelling Engali along with Samira Zaidi.

Lyshus—A drushkan child with a unique bond to Shiv.

Mamet—Plains dweller, Engali, and Samira Zaidi's lover. Once tortured by Fajir, she is now at home with the Engali along with Samira and Lydia Bauer.

Marie Martin, aka the Contessa—Deceased requisitions officer on the *Atlas*, god of the Deliquois Islanders, and telepathic. Killed by Dillon Tracey.

The Moon, aka Meredith Marlowe—Former lieutenant on the *Atlas*, god of the Sun-Moon worshipers along with the Sun, telepathic, macro-psychokinetic, and permanently bonded telepathically with the Sun.

Naos—Entity who took over Patricia Dué's body during the *Atlas* accident. Macro- and micro-psychokinetic, telepathic, prophetic, and pyrokinetic. The only person still living in space on the *Atlas*.

Natalya Conti—Deceased macro- and micro-psychokinetic yafanai. Killed when Patricia Dué took up residence in the body of Kora.

Nau—The third drushkan queen.

Nettle—A drushkan hunt leader, Cordelia Ross's lover, and one of Cordelia's renegades under Pool.

Nico—A Sun-Moon worshiper, widow, and second in command to Fajir.

Pakesh—Former plains dweller, telepath, and macro-psychokinetic. Now receiving training from Simon Lazlo and Horace Adair.

Patricia Dué—Former copilot on the *Atlas*, macro- and micro-psychokinetic, and telepathic. Fled her former body, which had been taken over by Naos, and now resides in the body of Kora. She revived Dillon Tracey's old body, turning him into her servant Jonah.

Paul Ross—Deceased mayor of Gale and Cordelia Ross's uncle. Killed by Dillon Tracey.

Pool—The Anushi (first) queen of the drushka, Shiv's mother, and bonded with the youngest tree of the original nine drushkan queens. She has a special bond with Cordelia Ross and Simon Lazlo and hosts Cordelia's renegades.

Reach—Former drushkan ambassador to Gale, a shawness (healer), Little Paul's mother, and one of Cordelia Ross's renegades under Pool.

Samira Zaidi—Macro-psychokinetic yafanai, Simon Lazlo's best friend, and Mamet's lover. Now living with the plains dwelling Engali along with Lydia Bauer.

Shi—The ninth drushkan queen, leader of all drushka except Pool, and responsible for the poisoning of Gale.

Shiv—A young drushkan queen with a young sapling, Pool's daughter, and Liam Carmichael's lover. Has a unique bond with the child Lyshus.

Simon Lazlo—Former botanist and biologist aboard the *Atlas*, micro-psychokinetic, Horace Adair's lover, and Samira Zaidi's best friend. Traveling with Cordelia Ross and Pool.

The Sun, aka Charles Christian—Former lieutenant on the *Atlas*, god of the Sun-Moon worshipers along with the Moon, telepathic, pyrokinetic, and permanently bonded telepathically with the Moon.

Thesta—Drushkan second in command to Enka.

Wuran—Chafa (chief) of the plains dwelling Uri.

Yuve—A chafa (chief) of one of the numerous clans of the plains dwelling Engali.

CREATURES AND TERMS

Ahya/Ahwa—Drushkan terms meaning emphatic affirmative/negative.
Boggins—Squat, swamp dwelling creatures that nearly destroyed Gale.
Geavers—Very large, long-necked pack animals used by the plains dwellers.
Grelcat—Furred predators that stalk the plains.
Hoshpis—Large beetle-like creatures that the Galeans use for meat, leather, and mead.
Nini—A drushkan pacifier meant to be bitten.
Ossors—Large, two-legged insects that the Sun-Moon worshipers and plains dwellers ride.
Pross Co.—The company that originally sent the *Atlas* into deep space.
Progs—Large, long swamp predators that nearly destroyed Gale.
Shawness(i)—Drushkan healers.
Shi'a'na—Drushkan word for mother.

About the Author

Barbara Ann Wright writes fantasy and science fiction novels and short stories when not ranting on her blog. *The Pyramid Waltz* was one of *Tor.com*'s Reviewer's Choice books of 2012, was a *Foreword Review* BOTYA Finalist, a Goldie finalist, and made *Book Riot*'s 100 Must-Read Sci-Fi Fantasy Novels By Female Authors. It also won the 2013 Rainbow Award for Best Lesbian Fantasy. *A Kingdom Lost* and *Thrall: Beyond Gold and Glory* won the 2014 and 2016 Rainbow Awards for Best Lesbian Fantasy Romance, respectively. *Coils* was a finalist for the 2017 Lammys.

Books Available From Bold Strokes Books

A Heart to Call Home by Jeannie Levig. When Jessie Weldon returns to her hometown after thirty years, can she and her childhood crush Dakota Scott heal the tragic past that links them? (978-1-63555-059-7)

Children of the Healer by Barbara Ann Wright. Life becomes desperate for ex-soldier Cordelia Ross when the indigenous aliens of her planet are drawn into a civil war and old enemies linger in the shadows. Book Three of the Godfall Series. (978-1-63555-031-3)

Hearts Like Hers by Melissa Brayden. Coffee shop owner Autumn Primm is ready to cut loose and live a little, but is the baggage that comes with out-of-towner Kate Carpenter too heavy for anything long term? (978-1-63555-014-6)

Love at Cooper's Creek by Missouri Vaun. Shaw Daily flees corporate life to find solace in the rural Blue Ridge Mountains, but escapism eludes her when her attentions are captured by small town beauty Kate Elkins. (978-1-62639-960-0)

Twice in a Lifetime by PJ Trebelhorn. Detective Callie Burke can't deny the growing attraction to her late friend's widow, Taylor Fletcher, who also happens to own the bar where Callie's sister works. (978-1-63555-033-7)

Undiscovered Affinity by Jane Hardee. Will a no-strings-attached affair be enough to break Olivia's control and convince Cardic that love does exist? (978-1-63555-061-0)

Between Sand and Stardust by Tina Michele. Are the lifelong bonds of love strong enough to conquer time, distance, and heartache when Haven Thorne and Willa Bennette are given another chance at forever? (978-1-62639-940-2)

Charming the Vicar by Jenny Frame. When magician and atheist Finn Kane seeks refuge in an English village after a spiritual crisis, can local vicar Bridget Claremont restore her faith in life and love? (978-1-63555-029-0)

Data Capture by Jesse J. Thoma. Lola Walker is undercover on the hunt for cybercriminals while trying not to notice the woman who might be perfectly wrong for her for all the right reasons. (978-1-62639-985-3)

Epicurean Delights by Renee Roman. Ariana Marks had no idea a leisure swim would lead to being rescued, in more ways than one, by the charismatic Hudson Frost. (978-1-63555-100-6)

Heart of the Devil by Ali Vali. We know most of Cain and Emma Casey's story, but Heart of the Devil will take you back to where it began one fateful night with a tray loaded with beer. (978-1-63555-045-0)

Known Threat by Kara A. McLeod. When Special Agent Ryan O'Connor reluctantly questions who protects the Secret Service, she learns courage truly is found in unlikely places. Agent O'Connor Series #3 (978-1-63555-132-7)

Seer and the Shield by D. Jackson Leigh. Time is running out for the Dragon Horse Army while two unlikely heroines struggle to put aside their attraction and find a way to stop a deadly cult. Dragon Horse War, Book 3 (978-1-63555-170-9)

The Universe Between Us by Jane C. Esther. Ana Mitchell must make the hardest choice of her life: the promise of new love Jolie Dann on Earth, or a humanity-saving mission to colonize Mars. (978-1-63555-106-8)

Touch by Kris Bryant. Can one touch heal a heart? (978-1-63555-084-9)

A More Perfect Union by Carsen Taite. Major Zoey Granger and DC fixer Rook Daniels risk their reputations for a chance at true love while dealing with a scandal that threatens to rock the military. (978-1-62639-754-5)

Arrival by Gun Brooke. The spaceship *Pathfinder* reaches its passengers' new homeworld where danger lurks in the shadows while Pamas Seclan disembarks and finds unexpected love in young science genius Darmiya Do Voy. (978-1-62639-859-7)

Captain's Choice by VK Powell. Architect Kerstin Anthony's life is going to plan until Bennett Carlyle, the first girl she ever kissed, is assigned to her latest and most important project, a police district substation. (978-1-62639-997-6)

Falling Into Her by Erin Zak. Pam Phillips, widow at the age of forty, meets Kathryn Hawthorne, local Chicago celebrity, and it changes her life forever—in ways she hadn't even considered possible. (978-1-63555-092-4)

Hookin' Up by MJ Williamz. Will Leah get what she needs from casual hookups or will she see the love she desires right in front of her? (978-1-63555-051-1)

King of Thieves by Shea Godfrey. When art thief Casey Marinos meets bounty hunter Finnegan Starkweather, the crimes of the past just might set the stage for a payoff worth more than she ever dreamed possible. (978-1-63555-007-8)

Lucy's Chance by Jackie D. As a serial killer haunts the streets, Lucy tries to stitch up old wounds with her first love in the wake of a small town's rapid descent into chaos. (978-1-63555-027-6)

Right Here, Right Now by Georgia Beers. When Alicia Wright moves into the office next door to Lacey Chamberlain's accounting firm, Lacey is about to find out that sometimes the last person you want is exactly the person you need. (978-1-63555-154-9)

Strictly Need to Know by MB Austin. Covert operator Maji Rios will do whatever she must to complete her mission, but saving a gorgeous stranger from Russian mobsters was not in her plans. (978-1-63555-114-3)

Tailor-Made by Yolanda Wallace. Tailor Grace Henderson doesn't date clients, but when she meets gender-bending model Dakota Lane, she's tempted to throw all the rules out the window. (978-1-63555-081-8)

Time Will Tell by M. Ullrich. With the ability to time travel, Eva Caldwell will have to decide between having it all and erasing it all. (978-1-63555-088-7)

Change in Time by Robyn Nyx. Working in the past is hell on your future. The Extractor series: Book Two. (978-1-62639-880-1)

Love After Hours by Radclyffe. When Gina Antonelli agrees to renovate Carrie Longmire's new house, she doesn't welcome Carrie's overtures at friendship or her own unexpected attraction. A Rivers Community Novel. (978-1-63555-090-0)

Nantucket Rose by CF Frizzell. Maggie Jordan can't wait to convert a historic Nantucket home into a B&B, but doesn't expect to fall for mariner Ellis Chilton, who has more claim to the house than Maggie realizes. (978-1-63555-056-6)

Picture Perfect by Lisa Moreau. Falling in love wasn't supposed to be part of the stakes for Olive and Gabby, rival photographers in the competition of a lifetime. (978-1-62639-975-4)

Set the Stage by Karis Walsh. Actress Emilie Danvers takes the stage again in Ashland, Oregon, little realizing that landscaper Arden Philips is about to offer her a very personal romantic lead role. (978-1-63555-087-0)

Strike a Match by Fiona Riley. When their attempts at matchmaking fizzle out, firefighter Sasha and reluctant millionairess Abby find themselves turning to each other to strike a perfect match. (978-1-62639-999-0)

The Price of Cash by Ashley Bartlett. Cash Braddock is doing her best to keep her business afloat, stay out of jail, and avoid Detective Kallen. It's not working. (978-1-62639-708-8)

Captured Soul by Laydin Michaels. Can Kadence Munroe save the woman she loves from a twisted killer, or will she lose her to a collector of souls? (978-1-62639-915-0)

Under Her Wing by Ronica Black. At Angel's Wings Rescue, dogs are usually the ones saved, but when quiet Kassandra Haden meets outspoken owner Jayden Beaumont, the two stubborn women just might end up saving each other. (978-1-63555-077-1)